Love
and
Loyalty

"The Traits That Made Lincoln Great"

Florence W. Biros

MANDEL MURPHY CHI

Love and Loyalty -
The Traits That Made Lincoln Great
© 2003 Florence W. Biros

ISBN 0-936369-92-2

SON-RISE Publications & Distributing, Inc.
51 Greeenfield Road
New Wilmington PA 16142
1-800-358-0777

Acknowledgements

Deep appreciation goes to Jim and Donna Jackson of County Lane Graphics, New Castle, PA for all of the design and setup; to Ashley Ceremuga for the portrait of Lincoln on a horse; to Bryan Bennett for his eagle pen-and-ink drawing; to W. L. McCoy for his photos of the Lincoln Museum at Hodgenville; and to all those who contributed to *Lincoln Album of Immortelles* and are used here.

*   *   *   *   *

This book is dedicated to all those whose
love and loyalty has made it possible.

*   *   *   *   *

Table of Contents

A MAN of great ability, pure patriotism, unselfish nature, full of forgiveness to his enemies, bearing malice toward none, he proved to be the man above all others for the great struggle through which the nation had to pass to place itself among the greatest in the family of nations. His fame will grow brighter as time passes and his great work is better understood.

(U. S. Grant)

LOVE AND LOYALTY
The Traits that Made Lincoln Great

Memories of the old Prospect Heights School in Sharon, PA flood my mind every February. As students we painstakingly cut out silhouettes of George Washington and Abraham Lincoln and displayed them on the windows. We spent a lot of time in the classrooms learning about America's first President and Lincoln, the Great Emancipator. The Preamble to the Constitution and the Gettysburg Address had to be memorized in order to pass American History. Something about the lives of the first President and the one who managed to preserve the Union gave us a sense of well-being that God had been the basis for the roots of our United States of America. Learning the reason for the words, "And the flag was still there," from the *Star-Spangled Banner* following the battle at Fort McHenry also made a sense of awe sweep over me as Old Glory passed by and we stood with our hands over our hearts and pledged allegiance to the flag.

Since that era America has been eroded of its morality and its Godly basis. In the name of "progress" the old school on Spruce Street has been replaced with a more modem edifice. Government offices now close down for a three-day holiday in February to commemorate "Presidents' Day" which seldom falls on either George Washington or Abraham Lincoln's birthday, but it appears to be set strictly for the convenience of our country's citizens to enjoy a vacation from work. The emphasis now seems to be on the sales events. "We've chopped prices down to the bone," appears over and over on television, newspaper and radio. Visual ads often show a silhouette of George Washington, even though many students today never heard the story of our first President and how history says he admitted to chopping down the cherry tree, saying, "I cannot tell a lie."

How I wish I could rekindle the flame of patriotism in America's young people! In my first Civil War novel, *DOG JACK*, I renewed my own interest in our forefathers, and in the great conflict between the North and the South in particular because Dog Jack had been the mascot of the 102nd Regiment of the Pennsylvania Volunteers. As I researched that novel and visited the reenactment of the 125th anniversary of the Battle of Gettysburg, the pathos of that memorable period in our history came back to me, and I found myself so caught up in the struggle that killed so many of our American boys from both the North and South that I actually wept.

DOG JACK has become popular with Civil War buffs, dog lovers, Home Schoolers, and even students in the public schools, so it was most thrilling to be able to capture a heart-touching story sharing such an important segment of our country's history and making folks aware of its significance once more. Recently I found a book in my husband's vast library of literature, and it was difficult to believe that I had not discovered it before: *Lincoln Memorial Album of Immortelles*. Once I opened the cover, I discovered nearly 600 pages of unbelievable tributes to Abraham, many of which gave anecdotes of acquaintances' personal encounters with the great leader. The year and the place of printing? 1890 at Springfield, Illinois by the Lincoln Publishing Company!

As I read through Lincoln's speeches and the writings dedicated to his memory, many facts and stories that are not commonly known surfaced, so my mind began to put together another book, this one to tell the little known facts about the character of the man who determined to preserve the Union. Some of the tales about him sent me scurrying to other sources to find out more of their background, and it is with great pleasure and enthusiasm that I offer you the contents of *LOVE AND LOYALTY-The Traits that Made Lincoln Great*. May it take you back in time to relive that era of American History which tore the nation asunder, yet it is my hope that this novel will help you understand the man who proved to his country that poverty and deprivation cannot stand in the way of a soul destined to work and change the face of the nation. It is my prayer that anyone reading this will find the faith to believe that through hard work and studying, any American can make his mark in this world regardless of his circumstances. *LOVE AND LOYALTY-The Traits that Made Lincoln Great* is meant to prove that premise.

MEMORIES

On February 12, 1818 a tiny column of smoke curled out of the log cabin chimney, the only indication that the small hand-hewn building on Pigeon Creek might contain human habitation. Twilight was settling in on the pastoral scene located at the base of an Indiana hillside. Fresh snow had already covered the footprints that Tom Lincoln and his son Abe had created earlier in the day while they were splitting logs and feeding the horse, the cow and the few chickens that were housed in the shed at the side of the cabin.

Inside the log building more merriment than usual was taking place; Father Tom had slipped out with his nine-year-old son and his rifle in the morning. Abe had returned in a jubilant mood as he presented the rabbit his father had bagged, so that his mother could roast fresh meat for supper. This unexpected bounty had put the family in a festive mood.

During grace that evening Tom Lincoln gave special thanks for the occasion and the reason for the delicacies. Abe's mother had outdone herself for her son's birthday, adding carrots to the stew. The carrots *had* been taken from the garden, then painstakingly buried in a root cellar that past summer. Abe knew all too well how his mother tried to stretch their meager food supplies by rationing them all winter so that she'd have enough essentials to last until spring.

The Lincolns' only living son grinned at his mother as she brought out a steaming pan of corn bread from the miniature cookstove beside the fireplace. "Mama, thank you. Thank you!

You know that johnny cake is my favorite." Then glancing at his father, he added, "Thank you, too. I know how hard it is to pick and grind the corn into meal."

A rare smile crossed Tom Lincoln's face as he answered, "You ought to know. You worked hard, too, to harvest the crop."

Those words caused Abe to stop eating for a moment. His father had smiled and given him a word of encouragement! My, this was a festive occasion!

Both his mother and sister planted a kiss on his cheek, and then, to Abe's amazement, his father joined in to put his arm around him and say, "Happy birthday, boy. I can only give you a hug, I wish I could give you a toy." Abe could not believe his father's kind words which were so unlike Pa's usual gruffness. Abraham Lincoln grinned. He decided he would never forget his ninth birthday. Later Tom Lincoln even joined his wife and two children as they sang a couple of nonsensical choruses. Abe felt as though he must have touched heaven. His father seldom joined in family fun functions. He surmised that it was because of his tremendous responsibilities just housing, feeding and clothing his mother, his sister, Abe and himself. Would he withdraw from everyone if he had the burdens his father had to bear? He wondered that every time he tried to communicate with his father. Abe hoped not!

As Nancy Lincoln began to sing the words from the hymn, "Coming Home," everyone's mood became more tranquil. The first stanza brought the impact of the fact that earth was only a temporary residence for she sang, "Ask me not with you to stay, Yonder's my home." The four members of the Lincoln family had fresh wounds about death for they had witnessed a tragedy close by. Luke, a neighbor lad who had befriended Abe, had come down with a sudden illness. Within hours his nausea had come to a point beyond human endurance despite everything his parents had tried to do for him. Abe had lost someone he cared about, but illnesses often took place in that remote wilderness in Indiana. Death often came and snuffed out a life in an instant, so Abe learned early not to dwell on death.

His mother had told him when he was quite young, "Life is

for the living, Abe, you need to read and get all the knowledge you can out of books. I wish I could read better, but I'm trying to see to it that your sister and you know how, but I've been unable to get you very little actual schooling. At this point Sarah knows more than you. If you can't get your formal education, she'll continue to teach you."

Abe soon learned that his mother was right. He began to realize that his father had no knowledge except to be able to eke out an existence as a dirt farmer. To be equipped to have some other vocation, he needed to have more education. "Maybe, Mama," he said to her one day, "Maybe I can study hard enough to become a lawyer or something."

His answer came, in the form of a hug and the affirmation, "Son, you can do anything you set your mind to." Abe was certain that she believed what she said, but how often he'd ached for some word of encouragement from his paternal parent. Somehow, on that night of his ninth birthday, he felt as though Tom Lincoln might begin to encourage him more. He'd already given him a hug and a word of praise!

Once the singing ceased, Sarah and his mother washed the dishes and put them away, then both picked up some mending. Abe went to the makeshift book shelf beside the stone fireplace and tried to decide which one of the books he wanted to read. His small library consisted of copies of *Aesop's Fables*, *Bunyan's Pilgrim's Progress*, and an anthology of poems by Tom Burns. His copy of *Ween's Life of Washington*, was well worn. The Father of America was his favorite hero except for the biblical character, David. He read aloud from the Bible to his mother almost every evening because he enjoyed reading about all the dramatic events he found inside its covers. Abe was reaching for his Bible when his father spoke,

"Abraham Lincoln, it's time I told you about your heritage. Yes," he added, "it's time."

Young Abe spun around, searching his father's face for a clue as to why he was addressing him by his full name. Never before had he spoken to him in such a formal fashion. Had he done something to displease him?

"Come here, son," his father directed as he patted a spot on the wooden bench where he was sitting.

As young Abraham seated himself by his father, he did so with apprehension. Try as he might, he couldn't think of anything he'd done that would have such a sobering effect on the man who he sometimes felt endearing enough to address as "Pa."

Baffled by his father's unusual behavior, he decided to get brave enough to inquire, "Pa, have I done something wrong?"

A soft look spread over his parent's face as he reached out and clasped his own hand over Abe's who tried not to draw back. That move came as a total shock. Twice in one evening! His father had never touched him before that he could remember.

"Oh, no, son. It's just that I've been waiting for the right time to tell you about our family history, and what I'm about to tell should have an impact on you and what you do with your future years."

Before Abe could say anything further, his father continued speaking in that solemn voice. "Son, you've always been told you were named for my father."

Abe nodded. That was no new revelation to him. "But," Tom Lincoln said to his only male offspring, "You've also known that your grandfather is no longer alive."

Abe nodded his head again. His father spoke on, "I've never told any of you what happened to him, not even your mother," then turning in her direction, he said, "I'm sorry, Nancy." He added in a husky voice as if his emotions were overwhelming him, "but it was as though the whole experience was some kind of a nightmare. I felt as though I could never share the haunting memories with anyone, yet somehow I feel like Abe deserves to know about it since he is his namesake."

Tom Lincoln seldom addressed his wife by her first name in front of the children, so Abe's curiosity was whetted even more. Usually his father called his mother "Mother" or "Ma." It seemed to Abe that neither was a term of endearment.

Abe's father appeared to be so caught up in his own feelings, he didn't seem to notice that the womenfolk were neglecting their mending and all eyes and ears were tuned toward him.

"Around 1781 my father had emigrated from Rockingham County, Virginia to Kentucky while he was still a boy. Daniel Boone had become a hero there and had gained great notoriety as a celebrated Indian fighter. Your grandfather, the first Abraham Lincoln, was one of his contemporaries.

"Kentucky was a wild and wooded territory then and became the scene of some fierce and desperate conflicts between the settlers and the Indians, so much so that it earned the name 'The dark and bloody ground.'"

The cabin remained quiet while the rest of the family sat in rapt attention as the story continued. Even though Abe understood that he had been the intended target of the conversation, the look on Nancy and Sarah's faces assured him that the strange tale kept all of them wondering what was next. What was Tom Lincoln about to say that would cause him to act so much out of character and use words Abe never knew he had in his vocabulary?

After a brief sigh, Tom continued, "I was only six when my pa and I were out working in the cornfield. I glanced up, and to my great horror, I spied an Indian sneaking up on us with a rifle aimed straight at my father. Scared almost to death, I couldn't even get out a squeak to warn him. The Indian fired. My father crumpled and fell to the ground. My heart beat so fast that I thought my chest couldn't contain it.

"Your Uncle Mordecai, my older brother, witnessed the whole episode from a place where he was working close to the cabin, but the intruder never noticed him as he ran inside and grabbed his already-loaded rifle. When he peered back outside, he panicked.

"Mordecai said the scene scared him beyond words. Not only was his father dead, but the Indian had grabbed me and was carrying me away!" With those words Abe's father had to stop to gain his composure before starting again. "A stack of firewood was close to the door and he spied a small opening to see through. Without much thought he took aim at a silver metal that shone on the Indian's chest. Bang! A shot rang through the air. The Indian dropped me and he fell to the ground just like your grandfather did. Mordecai told me later that all he had time to do was cry inside, 'Please, God'."

Abe's father acted as though he couldn't stop sharing his story, for he said, "My brother's shot could have killed me, too, but he was an expert marksman. Thank the Lord his prayer was answered. Otherwise I'd have been dead.

"Instead I ran to my mother's arms, as she stood watching in the cabin door. She scooped me up and I think I never appreciated more the comfort that she gave me at that moment."

Silence fell in the small cabin. Tom Lincoln glanced around at the faces of the other members of his family. For the first time he seemed to comprehend the fact that the entire family had been listening and were overwhelmed emotionally by his dramatic story.

Everyone appeared to be in deep thought until Abe interjected his personal thoughts, "Pa, I count it a privilege to be named after your father and I will do everything I can to make the name 'Abraham Lincoln' always deserve deep respect."

Later when the rest of the family was bedded down for the night Abe's mother came to pray with him.

"We didn't get to read the Bible tonight," Abe whispered. For a second his throat tightened and he could hardly swallow. Tears misted in his eyes. Oh, how he wished he could convey to his mother the depth of his feelings for her.

"Mama," he whispered, "I love you. You've tried so hard to see to it that Sarah and I had book learning, and you've made it so we could go for a few months every time an itinerant teacher came by so that we could both be able to read. You've taught me that I must be honest and true to everything that's right. Oh, Mama, how can I ever thank you?"

His mother didn't answer at once, making Abe certain that the events of the evening had touched his mother, too. He could not see Nancy Lincoln's face, but her next words came out in a hoarse whisper, "Abraham Lincoln, you never need to thank me. I am ever so grateful that the Lord gave you to me as a son. I am most pleased to be the mother of such a kind and thoughtful boy. Some of what we heard tonight makes me understand your father better. We've a lot to think about, but I hope you had a nice birthday anyway. I love you and the Lord loves you. In your father's way, I'm sure he does, too." With that she planted a kiss on Abe's cheek.

Nancy Lincoln had started to move away when Abe whispered, "Mama, I've got too much on my mind to go to sleep right now. You too tired to talk?"

His mother stood beside him, forming a shadowy figure in the dim light of the glowing fireplace. "No, not really. Not if you want to." With that she sank down to sit on the feather mattress she'd made for him. "What're you thinking about, son?"

"Hodgenville, Mama. It seemed back there in Kentucky that Pa was always telling his tales and making people laugh. When we lived those years by Knob Creek everyone seemed happier. Remember how my friend Austin saved me when I got into water over my head and almost drowned?"

"I remember," Nancy whispered. "You had a close call."

Abe was quiet for a moment before he spoke again about something that had been bothering him for a long time and he had kept hidden in the corner of his young mind. He finally asked, "Mama, Pa took a job of rounding up slaves one time, didn't he?"

His mother sighed. "I'm sorry to say, he did, Abe, but your father soon decided it was like selling his soul for six cents an hour, so he quit."

Abe stopped as if sorting out his thoughts before speaking again. "Oh, how much I hated to see those men being driven like animals down Cumberland Road. Why did people treat them so badly? Because they were black? Why should they be any different than we are? Bet they have the same feelings inside."

"I'm sure you're right," Nancy agreed. "We need to pray that someone can change their lives and somehow change their miserable existence."

Abe's mind kept on a roll, so he asked: "Remember when Dennis came over and took a buzzard feather and made a quill pen out of it so he could teach me to make letters? Mama, I feel like he's the one thing that helps make it so we can stand this place. The other thing I miss is going to "blab" school. I learned a lot in the a months even though the teacher was the only one who had a book and all we could do was talk. I wish Sarah and I could learn more, but there's nobody around here to teach us."

"You can help each other by reading every book we have."

Abe giggled. "Mama, I've already done that. I even read them aloud when nobody's in the cabin. I think the pages are printed inside my brain."

His mother sighed, "Just like you did the preacher's sermons back in Kentucky. I think you memorized the sermons and all the words of every minister who came by."

"I miss that, Mama. When we came here and Dennis moved here with the Hanks, he and Pa built the lean-to so we had somewhere to sleep until we had a cabin built, I had no idea what was coming. That was such a terrible winter! I'll never forget shivering on leaves under the bearskin. Oh, how the wind howled as the snow drifted in on top of us."

Nancy stroked Abe's head as she whispered. "That's all behind us now, son. Things are going to be better. Come spring we'll plant crops and do fine. You've already forgotten the unpleasant things back at Knob Creek farm. There were some, you know. Remember how you walked behind Pa and Dennis and planted pumpkin seeds between their corn seeds? They'd just begun to take root when the creek overflowed and everything washed away. That probably was the thing that made your pa want to move, but son, I'll tell you now as I told him then, there's no place on earth that is perfect. The Lord put us here to make the best of every situation. Just trust in Him and He'll get you through whatever problem you find yourself in and finally He'll give you your just rewards. Life is fragile, so make the best of each moment of every day. If we get separated here on earth, then we'll meet again in heaven." With those words she planted one more kiss on her son's cheek. "Good night again. Pleasant dreams."

"Mama" he spoke in a soft whisper, "Promise me that we're not going to ever be separated."

For a moment she stood beside him, her image even more hazy as the fire was dying down.

Abe whispered, "Don't let Pa put logs on the fire tonight. I'll do that. He needs his rest, too, so I'll see to it that the fire doesn't go out. Please, Mama, please don't ever talk about separation again."

"Thank you, son, for all your concerns," she whispered back as she planted another kiss on his forehead. "You make me happy. As soon as you do your chores, make sure you get some good rest."

With that she left his side. After building up the fire, as he promised his mother, he soon fell fast asleep.

"What constitutes the bulwark of our own liberty and independence? It is not....the guns of our war steamers, or the strength of our gallant and disciplined army.... Our reliance is in the love of liberty which God has planted in our bosoms."

FROM A SPEECH
AT EDWARDSVILLE, ILLINOIS
SEPTEMBER 11, 1858

GROWING PAINS

Winter's snows washed away during the Indiana spring rains, and with the emergence of new life all around him, young Abe Lincoln found hope springing up inside his heart. He watched in amazement as their heifer gave birth to a miniature boy cow. It tickled him to see the newborn creature change from a spindly legged baby to an animal that seemed to be so inquisitive.

"Mama," he said with a laugh, "that little bull is growing so fast and he has his nose in everything."

His mother laughed with him, then replied, "He's not much different than my son. You're growing faster than the seedlings you've helped to plant. As for your curiosity, I'm sure it exceeds that of the nosey little bull calf."

Abe realized his search for answers about everything made his father impatient with his never-ending questions. On a trip to town for supplies Abe saw signs at the general store about upcoming elections, so he asked his father, "Pa, do you go to vote? I was reading that it's every citizen's duty to help elect good officials."

When his father didn't respond with an answer, Abe understood it was because of his father's lack of learning. Tom Lincoln could do little more than write his own name, but he did have some knowledge of numbers. How could that help him read a ballot? Often his son wished his father's pride would allow him to let his wife and children teach him the three R's, but he had enough insight to know that his pa could not accept their help. That would be too demeaning to him.

Abe also wished that his father could give him satisfactory answers, but instead his pa often retorted in a sharp voice, "Abe, you are just too big for your britches! No nine-year-old should be concerned about the government. We have work to do."

During the spring months Abe kept methodically weeding between the rows of new sprouts, but his mind continued to dwell on secret thoughts. Some day he was going to become a lawyer or a politician or somebody who could help the world be a better place.

Sure, he enjoyed being outdoors, but his goal was to be more than a dirt farmer. Yes, he appreciated all his father's hard work to improve their meager lot in life, but each day meant endless physical labor for the entire family with no time to do anything but work. *No fun at all,* Abe thought to himself.

In the summer of that year Abe stood in the cabin doorway and was startled to see Dennis racing toward the Lincoln cabin. Dennis and Abe had been friends in Hodgenville so he'd been thrilled to have him come to Indiana, too. One look at his friend's sheet-white face made Abe convinced that the illegitimate son of his mother's cousin was shaken up by something drastic.

"They're dying! They're dying!" he gasped as soon as be could catch his breath. Tears filled his eyes as he tried to speak "Both of them have taken to their beds. Neither of them can keep anything down. They can't lift their heads from their pillows. They're that sick!" Abe knew without an explanation that Dennis was talking about his own relatives who had taken his cousin in.

Without a word, Nancy rushed to get her cape. "Come on, Dennis. We can't waste time! Abe, you come, too. You can help Dennis get a doctor if need be."

The three of them rushed to the nearby cabin that Nancy's aunt and uncle built from the Lincoln's original lean-to's framework. As Dennis flung open the door, all three of the would-be rescuers stood, mouths gaping, at their two beloved relatives who lay, face up, staring at the ceiling. "They're dead, aren't they, Mama?" Abe whispered as he took in the reality that neither his great aunt or uncle had moved at all.

Nancy Hanks Lincoln shook her head in assent, then she walked over to the bed and touched her aunt's body, then her uncle's. Tears misted in her eyes. "You're right son. They're gone." Her answer back was little more than a whisper.

Dennis stared at his caregivers' bodies. He sobbed, "Now what's going to happen to me? They're the only ones who thought I was worth a plug nickel. My own mama didn't want me. My pa left before I was born. He didn't want me." His sobs seemed to engulf him as he blurted out, "They're the only ones who wanted me. Now nobody does!"

Seconds later Abe watched his mother react to the hurting young man. Encircling her arms around him, she cried, "Oh, Dennis, that's not so! God loves you and so do we."

Through more tears Dennis sobbed, "That doesn't give me a home. Who is going to take me in out in this God-forsaken wilderness?"

"We are! Dennis, shame on you!" Nancy Lincoln scolded. "You know we would never leave you alone without a roof over your head or food and love. We don't have much, but we'll share it with you. As long as I have breath you will have a home. Let's go now. We need to make arrangements to bury these two wonderful people."

Abe wondered what his pa would say, but to his amazement, Tom Lincoln welcomed Dennis with these promising words, "We can build a future together, son. You can stay as long as you need to."

Dennis' expression became grim again. "I don't know how to thank you. All I know is that my being here won't be easy for you. I know you have enough worries already, yet I will promise you one thing. I will do my best to help provide for you and myself in every way that I can."

The Lincolns and their new boarder bedded down for the night, knowing that in the morning they'd have to summon the preacher and then fashion two caskets.

The entire day Abe worked methodically through the building of the boxes out of crude pine, the digging of the one large grave, and later, after the service, the lowering of the caskets into the ground. He wished that he could think of words that might somehow console the lad who he'd always admired and thought of as a great cousin, but he could think of none.

In the days following Abe's concern for Dennis' hurt grew more and more. Abe sympathized with him often. "I don't know quite how you feel. I can't imagine ever losing Mama."

ROOT OF THE PROBLEM

Abe did his work as always, but his mind kept trying to think of words that might somehow console the older lad who he'd always admired. Just to look at Dennis, he knew he had a hurting heart from his great loss.

Because of Abe's concern which he expressed often, he and his cousin grew as close as brothers. Abe sympathized with Dennis often. When Dennis grew teary-eyed, he'd whisper in a choked voice, "I hope you never have to go through such an awful hurt."

The two boys were standing outside the Lincoln cabin early in the morning when Dennis turned to Abe and said, "No sense crying over spilled milk. I'll go get my rifle and we'll go get some game for your mama to cook. I promised your pa that I'd do all I could to help with my board and keep, so let's get going. Time's a wastin' again."

Abe laughed and declared, "You're right. Around here if nobody works, nobody eats."

Abraham Lincoln did all the mundane things to keep life going, but the sudden death of relatives he loved caused him to give more serious thought to life. It seemed to him that such a family tragedy had little long-term effect on the world. How he hoped that he could accomplish something in his lifetime that would make the world remember him.

His mother always showed her sensitivity to his moods. She'd share with Abe at great length her feelings about life and death during their ritual prayers before bedtime. He wondered how long their special time together would continue. After all, he was nine and growing up, yet she still listened to his prayers and tucked him in with a good-night kiss.

"Mama, you know I plan to do something great for humanity before I die," he assured her.

One night Nancy Lincoln reached over and stroked her son's forehead as she spoke in a soft, reassuring tone of voice, "In the Bible it says there is a time for all seasons—a time to live and a time to die—a time to laugh and a time to cry. You have such a fine sense of humor. I will be real honest. Sometimes I see little hope for our future, but then you tell a story and make me laugh. I don't know how your cousin would make it through his awful heartbreak if it wasn't for you and your laughter."

A few days after that conversation his mother had served the family their evening meal, but Abe noticed that a deep red flush covered her face.

"Mama," he cried, "are you sick?"

His mother looked toward him and nodded, "Abraham, I don't know why, but I don't feel well."

Tom Lincoln, who had already moved away from the table, came back and reached over to touch his wife's forehead. "Nancy, you have a fever. You're burning up! You need to get some rest."

Seldom had Tom Lincoln's son seen any consideration for his mother on his father's part, but Abe's concern for her well-being deepened as his father put his arms around her waist and helped her over to their bed.

Confused over what he should do to help, Abe grabbed a glass jar and ran outside to the pitcher pump to fetch fresh water to take to his ailing mother.

His concern deepened as he watched his mother's struggle to keep going, but she had constant bouts with nausea and stomach pains. The red flush from the fever never left. At the end of the week she appeared to have given up.

Desperate as to how to help, Abe kept running back and forth with water with the hope of somehow bringing her soaring fever down. He cried to his father, "Pa, can't you get the doctor? Can't you do SOMETHING?"

His father shrugged his shoulders. "Son," he answered with a pat on his shoulder, "It's no use. I'm certain I know what's wrong with her."

Tom Lincoln's answer frightened his son so much that he cried out in anguish, "Pa, are you saying that Mama has what killed Dennis' folks? Pa, you don't mean that, do you?" His father just stood with a look of anguish across his face.

Abe felt as though he'd been kicked in the pit of his stomach. "Can't you get a doctor? Is she going to die? Oh, Pa, do something!" he wailed.

"No one knows what to do for her problem. If I got a doctor here, he'd give the same answer. Abe, we can't save your mother."

Through tears Abe stumbled out of the cabin to get another jar of water and brought it back to his precious mama.

Nancy Lincoln lifted her head from the feather pillow long enough to take a sip, then as if that movement took every speck of energy she had left, her head fell back against the bedding.

"Abe, listen to me," She whispered, but then she became quiet.

Wide-eyed, her son waited until he could bear her silence no more. "Mama," he managed to get out in a hoarse whisper, "what do you want me to hear?"

For a moment she lay there, her eyes fixed on him. "You have great potential." Tears misted in her eyes as she tried to speak further. "Memorizing comes so easy for you."

After a brief silence she managed to go on, "You will become something great if you stay as close to God and are as loyal and honest as you are now. Someday the world will recognize the name of Abraham Lincoln."

She fell silent. Abe's heart kept thumping wildly in his chest as he waited for her to say something more. Her eyes finally met his when at last she spoke again, "And, son, look out for your sister and your father."

After those words which Abe knew came straight from her heart, she seemed to drift off. Then with a gasp, a slight smile crossed her face which assured Abe that his beloved mama had gone to meet her Maker, but the anguish in his heart was more than he felt he could bear.

"Mama!" he screamed, "Mama, don't leave us!" he pleaded over and over with her still form.

Tom Lincoln rushed in and touched her head. "Nancy! Nancy!" he wailed. "Please come back! I promise I'll be kinder! Oh, Nancy, please don't go!"

Standing beside his son, Abe thought his pa was waiting for a miracle, but his mother's body just remained still and lifeless so his father turned and swept Abe up in his arms crying. "Oh, son, she's gone! She's gone!"

Sarah had just come in from milking the cow. When she saw her father and brother in an embrace and her mother's still form lying on the bed, she flung herself between her menfolk where the three of them remained in a tight family circle, weeping at their loss. Abe wept until he could weep no more.

Neighbors heard and came to call, bringing food and words of sympathy. When the doctor-coroner arrived to sign the death certificate, he told Tom, "I am almost certain that your wife's death was due to milk fever, the same as your two neighbors. Nothing else I know of can explain the sudden high fever and quick death. I'm so sorry. We can only speculate that a plant is the source of the problem, but no one knows for sure. My own belief is that it comes from a cow eating the snake root plant and the poison is passed on through the milk."

Tom Lincoln stared into space for some time after the doctor left. Dennis had come in and was trying to deal with his own loss at the shock of yet another of his kinfolk passing on.

Tom Lincoln spoke to his daughter first; "Sarah, go throw that milk away."

"But, Pa, what are we going to do without it?"

Tom Lincoln's face clouded as he answered, "Sarah, I'm more concerned what we're going to do if we drink it. The doctor said your mother's problem could have come from the milk and we've had enough grief."

"Abe and Dennis, come with me. I'm sure I know where the culprit is. Dennis, do you remember the snake root plant down by your property? Some of it grew over on ours and I believe we'll have no more problems with milk fever if we get rid of it."

The three started out with hoes in hand. As they neared the property boundary line, Tom cried, "There it is!" With those words he began to dig into the hard earth until he was able to pull the plant out of the ground, roots and all. The trio worked together digging and tugging at plant after plant until there were no more left.

After trudging back to the cabin with their arms loaded down with the snake root plants, they spread them out on the ground to dry for a while in the hot sun. Once they were dried out; they doused the plants with kerosene and set them on fire.

The following day Dennis, along with Abe and Tom Lincoln, worked together to build a coffin out of rough pine lumber. Tears splashed on the finished box as Abe tried to comprehend that it would be the last gift of love, the final thing he could ever do for his beloved mother.

The preacher and the neighbors assembled together late in the afternoon around the grave that several men had offered to help dig the day before.

Abe stood between his father and sister while Dennis took his place beside her.

As Abraham Lincoln's mother was lowered into her grave, a feeling of unbelief swept over him. *The happenings of the past two days are just a nightmare*, he thought. *When I wake up, it will all go away. It has to be a dream.*

Yet, as he stood looking at the wooden box which housed his mother's remains, reality set in. *She is dead!* he cried inside as the last shovel full of dirt was thrown on Nancy Lincoln's coffin.

When Abe turned to walk away kind folks offered words of sympathy. Over and over he heard, "I'm so sorry, son" but nothing helped the gnawing emptiness he was experiencing. Neither Sarah nor Dennis seemed able to say anything to bolster his gnawing spirit. Nor did his pa. They all had too much grief of their own.

The day of the funeral Abraham Lincoln left the cabin to go

for a walk in the woods alone to try to sort out his feelings. Pictures of his dying mother and her last words kept flashing through his mind and he determined that if he was to live up to his precious mama's expectations he would have to study harder and somehow get over his deep, gnawing sense of loss and grief.

TRUE GRIT

At ten years of age Abraham Lincoln felt as though his heart had been twisted and torn from his body in the months following his mother's death. Such emptiness! He could not find words adequate to express his feelings when Dennis questioned him about them.

The bleak, dark winter did nothing to restore a zest for living in the Lincoln cabin. Nights seemed to stretch into eternity as the wind howled and snow crept through the cracks between the logs where the mortar hadn't held. Abe shivered beneath a bearskin rug, still the only covering he had to keep him warm.

Even though Dennis was another mouth to feed, he proved to be a great asset to Tom Lincoln, Sarah and especially to young Abraham. Abe soon realized that Dennis was capable of chiding Tom Lincoln into hunting bear and deer meat even though his father, much like himself and Sarah, had little-or-no desire to keep motivated, to endure the hardships of their pioneer existence after the loss of Nancy Hanks Lincoln.

Abe was certain no one could comprehend his hurt following his mother's death, but then he looked at Sarah and began to anguish over her state of mind. Sarah, at age twelve, was blossoming into a young lady so her brother understood that her need for a mother's love and encouragement was far greater than even his own, so he approached Dennis with the perplexing problem.

"I don't know how to help Sarah. She's overloaded with all my mother's duties plus she seems unable to shed any of her own terrible grief. Her continual unhappiness shows that her present life is too much to bear."

Dennis nodded in agreement. "I know what you mean. Looks like her chin's draggin' on the floor every time I look at her."

His remark sent a ridiculous mental picture flashing through Abe's mind; causing a grin to spread across his faces "You sure can change a sad situation into a light one, Cuz. Any ideas how we can give her a chin lift?"

It was Dennis' turn to smile. "I don't know, but I think she'd respond to a pet of some kind, maybe a fawn or something. Let's try to catch one for her."

The idea appealed to Abe so much that the next day the pair set out on a hunt through the densest part of the forest. "Shh," Dennis whispered, when they came to a clearing where a doe and her spotted fawn were drinking from a small stream. In a soft voice Dennis added, "You go in from the right and I'll close in from the left as soon as I give the 'go' signal. Then we'll try to catch the fawn."

When the "go" signal came Abe leaped into action. Aiming for the baby deer's feet, he tried to make a tackle. As he landed face down on the ground he attempted to encircle the spindly-legged little animal, but swish! With a burst of energy the fawn leaped from his encircling arms and high-tailed after its mother, leaving Abe sprawled out on the ground.

Dennis, still upright, howled with delight. "My, my, just look at you! I never realized before how awkward you really are. You're all arms and legs." With that he reached down to give Abe a hand.

Once erect, Abe grinned, too. "Must have made some sorry sight, didn't I?"

Dennis flung an arm around his shoulder and the two walked that way for a short while toward home.

"Care to try to act that scene over again, old buddy?" Dennis laughed. Abe drew away after that remark, but as they continued their trek homeward they both had to giggle.

A sudden thought occurred to Abe — they hadn't accomplished their mission to lighten poor Sarah's aching heart. His head bent forward, he was amazed to see a sizeable turtle in his path. Reaching down, he caught it by its shell so as not to let the animal bite him in protest. "I got it! I got it!" he cried.

His joy sent his cousin into a spasm of laughter. "Pokiest animal in existence! No wonder you caught it!"

"This turtle is something that'll cheer her up!" Abe insisted and when he presented it to Sarah back at the cabin her face lit up with pleasure, something he hadn't seen in a long time.

"It worked for now!" Dennis claimed, "but she needs something more lovable, something soft."

A few days later they came upon a baby coon after they'd spent an hour fishing. They'd been fortunate to have caught a few small fish for supper. "Where's your mama?" Abe asked while he dangled one of his catch on a string beneath the tiny animal's nose. As the coon lifted its head to grab at the entice-ment, Abe bent down and scooped it up in his hand. To his surprise the little animal began to squirm and wiggle and claw at him so hard that he had to force himself not to let go. "It's taking all I've got to keep this baby from 'scaping my grip," he complained to Dennis. "It's one scrapper."

"That's what we'll call him — 'Scrapper'!" Dennis cried.

To the boys' delight "Scrapper" brought tears of joy to Sarah's eyes when she first saw the little furry creature. What amazed Abe more was Scrapper's reaction to its new owner. The little coon settled down in Sarah's arms and the ring-tailed ball of fur drifted off to sleep, making Sarah giggle and say, "Some Scrap-per! All he needed was a woman's touch."

Dennis grinned as he retorted, "He just thought you reminded him of his mother."

Sarah's foot reached out to give him a kick in jest, but missed her mark so much that all three howled with glee.

Abe couldn't sleep that night so he lay awake thinking about their lives. Pa was little consolation for his children's emotional wounds. At times his lack of concern for them even deepened their hurt. Thoughts of spring planting and all the hard summer work made Abe wish the beautiful season wasn't about to hap-pen. Abe never thought of sassing his father, but deep inside he wondered what "hard work" had ever done for the Tom Lincoln family. Every day Abe willingly took an axe and split logs and chopped trees. He knew the value of a strong body, but he also realized the great worth of a keen mind. After Abe had read and consumed his biographical copy of George Washington's life over and over, he'd decided that he, the lonely country boy, would somehow reach a similar status in this country that Washington and his peers had established as a great nation.

"Oh, God," Abe sobbed as a tear fell onto his feather pillow, "I sure do miss my mama."

During the few months earlier when he and Sarah had been able to go to school, an itinerant teacher passed through. The classes had always started the day by reciting the pledge of allegiance to the flag. Sometimes Abe would be overcome with a feeling of patriotism as he saluted the banner that represented freedom to him. He realized that the stars and stripes were only symbolic of the "Republic for which it stands," and the words "with liberty and justice for all" meant so much to him. He prayed that someday he would be free from his father's demands and get himself into a position to aid and abet others on their search for free choices in their lives.

Hard pressed for family funds, Tom Lincoln had announced that he'd again accepted a job rounding up escaped slaves to help with their income. His pay? Six cents an hour. Abe stared at his father, unable to speak the anger that raged inside of him.

As his son, Abe had a difficult time understanding this temporary job, but how would his father react to any confrontation about it? Abe had always shown respect to him. Abe had seen few slaves in his life, but every time the scenes had bothered him immensely. One happened on a Saturday while he was getting supplies. He watched a man being driven to town by a black man. At the general store the slave's owner stayed in his supply buggy while his Negro servant went in to bring out their purchases. Abe could sense the owner's patience was diminishing, that agitation was brewing inside the man — so when the black servant came out laden with the heavy sacks, his owner took the whip from the seat beside him and cracked it across the man's bare back causing him to cry out in pain.

"That'll teach you to keep me waiting!" the owner snorted. "We haven't got all day!"

The slave stood for a moment, looking at the man he was forced to call "Master." Hatred surfaced in the black man's eyes, and Abe fought back his own burning desire to deck the man's so-called "Master." Instead, Abraham Lincoln moved on, loading his own wagon, fearing what his father Tom might say to him if he dallied too long.

That memory, along with a few other incidents that Abe had witnessed, was etched in Abraham Lincoln's mind. How could his father accept pay for making men go back and work under such oppression? The night his father announced, "I'm going to give up those wild goose chases—I can find better things to do," Abe felt a surge of relief flow through him and he felt more kindly to his remaining parent than he had for a long time. Abe soon found out what his father's new pastime was — he was certain that from the way Pa was dressing up, instead of searching for slaves his father had decided to hunt for a wife!

Spring soon sprang! After their backbreaking weeks of digging and planting, leaf lettuce appeared and then vegetables began to ripen, giving Sarah lots of good things to serve for her menfolk. Most of her cooking was good, but too often her attempts at baking turned into disasters.

One August morning Abe sauntered out and picked a bucket of blackberries for her. Later he was pleased to find her trying to roll out dough to make a pie crust so her brother informed the other two family members, "You know we can anticipate blackberry pie for supper."

The meal was served. When no pie appeared Abe turned to his sister to inquire, "Sis, are you going to make us wait forever for our dessert?"

Sarah burst into tears and ran outside, causing her brother to get up from his chair and run after her calling, "Sarah, Sarah, what did I say? What's wrong?"

With a sudden thrust Sarah threw herself into his arms. "Oh, Abe, I can't do anything right! Your berries and the pie are burnt to a crisp! I wish Mama was here!" she wailed.

Abe tried his best to comfort her, then as he turned to go back inside, he saw his father standing in the doorway.

"Sarah," he said, "no one can bring your mother back, but a year has gone by and I decided we need a woman in the house. I aim to find me a new wife soon to help relieve you of some of your burdens."

More than two months passed before Tom Lincoln talked about the subject again with his children at the dinner table. He directed his conversation toward his son. "I've been trying to decide how to tell you but I guess now is as good a time as any. I'm going to Kentucky to bring home a new wife. She is a woman that I used to see before I courted your mother. You'll like her. You'll like her name, too. Her name is Sarah, the same as your sister's."

While everyone was still seated around the table he continued to talk. All eyes focused on Tom Lincoln who seemed to decide he needed to explain further for he said, "I told her if she'd be my wife, our marriage would be one of necessity. Her husband was a jailer and he died, leaving her some debts and three small children all under nine years old. She needs a husband and I need a wife as much as you all need a woman to make this house a home. Dennis helped me write a letter. I didn't want you to hear about this from him so he agreed to keep the matter secret until I got a reply." He stopped and cleared his throat.

"It came today. She said 'yes,' so I'll be going in two weeks to fetch her and her belongings. I know all three of you will make Sarah Bush Johnston and her children welcome. She has two girls and her middle child is a boy named Ben."

That speech to them by his father was the longest Abe could remember except for the night of his ninth birthday. Because he knew it was so important to Tom Lincoln, it should matter to Sarah, Dennis and to him. Pa even seemed excited!

The next couple of weeks Sarah and Abe questioned each other often about the prospects of having a stepmother. Abe surveyed the interior of the cabin with its dirt floor and sparse furnishing. The crude building had no window and the only door was improvised.

"Sarah, I wonder, do you suppose her children have ever had to sleep under bear skins to keep warm?".

Sarah shrugged her shoulders. "I don't care about that. All I worry about is where are we going to put everybody?"

Harvest, canning, bunting and making a small effort to ready the cabin consumed them. The day in early December chosen for their father's new marriage arrived before they had time to ponder much about it and its possible consequences.

Abe did call his cousin aside to ask, "You don't suppose Pa has made her believe we have much more than we have? He has a tendency to build his meager belongings up in his mind so I wonder what she'll think of us when she first sees the real mess. None of us have had time to even scrub ourselves clean lately."

Dennis' answer was simple, "We'll see."

Tom Lincoln left no doubt in his son's mind as to his anticipation of his forthcoming merger. Abe decided that his sister didn't either. Sarah had taken great pains to launder the only clothing her father had that was suitable for the event, so even Abe had to admit, "You look pretty spiffy, Pa."

Before Tom left he informed his children, "I'm not taking you because I'll need all of the room in the wagon for Mrs. Johnston and her three children and her dresser and what furniture she has. You'll have to wait here with Dennis while I go and fetch your new ma."

It was getting dark two days later when Abe heard the clatter of the wheels and the sound of horse's feet.

"They're home," he heard himself speak in a hoarse whisper and couldn't help but wonder why he was so apprehensive. Somehow he wished they had a window so he and the other two who'd been left behind could get a glimpse of the newcomers before they came inside.

Minutes later Tom Lincoln stood in the doorway with his new bride who, as Abe had feared, wore a shocked look on her face. He shuddered at the thought of his stepmother's initiation into her new home. The scraggly, not-too-clean children and the cabin must have made a poor impression on the new Mrs. Lincoln.

Abe awaited her negative reactions but instead she reached out and pulled Sarah toward her, giving his sister a hug as she declared, "I didn't know I was going to have such a beautiful namesake."

Then, turning to Abe, he noticed the corners of her eyes crinkled as she exclaimed, "Your pa says you're only ten years old, but I can tell you're going to turn into a man who I'll have to look up to." Next she turned to Dennis and whispered something. Abe paid no attention to what she said, but he did notice a smile spread over their adopted cousin's face.

His father stood, beaming, in the corner of the cabin, with his new wife's three offspring.

For a moment so many people made Abe think of what he'd said to his sister before the bride and groom arrived, "All of us are going to be jam-packed in the cabin even more than our little frying pan would be crowded if we tried to squeeze in an extra chicken."

He still wasn't sure where everyone was going to sleep, but somehow the new lady of the house impressed Abe so much that she gave him the feeling that, regardless of all the horrendous circumstances, the new Mrs. Lincoln could overcome them all.

For the first time since his mother's death Abraham Lincoln had a sense of belonging to a family with a purpose and a goal. He felt at home. "Dear God," he prayed before closing his eyes to sleep, "I know with your help we can become a family."

FAMILY CALAMITY

Early the morning after his father's new bride's arrival Abe awoke with a sense that a tremendous difference had arrived in the atmosphere of the small cabin. Glancing over, he saw his new stepmother beginning to prepare eggs for breakfast.

Abe hurried to get dressed and ready and then was delighted to find Sarah Bush Lincoln placing a huge bowl of scrambled eggs on the table. His eyes shone with delight as he declared, "My, you are a blessing."

His new stepmother smiled with her reply, "So are you, Abe, but we're all going to have to work to bring this family together. After breakfast, which I see we'll have to eat in shifts, I've thought of a plan that will help all of us."

Even Tom Lincoln appeared pleased with her, and listened while she laid out her ideas for improving their lot in life. Much to his son's amazement he didn't even protest her ideas, so Abe realized her plan might come to fruition.

The new Mrs. Lincoln came right to the point. "This place needs lots of help and we have lots of us to make it so much better. First of all—you men—young and old alike — need to take a few days to cut trees and have them made into boards so that we can have flooring for in here. It'll make it much warmer this winter."

As time went by Sarah Bush Lincoln and Abe drew closer and closer together. Her understanding of his emotional needs was uncanny. She often assured him, "Abraham Lincoln, I see great potential in you. For a young boy you know far more than any child I have ever known at your age. You amaze me."

Those words reached deep into Abe's heart. The two were seated in front of the crackling fire, but the warmth he felt was not just because of the heat produced by the flames. The new Mrs. Lincoln had endeared herself to him from the start, but as winter had set in she and Abe had found more time to spend getting to know each other better.

To her remark about his potential Abe simply replied, "That's what my mama always said."

Sarah put her arm around his shoulder and gave him a quick squeeze, "I know you miss your mother and I do not hope to replace her, but Abe, I will echo her sentiments about your possibilities as long as I am here. Books and learning have always intrigued me, too, so whenever I can I will help you."

In the years following Abe found she kept her word. At times she would sit and dream with him when he confessed, "I want to become someone who matters — a lawyer maybe or a politician, but how can I when Pa expects me to sling an axe both night and day? Do you think it would be possible for me to become a surveyor? George Washington was one."

"You can do anything you set your mind to," Sarah assured him.

During his next trip to town he found a used book in the general store and purchased it. He rode home in the wagon to share his treasure with his stepmother.

"Mama," he called as he raced in the cabin door, "look what I found! It's a copy of the same surveyor's manual that George Washington used." The endearing term "Mama" came easy for him anymore. In every way Sarah Bush Lincoln deserved the title and he felt certain his real mother would be pleased.

The woman he chose to call "Mama" put down her rolling pin and threw her arms around him. "Oh, Abe, that can be your ticket to a better life! You'll learn surveying in 'no time'."

When she removed her arms Abe found flour prints all over his shirt. "You going to put me into a pie?' he joked.

Sarah smiled one of her joyous grins, "You'd make a good one. You're that sweet."

During the next few months Abe spent every spare moment poring over the manual. "You'll make a fine surveyor," his stepmother kept assuring him. "Abe, I see it as a means for you to earn money to pursue your dreams."

Abe looked up from his book. "Mama, how could I leave you? I promised my first mother I would take care of Pa and my sister. Now I feel I need to take care of you and Ben and the girls."

Sarah's usual amiable face clouded. "Abraham Lincoln," she scolded, "we can take care of ourselves. You need to quit thinking of others and consider your own future."

Abe's own expression changed from merriment to seriousness. "But what about Pa? I see that you are right that his eyesight is fading and I'm sure he is in a lot of pain to make him act so ornery at times."

"You can't spend your entire life doing his bidding nor making us your top priority. My prayer is that the good Lord will direct you to your greatest potential. Your father will become proud of you. Learn all you can about surveying and go lick the world. You can do it."

But how about his father? Abe felt as though he meant little more than a workhorse did for his pa. Tom Lincoln's outlook on life was fading along with his eyesight. His stepmother told Abe in private, "Your father's vision gets worse all the time. All we can do is pray for him."

And so, Abe had stayed at the Lincoln homestead out of loyalty, along with a great measure of concern for the family's well-being and the promise to his real mother to "take care of your father and each other." So often he wished that the deep-seated love he had for his father didn't exist so that he could release himself from the bondage he felt to stay with him. At twenty-one Abraham Lincoln hoped and prayed for a way out of his humble existence. He'd reached legal age to leave, but his emotional ties kept him in bondage to the family.

Sarah's son Ben had in truth taken on the role of a brother. Dennis had long since got past being thought of as an illegitimate cousin in Abe's mind. The two had become bonded to him so much during the years that Abe declared, "No one better not dare to pick on you."

As for his sister Sarah, he doubted that anyone could measure up to the place she had held in his heart ever since their real mother's death. She'd grown into an attractive young woman and Abe never minded reaching out to give her a quick hug. He liked his two stepsisters, too, but his blood sister had a special place in a corner of his heart.

He told her, "No fellow dare pick on you. You are too special to let any guy abuse you. They'll never get away with hurting you. I'll see to it."

Yet his sister told him over and over about her own desire to spread her wings. "Oh, Abe, I'd like to find someone who really loves me and I can get married and have some babies of my own."

Her brother understood her feelings, but he watched with a protective eye when a neighbor boy came courting. He didn't say anything, but his constant presence when Aaron was around made his sister protest, "Abraham Lincoln, don't be so protective! I'm not a baby! I can take care of myself. You're going to scare him away."

"That might be a good idea. You could get a far better catch."

Sarah laughed and gave her brother a quick squeeze in return. "You see me as so much more than I am," she protested.

"No," Abe answered. "You don't see yourself as the special girl you really are, but I'll back off if you want me to."

"You're going to have to let me go," Sarah declared.

Abe muttered, "I will, but I don't want to."

Aaron continued to court his sister until one day Sarah announced at dinner, "I'm going to get married."

Abe excused himself from the table, making his sister confront him later, "Aren't you thrilled for me? You know every girl's dream is to get married and have a family of her own. Please be happy about my decision."

Abe looked his sister in the eyes. "More than anything I want you to have a great life. I've tried to analyze my feelings and have to admit a part of me is jealous that someone else is so important to you. We have always been so close, even before Mama died."

Tears glowed in Sarah's eyes as she reached up to put her arms around her brother. "You will always be number one with me," she whispered as she embraced him.

Time went by and Abe found himself at his sister's small wedding. It seemed she had been married only a short time when she appeared with Aaron one day and made an announcement to the Lincoln family, "We're going to have a baby! We couldn't wait to tell you!"

Sarah Bush Lincoln reached out and pulled her stepdaughter toward her in an embrace. "My, that is news!" she declared while giving the new mother-to-be a quick kiss on the cheek.

Abe gave her no words of congratulations, but only asked, "Are you going to build a home of your own or are you going to be forced to stay on with his family?"

His sister's face clouded for an instant "Abe, it's all right. They are very nice to me and Aaron and I want to wait until after the baby's born to try to build a cabin of our own."

Abe wasn't pleased with her answer. His own opinion was that Aaron's family overworked and had little consideration for his beloved sister, but he deemed it best not to say so.

One morning at breakfast his stepmother told him, "Abe, I'm concerned about your sister. I saw her yesterday and it looks as though she'll have her baby today. Things she said just didn't set right with me."

Abe put down his fork as he thought of what his stepmother had said. "Are they having a doctor?" he asked.

"I think not. Aaron's mother has helped deliver other babies, so they're going to have her."

A flush crept over Abe's face. "What? They can't know she's having trouble and not get her a medical man to help bring the baby! What kind of people are they? I'm going over there right now!" With that, he slammed out the door, saddled the horse and raced to his sister.

Aaron met him at the door. Red-eyed with tears flooding his cheek, Abe knew without him saying what had transpired.

Abe's furor had not subsided. He felt no compassion for his brokenhearted brother-in-law. Instead he shook Aaron by the shoulders while screeching, "Why? Why would you be so ignorant as to refuse to get a doctor for your wife?"

With that Abe rushed to the bed where his sister's still body lay. The silent baby had been placed beside her.

Aaron and his mother and father stood by, silent tears filling each of their faces. Abe's furor was more than he could contain so he screamed, "You have no sense! You let a beautiful girl and her baby die because you would not get a doctor."

Aaron sobbed. "Oh, Abe, there is no money to pay for one. We didn't want this to happen. Remember they are my wife and baby!"

Abe spun around, mounted his horse and raced it toward home where his family was waiting. He knew that his expression told the sad tale. They didn't need to ask. Unable to talk, Abe stomped out of the house and made his way into the woods. "Why, God? Why? She was such a fine girl," he wailed.

After a while he returned home. He knew from his stepmother's expression that she'd heard the news, but Sarah Lincoln did not offer to console him. For that he was glad. Words or affection couldn't help the pain that gnawed at his insides.

Later that afternoon Abe decided he could contain his emotions enough to talk to his stepmother. "Mama, are you sure you can make it without me? Can you and Pa get along if I leave? Sarah's gone and that was part of my promise to my mother. Pa's the other one. Do you think you could make it without me?"

Sarah pondered for a moment before answering. Abe saw that she was trying to hold back tears, but then she spoke in a soft voice, "Oh, son, we both know you need to spread your wings and fly. You are too big a man for this little nest. Yes, your father and I can manage. Ben is here. Don't let family love and loyalty stop you from your destiny."

With those words she reached up high and kissed him on the cheek.

One day when he'd reached the age of twenty-two Abraham Lincoln looked at his reflection in the mirror in the General

Store which all the women who had funds enough to buy a new dress used to admire themselves. The image he saw made him more determined to fulfill his new commitment to moving on to something better in life than the pioneer existence he'd endured as long as he could remember.

His frame was too tall for the mirror unless he bent over. When he did, his thin, haggard-looking face stared back at him. *I'm twenty-two and I look like a has-been. What hope is there for me? The only thing I'm good at is wielding an axe.* He'd been thinking of something for a long time. Fellows had shared, "The inn over at New Salem has a lot going on. We ought to go there sometime." After staring at his mirror image, he decided the time had come. *Maybe,* he thought, *that'll give me an opportunity to do something else.*

ABRAHAM LINCOLN I regard as belonging to the same class with the judges in Israel. He was raised up by Divine Providence to be the deliverer of this nation in a time of great peril. His work done, God permitted him to be removed without conscious suffering, by the bullet of a most cowardly and wicked assassin. His name will stand on the roll of fame next to that of Washington as a benefactor of his race.

L. Scott

(L. Scott)

1880.

MOVING ON

Frustrated, and in despair over his dear sister's death at such a young age, Abe decided to walk all the way to New Salem that evening and go to the inn over there where folks often went to meet each other. Maybe he could get a lead on improving his life. Abe loved to spin yarns and be with people, but once he'd completed the long walk and entered the building, he decided to sit and take in the sights and sounds with the hope that he could learn something profitable to him.

One man managed to be the center of attention, and Abe soon classified him as a braggart until the other young man approached him. "Aren't you Abe Lincoln?" he asked.

Startled, Abe replied. "Yes, sir, how do you know? To my knowledge we've never crossed paths before."

The stranger smiled and extended his hand, " My name is Denton Offutt. You might not know me, but I've heard about your great strength and keen mind. I need such a man as you."

A tinge of red crept up Abe's lean face. Few people ever gave him any praise, so he had to admit to himself that this outgoing character caught his attention.

Denton Offutt wasted no time. "My plan is to take a barge of corn from New Salem to New Orleans. I can buy it cheap here and sell it for five times my investment down there. I need a couple of men with great strength to help construct the raft, load it and paddle all the way down the Mississippi."

Abe's mind began to race. "Are you planning to pay your help, or will it be an excursion just for fun?"

A scowl crossed the newcomer's face. "Abraham Lincoln, I'm an opportunist, yes, but never would I expect someone to work for me without adequate compensation."

"Well, then we're on," Abe agreed with a handshake. His new employer's grip was almost equal to his own.

"I'll meet you in New Salem tomorrow on the far side of the dam," Denton told him. "Eight o'clock. Bring help if you can."

"Won't be a problem. I'll be there." And it wasn't. He soon talked his two able-bodied relatives into going on the wild adventure. Not able to sleep, he rose early in the morning and rousted his stepbrother Ben and John Hanks, his cousin, to make the fourteen-mile trek on foot before eight a.m.

His long legs could make great strides when necessary, so he reached his destination even before the appointed hour. His shorter-legged relatives cried, "Abe, slow down! Your legs are twice as long as ours."

When they arrived at their destination Denton was there with small logs and heavy twine. "I knew what we needed, but we'll have to depend on your ingenuity to get a raft together," he told Abe.

The four worked industriously under Abe's direction until late afternoon two days later they had created what looked like a sizeable flatboat. The young men grinned as Denton boasted, "We did it! Abe, you're a genius!"

"We'll see. Let's put her in to make sure she can float."

To their amazement the raft-like creation stayed on top of the water.

"It does!" Denton shouted. "It floats! Now we have to load her up." Tugging at the rope, he pulled it ashore, then the young men all worked together to get their cargo aboard.

"We're off to New Orleans as soon as we get her over the dam," Denton cried.

His excitement was contagious. Abe and the other men all wore a grin.

The raft kept its great promise until it got stuck. Halfway-across the dam the bow raised up in the air. Water surged around and in the stern.

"It's going to sink!" Denton cried.

"Not if I can help it! "Abe retorted. "Push the load to the front." As the others worked to balance the boat, he ran to the local copper shop where be convinced Mr. Onstot, the owner, to lend him the tool which he used to bore a hole in the boat to let the water run out. After plugging the hole, the raft was able to be poled over the dam as it teetered above water level.

As the men worked, the crowd that had gathered for the performance cheered. As soon as the raft was clear, Abe went ashore to return the auger to the copper shop owner.

Mr. Onstot declared, "I hear you were quite a hero today. We could use a few young men like you around here. Some of our lads leave much to be desired."

Abe protested, "I couldn't do what I did if you hadn't been willing to lend your auger to a stranger. I consider you the hero."

The older man grinned and offered his hand. "You know my name, but I don't know yours. Mind if I ask?"

"No, sir. Abraham Lincoln."

"Like I said. What this town needs is more young men like you. Matter of fact, I think the whole country would benefit if all its citizens had your willingness to work and be honest, too."

Back on the raft, the young men made their final preparations for their voyage. "New Orleans!" Abe declared. "New Orleans! We're going to New Orleans!" His voice was high-pitched as though he couldn't wait for the trip to begin.

John Hanks grinned, "Abe, we all know where we're heading. If you don't grab a paddle and help us get through this miserable Sangamon and start south down the Mississippi, we're going to stay right here. We need you to steer the way."

Abe did as he was told. After a long struggle with the oars, the four young men caught a glimpse of the wide river. "There she is!" he cried. "We've reached the mighty Mississippi. 'Old Miss' herself!"

Glancing around at the other three crew members, he chuckled to himself.

"What's so funny?" John asked him.

A wide grin swept across Abe's face. "It's just that I sense you guys are feeling the spirit of adventure as much as I am."

When they finally reached one of the widest sections of the river, a look of deep concern crossed their employer's face. "Wow! Did you ever feel smaller than you do right now? This little flatboat has a lot of cargo and it's pretty big, but this raft seems like a toy bobbing along in an enormous tub of water. Sure hate to think of trying to swim to shore."

At dusk, just as the river narrowed again, Denton spotted a little inlet in the terrain. "Abe, the water's much calmer here so we can steer toward shore to tie her up for the night."

Abe shook his head in agreement. "Wouldn't want to be out here in the water adrift. We going to sleep on land?" he inquired.

"Look at this thing," Denton answered. "Where on this little rig could we find a flat place big enough to sleep four bodies? Besides, we need to rustle up some grub. Don't know about you follows, but I'm starved. We can build a campfire to cook on and then it'll chase the skeeters away plus keep us warm for the night. Gets cold along the water after the sun goes down."

The other three young men all took hold of their paddles while Abe tied a rope to the end of the raft. When the flatboat got close enough to shore he created a lasso out of the rope's other end. With expert aim he tossed the loop over a low tree, making a sort of anchor to keep their tiny raft in one spot. Handling the rope, he began to pull in the slack to maneuver the boat toward the shoreline.

"You'd think you were a seasoned seaman," John Hanks declared as Abe tied the rope to the tree so that the flatboat and its cargo couldn't drift away during the night.

"I'm starved," John declared. His words aroused a chorus from the others, "Me, too."

Denton had brought along some smoked ham which he heated in a flying pan over the fire that Abe had built from twigs. "Smells won-der-ful!" Abe's stepbrother announced. "Nothing like the great outdoors to give a fellow an appetite."

Bread had also been brought from the raft; so the four men indulged in ham sandwiches. While a pot of water was being heated for coffee to drink, they enjoyed some of the ginger snaps Denton had brought in a metal tin. While the others settled back to enjoy the food and the night air, Abe rose to add some sticks to the fire when whomp! A set of arms encircled his chest. Abe's reaction was immediate. With all the strength he could muster he heaved forward and brought his attacker to the ground. Thud! One glance around proved to him that his attacker was not alone. Four other black men were grabbing and fighting Denton and the others.

Abe's own three comrades had sprung to their feet, alive and immediately active, punching and kicking at the men attacking them. Abe got a glimpse of the face of the black man who'd tried to fell him as he threw him close to the fire. Fear! He had never seen such a frightened look on any white man's face. Abe's heart felt as though it was beating in his throat. Did he kill the poor man? What if he'd made a direct hit and the fellow had been burned?

During the moment when Abe pulled back, another of their unwelcome guests tried to attack him from the back, but Abe grabbed the man and then used all of his strength to bring him up and over his shoulders. Thud! The man landed with such force that he lay motionless on the ground for minutes.

Relief flooded Abe's body as soon as his intruder gained his strength and scrambled to his feet and ran into the thicket. His other comrades followed in hot pursuit.

"Well I'll be!" Denton exclaimed after they were gone. "Abe, they'd have done us in if you weren't along. What do you think they wanted?"

Abe's cousin replied, "I'm sure they wanted something to eat. My guess is that they were runaway slaves in frantic need of food. That ham sure tasted good to us. Just imagine how the smell of something to eat could get them that excited."

Abe didn't speak until his stepbrother inquired of him, "What do you think they wanted? Do you agree with John?"

For a while Abe sat silent, as if deep in thought. Then he said, "Yes, I agree that they were probably a band of runaway slaves, but the thing that bothered me the most was the expression of the first guy I decked when I could see it from the glow of the fire. Never in my life have I seen such a look of fear. I couldn't help but wonder how I'd act if I knew men and dogs were hot on my trail on a manhunt looking for me. What if I was starved and wondering where I could find food and a place to hide? Those men weren't criminals; they were just looking for a way to exist and were nearly starved to death."

Later, after Denton Offutt and Abe's stepbrother had drifted off to sleep by the campfire, John asked, "Aren't you scared, Abe? I'm afraid to close my eyes for fear that they'll attack again."

Abe took a stick and moved the coals in the fire. "I'm not afraid of them coming back. They were too scared to try again. That's not why I'm so wide awake. The thing that bothers me is the injustice of one group of men using the other group as slaves just to obtain the things they greedily want for themselves. God wouldn't approve. I don't either."

John sighed, "Oh, Abe. They're just a bunch of blacks."

The remark riled Abraham Lincoln's sense of justice making him inquire of his cousin, "And what makes you any different from them? What if your skin was black? Go to sleep, John. You're making me mad." With those words, both Abe and John sprawled out on the ground and drifted off to sleep after a short while. They'd had quite a day.

The rest of the trip was uneventful, but each morning the members of the crew of the raft headed south, were up and ready for their next lap of their great adventure.

Denton Offutt, even though he'd paid the other three their wages in advance, made no effort to flaunt his authority. He declared to the others, "'Abe's the boss. Whatever he says, goes."

When the raft neared New Orleans Harbor, the river lost the isolation they'd enjoyed for so many miles. The wake from the small boats caused havoc for the inexperienced crew, but they finally managed to get their flatboat in and tied to the dock.

The New Orleans harbor bustled with boats, sailors and people. Abe stared. He'd never envisioned so much activity in one spot. Denton had gone to meet the man who'd ordered the goods they'd brought down so Abe decided they'd best wait until the purchaser arrived with his wagon before they could unload. Along with his other remaining crew members, he stood and stared in awe at the masses of people and their bustling activity when everything came to a standstill as a burly man cried, "There she comes."

Abe, Ben and John all turned to see what had caused so much interest. A great ship was coming in, one so much larger than Abe could ever imagine. Abe and the others, caught up in the majestic size of the ship that was being anchored, stood in awe as the sailors began to unload her cargo.

"Watch where you're going!" one of the crew members snarled when a black man appeared on the gangplank. Seconds later another, then another came into view. Scantily clad, each was a bent-over black man who glanced around, the whites of their eyes made such a contrast to their very black skin that Abe could not help but notice the intense fear that harbored in them. Each man was fettered to the man behind him by a heavy chain. The chain of broken spirits seemed endless.

"Slaves. They are slaves!" Abe whispered, not wanting to acknowledge such things could happen in his beloved United States, but he and his companions were witnessing what Abraham Lincoln considered to be the scourge of the nation.

A man cracked a whip over a black back. "A-H-H-," the victim screamed in pain. His overseer had no mercy, but used the whip again after the would-be slaves's cry of anguish.

Abe's mind rolled as the scene of horror unfolded before his eyes. "John," he whispered to his cousin, "they must have brought them over in the bottom of the ship. Imagine the smell — the horrendous stench of human kind being confined in a hold in this heat."

John's reply was simply, "Abe, most folks don't think blacks are human. No need to fuss so much."

Abe's frustration turned into full-blown anger. "Look at them! The only difference between us and them is the color of their skin. For shame, John Hanks! You can't approve of this sight! It's — it's inhumane!" Abe couldn't think of words adequate enough to express his emotions.

"Shh!" John whispered. "Everyone's looking at us!"

"So what! Somebody has to protest somehow!" Abe cried. Anger stirred in him like a pot of water about to boil over.

The next scenario they witnessed did not help Abe's constitution. Women, most of them little more than girls, began to be herded off the ship like animals.

The frightened eyes of one young woman met his. The terror, the total anguish printed across her face was almost more than Abe could bear. Abraham Lincoln determined in his mmd that somehow he would help her.

Denton hadn't returned with his customer yet, so Abe and his other two relatives sauntered down the street behind the parade of slaves. Abe had heard that the slave traders auctioned them off like cattle.

As they stood in front of the auction block, his own eyes surveyed the crowd that had come to buy a slave for a pittance. "Hope they go cheap today," a voice said beside him. "They probably will — there's such a bunch of them."

Abraham Lincoln turned to glare at the man. None of the potential slaves gave him the feeling of nothingness that this swarthy, shiny-looking human being did. So incensed with anger, be fought his urge to deck the character.

His stepbrother must have read his mind, for he spoke under his breath, "Abe, don't do it. That'd make you no better than him."

Abe grimaced, then spoke, "You sure know how to settle me down, don't you?"

A tremendous commotion brought his attention back to what was happening. The young woman whose eyes had met his was brought in front of the crowd, the first of the potential slaves The disgusting character standing beside Abe snarled, "She'll be mine"

"Over my dead body!" Abe whispered to John.

"What do you think you can do about it?" came the reply.

"I'll buy her myself. He's not going to get her."

"What? Have you lost your mind?"

"No! That creepy character isn't going to have her!"

The bidding began. Abe's two comrades stared in disbelief as Abraham Lincoln kept raising the ante.

Total disgust showed in his competitor's eyes as the bidding went higher and higher.

All Abe had in the world of finances was the pay he had confined in a cloth bag tied into his hip pocket - the money he'd received in advance from the trip. His heart raced faster and faster. *What if he had to stop before the swarthy-looking character did? How could he live with himself if that grimy man became the girl's master?* With a snort and a look of disgust, he glared at Abe and then bid one more bid when the auctioneer came back to him, anticipating Abe's combatant would go higher.

He did not. Abe, with a sigh of relief; went to the cashier to pay for the girl. When she was released to him, she surprised him by speaking a little English, something most slaves imported from the Dark Continent had to learn.

"You buy me?"

"Yes," he answered, "I bought your freedom."

"Then I can do what I want to do—to go where I want to go?" Her dark eyes danced with pleasure.

"Yes," Abe answered.

Tears began to stream down her face as she added, "Well, then, sir, I go with you."

Her last remark caught Abe off guard. What could he say in return? He'd bought her. She had a right to expect him to care for her, but he was simply trying to buy her freedom. How could he make her understand? What on earth could he do with such a girl?

Turning to his relatives, he could see from the smirks on their faces that they were not going to be of any help. They were amused at his self-made dilemma.

At that point Denton Offutt appeared. "I've been bunting all over for you. If we don't hustle we won't be able to get everything unloaded before we have to catch the steamer north."

Abe turned to the girl, "I'm sorry. Go. You are free." With those words, he joined the others to finish their task.

Later that night he boarded the steamer in which Denton

had booked them passage home. Abe had a bunk to lie upon. He could not help but think about the slaves and their horrendous conditions on the huge steamer as the smaller ship headed north. Their inhumane treatment tore at his heart. He was most distressed about the girl who he'd given most of his own pay to buy her freedom from bondage. *Maybe, Lord,* he prayed inside as he drifted off to sleep. *Maybe I should have brought her with us. What chance does she have out in the world alone?*

Frustration tore at him. *What chance do any of them have? Oh, God, if there be some way for me to change this horrible injustice, please show me.*

The trip north to New Salem was uneventful until Denton Offutt spoke to Abe when they arrived back at their starting point,

"Abraham Lincoln, you've proven yourself a man of great strength and ability. I've just purchased the old general store here and the gristmill. How would you like to run the store and oversee the mill?"

Abe stood speechless for a moment, amazed at the words he was hearing. Gathering his wits he finally replied, "I take it you're offering me a job. You were most generous on this trip, so I am certain you will pay me well and we have no need to discuss wages. However, I will have to go home and tell my family good-bye, then I can start Tuesday. I will be back that noon. Is that soon enough?"

"Sure is," Denton Offutt agreed, then reached out to shake Abe's hand. "Deal?" he asked.

"Deal," Abe agreed and strode off toward Pigeon Creek. The fourteen-mile trek seemed short that day. *Mama will be so pleased,* he thought. He couldn't wait to tell her.

NEW HORIZONS

Late in July, 1831, Abe leaned over to kiss his beloved step-mother good-bye. He'd informed his Pa earlier that he'd be leaving that day so, as his son, he was not surprised that his father had risen early and left the cabin, something he seldom had done before. Abe was certain that Pa was furious about his decision to strike out on his own because a larger burden of the care of the family would be on his father's shoulders after Abe was gone. Having wisdom beyond his twenty-two years, Abe also understood that his father's reaction to his son's future absence was also from other emotions.

"Poor Pa," he'd told Dennis the night before, "he's suffering from mixed feelings of anger, fear and love."

When Sara Bush Lincoln looked up into the grey eyes of her stepson, Abe sensed she was trying to hold back her tears. He was having trouble with his own eyes as she spoke softly, "Go. lick the world. You have to make your mark." Her look of gloom transformed into one where her eyes danced with pleasure as she declared, "Now, get going before you're late for your first day at a real job!" Her last teasing remark made it possible for them both to part.

Since Abraham Lincoln had no horse of his own, he had no choice but to make the fourteen-mile journey on foot. On that extremely hot, humid day he took every short cut he thought was feasible, feeling it imperative that he arrive at the specified hour.

He'd been told that the town of New Salem had a population

of only a hundred people, and from the number of onlookers who were standing, gaping in his direction, he knew the time of his arrival and his reputation had preceded him. Denton Offutt must have been busy touting all of Abe's physical prowess to them or there wouldn't be so many on hand to see the stranger's arrival. Many, he realized, had been on hand to cheer him in his attempt to get the flatboat over the dam.

Abe chuckled to himself as he thought of what his first impression was making on the new curiosity seekers. He realized he was quite a sight with his mended deerskin pants and his slouch hat. Dirt, sweat and grime had accumulated on his skin and clothing during his trek there. He'd used every available shortcut through the woods. Whatever the folks in his new hometown must have been anticipating of their new storekeeper, mine overseer, Abe was certain he didn't live up to their expectations. He smiled as he thought of how they'd be even less impressed if they had known that Denton Offutt's new employee was also penniless.

He reached out to see if the muslin satchel that his stepmother had painstakingly made by hand as a going-away present was intact. Inside he'd placed all his other earthly belongings — a change of clothing, his coon skin cap for winter and his treasured books.

Even though he seldom stood tall and straight because of his years of backbreaking, rail-splitting jobs, besides the fact that he towered over nearly everyone, he made an effort to straighten up to his full six-foot-four stature before stepping into view.

Scanning the crowd, a surge of gratitude swept through him as a familiar face emerged. "Welcome, Abe," Denton Offutt declared as he extended a hand.

"Glad to see you," Abe replied, returning his new employer's firm grip. *Does Denton realize how glad?* he wondered.

"Come on," Denton urged. "Let's go look over the store. Like I told you, it's not much to look at, but you can set up your living quarters in the back room."

Abe noticed that the crowd was dispersing as he and his

employer moved away, but three tough-looking young men stayed to eye him up further.

"That'd be the Clary Grove boys?" Abe inquired.

Denton nodded, "Sure nuf. They've heard of your reputation so they're trying to size you up. Since they haven't pelted you with rocks or smart remarks, my guess is those tough guys feel as though they've met their match. Your bulging muscles are impressive."

Abe chuckled, "Well I'd like it to stay that way. One of them at a time wouldn't phase me, but I'd sure hate to have to tussle with all three at once."

Within a few minutes Abe noticed the so called 'tough guys' had drifted away, leaving Abe and Denton free to talk. Abe's new boss told him, "You realize you'll have competition. The whole town has been used to going to the Hill McNeil General Store. You'll have to break them of that habit." Denton had just spoken those words when their walk brought them to a worn wooden building with a faded sign over the door which said simply, "General Store."

"This is it," Denton declared as he mounted the steps to the large porch. "Come on inside and check it out."

The interior was no more impressive than the outside. Large wooden barrels had markings on their sides indicating their contents: sugar, flour, crackers, salt. Smaller metal containers had labels indicating they held other commodities such as coffee and tea. The floor looked as though it hadn't collided with a broom for several months.

"Come see your new quarters," Denton invited as he shoved an old curtain aside to reveal a barren room with a worn army cot, cobwebs, dirt and little else.

"It'll do," Abe conceded. His mind reeled back to the time in his childhood when his family had huddled together on a mattress of leaves under bear skins for blankets while the wind and snow howled around them. This current hole-in-the wall didn't have much to offer, but it certainly beat their housing during that horrible Indiana winter.

"I'll bring you some bedding," Denton offered, "but I can't

be here much. You'll have to work on your own most of the time, but I believe you're capable of doing anything."

Those words had a great impact on Abraham Lincoln. Few people beside his mother and stepmother had ever given Abe such a great vote of confidence, so Abe determined in his mind that he wouldn't ever let Denton down.

The next week Abe kept busy scrubbing and sweeping and trying to get his new business in order. The following Saturday be posted a sign beneath the original one outside, "Open-Under New Management."

A thin, aged man with a beard and intense brown eyes was the first to wander in. "Name's Joshua Mason. Friends call me Josh," he declared.

Abe spoke as he offered his new customer a grin, "I'm Abraham Lincoln, but everyone calls me Abe."

Josh made himself at home by sitting on a cracker barrel while he filled Abe in on all the local news. Abraham Lincoln made another mental note not to say anything to this elderly gentleman that he didn't want all of New Salem to know. As Joshua Mason watched Abe's every movement and quizzed him on his background, Abe realized his first assessment was right. He was having his first encounter with the town gossip.

As the new store manager he decided to make the best of Josh's role as town crier by finding out more about his competition for himself, "How's the Hill-McNeil store doing?"

Josh grinned. Wrinkles around his dark eyes deepened as he spoke, "Oh, each of them is a fine businessman, but both of them are acting like a couple of lovesick cows. I hear they're busting up their business because they both want the same woman, a girl named Ann. "My, my," he chuckled, "that's ridiculous."

Abe smirked and nodded in agreement. "I'd say so. I've never seen any girl that's worth all that. She must be something else."

Old Josh declared, "Rumor has it that she's chosen John McNeil. You'll like him, too. Reckon he'll saunter in, too. Most folks will."

Joshua Mason knew the people of New Salem quite well for

they did much of what he predicted. Before the first week was over many of the curiosity-seekers Abe had seen on his arrival found their way into the store. John McNeil was one of them. Abe took to John immediately and was quite pleased when he explained, "I'm not going to be a partner in the store anymore so I thought it would be great if we'd become friends."

During ensuing visits Abe found his former competition to be intelligent, witty and charming. John soon broached the subject of his love affair himself. "Abe, I've fallen for such a wonderful girl named Ann. Sometime soon I'll tell her to stop by so you can meet her."

"That'll be nice, but I've never had much interest in women. My goal is to learn so much that I can build a worthwhile career. I'm really pleased when I'm not too busy and can study my books." Abe's face flushed as he explained further. "I often get so engrossed that I don't even hear folks come in. I put that bell over the door to let me know when I have a customer."

People always made Abe feel alive and he loved to spin yarns and tell stories that made them laugh. His tale-telling ability enticed both men and women to come and stay just to listen, making Abe's book-learning time more limited. Still sales didn't improve much. Abe admitted to Josh who'd become a daily visitor, "I'm afraid most people don't want to be customers, but they come for entertainment."

Early one morning Abe had just opened for business, but was in the back studying since most of his clientele usually came later in the day. The bell rang, summoning him to the front of the store.

Upon pulling back the curtain, his eyes focused on a young woman standing in the doorway. Sunlight streamed around her, giving her auburn hair a brilliant sheen. There she stood with an infectious smile that made her whole being seem to radiate. *Almost like an angel,* Abe thought.

Seldom at a loss for words, he had to force himself to speak, "May I help you, miss?"

As she moved closer Abe noticed the sparkle in her blue eyes that were accented by her matching dress. Extending her hand she spoke softly, "I'm Ann Rutledge and you must be Abe. John has told me so much about you."

Abe clasped her small hand in his giant one. *Never have I felt more like an overgrown giant,* Abe noted in his mind. "I'm so pleased to meet you, too," he assured her. They chatted for a while, then Ann dismissed herself, making Abe's twenty-two-year-old heart and mind wish that he was not so fond of John McNeil. Abe had no notion that he wanted to break up his friend's relationship with Ann so he made himself concentrate on other things.

Denton Offutt bragged incessantly about Abe's physical prowess. Abraham Lincoln cringed as he heard, "My man can outrun, out-throw and whip any man in town."

Abe overheard the Clary boys, "We know he's smarter but how strong he is has to be proven. We don't give any physical honors here until they are won."

It took no time for Jack Armstrong, the Clary boys' chosen leader because of his physical strength, to challenge Abe.

"We'll see how well you do in a wrestling match."

Not much excitement took place in New Salem, so Abe was not surprised when nearly the whole town arrived to witness the match. He watched as Bill Clary and Denton Offutt laid a huge bet of ten dollars; others wagered knives, money and trinkets.

Abe surveyed his heavy-set, experienced opponent who he towered above, but he himself weighed only 185 pounds. They circled, grappled until Abe had Jack Armstrong in his grasp. Then the Clary boys joined the fight. Abe was incensed as he was backed against Offutt's store. "That's it! I'll fight any of you singly, but I'm not going to be at the mercy of the whole mob."

Since no one accepted his challenge, Abe finally declared, "All right, we'll call it a draw."

That match gave him a reputation for courage and strength and acceptance into the Clary boys' gang which included "Slicky Bill" Greene as well as Jack Armstrong.

Along with admiration for his strength, Abe soon gained their respect for his honesty and integrity. Often they asked him to lead in whatever they tried to do. Sometimes he oversaw their fights, but more often persuaded the combatants to settle their differences verbally.

Abe was accepted in New Salem. Folks loved to hear his anecdotes and stories and his amusing way to settle a problem. A small man's friend had been whipped in a fight. The little fellow had too much to drink, so he challenged Lincoln, "Abe, my man licked yours and I can lick you."

Abe tried not to smile as he replied, "I accept the challenge if you will chalk your outline on me and agree not to hit outside those lines." Abe was relieved when the inebriated man didn't know what to do with such an offer and gave up.

During early winter in 1831 Abe was asked to join the New Salem Debating Society, something he welcomed since he'd always enjoyed public speaking.

He laughed after he'd been issued an invitation by Ann Rutledge's father, "Sir, I'm not sure if you want me. My own pa said he could never get me to shut up once I started and he couldn't get any of his helpers to think about their work."

After he joined, Abe found he enjoyed debating. While visiting over in Macon County he upset a politician by giving an impromptu speech on the navigation of the Sangamon River.

From past experience he knew his listeners anticipated some of his amusing stories, so he opened up the discussion of his subject, followed through with answers to their questions, and summarized it so well that even he was amazed.

Lincoln learned later that the President of the debate society told his wife, "There is more than wit and fun in Abe's head. He is already a fine speaker. All he lacks is culture to enable him to reach the high destiny that he has in store for him."

Hearing this, Abe decided to improve his education. Fewer and fewer folks flocked to Offutt's store so Abe had more and more time to read.

Mentor Graham informed him, "John Vance owns a copy of *Kirkham's Grammar*. I'm sure he'll let you borrow it," so Abe walked many miles to obtain the book. Never a 'know-it-all,' he went to Mentor Graham when he didn't understand a passage.

Bill Greene volunteered to ask questions from the book and

Abe would tell answers and definitions in return.

Because of his analytical mind, he turned his attention to mathematics, but his interest in literature was stimulated by the philosopher of the village, Jack Kelso. After leaving Offutt's employ, because the store went broke, Lincoln boarded with him and his wife.

Kelso quoted often from Shakespeare. "The quality of mercy is not strained, it droppeth like a gentle rain from heaven," was one of his favorites, but he repeated all Shakespearean lines with such fervor and gusto that Abe whispered to Jack's wife, "I do believe he missed his calling, he should have taken up acting."

Although Abe learned from Kelso, he'd be the first to admit, "Mentor Graham did more for my education than anyone."

Needing a job, Abe decided that he'd become popular enough with his neighbors that he might win a seat in the State Legislature, so on March 9, 1832 he declared his candidacy in a circular sent to all the voters in the county and in the *Sangamon Journal*. He asked McNeil and Graham to help put his message together. Abe was not at all sure of his own expertise at that time.

Abe told Graham, "I've made no secret of the fact that I'm for Clay for President, but I find the voters here are only interested in local issues and contests, so I'm going to avoid the national scene."

Graham had chuckled before saying, "Abe, some of the folks here have you pegged. They say you are a born politician."

Political parties lacked organization in the frontier. If a man wished to run, he tried to talk his friends into inserting an announcement concerning his candidacy. Some sought the backing of influential politicians, but Lincoln declared to Graham, "My decision is to make a direct appeal to the voters," which he did.

When Abe attended a town meeting he enjoyed the opportunity to address the voters. Looking at the faces of possible supporters, he decided to hit them full force with the things that affected them most: "We need to consider deepening and straightening the Sangamon River. My personal knowledge makes me believe that if we cut through some of the bends and dig a straight, shallow ditch of sufficient width through its lower course, and damming the old channel, the river won't clog with driftwood. This would be cheaper than roads or railroads."

He went on to say, "Education is the most essential subject voters have to consider. Every man should have an education sufficient to enable him to read the history of his own and other countries, by which he may duly appreciate the value of our free institutions; to say nothing of the advantages and satisfaction to be derived from being able to read the Scriptures, and other works, both of religious and moral nature, or themselves."

He concluded by saying, "Every man is said to have his peculiar ambition. I have no other so great as that of being truly esteemed of my fellow men, by rendering myself worthy of their esteem. How far I shall succeed in gratifying this ambition, is yet to be developed. I am young and unknown to many of you. I was born and have ever remained in the most humble walks of life. I have no wealthy or popular relations or friends to recommend me. My case is thrown exclusively upon the independent voters of the county, and, if elected they will have conferred a favor upon me, for which I shall be unremitting in my labors to compensate. But if the good people in their wisdom shall see fit to keep me in the background, I have been too familiar with disappointment to be very much chagrined."

McNeil congratulated him later in January. "Abe, your backing of the improvement of the Sangamon is well-chosen and well-timed. Captain Bogue of Springfield says he is going to bring the Talisman up the river as soon as the ice melts. Word is out and already new settlers are arriving. Land value has boomed. These new folks see that navigation of the river will mean cheaper goods and more accessible markets. Your prophetic words are coming true."

Lincoln was on hand when a letter arrived from Captain Bogue, "I will need several men to meet me with long-handled axes to cut off overhanging limbs and clear twigs from the river."

"Come on, we can get in a boat and clear the channel as we go," Abe coaxed his friends.

Abe felt his plan to prove that the Sangamon was navigable was at hand. Washington Iles led the boatload of enthusiastic men down the river, clearing the channel as they went.

On shore, men and boys cheered as the steamboat puffed through the water. Abe realized that the Talisman was the first steamboat that many of the onlookers had ever seen.

After passing New Salem, the boat was tied up at Bogue's Mill at Portland Landing, about five miles from Springfield. Abraham Lincoln felt like a celebrity as he entered the hall where all of Springfield seemed to be celebrating the Talisman's arrival. He whispered to Washington Iles, "Everyone's excited about our accomplishment."

Iles grinned in return, "So are we, Abe. We ought to be. It's quite a fete!"

The Talisman stayed tied up at Bogue's Mill for about a week when a major problem arose — the water was receding and the boat had to start its return trip or it would be hung up where it was anchored.

Rowan Herndon, Abe's friend, was hired because of being an expert boatsman. "Come along and help me get her down river again," Rowan Herndon coaxed.

"You don't need to coax me," Abe answered. "I'd be pleased to do the job."

Their task was not an easy one. The river kept falling. Time was running short. At New Salem Herndon consulted Abe, "We have no choice. We are going to have to break down part of the dam to let the old gal pass. Any other suggestions?"

"We barely kept her afloat on the way here. Four miles a day isn't much so we have to dismantle part of the dam or we won't be able to move her at all," Abe replied.

Once they were in agreement, they had no choice but to break apart enough of the dam to get the Talisman downstream to Beardstown.

When Beardstown finally came into view and they maneuvered the ship into the dock, Herndon shook Abe's hand. "We did it, partner!"

"Sure did," Abraham Lincoln agreed. "We each *earned* our forty dollars on this one!"

MILITARY DIVERSIONS

Later in New Salem, Lincoln met Ann Rutledge on the street. His heart skipped a beat but then she spoke, "Abe, I want you to know that John and I are very much in love. Aren't you thrilled for both of us?"

"That's just great for both of you!" he exclaimed in the manner he knew she expected. He resisted the urge to add his heart's cry, "I wish I was the one you chose," but he did not. After a short chat with the exuberant girl whose blue eyes seemed to sparkle in the sunlight he sauntered down the road deep in thought. *Why had no other girl ever meant so much to him?* He had no answer.

His deep concentration came to an abrupt stop when a voice called from behind him, "Hey, Abe, you know we got to go? You signed up and we're going," Bill Greene hollered.

"Go where?" for a moment Abe was completely befuddled. Where was this friend who ran around with the Clary Grove boys wanting him to go?

"Old buddy, wake up! Chief Black Hawk told the government that he crossed the river to plant corn, but he brought along three or four hundred braves decorated with war paint and armed to the teeth with swords and guns. Needless to say, the natives are scared! You knew our governor called for volunteers."

Slick Bill's remarks made him remember. He'd become so involved in helping to move the Talisman that he'd put the Indian crisis out of his mind. In 1831, hostilities were avoided when the Indians agreed to move west of the Mississippi and not cross back over without permission of the Governor of Illinois or the President of the United States, but Black Hawk had broken his word.

Abraham Lincoln shared with his friend, "I signed up when the governor asked for recruits. The store was winking out and I knew that I'd have to do something to sustain myself. It's most difficult when you don't know where your next meal is coming from. Besides, there was little choice."

Greene chortled, "What do you mean, no choice? You could either claim you were a coward and wouldn't fight and you'd have to pay the government a fee every year because you didn't. Since we're eighteen to forty-five, seems like we're stuck."

"I'm willing to go. I told them I would. Besides I need what they'll pay me."

"Okay, Abe. We're having a meeting tonight to see who we'll pick for our leader."

To Abraham Lincoln's utter astonishment the men picked him to head the pack by an overwhelming majority. And "pack" it was. Hard-looking, unshaven, they went off to be part of the militia and rid the land of the "pesky" Indians. They assembled at Beardstown and the new brigade marched to Rock Island where they were officially sworn in as a part of the Fourth Regiment of Mounted Volunteers on May 9.

Abe's "soldiers" had their own concept of military life. To Lincoln's very first order they replied, "Go to the devil."

One night he was aroused from his sleep by a lot of revelry. Opening the flap of his tent, he was certain his so-called "subordinates" had broken into the officer's quarters and consumed their liquor which put them in a wild state.

The following morning they wouldn't respond to Abe's prodding, "Get up!" he commanded, but all he got in response was, "Leave us alone."

Because his brigade did not march that day his superior officer called him in and snarled, "You are under arrest for this outrage your men have committed and you will have no choice but to carry a wooden sword around with you for two days."

The day after his sentence was over, the boys from Sangamon County decided that Abe had such physical strength that he could throw anyone. They bragged to the men from Union County, "Your great Thompson wouldn't stand a chance if Abe decided to do him in. Set up a time and Abe'll be there to finish your famous athlete and wrestler."

Abe moaned when they brought the proposed match idea to him "You fellows will be the death of me yet. Don't you know of Thompson's great reputation?"

"We do," Bill Greene answered, "but, Abe, you won't back off. You're no coward."

And so Abe found himself pitted against a man of great strength while the Clary boys and others on both sides waged their well-worn quarters and even empty bottles on the match.

"Lincoln versus Thompson," Bill Greene announced. "Let the best man win."

Struggling with all his might, Abe still went down for a fall. The second bout Abe again bit the dirt, but the Clary Grove boys kept yelling, "That's a dog-fall," but Thompson's backers yelled, "Pay up! Our man won!"

For a minute Abe thought the fight was going to be multiplied a hundred times, that everyone was going to get into the melee but he got up, dusted off his jean pants and said, "Boys, give up your bet; if he has not thrown me fairly, he could." Peace was restored in a matter of minutes.

Not long after that some of his men came crying, "Abe, there's a real injun here! Come on! We've got to get him!"

Abe went out and met the Indian, who handed him a letter from General Cass saying he was friendly to whites, so Captain Lincoln turned to his men and ordered, "You leave this old Indian alone."

The men screamed. "What? Abe, when did you get to be a coward? The only good Indian is a dead one!"

Abe felt a rush of color come to his face, "Listen, you uncouth characters!" His voice grew higher as he screamed, "You know I'm not a coward, and if you doubt it, give me a chance to prove it. I'll take on any ONE of you! This lonely old Indian can go."

The Clary Grove boys moved close to their Captain Lincoln, their eyes defying anyone who would cross him, amusing Abe who thought, *They can do anything to me, but they're all loyal when it comes to defending me. I need to be defended.*

The Indian left. None of the other so-called "soldiers" disputed his exit. Abraham Lincoln's men took on a more dignified manner after that, giving up most of their wrestling and playing pranks on each other, but tended to sing more often during their leisure hours instead of causing such chaos.

Abe had a difficult time teaching them military terms and tactics since his own knowledge of such things was so limited. Once when he had twenty of them lined up to march across the field, he couldn't think of the terminology to get the men to go in single file which they needed to do to get through the gate. Captain Lincoln used his own ingenuity by ordering, "Halt! This company will break ranks for two minutes and form again on the other side of the gate." It worked, much to Abe's delight.

The company's enlistment was over on June 16, but he re-enlisted as a private under Captain Elijah Iles which had more distinguished men — generals, colonels, captains and other men who had distinguished themselves in private and military life. Iles told him, "We are a scouting detachment or even a so-called 'spy battalion'."

Once while they were encamped near Ottawa, a scout sped into camp on horseback yelling, "The Indians are in Galena! They've cut off the town!"

Within minutes the company was on its way, hearts thumping in time with the drums as they marched, but no one saw a trace of an Indian. Reaching Galena, frightened men, women and children left their hiding places to meet them.

Elijah queried the man who claimed to be the town mayor. "Were they here?"

The wide-eyed, mustached man answered, "OH, YES, SIR!"

"Where are your wounded?" Elijah asked. "My medical men will take care of them."

"They don't need to, sir. Thank God, they didn't harm anyone except Widow Greene who was certain she was having a heart attack, but once they left she miraculously recovered."

On June 16 Abe decided to reenlist for yet another thirty days. While in Jacob Early's company he saw no fighting, but at Kellogg's Grove he and some other soldiers came upon a scene that horrified the men. All of them stood staring at the sight, "There's five, isn't that right?"

The man to his left answered, "You're right. There's five all told."

Early strode in and looked at the five white men who had been scalped. "All right. We can't help them now! Get busy and get them buried."

Abe knew how to shovel. To him it wasn't much different than swinging an axe. That day he shoveled dirt with such fervor that one of his comrades commented, "Abe, what's the rush? They're dead."

Abraham Lincoln stopped only long enough to cry in protest, "I hate it! I hate any man's atrocities against another! Back in my company I had to stop the boys from killing an old defenseless Indian."

His enlistment soon came to an end after that episode and Abe was mustered out of the service at White River, Wisconsin on July 10, 1832. Along with his messmate George Harrison, they ran to get their horses.

"Mine's gone!" Abe cried.

"Mine, too!" George moaned.

"Must have been stolen last night," Abe declared. "They were still here late in the evening."

"We're going to have to hoof it ourselves. The army doesn't give a hoot about us now but I understand they're going to give each of us one hundred and sixty acres of land for part of our pay, but we've got land to cover on foot before that."

The two men laughed as they started. Abe began his own version of the old song, instead of Tipperary, he began, "It's a long, long way to Peoria."

The rest of their company rode alongside them, laughing at their antics and giving them turns on their mounts.

When they reached Peoria, Lincoln and Harrison bartered

and bought a canoe, then paddled down the Illinois River to Havana where they began their cross-country trek to New Salem.

George asked him on the tiring walk, "What're you going to do when you get home, Abe?"

"Didn't want to get out of the war and be bored, so I'm taking on a new occupation—politics. My military career was not a waste. I met some rising young men in the Illinois political arena. They agreed to support me in the race for the legislature before I ever left camp. John Stuart and I got along famously. Like I said, George, it wasn't a waste."

OTHER DIVERSIONS

Since Abraham Lincoln returned home only two weeks before the election, he resumed his election campaign in earnest. He knew how to win friends and influence voters so he went house to house soliciting their votes. In rural areas where he met farmers hard at work, he literally pitched hay to help them as he pitched his candidacy.

Horseless, he could only go so far, but decided it would benefit him if he made his way about eleven miles to Pappsville where the folks were gathered for an auction. Abe arrived on the scene just as a bully had whipped his friend Rowan Herndon. The crowd was about to erupt into a full-scale battle when Lincoln grabbed the culprit by the scruff of his neck and the seat of his pants and tossed him several feet as though he were nothing but a sack of potatoes.

When Abe got up on a box, he got everyone's attention because he was towering so high over the people. He made quite a sight with his trousers not meeting his ankles by several inches, one suspender over a shoulder, and an old straw hat topping his dark hair.

Everyone listened as he spoke: "Fellow citizens, I presume you all know who I am — I am humble Abe Lincoln. I have been solicited by many friends to become a candidate for the legislature. My politics are short and sweet, like the old woman's dance. I am in favor of a national bank, in favor of the internal improvement system and a high protective tariff. These are my sentiments and political principles. If elected I shall be thankful; if not it will all be the same."

Sangamon County was entitled to four men in the legislature. On election day Abe waited for the outcome after the polls had closed. The final tally put him eighth out of the thirteen candidates. Even though the overall count was discouraging, he was thrilled with the total of votes he received in New Salem. Jubilant, he told his friend Bill Greene, "I've only been here for a year and the town gave me 277 out of their three hundred votes!"

Regardless, the election left him jobless. He'd always noticed that a village storekeeper was held in high esteem, so he wished he could clerk in a store again or seriously study law. Neither option seemed feasible. No stores in New Salem needed a clerk; he felt his education was too limited to become a lawyer in that summer of 1832.

Out of the three general stores, only his friend Rowan Herndon showed any interest in selling his part of the one Herndon and Berry owned, and Abraham Lincoln had no assets on which to borrow money.

Abe spoke to Herndon in his usual factual, honest manner, "I have no job, nor any money. If you'll give your interest to me on a promissory note. I'll pay you in the future. We can make a deal."

Rowan offered him his hand to clinch the arrangement after he drew up the necessary papers to put Lincoln in a partnership with Berry. Abe clasped Herndon's hand in his own, then with a hearty grin, signed, "A. Lincoln."

That January Lincoln and Berry bought out Reuben Radford who'd had his store nearly demolished by the Clary Grove boys. So discouraged, Reuben sold his remaining stock to Slick Bill Greene from whom he'd rented the store. Lincoln and Berry bought what items were left saleable from Greene.

The unlikely business partners couldn't make a go of it. Berry, even though he was the son of the Reverend John M. Berry, devoted his time to the consumption of liquor, while Abe Lincoln spent most of his days talking, joking and reading books when he didn't have a customer audience. As he declared to Bill Greene later, "It's no wonder we got deeper and deeper in debt." In April of 1833 Abe sold his interest to Berry.

Lincoln mused about his joblessness. *I'm going to have to do some menial labor to keep body and soul together.* He found no trouble finding work for he was skilled in many ways and folks enjoyed his company.

Rowan Herndon told him, "A good farm hand gets about $120 a year; a poor one $100 with bed and board." Abe knew he could qualify as a 'good one.'

Yet Abe wanted a position where his brains meant more than his brawn so he rejoiced when on May 7, 1833 he was appointed as Postmaster of New Salem. When friends asked, "How did you get President Jackson to give you a position when you're such an avowed Clay man?"

That question aroused Lincoln's sense of humor, so he answered, "The appointment is too insignificant to make my politics an objection."

Rumor had it that Abe was appointed because of a petition made by the women. One of the ladies told Abe later, "When Hill held the office he neglected to distribute the mail. He was too busy serving liquor to the men." Abraham Lincoln learned he had to post $500 bond, as all postmasters were required to do, so he signed the document which in effect could put him in debt even more.

As the head of the local post office Abe was to charge for a letter according to the distance it traveled plus its weight. A single sheet cost six cents for the first 30 miles; ten cents for 30 to 80 miles; on up to twenty-five cents for more than 400 miles. Two sheets doubled the price, three sheets tripled it. Abe's duty was to charge the person receiving the letter the sum that was placed in the upper right hand corner.

The new postmaster bragged to the Clary Grove boys, "I don't have to respond to any jury or militia calls, receive all my letters free and get one newspaper without any charge."

"A. Lincoln," as he signed all the mail, enjoyed accommodating people. Since he'd learned to survey, he would often take mail along in the top of his hat while walking to a surveying job.

Because he had access to the local newspapers in his part of the country, he took up reading all of them in order to know how public opinion was going on political issues.

Once he'd put himself in that arena, he never got it out of his system. He served as clerk for a dollar on election day, then returned the poll book to Springfield for two dollars and a half.

In late 1833 he became a deputy surveyor, a job he was recommended to get by a Democrat. Even though his overseer, John Calhoun, was a staunch member of that party, Abe decided to take the job once he was assured that it would not involve any political commitment.

Former Army Captain Abraham Lincoln received $125 for his service in the Black Hawk War plus several acres of land. His partner, Berry, also received pay for his military service. He began to sign notes and speculate on high financial transactions.

Instead of the pair paying off some of these debts, they invested in the cargo of the Talisman, whose owner, Vincent Bogue, had fled the country because of the failure of the steamship to reach his expectations and other poor business speculations.

Bogue wasn't the only one caught in a web of financial difficulties. Their chain of poor investments left Lincoln and Berry in a mess. When the sheriff notified the two about law suits demanding payment of what had become a burdensome debt, Abe declared to Berry, "We've certainly dug a deep hole. Do you suppose we'll live long enough to pay off our own 'national debt'?"

Abe declared, "We can't run away from our responsibilities. These folks are our friends and we need to reimburse them for their willingness to trust and believe in us."

April 19, 1834 Abraham Lincoln was first on the list of the men running for the state legislature. Although Abe was an avid Whig at the time, Bowling Green, a local Democrat leader and justice of the peace said, "Abe, I do believe in you. I'd like to help your campaign."

After consulting with the Whig leader, John T. Stuart, he gave his reply to Bowling Green, "Upon deep consideration with fellow Whigs, I thank you for wanting to back me and would appreciate any help you can give."

Abe's wit, his storytelling, kindness and vast knowledge made him popular as he went about, as he told Bowling Green, "All I have to sell is myself."

"Politics can be dirty," Abe admitted to Stuart when they were at a meeting on Clear Lake. "I need to tell you that some of the Jackson men came and proposed to me that they would drop two of their own men and get votes for me so they could beat you. They said they'd back me because they were afraid you would run for Congress later against them and win."

To this exposé Attorney Stuart told Abe, "Take their votes. I so appreciate your honesty in telling me their scheme, but I will risk it. My friends and I will concentrate our fight against Quinton, my opponent."

Abe made no formal declaration of his beliefs. His campaign was person to person, talking to farmers as he walked to his surveying jobs asking for votes as he delivered the mail.

At Island Grove Abe visited Rowan Herndon, a man he had befriended while trying to rescue the Talisman. Abe sauntered into his farm at harvest time. Rowan took Abe out to speak to the thirty men working in his field. "This is Abraham Lincoln. He'd like your vote for the legislature."

One of the hands hollered, "We don't vote for any man who won't show us he can do some tough job."

Abe took hold of their hand machine and worked it with no strain, then grinned and declared, "Well, boys, if that's all it takes, I am now sure of your votes."

Attorney John T. Stuart had been watching Abe. He declared, "I marvel at your rapport with people during this campaign. I am certain your honesty would make you a tremendous lawyer."

To this comment Abraham Lincoln answered, "I have given it some serious thought. Even as a child I told Mama I wanted to be a lawyer, but I have so little education."

Stuart declared, "But you have such a keen mind. I can help you."

With that encouragement, Abe went and bought a book of

legal forms. Using the instructions inside, he began drawing up mortgages and deeds and wills for his friends, providing them free gratis while saying, "I have to practice on somebody."

Squire Bowling Green, at age forty-four, was a delight to Lincoln as he watched the merry 240-pound man's stomach roll when he laughed. The squire showed no objections to friends' references to his obesity by calling him "Pot."

Often the Greens invited Abe to dinner, and delight surged through their guest when Pot said, "Abe, I think it's time you try a few minor cases in court. I see you snooping through my books and it is evident from your gift of gab that you are destined to become a lawyer."

The election results were in, but fearing defeat, Abe did not hang around for the results. It wasn't until the next morning that Pot exclaimed, "We showed them Abe, you made it! You came in second! You WILL BE our new state representative!"

Later Abraham Lincoln looked up the tally in the newspaper. "Second!" He cried aloud to Pot, "I came in only fourteen votes behind Dawson who was at the top. By Jove, that's amazing!" All Pot did in response was chuckle heartily and let his belly roll.

His win at the election polls sent Abe into a literal frenzy. He studied every law book he could get his hands on. At Stuart's invitation he went to his law office and read and consumed every bit of knowledge on the subject he could find.

He exclaimed to Stuart in a tone of voice equal to an excited small child with a new toy, "I've mastered forty pages of Blackstones today!"

On the road from Springfield to New Salem he'd read and recite from books he carried open in his hand until he reached a tree near a store, then sprawl out and put his bare feet on the trunk and read from Chitty or Blackstone.

One of his friends stopped to inquire as he watched him, "What are you reading?'

Abe's reply showed his indignation to the query, "I'm not reading. I'm studying law."

In November he interrupted his studies to borrow $200 from

a friend for some decent clothes, travel expenses, and to help keep his creditors from hounding him.

On November 22, 1834 he was delighted to be elected as one of the ten delegates to the State Education Convention to be held at the state capital of Vandalia.

Arriving in Vandalia, he surveyed the town. *Not much to speak of,* he told himself. The State House impressed him even less.

As he toured the dilapidated two-story place, his guide informed him, "The House meets on the first floor and the Senate on the second."

The Vandalia Inn had a 40 x 20 dining room, and the two weekly newspapers — one Whig and one Democrat — shared the state's political views. Those were the most impressive things to Abe as he settled into being a resident in that town of about 600.

Yet as time went on, other events of interest took place. Not only the legislature, but the State Supreme Court and the District of Illinois Federal Court all held sessions at Vandalia, so Abraham Lincoln told his friend Pot while on a visit to New Salem, "I get to rub elbows with legislators, judges, great lawyers, yes, even lobbyists. Do you think I'd make a good lobbyist?" he asked the squire, knowing that the question would bring on his all-encompassing chuckles.

It did. "You could sway a man into giving up his claim for gold," Pot replied. For the next few minutes the two howled with glee.

With Abe's determination to do the voters' belief in him justice, he gave his all to his new position in Vandalia. The process of seeing politics in action overwhelmed him so he kept a low profile, absorbing all the tactics the lobbyist used to persuade a man to vote for their cause. Unlike his usual outgoing self, he was more subdued. Abe Lincoln dropped into court sessions and listened to arguments. He seldom missed a roll call. After he'd taken in much knowledge, he was given a few minor assignments and later drafted a number of bills to be brought before the House.

As he told his friend Bill Greene when he dropped by, "I'm

getting three dollars a day for a job that I love!"

For the first time in his life he met men with vast education and breeding. Most had amassed a sizeable fortune, and Abraham Lincoln, more determined than ever to get a law degree and pay off his own staggering debts, returned to New Salem when the session ended in February.

There he resumed his legal studies with such fervor that one of the Clary boys growled at him, "You're going to kill yourself studying. What you think you're going to be? You don't think they'll want you as a lawyer, do you? Come on, let's have some fun."

"Not now," Abe answered. "If I'm going to be what I hope to become, I'll have to pass on such frivolities for a long time to come."

His unlearned friend walked away mumbling, "Now I'm a frivolity. What in thunder is that?"

FIRST LOVE

Back in New Salem Abe pondered the state of his own life. After his first step into the political arena, he thought often about seeing the judges and senators and the men who had reached places of recognition because of their abilities, so he determined in his own mind that he'd work hard enough and study law until he reached their status. He'd seen them arrive at parties with their wives at the Vandalia Inn, and he'd watched with envious eyes. How he wished he'd been able to take Ann Rutledge to such an event. How could he? When she'd told him about his friend John and how she loved him, her sea-blue eyes glistened with joy.

He often scolded himself. *There's more fish in the pond. Look around. You're twenty-six. Are you going to spend your life hankering for a girl who loves another man? Abraham Lincoln, wake up!*

Yet, back home, he had that old familiar feeling the moment he laid eyes on Ann Rutledge. A sickening feeling swept through him as he noticed a diamond ring on her hand when she smiled at him and declared, "Oh, Abe, you haven't been around and we've all missed you."

She said she missed him! Taking her outstretched hand in his, he decided he needed to act like something different than a love-sick school boy, so he said, "I see John has you branded." He spoke in jest, trying to make light of her engagement ring.

"Abe, I really did miss you. Heard you were in town and needed a room. Papa has one open at our boarding house. He needs help sometimes, so he might let you work out part of your room and board. Besides, I'm in a terrible dilemma and I need someone to talk to about it. You were always willing to lend an ear."

Abraham Lincoln responded with, "Of course I'll listen to you. I must admit that I missed you, too, but I'll have to consider the room proposition. I'll let you know soon."

Walking away from her, he knew his answer. How could he resist not staying at a place where he could see her every day? That afternoon he packed up his clothes to go to the Rutledges.

Ann welcomed him with a smile, and a declaration, "I knew you'd come! You always give me such good advice."

The two were standing on the front of the wide porch that went around the entire place. "Let's go out back where we can be alone and talk without any of the gossips hearing."

Abe's heart raced. She wanted to be alone with him! Did that mean she'd changed her mind about John McNeil?

He soon found out Ann's expression became sober. Her eyes clouded. "Oh, Abe, this story is like one out of a novel. You knew John McNeil quite well, didn't you think?"

Abe nodded, then she went on, "I thought I knew him, too. In fact, I was certain I knew his moods and his thoughts. If I hadn't I certainly wouldn't have agreed to become his wife, but he gave me this ring. He told me this story, and then he left. Oh, Abe, that's nearly two months ago. He said he'd love me forever, but he's never even written a word. What am I to do?"

"Oh, Ann, I'm sure there's some explanation."

Tears glistened in her eyes. She seemed to try to regain her composure as she continued to share her concerns with him, "Before he left he admitted a fact that nearly floored me. He said that John McNeil isn't even his real name, that in fact, he was christened as John McNamar. Abe, what a revelation. He'd asked me to be his wife and I didn't even know until then that my name wouldn't be Mrs. John McNeil," she sobbed.

Sitting beside her on that porch bench, Abe couldn't resist putting his arm around Ann, assuring himself that it was just a gesture to console her.

His heart beat faster as she leaned against him, wailing,

"Oh, Abe, what would I do without you? I'm so glad you came home."

For a brief moment she sat still until she pulled away. Her expression changed to one of anger "Can you imagine? He said when he left New York he changed his name because John didn't want his family to find him until he made his fortune, then he'd go back."

Abe said simply, "That's quite a revelation but, Ann, I'm sure. There's a reasonable explanation for John not writing to you. We'll just have to wait and see."

Abraham Lincoln decided he really didn't want John to return, that way Ann might respond to his attention and her missing fiancé wouldn't be wounded if he stayed away.

Every day he checked on the status of how Ann was feeling, and in truth he had to admit to himself he didn't want Mr. McNamar, alias Mr. McNeil, to show up.

As time passed Ann confided in Abe more and more. One day after John had been missing six months she threw herself into his arms wailing, "Oh, Abe, I've been such a fool. Why would I place my future in such a man's hands if he didn't care enough about his family to keep their name and why would I ever expect him to be loyal to me?"

Abraham Lincoln held her close, and whispered, "It's all right, dear Ann. We need to pray that things will work out."

He fought many emotional battles in his mind. John had been gone for six months without any communication. "Lord," he prayed, "Would it be agreeable to You if I shared my feelings with Ann now? It seems John has abandoned her."

Ann moved to Sand Ridge and Abe went to her there and admitted for the first time on a moonlight walk, "Ann Rutledge, I am head over heels in love with you, but I don't know how you feel about me." He leaned down and she made no effort to resist him as he tried to kiss her. His heart began dancing.

Distance loomed between him and Ann since her move, so Abe began to spend weekends with "Uncle Johnny" Short so he could court her more.

One night when he went to call, he was thrilled that her

engagement ring was missing. That night he felt heaven come down as she looked up at him and whispered, "Oh, Abe, I finally realized how much I love you, that John is almost a dream that never happened."

"If that's true, will you marry me? I promise I'll never leave nor forsake you, but will cherish you as my wife as long as we both shall live."

A wistful smile crossed her face. "That sounds like wedding vows and yes, I'll be thrilled to share them with you and be your wife, but Abe, dear sweet Abe, you'll have to ask Papa for my hand."

Abe laughed and swung her in the air, "That, my darling, will be my pleasure."

That same night they traveled to the Rutledge home where Abe found her father in the kitchen preparing some food for his customers. "Well Abe, good to see you. What's going on? You look like the cat who'd swallowed the canary."

"May I speak to you in private?"

Turning to his daughter, he said, "Ann, will you take this plate to the man beside the counter? Abe, let's go out on the porch."

Once outside Abe asked, "Will you give me permission to marry your precious Ann?"

"Her mother and I both feel you will be a devoted husband and take good care of our little girl." His words made Abe feel as though he'd taken wings and could fly!

Back in New Salem his old friend Josh met him in the Berry store. "Abe, did you hear? John McNeil has come back to claim Ann for his bride. Seems as though he'd met up with some hard luck on his journey home — got sick on the way, so sick he thought he'd die. When he recuperated, he made his way to New York, and then his father died so his mother begged him to stay and help her get adjusted to widowhood. Poor guy. He was despairing because he had made no contact with his bride-to-be."

Abe stood, speechless. Why hadn't John stayed away? How he wished that he hadn't heard Josh's tale, but he knew the old gossip usually had his facts right.

Half-sick from the news, Abe ran to the stable to rent a horse, hoping he would get there before John. But as he neared Sand Ridge, his heart sank. He could see John McNeil mounting the steps.

After tying the horse to the hitching post, Abe waited. He felt he had no choice but to let John explain himself, then let Ann do her choosing. Eternity passed, it seemed, before John opened the door to leave, walked down the steps, but never acknowledged Abe who was sitting on the stairs.

Ann came out and sat beside him," Oh, Abe, I feel so sorry for John. I told him I was sorry to disappoint him, but I'm in love with you and I want to become Mrs. Abraham Lincoln."

Those words sent Abe's heart dancing again. Sweeping the girl of his dreams up in his arms, he hugged and kissed her and nearly burst with joy. "Oh, Ann," he cried in delight, "You've made me the happiest man alive."

For weeks after that their lives were filled with plans and dreams until the day Ann's face clouded as she declared, "My parents want me to go to the Female Academy in Jacksonville for a year so that I would be able to make a living if something should ever happen to you."

What? Abe cried inside. *How could such a thing pour so much cold water on my great plans for the two of us?* Yet her words made him ponder. He'd spent nearly every penny he'd earned just to capture Ann's heart and start to pay off his huge debt. "It might be good for me to work at my law career and build a little nest egg for us. Can't say I like it, my darling, but I'll continue to dream of the day when you'll be mine. Oh, Ann, my love, my you fill my life with gladness."

Having agreed on that, Ann made her plans for more schooling and Abe put all of his efforts into building a brighter future for the two of them by taking on extra jobs and studying with renewed fervor.

In the summer of 1835 Ann's father visited him. Abraham Lincoln was not prepared for what he had to say. "Abe, Ann became ill, so sick we brought her home." Then he begged Abe,

"Please don't try to visit her. The doctors claim that any excitement would worsen her condition."

Abe wept when he heard she was racked with fever and getting pale and emaciated. "How could they expect me to stay away?" he cried to a friend. "Only part of me exists when I'm not with her."

He kept constant contact with her parents. On one of his many trips to their home to consult with her father about her well-being, he watched Mr. Rutledge's expression grow grim and grave — tears formed in his eyes. "Abe, we fear for her life. If her fever goes up any higher the doctor says she could die. As much as you'd like to see her, we'd like that, too, but the doctor claims it is best that you don't see each other. She might have a relapse because of it."

"A relapse? Oh, sir, I would not want to be the cause of more problems."

In spite of his feelings, Ann's health was foremost in his mind. Abraham Lincoln found he could barely function. His heart was being wrenched every day for each time he got a report it was worse than the one before.

After three weeks of agony, a messenger came to his door with a note, "Abe, the doctor tells us that her condition is hopeless. We can do nothing more so you are free to come and see Ann. Besides, Ann desperately wants to see you." These were words written by her father. Abe was certain that Mr. Rutledge and his wife could not have spoken them without emotionally breaking down themselves.

Casting everything aside, he rushed to his beloved's bedside. Words of endearment were passed between Abe and the auburn haired girl be loved with such fervor. Tears rolled down his cheeks as he looked at her once vibrant face and zestful eyes. As she spoke to him her words, even though little more than a whisper, were clear and concise. "Abraham Lincoln you are destined to be a great man. Don't let the world down. My love and my prayers will always go with you."

After trying to control his grief and the very thought of her dying, he placed his long angular face close to her and sobbed,

"Don't leave me, my darling. I can't bear thinking of life without you." He could see from her eyes she shared the anguish of her plight, which was almost too much for the two of them to bear. On that hot, humid day, August 25, Ann Rutledge closed her eyes for the last time.

Abe, numbed from the emotional pain, went through the motions of burying his beloved. Part of the epitaph on her tombstone even intensified his grief for it read:

"I am Ann Rutledge who sleeps beneath these weeds. Beloved in life of Abraham Lincoln. Wedded to him, not through union, but through separation."

As Abe Lincoln walked, sobbing away from her grave he wailed, "My heart lies there."

For weeks after the funeral Abe visited her grave but had no unction to work or eat. And others who saw him tried to change his emotional state by saying, "Abe, you're going to have to get a hold on yourself. You have to eat and sleep and rest or you will join her."

One close friend warned him, "Abe, be careful. You're losing your sense of reason. Life must go on. Ann wouldn't want you to give up. She always said you had the potential to become great."

Somehow those words finally penetrated the brokenhearted Abraham Lincoln so he decided to go away to the town of Bowling Green. He could stay with some acquaintances who had offered him refuge there when they saw the extent of his mourning and begged, "Abe, come stay with us for a while and sort out your feelings."

During that time he sought some consolation from the scriptures, especially dwelling on the segment in Ecclesiastes chapter 3 that said,

1. To everything there is a season, and a time to every purpose under heaven.

2. A time to be born and a time to die, a time to plant and time to pluck up that which is planted.

3. A time to kill and a time to heal; a time to breakdown and a time to build up.

4. A time to weep, and a time to laugh; a time to mourn, and a time to dance. *He wondered if he could ever laugh or dance again.*

5. A time to cast away stones, and a time to gather them together, a time to embrace and a time to refrain from embracing.

6. A time to get, and a time to lose, a time to keep and a time to cast away.

Abe dwelt on these words. His precious Ann had been plucked out and cast away from his life, but the Lord said there was a purpose for everything. Slowly Abe began to put the broken pieces of his life back together and returned in two weeks to New Salem with new grit and determination. Somehow, someway he would become the man that his sainted mother and his precious Ann had expected him to become.

"Please, Lord," he begged, "help me find a reason and purpose to live."

ATTORNEY AT LAW

After that, Abraham Lincoln immersed himself in studying his law books. He started the day with a prayer before he went to the cabin courthouse in Springfield to take the test to become a member of the Illinois bar in the year 1837. His long, thin face gave the appearance of one who radiated confidence, yet underneath his mind was churning because of the pressure. Abe knew that he had studied with as much fervor as was possible in order to pass the exam, a stepping stone necessary to fulfilling his goal of becoming a bona fide lawyer. He knew all too well that determination was the one thing that could keep him focused on the task at hand. He prayed for divine wisdom to ease his nerves and carry him through.

After completing the written part of the test, he turned the paper in to be graded for accuracy and depth of understanding the meaning of the law. Oral questions bombarded him next, yet he never lost his train of thought and was able to answer everything he was asked. A great sigh of relief passed through him when his interrogators concluded their questioning and he heard the announcement that he had also passed the written portion of the exam. A smile flooded Abe's face for the first time during that trying day. Abraham Lincoln, who had been born into poverty in an obscure cabin in Kentucky, was about to be accepted as a full-fledged Illinois attorney.

He felt every inch as tall as his six-foot-four stature when he arose to take the oath of office and place his hand on the Bible, then swear to uphold the law of the land. Not one to spend a lot of time being concerned about personal appearances, he'd given much thought as to what he should wear for such an illustrious occasion. Abraham Lincoln wanted to appear as a man fit for the legal profession. For years he had sacrificed to make this long-awaited dream come true. Few people, doubtless any person who witnessed his admission to the bar, had any concept of the dedication this new lawyer had to apply to get this prize. With his meager total of twelve months of formal schooling and his lack of any university or college training, he wondered if he was perhaps the only person with that background to ever receive such a degree. This accomplishment came when Abe was twenty-eight years old.

Limited finances kept him from getting a plush, new office. He had no choice but to put out a hand-carved shingle to advertise his new profession. It read simply, "A. Lincoln, Attorney at Law." No one seemed to care that he had deprived himself of so many creature pleasures for so many years just so he could attain this goal.

Abe soon learned despite his undaunted efforts to succeed, being accepted as a lawyer did not mean popular acclaim or financial success. Not one to sit idly by and not get things accomplished, be tried to fill in time by reading the Bible during this waiting game, and prayed that God would show him how to get people to come to his little dingy office. Over and over he found himself repeating his own mother's encouraging words that she had told him so often during the nine years he had her to inspire him, "You can do anything you set your mind to, Abraham Lincoln."

When it became obvious that no one was going to beat a path to his office door, he decided he would have to move out and drum up some business. After praying that the Lord would show him how, Abe hit upon an idea. Since he had learned surveying in order to obtain funds to keep life and limb intact while he was studying law, why not incorporate that knowledge to get clients' interest?

Leaving the office with a sign saying when he would return, he went in search of folks who might be having border disputes.

He soon found two pioneer neighbors who had been haggling over the markers on the corners of their properties. Abe learned from them that not even the surveyors could be certain which of the boundary markers were man-made, and which were gopher creations. Common practice at that time was for men to make small mounds of dirt to point out the ends of their properties, but the gophers were busy making similar hills themselves. After surveying the evidence, Abe determined which he thought were authentic markers and which looked as though they were made by industrious gophers. The newly-appointed member of the bar decided to represent the one he felt certain was the real property owner.

To reassure himself and his client about his decision, he rushed to town on his horse. There he amused a friend by asking to borrow a book about the life of the gopher. Inside its pages he found what he considered to be accurate proof about his beliefs; so he went to court with the mental assurance that he could win the legal battle.

When the session began, Attorney Abraham Lincoln stood before the jury and argued his case. Snickers rippled through the log courthouse as soon as Abe proclaimed, "I have proof that my client's boundaries are authentic surveyor's mounds, while his opponent has no more than stacks of gopher dust marking his boundaries."

He then explained, "The gophers burrow and I could determine the difference between the two kinds of hills by the fact there are tunnels beneath the creature's creations and I found such evidence beneath my opponent's landmarks." Lincoln was thrilled when the jury's verdict agreed with his explanations.

A few days later an irate old farmer named Mr. Case came storming into Abe's office. "They promised!" he cried. "I took them at their word that they would pay me for my prairie plow and my team of oxen. Those Snow brothers claim they don't have to pay me the two hundred dollars they'd promised! They said they'd pay me as soon as they got paid. I know they've already got their money, but they haven't given me a red cent!" His voice gained momentum and volume as he continued with his tale of woe; his face reddened from his obvious frustration. "They say they don't have to pay me a penny because they signed a note when they are not of legal age! Legal age, ha!"

Concerned that the poor man was about to have a stroke, Abe tried to pacify him. "We can take them to court and win," Abe assured the frustrated seller, then he added, "What they're trying to do is a form of legal theft, but we're not going to let them get away with it."

A frown furrowed across the farmer's brow. "But they claim a lawyer told them that I have no recourse because they were both minors when they signed the note, and nothing can be done about it because that's the law."

Abe placed his hand under his chin as though deep in thought. As if a sudden spark came from inside his head, a twinkle appeared in his eye. His face took on a look of pleasure as he spoke to his client, "Don't fret. We can win regardless of the fact that they were under legal age when they signed the document. Trust me."

The day came for the case to come to trial. Abe looked around the court room and noted that the Snow Brothers had hired counsel of their own. Their attorney was the first to share his clients' case before the jury, stating: "My clients do not deny making the note. However, Mr. Case was most aware that they were both minors at the time of the conveyance and the contract."

Attorney Abraham Lincoln could not dispute that fact legally, so he used his turn to begin with agreeing with his opponent by saying, "Yes, gentlemen, I guess that's so."

The Snow Brother's lawyer retaliated by reading the Minor Act aloud. Once more Abe stood and agreed to its validity, causing him to realize his ability to defend Mr. Case on legal terms was in jeopardy, so in slow motion he half-sat, half-stood as he began to address the court in his clear, unassuming accent, "Gentlemen of the jury, are you willing to allow these boys to begin life with this shame and disgrace attached to their character? If you are, I am not. The best judge of human character that ever wrote, had left these immortal words for all of us to ponder:

"Good name in man or woman, dear my lord,
Is the immediate jewel in their souls.
Who steals my purse, steals trash; 'tis something, nothing,
'Twas mine, 'tis his, and has been slave to thousands.
But he that filches from me my good name,
Robs me of that which enriched him,
And leaves me poor indeed."

Then, rising to his full towering height, he turned and looked down upon the Snow Brothers. Stretching his long right arm toward his opposition, he continued on with the discourse, "Gentlemen of the jury, these poor innocent boys would never have attempted this low villainy, had it not been for the advice of these lawyers."

For the next few minutes he decreed, "Even the noble science of law could be prostituted, belittling the great legal profession if the young men got away with such an act." In conclusion, he added, "Gentlemen, you have it in your power to set these boys straight before the world." In his final words he pled for the young men only. Not once did he ever mention his own client's name.

Glancing at the jurors, their faces registered the indignation Abe had hoped to convey. The jurors never left their seat to decide that the Snow Brothers needed to pay their debts. More amazing, even to Abraham Lincoln, was the realization that he had put those two conniving minors under such conviction that they were willing to pay off the debt they owed the farmer, legal or not. A. Lincoln, attorney at law, had wrapped up that case in his favor in less than five minutes. It was at that point that he realized his wit and humor, his quaint and homely illustrations, his inexhaustible store of anecdotes which always brought out a point, added a great deal to his power as a jury advocate.

After he'd been established for a while he spoke with fellow lawyers about the tariff, amusing his acquaintances by his own zany interpretation of the problem, "I confess that I have not any very decided views on the question. A revenue we must have. In order to keep house we must have breakfast, dinner and supper, and the tariff business seems to be necessary to having them. But yet, there is something obscure about it. It reminds me of the fellow that came into a grocery down in Menard County, at Salem, where I once lived and called for a picayune's worth of crackers, so the clerk laid them out on the counter.

"After sitting awhile he said to the clerk, 'I don't want these crackers, take them and give me a glass of cider.' So the clerk put the crackers back into the box, and handed the fellow the cider.

"After drinking, he started for the door. 'Here, Bill,' called the clerk, 'pay me for your cider.'"

'Why', asked Bill, 'I gave you crackers for them.'

'But I haint had any,' responded Bill.

'That's so,' said the clerk. 'Well, clear out! It seems to me that I've lost a picayune somehow, but I can't make it out exactly.'

"So," said Lincoln after the laughter had subsided, "it is with the tariff. Somebody gets the picayune, but I don't exactly understand how."

PROMISED LAND

Abraham Lincoln held little hope for his future. It seemed everything he'd tried had turned sour. He'd taken the job of surveying the town of Petersburg, but his pay had only put a small dent in the money he owed folks back in New Salem. With no immediate prospects for employment or money for his pockets, he asked the Lord, "Father, I don't know what to do or where to turn. I've struggled all these years to become a lawyer, but now I'm so broke I don't have enough to feed myself my next meal, let alone keep up a new law office. All I've done so far with my learning is to get people to listen. Even though I've made a name for myself in the court room, what good is that?"

Dejected, on that April 15, 1837, he continued to seek direction as to what he should do next. To his total astonishment, the answer came to him in the form of Attorney John Stuart, one of the most renowned lawyers in Springfield. He found Abe sitting on a cracker barrel in the general store in Petersburg, brooding over his dilemma because his job of surveying the town had come to a close and he was in a quandary as to what to do next.

Abe was feeling of little worth when the attorney strode over to him, "Abraham Lincoln, there you are!" he exclaimed.

Amazed, Abe sprang to his feet and grasped the man's hand. So startled he couldn't even remember his visitor's first name, but his smile and demeanor assured him that Attorney Stuart was there for good, not to collect a client's debt or sue him for some wild thing. For that Abe was grateful. He had enough negative financial and mental problems to deal with these days. He had amassed enough bills to call them, "My national debt." After being caught off guard he realized that John Stuart not only had been the one who had befriended him during their time serving in the Indian War but had encouraged him later to become a lawyer.

John Stuart went on, "Abe, I've given it much thought,. You know I'm running for political office, and I'm certain you can service the clients while I have to be out campaigning. I'd take you on as a junior partner in the firm. You can share my new office on Hoffman Row." Abe's heart beat faster. No mention of the partnership requiring any investment on his part made him thrilled to accept

"I'm broker than a saddle tramp," Abe confessed later to one of his many friends in Petersburg, "except for one thing — I don't even own a horse."

The friend offered to lend him his own steed, so Attorney Abraham Lincoln headed to his new occupation riding on a borrowed horse with all of his earthly possessions loaded into two saddle bags.

Once he reached Springfield he noticed a sign saying, "A.Y. Ellis Company General Store," so he hitched the horse outside and sauntered inside. The clerk's face shone with pleasure as Abe approached the counter.

"I'm Joshua Speed," the store clerk said as he offered his new customer a handshake. Abe could sense the excitement in both the eyes and the voice of the young man as he continued, "And you, I know you are going to be the new lawyer in town. I'm so glad! Mr. Lincoln, I've heard you speak and I consider you to be a great orator!"

Abe flushed, partly from the compliment, but mainly because of his financial dilemma. Although he did not want to, he felt compelled to ask his new-found admirer a tremendous favor, "My need is to have a mattress, pillow and some bedding. Can you give me the cost of these much-needed sleeping essentials? I'm sorry, but you will have to trust me for payment until I make enough in my new occupation. I don't even have a place to put my belongings."

The clerk's next offer compounded Abe's pleasure, "I have a large room with a double bed upstairs which you are welcome to share with me."

"Then I won't even need all that stuff!" Abe cried with delight. Without another word, he turned and mounted the steps two and three at a time, as fast as his long, lean legs would allow. A minute or so later he returned, a grin plastered across his face "Well, Speed," he declared, "I have moved."

After thanking Joshua Speed for his kindness and generosity, Abe walked out onto the main street in Springfield. An unrestricted pig looked up and snorted at him, others ambled down the dirt road, rummaging at any debris they could find.

A few brick buildings stood out from among the many log cabins. Abe gave little heed to the nostril-burning aroma of manure emanating from outside the stables at the edge of town. His frontier days during his childhood had made him accustomed to that obnoxious smell. As he surveyed the sights, sounds and smells of Springfield, a glimmer of hope for his future began to form in his mind. His precious Ann was gone, but she had wanted so much for him to amount to something greater than he had been in New Salem. *Lord* he thought, *It's taken me a shorter time than Moses, but I see Springfield as my promised land.*

Speed had given him directions to his new office which was housed in the second floor of a building on Hoffman Row. When Abe opened the door and entered the room, he felt a surge of gratitude. Attorney Stuart was there to greet him. "Abe, I think this will work out very well for both of us."

To this statement Abe heartily chimed in, "I'm sure it will."

"My, things are looking up!" he told Speed later. "You've furnished good quarters and I have a job of my liking."

In the ensuing months Joshua Speed and Abraham Lincoln became confidants, Abe even told him of his hopeless feeling when his precious Ann was sick and how devastated he'd felt after her death.

Speed listened intently, then declared, "That's what you need, a replacement for Ann."

Abe just shook his head, "Old pal, you don't understand. I

do not feel at ease around women. Spinning a yarn for mixed company comes easy, but I get panic-stricken and choked-up when left alone with a female."

"What!" Speed demanded. "You were planning to marry Ann Rutledge, but you claim you get tongue-tied with a woman. How do you explain that?"

Abe sighed. "Remember, she and I had become great friends for years before we fell in love, so she didn't intimidate me at all."

"Well, then it's time for you to have a social life and meet new people. There's a dance at the Edwards' house on Saturday night. You're going."

"No!" Abe protested. "You are handsome and well-built. Look at homely, gangly me. You have everything going for you, including money. We both were born in Kentucky, but our similarities end there. The Lincolns were dirt-poor with next to no education and the Speeds had money enough to get you a college degree. You still have money. My supply is almost nil."

Joshua Speed laughed, "You're a lawyer and most folks think anyone practicing law is rich, so no one needs to know that you are almost broke. That gives you access to society."

Abe hung his head. "You were born into society. I was not. If I became the President of the country — which is a laugh — I would never belong."

The color of Joshua Speed's face began to change. Red blotches appeared, so Abe knew he'd protested too much. Speed's next words were angry, tart: "That's enough! You have no choice. I've made up my mind you're going to join the world and not be buried in books. They're great, but they're supposed to prepare you for real life. Now, that's all there is to it! We'll leave here at 7:30. The party starts at 8 o'clock."

Abe decided that he had to get over his lack of self-esteem and the feeling that he didn't belong in society. "Okay, if you go, I'll go, but don't abandon me in some place with a bunch of strange women."

His friend howled with delight, "Once you get used to the company for the evening, you'll start telling your tales and I'll feel that I'm the one left out."

To this Abe simply replied, "You dreamer, you."

The following night he went to great pains to look like society, but as he leaned far enough down to inspect his image in the mirror, he shook his head and told his companion, "You can't make a silk purse out of a sow's ear. If I had on a swallowtail coat, I'd still look like a country bumpkin."

He could sense Speed's exasperation at hearing that last comment, so he chose to be quiet.

After a short carriage ride they got out and walked up the steps to the most fabulous residence Abe had ever visited; in fact he doubted if he'd ever seen better.

A black butler met them at the door. "This way, sirs," he said as he led them toward a room where piano music was being played. The exquisite sight before him caught Abe's breath for a moment. Elegant tapestry couches lined the walls, and to his total amazement, beautiful girls in elegant silk gowns adorned many of them.

HE was the true American, at one with the people in his origin, his simplicity of character, his rugged manliness, and his stern devotion to the cause of civil liberty. While he lived, he was the friend of his country, and when he died the sense of personal bereavement darkened every American home. In the supreme crisis of American history, his faith in the ultimate triumph of popular institutions never failed him. By that faith he saved the nation, he widened the bounds of human freedom, and he rendered forever sacred those principles of government which rest upon justice and the equal rights of man. His real epitaph cannot be written. It has received its truest expression in the silent memory of those great historic deeds with which his name is associated, and which can never, as long as liberty is cherished by man, be effaced from the records of time.

William C. Morey
(William C. Morey)

UNIVERSITY OF ROCHESTER, 1880.

CHANGE OF HEART

A woman dressed in a swirling orchid silk gown approached the two men wearing a warm, inviting smile. "Good evening. So nice to have you, Josh. This must be your friend Abe. Isn't that the name?" Her question was really directed at Abe, so he answered, "Yes, ma'am. It's Abraham Lincoln."

A pleased look crossed her face as she extended her hand, "Your friend thinks so highly of you. I'm your hostess, because I'm married to Mr. Edwards. My name's Elizabeth. Welcome, Abraham Lincoln. Joshua, please introduce him to the other guests."

As Abe's eyes scanned the huge room, they came to rest on a familiar figure. "Speed, that has to be Judge Stephen Douglas! You don't know the girl who's making eyes, at him, do you?"

Joshua looked over at the young woman dressed in a deep blue taffeta dress. "Oh, her! That's Mary Todd, Elizabeth's sister. She can talk politics like any man who studies the subject."

A quizzical look crossed Abe's face. "Why would that interest her? Women here can't even vote."

Joshua Speed chuckled. "Maybe so, but I think she has political ambitions of her own. She wants to marry a politician. Elizabeth says she always told her family back in Kentucky that someday she wanted to be married to the President of the United States. That's probably why she has the judge cornered. He has that kind of potential."

Abe sighed, "Indeed he has." He watched as Mary Todd waltzed with Judge Douglas who then seemed to excuse himself to go to dance with the other girls, leaving the hostess' sister alone for a moment. Abe, determined to make her acquaintance, somehow found the nerve to approach her and say, "I've been dying to dance with you."

He had to lean over to put his arm around her. He thought, *I must be over a foot taller than this girl.*

Yet, as they danced, he had none of the problems talking with her for she was vivacious. Her eyes danced as she giggled and chatted with him about everything, but seemed to enjoy talking about politics most. Abe soon found that all he needed to add to their conversations was either "yes" or "no." He had to admit to himself that yes, indeed, Mary Todd had him under her spell.

He bid her good night later, and riding back in the carriage toward their room, he knew Joshua Speed was going to tease him so he was ready for the chuckle and remark from the young man sitting beside him. "Looked to me as though you didn't suffer too much. Not bad, is she?

Abe realized exactly who he meant. "No," he answered, "not bad at all, but what chance do I have? The odds are stacked in the judge's favor."

"Not from what I saw tonight. For heaven's sake, old buddy, don't give up before you get started."

And so he didn't. He began to spend time doing what he called "frivolities" more than he ever had before — going on horseback rides, dinner parties, the theatre — all with Mary or where he knew she might be.

They learned much about each other. Her background was much like Josh's. She'd been born in Kentucky, went to private schools. Her mother had died. When her father remarried she did not get along with her stepmother, something Abe had a difficult time understanding because of his close bonding with Sarah Bush Lincoln.

She claimed, "I support the Whigs and prefer Henry Clay for President, but I'll have to back William Henry Harrison because he is the party's choice."

In the meantime Abe began to realize how much his law

practice was helping him to rise a step higher with his political ambitions. Mob violence across the country had his dander up, especially when he read in the newspaper about a vigilante outbreak in Mississippi where so many gamblers were executed by dangling them from the trees. The article also told about a mulatto man who'd been burned to death by a mob. Lincoln was irate, "They never held a trial, Speed!" he cried as he read the news aloud. "Men must NEVER take the law into their own hands!"

Episodes such as these caused him, Abraham Lincoln, as an attorney to find public places to get up and promote the cause of justice before the people. "Man must obey the laws of the land or we will be nothing more than cannibals."

Through his knowledge of the law, Abraham Lincoln also began campaigning against graft in both Springfield and the government of the state of Illinois. People listened. Mary Todd admitted to Speed that she'd begun to see Abe as her political and romantic hero. Their joint interest in politics brought them closer and closer together.

Joshua Speed had also taken a great fancy to a girl named Fanny Henning and shared with Abe that he was contemplating marriage. The two close friends discussed at great length both of their love lives and the weighty decisions they had to make.

Abe joked, "To marry or not to marry, that is the question." After a long walk on a moonlit night, Abe waited until they were seated in her sister's living room before he found the nerve to ask, "Sweetheart, would you like to become Mrs. Abraham Lincoln?"

"Yes!" she cried, giving him a huge kiss. It seemed to Abe that she came more alive as she twirled her dress and danced around the room.

Her willingness scared Abe. He began to wonder to Speed later, "Do I really love her?"

Josh was pleased to tease him about his uncertainty. "Abe, you'd have been knocked for a loop if she'd said 'no.' Instead, you're just a chicken who's afraid to get married."

"I suppose you're not," Abe quipped back.

"No, I am NOT! If Fanny will have me, I'll be a proud rooster!"

After many sleepless nights Abe decided he had to renege on his offer so he went to Mary and told her, "I don't know what to say. I guess I'm just not the marrying kind." Mary's reaction was not what he expected. She sat, stunned, on the sofa. It was her turn to be devastated. Abe was shocked. For the first time since he'd known her, she seemed unable to speak. Tears flowed. He kissed her good-bye, but she still sat speechless. Abe tiptoed out the door.

After that episode Abraham Lincoln went to pieces. He never liked to offend anyone, let alone someone he cared about. On top of it all, his dear friend Speed was moving back to Kentucky and Abe felt as though his whole life were falling apart. Depressed, Abe found himself incapable of doing menial tasks or everyday business.

Speed took the opportunity to taunt him by letter, "You, the great orator, look at you! Don't you realize it's because you love the girl? Good heavens, man, you'd have thought she'd spurned you, but she said 'yes'!"

Still Abe's melancholy moods continued, but Speed also found himself with a case of "cold feet," declaring in another letter that he wasn't certain of the depths of his own love.

That letter brought one of protest back from Abraham Lincoln. "You know very well you love Fanny. Her sweet personality, her deep faith and beliefs and all her goodness have all been points that made her catch your fancy from the beginning."

After sending that letter he thought, *Wise up, Abraham Lincoln, or you may lose the woman who was meant to be your wife.*

He began to do some serious contemplation about his own life. Miserable! That was the only way to describe it. He had to get a grip on himself.

Abe decided that perhaps a visit to Joshua Speed in Kentucky would improve his melancholy mood so he boarded a train and headed south. *Maybe,* he mused to himself as the wheels began to clang and the engine started to hiss and blow off steam, *maybe Josh can help me out of this mood.*

He found his friend Speed extremely busy in a new job, so

Abe befriended one of the servants who he enjoyed talking with so much. Samuel, the Speeds' cook, offered him words of encouragement, "A man of your stature should have a missus! The Good Lord meant for everyone to have a mate. His Book says that it is not good for man to be alone." White teeth shone as Sam grinned and patted Abe on the back. "You just havin' love miseries. Go on home and make up with your sweetheart. Mistah, look at you. You'd think that she turned you down instead of you backin' out. Just cause I'm black doesn't mean I don't understand your feelings."

Abe stared at the man who seemed to have so much wisdom. Before he spoke again, he reasoned in his mind, *How does someone with so little opportunity know so much?* After thinking that thought, Abe reached out and clasped the man's hand in his. The two stood there with Abe's gnarly white hand and Sam's muscular black hand held together in a firm grip. Abe could not help but be amazed as the two stood with their hands intertwined. He had never touched a black person before, but felt no difference in the cook's skin from his. After talking to Sam, he realized their feelings weren't much different either.

At last Samuel laughed, then boomed out in a voice that sounded like an order, "Go Home! Your miseries will be over once you ask her to forgive you and hear her say again that she wants to be your missus!"

After that the two men parted. Abe had no other opportunity to talk to him before leaving, but his new friend's nudgings were foremost in his mind on the train ride back to Springfield.

Back home Dr. Henry, who Abe had consulted because of his mental state, finally talked him into attending some social functions. Springfield society was so small that he couldn't help but run into Mary. She was always there.

Speed decided he did indeed want to marry his Fanny. Abe smiled when he read the letter announcing Joshua's forthcoming marriage. Along with his congratulations he told Joshua Speed, "You try it. If you like it, I might try tying the knot too."

Abe realized he was afraid of a marriage commitment. He knew himself well enough to understand he could never break such a sacred vow, so he struggled with uncertainty.

Mary's sister and brother-in-law, the Edwardses, showed their disdain for Abe since spurning Elizabeth's sister. Abe understood that their family's pride had been wounded.

Yet others were determined to bring the two back together, and Abe found himself in Mary's company at a dinner party where Mary Todd was seated beside him so Abe realized that the hostess was playing cupid. As the evening progressed he once again became enchanted with Mary's charm and intelligence.

Speed assured him months later, "I love Fanny and being married to her. I'm glad you decided to try it yourself."

That word of encouragement was all Abe needed, and he Mary once again on a moonlit night. "Will you marry me? This time I'm sure I want to love you forever."

"Yes!" she declared as she let him hold her close and kiss her. "Oh, Abe, yes!"

They began to make plans. Mortified by his jilting her, Mary had made such a fuss about Abe's decision to break off their relationship that he'd heard by way of a letter from Speed in Kentucky that the Edwards family deemed him an incompetent.

Joshua Speed had also informed Abe, "Her family does not envision a member of the Lincoln clan to be a suitable match for one of the Todds."

That had been a major reason for Abe to stay away from Mary Todd for such a long time, but she assured him often as they'd begun their secret dating, "Oh, Abe, you have such fantastic ability! You can do anything you set your mind to."

That is what Mary claimed, yet she seemed embarrassed at Elizabeth and Nivian's disapproval. As Abe had told Speed, "She tore me to pieces verbally when we parted so her sister and her husband feel they have just reasons to think as they do about me. She made her own dilemma. Guess she'll have to fix it herself."

Abraham Lincoln still had mixed feelings at intervals before their marriage, but as he told Speed, "There's no female who I've ever met that understands my bent toward politics. Sometimes I feel that she's more knowledgeable than I am. She doesn't even have the right to vote, and that's a shame. Women shouldn't be treated any different than men."

Speed howled with delight. "Oh Abe, wouldn't life be boring without the girls? The world wouldn't last long without them."

Abe laughed with his friend before adding, "I've put my hand to the plow. In the Bible it says that once you do that, you shouldn't turn back. That is true. I've already hurt her deeply because of my indecision and I will not do it again. She isn't Ann, but she's a brilliant woman and I am going to marry Mary this time, no matter if my feelings go up and down with her moods. I can't say anything, I'm too moody myself."

Speed declared, "You are serious, aren't you?"

Abe nodded his head, "I had to reach this point. You know that when I make a vow, I will keep it. The marriage vow should never be taken lightly."

Nearly three long years after they met, Mary and Abe began making definite plans to become man and wife and set November 4, 1842, as their wedding day. Nervous because of bad feelings Mary had aroused in both her sister and her husband, the bride and groom-to-be finally gathered enough courage to go to them and tell them of their plans.

Elizabeth Edwards showed her disgust at first, but Mary assured her and her husband, "I have thought the whole thing through and through and I am proud to say I want to become Mrs. Abraham Lincoln."

Her sister threw her hands in the air in a gesture that Abe knew meant her sister's marriage to him was exasperating, but then Elizabeth declared, "Mary, if you are determined to have this man who is ten years older than you, then I am just as determined that you will use our parlor for your exchange of vows."

She got her way. Abe and Mary became man and wife there during a ceremony with an Episcopal minister officiating. Abraham Lincoln placed a gold ring on his new bride's finger. He'd had the words "Love is eternal" engraved inside.

The newlyweds went to live in a room at Globe Tavern, where

they decided they needed to stay for some time.

As Abe put it, "Mary, it's only four dollars a day and if we stay here, we can help work off 'My National Debt.' I have no intention of not paying off everything I owe back in New Salem."

Within two months Mary found she was pregnant, but she refused to go to her sister's home to have the baby. On August 1, 1843 when it was time to give birth to her child, her pride would not let her budge from the tiny room.

She told her husband, after they named the child Robert Todd after her father, "We need to get more room for us and Bobby. You know that anyone of any importance looks down his nose at us."

Abraham Lincoln felt as though he had finally been fulfilled, having a wife and baby. He began to work diligently to get ahead. He'd reached an amazing $1500 a year so he bought a bungalow on the corner of Eighth and Jackson streets where Bobby had a play-yard. He hired a maid for Mary, and they had their second son. "Eddie" was named for Edward Baker, Abe's friend.

Mary, always afraid of being poor again and being frowned on by society, went through manic stages of saving and scrimping and haggling over prices to spending money like a drunken sailor, both of which frustrated her husband who did not like fussing or confrontation.

Usually he liked to dote on her, calling her "my Molly" or "my little woman," but most of all she loved being called "my child wife."

As long as Abe catered to her and her demands, which he usually did, they had a relatively stable, happy marriage. He tried, whenever possible, to please his wife who in so many ways often lived up to the "child" part of the nickname he had given her.

POLITICAL MANEUVERS

The new Mr. and Mrs. Lincoln had such limited funds that after they set up housekeeping in one room at the Globe Tavern. Mrs. Lincoln never stopped complaining, always reminding Abe, "I am not accustomed to such a humble existence," so Abe decided to run as a Whig candidate for Congress. Having a family inspired him to want to obtain a good living for them.

Mary was thrilled with the idea of a means to higher prestige and more funds, but she exclaimed, "Abe, John is going to run for the same office! He's only thirty-three and not only is he my cousin, but he's a formidable foe."

Abe sighed, "Not only him, but my friend Edward Baker is going to run."

The political rumors about him caused Abe to laugh and tell Hay, his new office aide, "It's a good thing I can see humor in what they say about me — that I'm a candidate of pride, wealth, and aristocratic distinction. What's even more ludicrous — they're saying that I support drunkenness when I've been a teetotaler all my life."

It came as no surprise when Mary's cousin John Hardin won the election, but Abe signed the Pekin Agreement saying that he would be the candidate selected for Congress in 1846.

After the campaign he returned to Springfield to set up office. His choice for a partner? William Herndon, whom he'd met when Speed was clerking at the store.

Mary was horrified at Abe's choice. "Abraham, I wish you'd have consulted with me. That man is a nonstop chatter box. He winds up in the morning and never stops all day. He probably talks in his sleep!"

Lincoln shrugged, "You may not approve of his attire — the high silk hat and his shiny patent leather shoes, but he's meticulous and should help keep the office in order. The die is cast. I've asked him and I won't go back on my word."

Mary gave him what he called her "disgruntled look" and declared, "He also buries himself in a bottle. You'll be sorry."

When Abe shared the little second floor office across from Springfield's public square, "Billy" did not live up to his partner's expectations in many ways. Herndon cluttered as much as the man he always addressed as "Mr. Lincoln," and only occasionally protested Abe's ritual of reading the newspapers aloud every morning while sprawled across the sofa with his feet propped up on chairs at the end.

"Why do you do that?" Bill Herndon asked one day.

"Do what?"

"Read aloud. Can't you read to yourself?"

"I could, but you wouldn't get any benefit from it. Besides, both my eyes and ears together duplicate their good when I read out loud."

In 1845 Abe began working toward his goal of becoming a member of Congress. His friend Edward Baker assured him that he'd step aside and let Abraham Lincoln become the next Congressman. However, Hardin, Mary's cousin, did not want to live up to the Pekin Agreement and gave Abe a difficult time. Abe told Mary, "I'm afraid your relative enjoys his Washington position too much to do so without a fight."

Hardin finally conceded defeat in February. In May, Abe heard in the Whig's district convention, "We hereby proclaim our candidate for a seat in Congress to be the Honorable Attorney Abraham Lincoln."

"Time to get on the road again," he told Mary. "The Democrats have nominated Peter Cartwright, the Methodist circuit preacher, for their candidate."

Rev. Cartwright claimed, "My opponent is an infidel. He does not even belong to a church."

In response Abe put out a signed flyer confessing, "I am not a church member, but I believe in a Supreme Being and have never denied the truth of the Scriptures. I would not support an atheist for public office since no man has a right to injure community feelings and morals."

On August 3, 1846 he listened as the results were tallied. He'd polled 6,340 votes to, the pastor's 4,829 — an unexpected majority for the district. Even so, he wrote to Speed about the election results saying at the closing of the letter, "I am not as pleased as I had expected."

In early December, 1847 the Lincolns took up residence in Mrs. Spragg's boarding house across from the Capitol.

In Washington, Mary had a difficult time feeling important. Abe was either melancholy at meals or busy entertaining other members of Congress with his witty stories around the boarding house table during meals.

His wife had fits, announcing, "I can NOT endure staying in one room all day with the boys! We might as well be back at the Globe. Abe, these congressmen are sickening. This little town is crawling with saloons and women of ill repute."

Abe told her, "Mary, now listen, I came to Washington to fulfill my job. I can NOT spend my life trying to pacify you."

And so, Mary carried out her, threat. After three months in Washington she exclaimed, "I've had it! I'm packing up the boys and taking them home to Kentucky."

With her departure, Abe worked at his duties and became unpopular back in Illinois because of his dispute with President Polk over his policies about Mexico during the United States' war with the Mexicans. In fact, he made a speech about it, claiming that Polk had failed to end the war as he should.

Abe waited several weeks, then told Hay, "Not one single Whig has backed me up. They're criticizing ME back home about being critical of the President. Even Billy Herndon wrote to tell me that I'm misguided; that Polk has a right to dispatch troops to guard against a Mexican invasion. Mary's not here. The boys are gone and I'm miserable!"

When spring came, Abe's enthusiasm blossomed along with

Washington's fruit trees, causing him to put all his zeal behind the Whig candidate for President, Zachary Taylor. Even though he himself was an avid Clay man, he backed Taylor in order to support the Whigs.

Abe stumped in New England by train, making certain to appeal to his audience. "As conscientious Whigs, don't abandon the party so we can keep slavery from expanding."

At Boston's Tremont Temple Abe shared the platform with William H. Seward, the former Whig governor of New York. Abraham Lincoln was impressed with Seward's message even though the man only ceased his cigar-smoking habit long enough to speak for the Whigs and then add his comments declaring, "My concern is about the Southerners controlling the Union and the slavery issue."

Lincoln, impressed, told Seward, "You are right We've got to deal with the slavery question and give it more attention than we have been doing."

Taylor did win. Lincoln went home to Illinois to be with his family for the holidays where Mary and the boys were once again. "It won't be long now, Mary. I'll be home to stay soon. You know that this is my last session." After a kiss, he boarded a train and returned to Washington alone.

In Congressional debates, even fistfights flared up about the slavery issue. At Mrs. Spragg's dinner table Abe sided with Joshua Giddings about the slaves.

"The view out the window of the 'Georgia Pen' across the street from the Capitol nauseates me. They drive in the Negroes where they collect and keep them until they are taken like droves of horses to the Southern markets."

Abraham Lincoln became so incensed with that sight that he informed the House, "I am getting prepared to introduce a bill to ban slavery in the District of Columbia and fifteen of the Capitol's top citizens agree with my plan."

To that remark Southerners screamed, "Who are they? Give us their names."

Arguments and fights ensued. John C. Calhoun and others threatened to boycott Congress. In a speech Calhoun declared about the two races, "They cannot live together in peace, or harmony, or to their natural advantage, except in their present relation."

Conservative Whigs warned Abe, "Your abolition bill will only drive Southerners to even more dangerous threats."

Abraham Lincoln relented and gave in to their ideas but he was somewhat disheartened with himself.

His last session of Congress ended in a deadlock with neither side giving in on what Lincoln called "the destructive question on slavery." That was on a Sunday morning.

The following day, March 5, 1849, Abe attended Zachary Taylor's inauguration and the ball which followed.

He waited again. This time he expected Taylor to give him a cabinet post, but he received none. A mix-up with his dossier, which the President had asked him to compile, caused him to lose out on another appointment, this time to Justin Butterfield from Illinois who had actually opposed Zachary Taylor during the election.

Lincoln couldn't believe the news when he heard it. Perplexed, he turned to Hay to ask, "Where is the justice? Taylor gave the appointment to a man who campaigned against him."

Abe received a communiqué telling him of the President's regrets, saying, "I'd like to offer you the opportunity to be Secretary of the Oregon territory."

Abe turned it down. Indignant, he declared to Hay. "They might as well send me off to Alaska with the Eskimos. Thanks, but no thanks."

Mary agreed, "Papa died, Eddie's not feeling well, and we don't need to take arduous trip out west."

Returning to his family and friends in Springfield, he told Herndon, "Billy, I don't know that my system can endure politics. Langdon will run for my seat and probably win. Let's you and I knuckle down and make a prosperous law practice out of this place."

ABRAHAM LINCOLN is one of the most commanding figures in history. That his elevation to the Presidency was at first viewed with aversion by a large and influential body of his countrymen there can be no question. But events vindicated the wisdom of the choice. The world has confirmed and history has recorded it. When he died it was as a conqueror. Like Wolfe, at Quebec, Abraham Lincoln expired in the arms of victory.

Saml Adams Drake

MELROSE, 1882.

(Samuel Adams Drake)

RENOVATION DILEMMA

While living in Springfield Abraham Lincoln decided that he had to be away from his family far more than he chose if he was to further his political career and, that he needed to ride the circuit as a lawyer in order to make a living for his family. Although Mary often spoke of her determination "to be married to the President of the United States," Abe deemed even the thought of such a thing ever taking place as ridiculous.

"Mary, Mary," he'd say, "if you wanted to be married to a man in the highest office in the land, then you shouldn't have hitched up with a fellow from the lowest end of the social ladder."

"Abe Lincoln," she protested, "with your charm and intellect I know you can do anything you set your mind to — so set it for top billing."

"As your husband I don't want to laugh in your face, but I have to tell you such dreams give me a secret chuckle. Do you know how many times I've been defeated in business and a run for office? At one point I couldn't get elected for dog chaser." Abe's grey eyes twinkled as he tried to squelch some of his wife's enthusiasm so she wouldn't be disappointed when her big dream evaporated.

His friend Speed had dropped by to chat when Mary wasn't home. Joshua Speed had moved out of town but he still remained one of Abe's close confidants. The pair was sitting in the Lincoln kitchen sipping tea and swapping yarns, when a look of amusement surfaced in Abe's long, drawn face. "Speed, you'll love this one! Mary thinks I'm Presidential material — not for the local lodge but for the WHOLE UNITED STATES."

Abe chuckled.

Putting his tea cup in his saucer, Abe's friend looked directly in his eyes. "Never thought about it, but why not? You have the brains and the stamina to do anything. Sure, you can do it!"

Abe stared. "Have you gone crazy along with her? Don't you remember the penniless pauper on the borrowed horse that you took pity on and shared your quarters with him?"

Speed's gaze never wavered. "You can if you set your mind to it. Look how far you've come."

Abe smiled again. "Well, Mary's political ambitions have given me some advantage. I need to go on a campaign for six months. I hate going away from my family for even a short time, but I need to if I'm going to get anywhere in politics and I must make a better living. At least I won't have to listen to her nag about my leaving, but I know she won't just let me go without paying some kind of price. I know her too well to think she'd just agree to just let me leave for so long without some colossal favor."

Mary entered the kitchen then with Robert and Eddie in tow. "Speed, how nice to see you," she greeted Abe's friend. "Would you like to stay for dinner?"

"No thanks, Mrs. Lincoln. I need to be moving on."

Mary reached and hugged Abe around the waist. "Here's the newspaper, dear. I picked it up for you. Why don't you go in the living room and enjoy reading it until dinner is ready."

As he sat down to read the paper, he thought, *My cunning wife is up to something. When I get treated this well I ought to prepare myself for a Significant Demand.*

Mary seldom disappointed him. In the midst of one of her best meals, while she was serving his favorite Johnny cake, she cooed. "Abraham, dear, look at this house. You need to think about the fact that this house is not of the caliber for a man of your stature. It needs major remodeling."

Her request came as no surprise. "Mary, you know that we're in no financial situation to do such a thing right now. I'm going to be gone, but our income is going to be almost nil. We CAN-NOT do anything major, let alone revamp this house." That was his answer, but he knew Mary Todd Lincoln well enough to expect her to continue to work him over before his planned departure.

His spouse did not disappoint him. Every breakfast, lunch and dinner she continued her badgering, each time getting a little more vociferous and forceful.

Then the day arrived when an exuberant Mary met him at the door squealing with delight. "Darling, we can do it! We can do it! I've inherited twelve hundred dollars." With that, she placed a letter declaring that she was indeed inheriting that large sum of cash in his hand.

"I'll get my friend to give us a bid," he told her. "We'll see what we can do, but don't get your hopes up too high."

Abraham Lincoln decided to get his building contractor friend to help him with his plan. Going to John's office, he stated his case, "Friend, I have an outrageous favor to ask of you. My wife has this dream of making our little house on the corner into some sort of palace, but I need your help to stop her. Would you please go and look over her ideas and then give us some outrageous bid so that I can get her to agree that we never could afford to have those vast renovations done?"

John, the contractor, laughed as he declared, "I understand now why you win all the cases you do."

Offering his hand, Abe grasped it firmly, "I take this shake as a form of agreement on my proposal. We men have to stick together or the women would make us fall apart."

During the next week contractor John did Abe's bidding and offered his bid of thousands of dollars.

Abe tried to console his wife's depressed mood over the situation, "Don't worry, dear, we'll do something to fancy up the place when I get back."

Expecting a war to erupt, he was amazed that she didn't even mention the idea again. He was the one who finally brought the subject up. "You see, Mary, I was right. I'm sorry, but you'll just have to wait until I'm bringing home more money. Yes, it would be nice to have more room for the boys, but we can't do it now."

She simply kissed him. To his amazement she never brought up the subject again. She didn't even seem to resent his decision. Her usual treatment was to ignore him when she felt inconvenienced, but she administered no such punishment this time. Instead she busied herself washing and ironing and packing his clothes. Thrilled with her seemingly selfless efforts, Abe again thanked and commended her "My, but you have been so kind. I'm so sorry I have to leave you."

The day of his departure the two of them stood in the doorway of their little home.

After lifting up Robert and Eddie and giving each a special hug, he leaned over and planted a special kiss on his wife's check. "Promise you'll write often," Mary pleaded.

"Of course I will," he agreed, then lifting his suitcases he went out the door of their bungalow home. Turning to wave good bye, he felt a special attachment to his family. While he traveled by train to the first stop on his long journey a warmth for his wife flooded his mind and he began thinking their marriage was starting to mature.

During the interim between his departure and his homecoming the Lincolns exchanged many letters sharing about their two sons and politics, the two things they had in common. Mary never mentioned the house for which Abe was grateful. He certainly was not going to bring up the subject. Abraham Lincoln began to breathe easier about the homefront. His Mary's fancy must have turned elsewhere.

Upon his return to Springfield in 1844, his steps quickened as he reached the corner of Eighth Street and Jackson. For a moment he stood, baffled at the edifice standing before him. Both the houses on the right and the one on the left of the corner were the same as he remembered, but the one he and Mary had called home was not!

Spying a familiar neighbor he joked, "Do you know where Mr. Lincoln lives?"

The pair stood together looking at the two-story home with

a completely changed exterior. The neighbor patted Abe's arm, "That wife of yours can do quite a job on anything if you let her loose. I think she could change the course of history if she decided that was her aim. Don't you think so, Abe?" he queried.

Abe shook his head. "I think I'd better check out the inside, too." With that he bid his neighbor farewell and went to the door.

Anger, betrayal seethed inside of him as he knocked at the door of the strange dwelling but once it was open all bedlam broke loose.

Robert and little Eddie squealed with delight, throwing themselves in their father's arms. As he scooped them up together, Mary joined them in the melee. As soon as he put down his excited little boys, she hugged him and he reached down and gave her a kiss.

"Abe, come, come see how marvelous it looks." He followed behind as she escorted him up the newly constructed staircase.

"See, Papa, see," Robert cried excitedly. "Each of us has our own room."

Mary and the boys great pleasure calmed his anger. She beamed as she showed him the rest of the house's interior and he decided that he would do or say nothing to thwart her enthusiasm. "Look, dear, I even made drapes for the windows myself. I'm so proud of how everything looks."

He loved to see her happy so he decided that he would not ever mention the financial mess. Somehow he'd manage to cover her extravagant taste. He always did.

FOR the fame of Lincoln it is only necessary to say that he was contemporary with the permanent establishment of human freedom in the United States, and identified with its final accomplishment.

Fernando Wood

(Fernando Wood)

NEW YORK, 1880.

POLITICAL DREAMS

Not long after that the Lincolns were eating in their kitchen when Mary waved an envelope in front of him. A smile spread across her face as she opened it. "Oh, Abe," Mary cooed, "We're invited to the Governor's Ball."

Abe knew that Mary enjoyed such prominence because of her desire to be socially important, but as an aspiring office holder he went to such functions to discuss the political arena with men such as the Illinois Republican Governor, William Bissell. His aim was to learn all he could about the slavery situation in the early spring of 1857.

Abe discussed the problem with his many Republican friends, men he'd teamed up with when the Whigs began to lose out. After the gala event he declared to Mary, "I know you go to dance. I go to waltz into information about politics. On March 4th President Buchanan announced that his new Supreme Court was going to resolve the slave problem for all time. Along with new appointees there are five Democrats and only two Republicans all told because of the President being a Democrat himself."

Mary eyed him curiously. "You knew that was a great probability. You'd appoint Republicans if you were in his place. Why are you so concerned?"

Abe's expression became grave. "I'm concerned about the Dred Scott decision. I'm afraid of how they're going to vote on it."

It wasn't long before he read in the newspaper words that

he was certain would send the Republicans into a spin. "Mary, Mary, I told you! Chief Justice Taney and the other six Democrats declared that free Negroes were NOT and NEVER HAVE BEEN U.S. citizens. He claims that the Constitution and the language of the Declaration of Independence never embraced them as Americans."

Abraham Lincoln's tone of voice grew more and more indignant as he continued, "Negroes are said to be inferior and totally unfit to associate with the white race politically and socially and the court declared in a vote of six to two that the Declaration of Independence has nothing to do with blacks."

For once Mary held her tongue. Abe knew she'd grown up with slaves tending to her needs back at the Todd estate in Kentucky, but his childhood and early years had been marred by mental pictures of men driving slaves up a hill, of his father demeaning himself by rounding up slaves for a pittance.

Abe closed his eyes as he sat back in his rocking chair in his Springfield home.

The encouragement and insight he'd received from Speed's black chef came into his thoughts. In Abe's mind's eye he could see the grateful face of the girl he'd purchased freedom for in New Orleans. He hadn't taken her with him so he'd always wondered if he'd been wrong. Where could she go? Where did she go? What chance did she have for any kind of decent life?

As he pondered the Supreme Court decision further, the frantic faces of the black men who attacked them by their river boat also came to his mind. Their desperate fear had shown in their frenzy for the bare essentials for survival. "Oh, God," he prayed, "no one has a right to determine another man's fate. How could anyone decide who was classified as a human being?"

His mind kept coming back to Speed's servant who Abe had befriended on his trip to Kentucky; a man who proved to Abe that black folks not only had brawn, but they possessed brains and a keen sense of humor.

Abe didn't talk about politics any more that day. Mary had supported Filmore for President. Abe had given over fifty speeches for Freemont, the Republican candidate who the Democrats chose to call a fanatical "black abolitionist."

Neither of their candidates had won, so they had no choice but to wait and see what Buchanan would do. To Mary and Abe Lincoln the new Democratic President couldn't have made a poorer start for his term of office so Abe told Hay the next day following the election, "I'm going to have to stick here in the office to increase the coffers again, but I'm in full accord of unseating Douglas in the Senate race in 1858 and Buchanan in 1860."

W ITH profound reverence for the life and character of Abraham Lincoln.

J. A. Garfield

(J. A. Garfield)

MENTOR, OHIO, JULY 2, 1880.

THE GREAT DEBATES

When the Whig party had become inconsequential, Abe had joined the Republicans who professed much of their same ideals and platforms, yet he was astounded when the Republican party chose him to run for the United States Senate against the famous Democrat and orator, Stephen Douglas, in July of 1858. He knew the judge well and had the utmost respect for his abilities. Why would they choose him to run against such a man?

He began to think of strategy for such a race. Abe was certain that his opponent for the state of Illinois senatorial seat would respond to his challenge to him, "I propose a series of joint debates to be held in our principal towns."

Stephen Douglas' reply was immediate, concise, "I agree to this challenge. After deep consideration I also suggest that each discussion will last three hours; that Mr. Lincoln and I should speak for three hours all told, and we should alternate in each opening and closing. The opening speech should last one hour, the reply an hour-and-a half, and the closing half-an-hour."

Abe read his opponent's suggestion and grinned, "Good plan. Couldn't improvise a better one myself. However, I'd like to add that these meetings be held in the open air. No hall could hold so many inquisitive spectators." He knew Judge Douglas always drew a crowd.

And so, almost on the agreed terms of a duel, the meetings began. The first confrontation between Abe and his competitor shocked the Republican party candidate. Abe whispered to his friend Nicolay who was standing beside him, "Look at them!

Did you ever see so many reporters? Douglas claimed that all the major newspapers across the country would send their own newsmen, and I believe from the looks of the number of men who are wearing 'press' badges, that he was right."

Not only the reporters, but the masses of curious people who stood for hours at each speech were greater than any crowd he could have imagined. To his amazement, the contents of his speeches were published verbatim across the country alongside those speeches made by Stephen Douglas.

Concerned about Douglas' great natural speaking skills, Abe's friends urged him to share his amusing stories to his audiences, but he objected, "These occasions are too serious, the issues too grave. I do not seek applause, nor to amuse the people. I want to convince them against the extension of slavery with the greatest conviction, that on the result, hangs the fate of our great country."

After Nicolay had surveyed the first of the verbal duels, his ardent fan spoke to his friend, "You have two great advantages — you have the best side of the question and the best temperament. Abraham Lincoln, you are skilled at telling an apt story to illustrate your point. Your adversary gets most irritable when he's hard pressed."

"We'll see," Abe answered. "The proof of the pudding is in the eating." He knew that Nicolay understood that nothing is certain about the results of a speech until it is over. "They'll have to taste test it a while. Then they'll decide."

During the first of these debates at Ottawa, Douglas bombarded Abe with questions that he could not ignore. Cheers and jeers arose from the crowd every time they agreed or disagreed with each of the men. Abe couldn't help but think he was performing in a two-ring circus, Stephen Douglas, the "Little Giant," in one, Abraham Lincoln, the tall, gangly "Rail-Splitter," in the other.

Consulting with the state's top political leaders, he was advised, "Be aggressive and put your opponent on the defensive!"

Nicolay laughed, "Mr. Lincoln, they want you to get in the ring like a boxer and make certain you get in the first punch, then you're supposed to knock him out before the fight ends."

Abe chuckled at his friend's comparison, but he decided to put the politician's suggestions into action in the next debate at Freeport and into those that followed.

Abe knew he had help from the newspapers and other Republican speakers — Trumbull, Swett, his ardent supporter Lamon, Davis, and his long-time law partner and friend, William Herndon who he affectionately called "Billy." Even Frederick Douglas, the famed Negro editor who fought for the abolition of slavery, came out from New York to join in the "get-Douglas fight." The black editor was esteemed by many whites because of his intellect and powers of persuasion.

August 27 was late summer, but the day was damp and chilly as Abe stood before an audience of about fifteen thousand pro-Republicans. He declared, "Yes, I am against the addition of more slave states" Then he added, "No, I am not pledged to the abolition of slavery in the nation's capital."

After that he thrust two quick punches at Douglas, "Can the people of a territory in any lawful way include slavery before statehood? If the Supreme Court ruled that a state could not prohibit slavery, would you abide by the decision?"

Douglas threw out some punches of his own, which became known as the Freeport Doctrine because of it being established during the two candidates' speeches there. "Of course the people of a territory can exclude slavery before statehood through the principle of 'unfriendly legislation' that will allow them to refuse to enact the necessary protective measures. I have argued this doctrine all over the great state of Illinois for years, so there is no excuse for my opponent pretending not to know my position now. As to his question about the Supreme Court, I am certain it would never hand down any such decision as Lincoln described. That would be an act of moral treason to which no justice would assert."

Douglas then dealt what Lincoln considered to be a low blow, "You Black Republicans," he began, but to Abe's amazement the crowd yelled back, "White! White!"

Douglas' next punch bit Lincoln as though it were lethal, at least below the belt. "The last time I came here to make a speech, while talking to you people of Freeport, I saw a magnificent carriage drive up and take a position on the outside of the crowd. A beautiful young lady was sitting on the box seat while Fred Douglas and his mother reclined inside, and the owner of the carriage acted as driver."

Abe noticed that the audience seemed to be confused. Some cried, "Right!" and others, "What of it?"

Douglas bellowed a reply, "If you Black Republicans think that the Negro ought to be on a social equality with your wives and daughters, and ride in a carriage with your wife, while you drive the team, you have a perfect right to do so, and, of course, you will vote for Mr. Lincoln."

The applause after the judge's speech sounded to Abe like thunder rolling across the huge throng, yet at the end of his own oratory, the audience seemed to be thoughtful, contemplative.

After the crowd had dispersed, Abe turned to Nicolay. With a shrug of his shoulders, he declared, "I gave it my best"

"It'll have a greater impact than what you think. Everyone left in a far more contemplative mood. Things will go better when you two go at it again in Little Egypt."

Abraham Lincoln traveled later to Jonesboro near the Kentucky border. On that star-studded night of September 14 he sat in front of his hotel for about an hour. His own mood was contemplative, wondering what would transpire the next day. Donati's Comet streaked across the heavens with its tail of fire. Abe wondered, *Am I going to ignite the world with fire as that comet's doing, or are my ideas going to fizzle and give out, leaving this country which was meant for greatness in such a sorry state?"*

Nicolay sat beside him, allowing Abraham Lincoln to pursue his thoughts until Abe turned and sighed, "I shouldn't worry about Little Egypt since my beginnings were just east of here in Indiana. I'm part of these people." He went to bed, reassured in his mind.

His assurance changed when he faced the new crowd. Nicolay made a quick count. "Only twelve hundred people. Most of them are wearing badges claiming 'Buchanan for President,'

Mr. Lincoln, that means most of them are Democrats, probably in favor of the judge."

Douglas took advantage of the crowd's favor toward him, never giving up on his punches against Lincoln's speech declaring 'A House Divided Cannot Stand' which advocated unity of the country on the slavery issue.

When Abraham's opportunity came he threw a few punches of his own, saying, "My opponent tells what is most suitable for the area in which he is speaking. First he says that it is up to a territory to vote to keep slavery out, but when asked if it is possible for this to take place before statehood, the judge says it is up to the Supreme Court to decide. Now, Judge Douglas, you can't have it both ways!"

Abe knew the rules made it impossible for the judge to retaliate then since it wasn't yet his turn, so he threw out another punch, "He has his own opinion about the Supreme Court's ruling on the Dred Scott Decision which says a territory cannot prohibit slavery at all."

Abe drew a breath before placing his next blow, "The honorable judge shifts his ground again, telling the voters that they can still ban slavery through what he calls 'unfriendly legislation.' Now, what is that? It's as unreal and deceptive as Douglas' other doctrines. Slavery has plenty of vigor to plant itself in the territories without police measures. It takes not only law, but its enforcement to keep it out."

With that, he turned to his contender in the verbal match, "if slave owners in a territory demand Congressional legislation to protect slave property, will you vote for or against such a measure?"

Douglas' reply was somewhat evasive, "I do NOT believe that Congress has a right to intervene in the territories." The 'Little Giant's' voice gained momentum as he threw another jab toward Lincoln, "No matter what my opponent says, the Freeport doctrine and the Dred Scott Decision are not contradictory. The Supreme Court recognizes the right of a man to take slaves into the territories, it remains a barren, useless right unless the government there has enacted local protective legislation. Refusal will exclude slavery just as effectively as if there was a constitutional provision against it."

The verbal boxing matches continued, each of the two participants attempting to win. Their next stop was in central Illinois at Charleston.

Previous to that debate Lincoln had read that Kansas voters had rejected the Lecompton Constitution which had ensured it would eventually become a free state.

When Nicolay and he had discussed this, his friend had informed him, "Federal troops had to oversee the voting, the fray was that bad. Because of Southern opposition to their decision in Washington, Kansas won't be admitted to the Union until 1861."

At Charleston Lincoln arrived in a noisy parade through dust thrown up from the horses' hooves of Lincoln's carriage and a flower-covered wagon filled with women, each carrying a banner representing the 32 states. That ridiculous sight, because of the voting on August second, was the end of the boisterous parade — a young woman on horseback with a sign which read, "Kansas — I will be free."

During that debate Lincoln wasted no time getting to the Negro question, "The moral question of slavery in a country with its own Declaration of Independence, that is the central question between Douglas and myself."

Judge Douglas countered with a punch aimed to get the sympathies of the whites in the audience, "I am not for Negro equality and intermarriage. Lincoln is a racial hypocrite. Like a chameleon, he changes to suit his surroundings. In northern Illinois he declared the Declaration of Independence applied to Negroes. Down here he's not for political social equality with them. These Republicans! Their principles in the North are jet black!" At that point the audience howled, causing Douglas to add, "In the center they are in color a decent mulatto." This inspired the crowd to laugh again so Judge Douglas added, "In lower Egypt they are almost white." Howls of laughter followed. When it finally subsided, Douglas added, "Well, Lincoln was right. A house divided against itself cannot stand."

Lincoln rose for his next punch of retaliation, "I never said I favor Negro citizenship as my opponent has charged, and as to my stand on the race issue, I have said the same thing in all three sections of this grand state."

And so, the bouts went on. In Galesburg he rose to speak to a crowd of twenty thousand who had gathered to hear a debate first hand in spite of a frigid, icy wind.

Alton, Illinois was the last stop for the debates between the two Senatorial candidates. Both candidates suffered from exhaustion. The campaign trail had caused the Little Giant to suffer a tremendous loss — his voice almost giving out on several occasions, yet he summarized his feelings by saying, "This government can endure forever, divided into free and slave states as our fathers made it, each state having the right to prohibit, abolish or sustain slavery just as it pleases."

Lincoln's summary showed the contrast between the two men who'd been in the ring so long that they were ready for the decision as to who was the winner to be announced. He declared, "Slavery is the only issue that ever menaced the Union, but a threat is not removed by extending it and making it larger. You may have a cancer upon your person and not be able to cut it out lest you bleed to death, but surely it is no way to cure it, to engraft it and spread it over your whole body.

"My heart's desire is that we not only have free territories just for native-born Americans, but for all other men from all over the world who want to find new homes, a place to better their conditions in life."

Back in Springfield he had no choice but to get back to his law office as he had not made any money since the beginning of the campaign and his household expenses loomed high and heavy before him. He hadn't seen his family except for Robert and Mary showing up as a delightful surprise for a parade in Alton where Robert marched with the Springfield Cadets. A sense of pride in his family's ardent support had overwhelmed Abe then, making him even more pleased to be home.

Reaching down be scooped his wife and offspring into his arms upon his arrival with the exclamation, "Oh, you'll never know how nice it is to come home after my private war!"

Mary laughed, "It was a battle, wasn't it, Abraham? Do you know if you won?"

Abe contemplated her question, as he so often did when he wasn't sure of himself. "Mary, I don't know. I gave it my all. The rest is up to the voters."

November 7 arrived, the day when Abraham Lincoln knew the decision as to whether he would hold a seat in the United States Senate had come. The day was not one to build up his morale. Damp and cold, the rain drizzled as he made his way to the polling place to cast his vote early in the morning.

At the Lincoln-Herndon office he attempted to go through the necessary papers of his agenda there, but he did not attempt to make any major decisions. His thoughts were too directed toward the outcome of the election. *Will I or the "Little Giant" become the next United States Senator from Illinois?*

That evening he made his way to the telegraph office with Herndon. "Billy, I somehow don't feel you need to worry about losing your partner. This doesn't seem to be the time."

Herndon looked at him, "Abe, I'm surprised at you. I've never seen you give in to a fight before the last bout."

Abe trudged through the light drizzle feeling as downcast as the twilight as it set in. "I didn't. I stayed in till the last punch was thrown and gave it my all. We'll see."

Other friends and politicians had gathered in the little telegraph office to wait for the news. One telegram after another came in. "Abe," Billy cried joyously, "it looks as though you're winning the race!" Excitement ran high as the final popular vote for Republicans came over the wire. Nicolay had joined them. "Mr. Lincoln's candidates have 190,000 votes all told! Douglas has only 176,000." His voice was jubilant.

Abraham Lincoln was not rejoicing. "We'll have to wait. The legislature is full of Democratic holdovers, outnumbering Republicans 54 to 46. That's how the balloting for Senator will go. No self-respecting Democrat would ever vote for me, not even a Buchaneer."

His last prediction came true. In the final countdown, he

lost four months of campaigning, writing the best speeches and delivering them with great eloquence and have the backing of top Republicans, appeared to be in vain.

He had little to say when he arrived at home. Mary must have known of his defeat beforehand for she read the tribute to him in the Chicago Press and Tribune "Oh, Abe, it says here, 'The Republican party owes Abraham Lincoln a great deal for he steadily upheld the principles of Republicanism and contributed speeches that could become landmarks in our political history'."

"Mary," he said, "those are quite fancy words, but somehow my efforts did not sway several whose endorsement I needed so much. I cannot blame any man for what he believes."

After a day of musing, Abe picked up his pen in the office, dipped it in the ink well, and sent a letter to an old friend, Dr. Anson Henry. In it he said, "I am glad I made the late race. It gave me a bearing on the great and durable question of the age, which I could not have had any other way, and though I now sink out of view and shall be forgotten, I believe I have made some marks which will tell for the cause of liberty long after I am gone." He sent it, believing that he had made one last mark.

In February freezing cold had settled into Springfield and Abe had settled into believing he had no political future when friends dropped in at his law office. He realized that he'd lost his spark as he confessed, "I feel like the boy who stumped his toe. I'm too big to cry and too badly hurt to laugh."

In his inner being he felt as though he had reached the bottom, that any hopes he had for making his mark on the national scene were over.

THE Martyr President seals with his blood the emancipation of a race, and grasping four millions of broken coffles, ascends to the bosom of his God, thus consecrating the land of Washington as the home of the emigrant and the asylum of the oppressed of every clime and of all races of men.

(Galusha A. Grow)

PHILADELPHIA, 1880.

ABRAHAM LINCOLN was the right man in the right place, at the right time. The whole country owes him a debt of endless gratitude.

(W. W. Goodwin)

CAMBRIDGE, 1880.

OPPORTUNITY KNOCKS

In the fall of 1858 Abe noticed that Mary took great interest in the newspapers when she read extracts from the Lincoln-Douglas debates printed first in the Chicago papers then re-printed across the country, even in the *New York Tribune*. One evening after dinner she sat down to scan the papers, then put them aside on the table beside her.

"Abraham Lincoln," she sighed, "I think my dream might come true. Your ideas are making national headlines! Just imagine — I can be the PRESIDENT'S wife!"

Abe never glanced up from the book he was reading but replied in a soft tone, "Mary, you dream too much." He hoped that would end the conversation, but he knew her too well to expect it to stop there.

"Abraham Lincoln, wake up!" she cried in a shrill voice. "Your debates with Douglas have put you right in the center of the stage to have a chance at the Republican nomination."

"Mary, Mary," he sighed. "Do you realize how many great men qualify for that opportunity? There's Chase and Seward and a long list of potential candidates. I don't have a squeak of a chance against these giants in the national political arena. It is a God-given miracle that I might manage to get a seat in Congress."

His spouse was not one to give up on something she hoped for. Abe's own hope at that moment was that her interest could be sparked by something else besides him capturing the Presidency. "Sweetheart, it's wonderful that you think I am such top-grade material, but please remember I grew up in the rough frontier with a minimal amount of education. As much as I hate to admit it, all these men know far more than I do about running the nation. Please don't get your hopes flying. Someone is sure to shoot them down."

Not long after that he was coming out of a meeting at the courthouse on the south side of the public square when a voice called out from behind him, "Abe Lincoln, is that you walking around here at dusk?"

Turning to greet the man whose voice Abe recognized, he said, "You guessed right, Jesse Fill."

When the man came close he admitted, "I realized when I saw the tall form that was emerging from the building it had to belong to you. But how did you know the voice was mine?"

Abe laughed and declared, "I guess it's because I've heard it so many times."

"Well, you're just the man I wanted to see. Will you come over to my brother's law office up over the Home Bank so we can discuss what's on my mind?"

"Sure," Abe agreed. "No reason not to join you."

At twilight the two men sat down across the room from each other to talk. Abe waited for his host to start the conversation, which he did almost immediately by saying, "Lincoln, I have been east as far as Boston and up in the New England states except for Maine. In New York, New Jersey, Pennsylvania, Ohio, Michigan and Indiana — everywhere I hear you talked about and often asked: "Who is this man Lincoln from your state canvassing in opposition to Senator Douglas? Being, as you know, an ardent Republican and your friend, I usually told them we had in Illinois two greats instead of one; that Douglas was the *little one*, as they all knew, but that you were the *big one*, which they didn't know."

"But seriously, Lincoln, Judge Douglas is so well-known that you are getting a national reputation through him as a result of your speeches with him which have been extensively published in the East. Discriminating minds claim you are quite a match for him in debate. Truth is, I have a decided impression that if your popular history and efforts on the slavery question can be sufficiently brought before the people, you can be made a formidable, if not a successful candidate for the Presidency of the United States of America."

Lincoln sighed as if in desperation. "Oh, Fell, what's the use of talking of me for the Presidency, while we have such men as Seward, Chase and others, who are so much better known to the people, and whose names are so intimately associated with the principles of the Republican party? Everybody knows them. Nobody, scarcely, outside of Illinois, knows me. Besides, is it not, as a matter of justice, due to such men, who have carried this movement forward to its present status, in spite of fearful opposition, personal abuse, and hard names? I really think so." Abe had used the same argument with the men who had hopes of making him President as he had with his wife when she expressed the same dream.

Fell argued back, "There is much truth in what you say. The men you allude to, occupying more prominent positions, have undoubtedly rendered a larger service in the Republican cause than you have. The truth is, they have rendered too much service to be available candidates. Placing it on the grounds of personal services, or merit, I concede at once the superiority of their claim. Personal services and merit, however, when incompatible with the public good, must be laid aside. Seward and Chase have both made long records on the slavery question, and have said some very radical things which, however just and true, and however much these men may challenge our admiration for their courage and devotion to unpopular truths, would seriously damage them in the contest, if nominated. We must bear in mind, Lincoln, that we are yet in a minority; we are struggling against fearful odds of supremacy. We were defeated on this same issue in 1856, and will be again in 1860, unless we get a great many new votes from what may be called the old conservative parties. These will be repelled by the radical utterances and votes of such men as Seward and Chase.

"What the Republican party wants, to insure success, in 1860, is a man of popular origin, of acknowledged ability, committed against slavery and aggressions, who has no record to defend and no radicalism of an offensive character to repel votes from parties. Hitherto adverse, Judge Douglas has demonstrated your ability and your devotion to freedom. You have no embarrassing record; you have sprung from the humble walks of life, sharing in its toils and trials. If we can only get these facts sufficiently before the people, depend upon it, there is some chance for you.

"Now, Mr. Lincoln, I come to the business part of this interview. My native state, Pennsylvania, will have a large number of votes to cast for somebody on the question we have been discussing. Most of Pennsylvania won't like New York and her politicians. She has a candidate Cameron, of her own; but he will not be acceptable to a larger part of her people, much less abroad, and will be dropped. Through an eminent jurist and essayist of my native county in Pennsylvania, favorably known throughout the State, I want to get up a well-considered, well-written newspaper article telling the people who you are and what you have done, that it may be circulated, not only in that state, but elsewhere. This will help in manufacturing sentiment in your favor.

"I know your public life, and can furnish items that your modesty would forbid, but I don't know much about your private history: when you were born, the names and origin of your parents, what you did in early life, what opportunities for education you had. I want you to give me these. Won't you do it?"

Abe's face began to show a trace of hope. "Fell, I admit the force of much that you say, and admit that I am ambitious, and would like to be President," he declared. "I am not insensible to the compliment you pay me and the interest you manifest in the matter; but there is no such good luck in store for me as the President of these United States. Besides, there is nothing in my early history that would interest you or anybody else; and, as Judge Davis says, 'It won't pay.' Good night."

Jesse Fell called after him as his giant form, wrapped in a dilapidated shawl, disappeared in the darkness, "This is not the last of it; the facts must come out." The next year, 1859, Fell was engaged as the corresponding secretary of the Republican

State Central Committee traveling over the state and carrying out plans for a more thorough organization of the Republican party, preparatory for the great contest of 1860. Rumors in the Republican party came to Abe about Jesse Fell visiting personally a large majority of the counties in Pennsylvania, and nearly everywhere had the satisfaction of learning that, though many doubted the possibility, most generally it was Abe's nomination that met with approval. When this fact became apparent to Abe he frequently met Jesse during his travels. In the month of December when the two met, Jesse assured him that it could pay. "Abraham Lincoln, nationally read newspaper articles about you will pay off." Because of this Abe began to consider sending Jesse a brief history of his personal life.

After much contemplation he wrote the following note to Jesse Fell:

"Springfield, Dec 20, 1859

"J. W. Fell, Esq.
"My Dear Sir:
"Herewith is a little sketch, as you requested. There is not much of it, for the reason, I suppose, that there is not much of me. If anything be made of it, I wish it to be modest, and not to go beyond the materials. If it was thought necessary to incorporate anything from any of my speeches, I suppose there would be no objections. Of course, it must not appear to have been written by myself
"Yours very truly,
"A. Lincoln"

After more thought he penned the following brief history of his background:

140

I was born Feb. 12, 1809, in Hardin county, Kentucky. My parents were both born in Virginia, of undistinguished families — second families, perhaps I should say. My mother, who died in my tenth year, was of a family of the name of Hanks, some of whom now reside in Adams, and others in Macon counties, Illinois. — My paternal grandfather, Abraham Lincoln, emigrated from Rockingham county, Virginia, to Kentucky, about 1781 or 2, where, a year or two later, he was killed by indians, not in battle, but by stealth, when he was labouring to open a farm in the forest — His ancestors, who were quakers, went to Virginia from Berks county, Pennsylvania — An effort to identify them with the New England family of the same name, ended in nothing more definite, than a similarity of christian names in both families, such as Enoch, Levi, Mordecai, Solomon, Abraham, and the like —

My father, at the death of his father, was but six years of age; and he grew up, literally without education — He removed from Kentucky to what is now Spencer county, Indiana, in my eighth year — We reached our new home about the time the State came into the Union — It was a wild region, with many bears and other wild animals, still in the woods — There I grew up. There were some schools, so called, but no qualification was ever required of a teacher, beyond "Readin, writin, and Cipherin" to the Rule of Three — If a struggler supposed to understand latin, happened to sojourn in the neighborhood, he was looked upon as a wizzard— There was absolutely nothing to excite ambition for education. Of course when I came of age, I did not know much— Still somehow, I could read, write, and cipher to the Rule of Three; but that was all— I have not been to school since— The little advance I now have upon this store of education, I have picked up from time to time under the pressure of necessity—

I was raised to farm work, which I continued till I was twenty-two— At twenty-one I came to Illinois, and passed the first year in Illinois— Macon county— Then I got to New Salem (at that time in Sangamon, now in Menard County, where I remained a year as a sort of Clerk in a store— Then came the Black-Hawk war; and I was elected a Captain of Volunteers— a success which gave me more pleasure than any I have had since— I went the campaign, was elated, ran for the Legislature the same year (1832), and was beaten— the only time I ever have been beaten by the people— The next, and three succeeding biennial elections, I was elected to the Legislature— I was not a candidate afterwards. During this Legislative period I had studied law, and removed to Springfield to practice it— In 1846 I was once elected to the lower House of Congress— Was not a candidate for re-election— From 1849 to 1854, both enclosure, practiced far more assiduously than ever before — Always a whig in politics; was generally on the whig electoral tickets, making active canvass — I was losing interest in politics, when the repeal of the Missouri Compromise aroused me again — What I have done since then is pretty well known —

If any personal description of me is thought desirable, it may be said, I am, in height, six feet, four inches, nearly; lean in flesh, weighing, on average, one hundred and eighty pounds; dark complexion, with coarse black hair, and grey eyes. No other marks or brands recollected —

Hon. J. W. Fell.

Yours very truly
A. Lincoln

Washington, D.C. March 26. 1872
We the undersigned hereby certify that the foregoing statement is in the hand writing of Abraham Lincoln.

David Davis
Lyman Trumbull
Charles Sumner

Once these two items had been finished he spoke aloud to himself as though someone else were present, "As I said — there isn't much of me." With those words he signed the letters, folded the papers, placed them in an envelope, then addressed it to Jesse Fell.

Sprawling out on the sofa, he uttered the words he'd taken to heart from years of studying Shakespeare "To be or not to be? — that is the question." Then, with a sigh, he added, "Time will answer the question."

Abe gave serious thought to what impact Jesse Fell's request and his own fulfillment of it might have on Mary. *To tell or not to tell? That is the question,* he thought before deciding to share the news with his wife, but finally determined he could live with whatever consequences that giving her the knowledge of Fell's interest in his possible Presidential candidacy, might cause.

The Lincolns were getting ready for bed when Abe made up his mind that late that night was the perfect time to spring the news without any fanfare. "Mary," he spoke almost in a whisper, "Jesse Fell asked me to submit a history of my life so he could use it in the upcoming campaign."

"What? Abraham Lincoln, how long ago did he ask you?' Her eyes spit fire so he steeled himself for a scolding.

"Oh, a couple of days ago, but I didn't get my answer together until today," Abe answered, trying to sound as nonchalant as possible.

Instead of getting the expected chastisement, she began dancing and twirling around the bedroom in her brightly colored floral nightgown, then she swung around and encircled his waist with her arms as he stood against the dresser. "Oh, Abe, I told you! I just knew my dream would come true!"

Abe looked down at her and moaned, "Mary, Mary, we have so far to go before I'd even be considered a viable candidate. Too many impediments stand in the way. Any betting man would call me a 'long shot,' a very, very, very long shot."

"Stop it! Stop it, Abe! No more negatives! We are going to occupy the White House!" she declared with a stomp of her foot.

For the next half-hour he tried to unwind his exuberant spouse. How he wished he hadn't told her about the material Jesse wanted to use for publicity. Whenever she didn't get her way, it was most difficult to live with her. He told Hay the following day, "Mary's possessed with the Presidency as much as a woman is who has a bee in her bonnet." He wished he'd never mentioned the possibilities.

TO BE OR NOT TO BE

Abe continued to cool his wife's enthusiasm after Jesse Fell approached him about the Presidency. "Mary, please don't get your hopes up. It seems to me that I'm more suited far the Senate than the Presidency. If nothing else cones my way, I'll run against Douglas in '64. In the meantime the Republicans need someone to unite and expand their party and I think that's a job for me."

Back at the office he contemplated his future, and tried to talk it over with Bill Herndon who could be an inspiration. If Abe listened carefully between his partner's chatter, he often had brilliant ideas. His suggestion this time made sense, "Why don't you gather all your speeches together and have them published? That'll keep your name and the party platform before the public."

Lincoln looked contemplative. "That's an outstanding idea, but you realize of all the men who are contending far the Presidency, the Democrat who defeated me for the Senate is going to give me the greatest problem." Having said that, be realized to his own amazement that he saw himself as a serious contender against Douglas for the President of the United States even though he hadn't beat Douglas for a seat in the Senate.

"The Lincoln-Douglas debates are still going on," he told Hay at the office.

John Hay laughed, "You are both adding fuel to top that fire. Every time you come up with something, he counterattacks and visa versa. The only thing is — now you don't appear on the same stump."

At one of his speeches he declared, "The Southerners claim their slaves are better off than the North's hired workers," Lincoln argued, "but the slaves have no opportunity to better their lot in life. Once a slave always a slave," he decreed.

He went on to say, "I was a hired laborer working for twelve dollars a month, but in the junues of the free-labor system a prudent, penniless beginner in the world leaves home with his capital — two strong hands and a willingness to work — and chooses his employer and mode of labor. His employer pays a day's wage far a fair day's work. He saves frugally for a couple of years, buys land on his own or goes into business for himself, marries, has sons and daughters and in time has enough capital to hire another beginner."

Abe grimaced as if what he was about to add was painful, "Pure slavery has no hope."

Northerners and Southerners bantered opinions back and forth, but in October when Lincoln was out working on the circuit court, the entire nation woke up to the headlines, "Harpers Ferry Raided!"

Abe analyzed thee account with acute interest, reading aloud as he always did, "John Brown who'd been the center of slave troubles in Kansas helped engineer an attack on the small town in Northern Virginia with the hopes of seizing the federal arsenal there.

"The invaders were mostly young. Five of them were black. Colonel Robert E. Lee and his militia captured the men, exposing John Brown as their leader when Brown warned the South that God had appointed him to liberate their slaves by some violent and decisive moves."

Abe folded up the paper with, "Well, God, I'm afraid the die is cast. The South will blame the Republicans for the whole mess."

The following months proved him right. Southerners lambasted Northern Republicans, claiming they were responsible.

Back home in Springfield Abe broached the subject with his wife, "At first I thought that the old fellow was mad, but the more I learn about his background, the more convinced I am that he is a man of great courage. However, I can never condone acts of violence where a man takes it into his own hands, so he must be punished."

On December 2 when John Brown was hung from the gallows in Virginia it made national news. The following day Abraham Lincoln told a crowd in Leavenworth, Kansas, "Southerners need to be warned! If constitutionally we elect a President, and they undertake to destroy the Union, we will deal with them as old John Brown has been dealt with."

Back home in Springfield, Lamon and other friends assured Abe, "You still have tremendous Presidential potential."

"I'd rather be in the Senate," Lincoln argued.

Many political maneuverings took place in the months that followed. The one that benefited Abe tremendously caused him to exclaim to Herndon at their law office, "Billy, Providence must be on my side. Judd has talked the Republicans into having the National Convention in Chicago!"

That January all of Lincoln's backers met at a secret caucus to launch Abraham Lincoln for President.

"I'm not certain, fellows, if I am not a more suitable candidate for the Senate, but if you wish me to run for the top position and you will give it your all, so will I. One of the pitfalls in my path is the fact that I need Illinois to win, but the Chicago Press and Tribune has definite leanings toward Chase. What can we do about it?"

Norman Judd, not only the head of the Republican state party, but a man of considerable tact and influence declared, "I have many friends at the newspaper. When I get through convincing them of your merits, they'll change their tune. Do you realize your Kentucky heritage will help get the votes of the border states? If we can get Jersey, Pennsylvania, Ohio, Indiana and Illinois to vote our way, we will have the most populous states in our pocket."

All that encouragement raised Abe's hopes, much as a thundering wave coming in to shore, but when he read stories about him being "too liberal" or "too inexperienced" for the Presidency his hopes weakened like a wave going back out to sea. His faith in himself was lost when Billy, his loyal partner for so many years declared, "Abraham Lincoln, I am always for you, but until you get this Presidential nonsense out of your head, I don't think we'll have too much in common." Those words stung Abe's confidence.

Regardless of the negatives, Abraham Lincoln was invited to New York to speak at Henry Ward Beecher's church in Brooklyn, but found that men who were against Seward for President had managed to get a crowd coming to the Cooper Institute instead. What amazed Abe even more was the tremendous reception he received from the Republicans there, even entertaining him at the elegant Astor House.

As he looked in the mirror prior to going on the platform, his attire pleased him. For once he was pleased that Mary had coaxed him to get a new broadcloth vest and shirt to put over his white shirt and adorn with a black bow tie.

He was certain that his attire and his stack of books gave him a sense of importance as he began to address the crowd of over a hundred who gathered there on a bitter cold night just to hear him speak.

Even though his hands shook and his voice trembled at first, he soon forgot his nervousness as he informed his rapt audience, "I want to demonstrate once and for all that Republicans and not Judge Douglas are right about the Founding Fathers and slavery."

To Abraham Lincoln's amazement he heard cheers coming from his audience as he continued to speak, accusing the South of malicious slander with their accusation that the Republicans were responsible for Harper's Ferry.

Next he challenged the Republicans, "Though we are much provoked, let us do nothing through passion and ill temper."

After his impassioned speech, Abraham Lincoln stood astounded at the standing ovation. Hats and handkerchiefs were thrown into the air. He noticed as the men from the press rushed out with their notes that Noah Brooks of the *New York Tribune* was one of them.

The Cooper Institute speech brought such positive publicity that Abe began getting invitations to address groups all over the New England States. Abraham Lincoln said he thought he'd enjoy going on such a circuit, making his ardent fan and friend Nicolay declare, "You're really pleased with that prospect, aren't you? Bet you'll find your way to visit Bob at Philips Exeter Academy in New Hampshire where he's studying, won't you?'

Lincoln laughed. "You don't think I'd miss the opportunity to see my son, do you?"

He didn't. Abe knew too well that his eldest child had failed fifteen of sixteen subjects on the entrance exam at Harvard, so Robert had opted to go to Exeter to prepare himself to try again. "You can do it, son. I know you can," Abe prodded his offspring when they met. "Robert Todd Lincoln," he assured him later, "I am most proud of your determination."

Abe decided to have Robert go along to Concord and Manchester where both father and son were astounded to hear the announcement, "We are pleased to present Abraham Lincoln, the next President of the United States."

Invitations kept flooding in. "Mr. Lincoln," Nicolay said, "they're from Pittsburgh, Philadelphia and Newark and all over," but Lincoln declined from sheer exhaustion.

Back at Exeter the two Lincolns went to church at Robert's insistence. At dinner as the father and son chatted together Abraham encouraged his son, "You will go to Harvard and succeed. How fortunate you are. Your father never had the opportunity to attend college."

"Meeting with you has just increased my homesickness and my desire to see Tad and Willie. I am going to write your mother that I'll be home soon."

After another speaking engagement he caught a train to Springfield. Upon his arrival at their corner home, Abe opened the door to screams of joy, "Papa's home! Papa's home!"

Mary, too, came running. As Abe encircled his family there in his arms, he nearly wept from joy. "Mary, love is what life is all about," he whispered.

Later he confided to her, "It does seem since the Cooper Institute that I have a shot at the seat. Even the Republicans here are saying that I might be Presidential timber after all."

Seward was gathering interest, getting delegates from the Western states of California, Wisconsin and Minnesota. Lincoln was appalled by that news, however, when Hay reported to him, "You'll be pleased, sir. Judge Douglas has lost the Democratic nomination. Your old adversary has been shot down this time," Abe found reason for hope.

Lincoln smiled "Things are looking more promising," he commented.

Feeling somewhat secure, Abraham Lincoln went to the Republican Convention. In a way he was not prepared emotionally to have his cheering fans lift him high and pass him from one to another over to the platform. The whole scene mortified him, but he was even more perplexed when his cousin, John Hanks, who'd accompanied him on his Mississippi trip, marched in carrying two fence railings and a sign, "Abraham Lincoln, the Rail Candidate for President."

Humiliated, Abe sighed and said almost in a moan, "I suppose I'm supposed to reply to that." Even though possible Presidential candidate Abraham Lincoln frowned upon the displays, he soon found the antics endeared him to the common man. His nickname, "Abe," which he had frowned upon for years, was picked up and became a household name along with his "Rail Splitter" image.

David Davis took over Abe's campaign, telling him, "You know that Seward is the top candidate and has one hundred fifty delegates pledged to him."

To Abe's question, "How many do I have now?'

"Twenty two. The other three candidates have about fifty apiece."

Abe's heart sank. "If I win, it certainly will be that the dark horse that won the race."

Abe and his new friends sat in his office speculating about Seward's possibilities. Nicolay stated his ideas, "I don't think he can get the nomination. He's considered to be a radical. He's joined himself with Republican liberals so his chances are going to be slim."

Hay added his viewpoint. "It's ridiculous, but the Democrats blame him for Harper's Ferry and some folks still think of him as an arrogant Whig. Can those hang-ups in his background make it possible for him to win?"

Abe simply shrugged shoulders and told his aide, "I'll use the age-old wisdom and tell you 'time will tell'."

Lincoln learned later that David Davis was like a man obsessed with one goal — to get the nomination for Abraham Lincoln. Abe fretted at home until he learned that his manager went without sleep, orchestrating the campaign by importing thousands of Illinois Republicans to demonstrate for "Honest Abe" and to make certain that Abraham Lincoln's name was so prevalent that everyone who came near the Convention Center had to be aware that Lincoln was the man of the hour.

Abe learned from the men that Davis sent his emissaries to talk to delegates with their sales pitch - "Lincoln is the only candidate who can win against the Democrats. He has no negative national image, has offended no Republican groups, and his background gives him an edge over all the other candidates to woo the important lower North."

Abe told Mary, "I have no desire to go to my slaughter," so he decided to stay in Springfield. He admitted, "I feel I have little chance to win. If Seward loses on the first ballot, the convention vote will undoubtedly go to one of the other two."

However, messages and telegrams from Lincoln headquarters in Chicago gave him some reason for hope. Knapp, the delegate from his home district wired, "Things are working; keep a good nerve — be not surprised at any result but I tell you that your chances are not the worst. Be not too expectant, but rely upon our discretion. Again I say, brace your nerves for any result."

Abe sat in his office discussing the message when another one came via Dr. Roy of the *Press and Tribune*. "A pledge or two may be necessary when the pinch comes."

Lincoln sighed and told Hay, "Send an urgent message to

Davis. Make no contracts that will bind me. If I do win no one is going to have me cornered with promises I can't keep. I know Davis will honor my request."

Abraham Lincoln rose early the morning of May 18. He chatted with Mary who assured him as always, "You know very well you have a great chance. Don't expect failure. Think positive. I am. You ARE going to be the Republican nominee."

"Little woman I wish I had your faith in me," he answered, but left shortly after he headed out — visiting another law office, then his own, where he chatted with law students who were there until the co-editor of the *Illinois State Journal* burst through the door, his face glowing with excitement. "Abe! Abe! You have 102, Seward has 173½! The other candidates votes aren't enough to matter!"

"Told you!" Nicolay cried. "We told you that you'd give them a run for their money!"

Abe tried not to let his excitement show, but he went back to the newspaper office with the editor to await the second ballot.

The newsroom went wild when the next results were read aloud, "Seward gained 11, but Lincoln picked up 79, including all the 48 Pennsylvania delegates."

When the last telegram came, it was given to Abe to open. For minutes he stood and stared while everyone waited.

When Nicolay could stand it no more, he cried out, "What is the verdict?"

Abe nodded and declared, "It says, 'Lincoln, you are nominated.' Out of the 466, I needed 234, but I received 354!" He stood silent for a moment, unable to grasp the true meaning of what he was about to say, "Mr. Evans, a delegate from New York moved that the nomination be made unanimous. I guess they were all excited." Again he hesitated before declaring with a wide grin, "Well, we've got it"

The newspaper office broke into bedlam. Cheers and hurrahs filled the place as congratulations flooded the wire. Church bells began to ring as he excused himself to hurry home "to the little woman down at our house who will want to hear this."

Mary cried, "I told you! I felt it in my bones. You ARE the

man of this hour! Oh, Abraham Lincoln, I WILL be the President's wife."

Before he could argue that the Republican nominee for President had to beat the Democrat, well-wishers began pouring in. All through the night the Republicans held a victory parade, winding up in front of the two-story corner house. Abe spoke to them, his face lit from their torches. "Thank you friends, I wish I had room to invite you all in."

With those words reality began to sink in. He'd prepared for defeat, but victory was his. He, Abraham Lincoln, was to be the Republican nominee for President of the United States of America!

154

NAVY GROUP OF STATUARY.   NATIONAL LINCOLN MONUMENT.

Representing a scene on the deck of a ship of war. The mortar is properly poised, the gunner has rolled up a shell ready to be elevated into the mortar, the boy, whose duty it is to carry cartridges to the piece, and who in nautical phrase is called the powder monkey, has elevated himself to the highest position. The two latter believing they are about to enter upon an engagement, are peering into the distance with manifest indications of excitement. The Commander, however, having taken an observation through his telescope, finds there is no cause to apprehend danger, and is calmly meditating.

THE LONG MARCH

"A flood! Mary, that's what's overtaking me. Even though I'm just a possibility for the Presidency, I cannot hide from them. Everyone who voted for me seems to think I owe then a favor. How can I get away from the favor-seekers? They all know where my office is and they've already worn out the steps." Every morning Abraham Lincoln groaned to his wife about the tremendous pressures brought to bear, his wife, he knew, would have a suggestion so it was no surprise when she advised him, "Get an office in the Statehouse and get yourself a private secretary. Abraham, you cannot possibly answer this deluge of mail."

Abe was sage enough to acknowledge that in some instances his wife had great insight, especially when it came to politics.

He had no trouble getting a room in the Governor's Statehouse, then he went to the Secretary of State's office where John Nicolay was employed as keeper of records. Nicolay had followed him and his campaigns and had often sparked up Abe's rallies by suggestions which met with approval because John was also a very gifted journalist and perhaps Abe's greatest admirer other than his family and Herndon.

"The hounds are chasing me," Abe told him. "I need help to keep them at bay. They want my picture, my autograph, my time and if I let them, I think they'd skin me if they could. Will you come and be my personal secretary? You have always seemed to be in and out of my life and concerned about me and my affairs. I would be thrilled if you could help me."

A grin spread across John Nicolay's face. "Mr. Lincoln, such an honor! Let me see if it will be feasible with my employers here to let me go." With that John left to talk to his bosses and came back minutes later exclaiming with joy, "They're thrilled for me, saying such an opportunity to work for the next President!"

"Presidential hopeful," Abe replied. "It's a long way between starting to march and defeating the enemy."

Since candidates did not go out and solicit votes themselves, Abraham Lincoln had to let others do his campaigning. Nicolay teased him, "Everyone wants to see you, get your autograph, paint your picture or give you a gift. You have been given enough wedges, log chains and axes to start a museum."

"That's true," Abe answered, "but the thing I resent the most is the reporters. Since they've dubbed me a 'dark horse' because they didn't have much to go on from my past. Now they're nosing into my house, my children, my personal life, who is going to be in my cabinet, what my policy is on slavery? They ask so many questions that I wouldn't be shocked if they wanted to know where I buy my underwear."

Everyone seemed to be so curious about him that Horace Greeley came to say, "Abe, we need some sort of biography so people will get to know you."

As the Presidential nominee Abe had concern when Scripps of the *Chicago Press and Tribune* offered to publish a short campaign biography. Nicolay was amused at the end result of Abe's autobiography where he talked about himself as "A." as a boy; "Mr. L." after he became a man. Even though his personal secretary had scoffed at the ridiculous style which he had to help put together, Nicolay had to shake his head at the tremendous response. "Can't believe it — they claim they've sold a million copies! Can't believe it," he echoed again.

Abraham Lincoln shook his own head in utter amazement. "Me, too!"

Proof sheets came from a biography *Follet, Foster and Company* hoped to publish but Abe refused to even look at them, saying, "I authorize nothing. I will be responsible for nothing."

Previous to the national election Abraham Lincoln had much

to pray and think about. "Republicans seem to have united in their thoughts about the nation and the election. I'm glad they're against the moral wrong of slavery. Even the so-called 'liberals' seem to be behind me."

"Good news!" Nicolay declared as Abe entered his state-house office after the political debate had been in full swing before that June 18. "The newspapers say there's a split in the Democratic ranks. The North and the South have split! Of course Judge Douglas is the Northern choice, but the South had their own convention and nominated Breckenridge."

One of those rare all-encompassing grins flooded Abe's face. "Best news yet! A house divided cannot stand, you know."

Parades, parties, social functions of every kind took up the Lincoln family time and also lessened their ability to fight off diseases. Willie contracted scarlet fever which caused his father to claim, "Mary, I must have an inferior form of that myself. My throat and my head are killing me."

His spouse responded, "Abraham Lincoln, I fear this whole campaign is hard on all of us. Oh, how I hate the scandalous things they're spreading about you. I don't know if either of us can withstand another defeat."

Feeling poorly, Abe asked Mary, "What do you think they're saying about me?"

"Oh, Abe, you always expect the best of people, but they're not living up to your expectations at all. The *Charleston Mercury* called you a 'horrid looking wretch' and a 'bloodthirsty tyrant.'"

On a visit to Abe's new office Bill Herndon affirmed Mary's negative speech, "Mr. Lincoln, you have a miserable reputation south of the Mason-Dixon line. They blame you for sending spies into the South, saying you belong to the Black Republican, free-love, free-Negro party. That's just a part of what they're saying down there; they'll make you look as bad as they can so you will not argue with their decision to secede from the Union."

A group of capitalists came to him. Their spokesman pleaded, "It is our hope that you will consider our needs. If you can fore-stall secession and offer the Southerners some sort of conserva-tive promises, it will help with New England's commercial and manufacturing interests. We can sway many votes in our states if you will do us this favor."

Abraham Lincoln's ire was inflated. "No!" he cried. "Why would I barter away all the moral principles involved in this campaign for the commercial gain of you and the South?'

With all the cartoons, the name-calling and the actual lies being told about him, he declared to Mary, "We've already won in Vermont, Maine, Pennsylvania, Ohio and Illinois. The Republican time has come."

November 6, election day, Abraham Lincoln showed no visible signs of being a candidate for the President of the United States. Amiable, joking, he made little reference to the outcome of the election which was foremost on his mind. Not wanting to appear over-anxious, he waited until nine in the evening when he and several friends sauntered over to the Springfield telegraph office to await the returns.

Abraham Lincoln chuckled to himself as he sprawled across the ancient sofa while the Illinois vote counts arrived. Grinning, he quipped to Nicolay, "If the voters could see me now, do you think they'd consider me as Presidential timber?"

Before his aide could answer, a new tape was clicking, causing great commotion as Jesse Du Bois read aloud, "It looks as though Lincoln has carried both New England and the Northwest! There's a hint about a Republican sweep in the upper and lower North."

Abe sat up on the sofa, laughing as he declared, "I don't want to be caught laying down on the job." He noticed there was also an air of excitement among all the tally watchers.

Du Bois was exuberant as he read a private message from Cameron, one of Abe's staunch supporters, "Pennsylvania is certain to go Republican. We need New York which seems to be in our pocket!" At that Lincoln's fans went wild. Abraham Lincoln couldn't contain himself and let out a noise that sounded much like a fog horn.

Du Bois grabbed the final telegram about the North, then ran to Lincoln's new office which was swarming with Republicans. Hats went up in the air; excitement got the best of some men so much so that they rolled on the rug.

When they returned to get the last of the returns, Lincoln declared, "Now, we shall get a few licks back."

Even though he was certain he was going to get almost all negative exposure down South, he knew that there couldn't be enough to cause him much trouble, so he joined Mary to go to a dinner that she had helped the Republican women prepare for him.

He smiled to the greeting, as he went in the door: "How are you, Mr. President?" They over-did their attention to him so he whispered to Mary, "Think I was the king or something," to which she whispered back, "You are."

Since he wanted to check on the final returns, he told Mary, "I'm going back to see how things ended. You go get some rest and I'll be home later."

At 1:30 in the morning he gave up and went to join her, satisfied that the Democratic split had made it possible for him to win. He had enough popular votes to defeat his combined adversaries in the electoral college. That pleased him. He had won on his own merits.

At home he found sleep was impossible. Republicans marched and sang in the streets. Inside President-elect Abraham Lincoln was going through a self-analysis. *How will he fare as the head of the nation? What can he do if the South does secede? Who will he appoint for his cabinet?* The parade of thoughts rambled through his mind as the parade of excited citizens continued to march through the streets. At four in the morning his corner house seemed to tremble from the roar and vibration of a cannon going off outside.

Abraham Lincoln rose early from his nearly sleepless night to head to his office in the Statehouse. Nicolay greeted him, "President Lincoln, Sir, I understand we have a problem. The South celebrated your victory in a sleepless manner, too. The streets down there were filled with citizens who cried they had to secede since you were elected President."

Abe's brow furrowed as he addressed those who had worked with such tenacity to help him win, as well as the newsmen gathered there, "Well boys, your troubles are over. My troubles have just begun."

The following photos are from the Lincoln Museum at Hodgenville, Kentucky. Abraham Lincoln, 16th U.S. President, was born February 12, 1809, about three miles south of there on the Sinking Spring Farm which is today part of the National Park System.

In 1811, the Lincoln family moved six miles east to the Knob Creek place from where Abe had his few years of formal schooling under Zacariah Riney and Caleb Hazel.

—— Photos by W.L. McCoy

The Museum building is on the National Register of Historic Places, located on the town square overlooked by the original bronze statue of Lincoln by A.A. Weinmann. The Lincoln Museum first level depicts twelve authenticated scenes of great importance in Lincoln's life and our nation's history. On the second level are exhibits, memorabilia, and the Lincoln Days Art Collection. Welcome to mementos of Lincoln's Birthplace.

SCENE 1: THE CABIN YEARS   1809-1816

SCENE 2: THE BERRY-LINCOLN STORE   1831

SCENE 3: THE RAILSPLITTER   1825

SCENE 4: THE MARY TODD HOME   1849

SCENE 5: LINCOLN VISITS FARMINGTON 184

SCENE 6: THE LINCOLN-DOUGLAS DEBATE 185

SCENE 7: EMANCIPATION PROCLAMATION   SEPTEMBER, 1862

SCENE 8: THE MATTHEW BRADY STUDIO   FEBRUARY, 1864

SCENE 9: THE SECOND INAUGURATION   MARCH 4, 1865

SCENE 10: THE GETTYSBURG ADDRESS   NOVEMBER 19, 1863

SCENE 11: SURRENDER   APRIL 9, 1865

SCENE 12: FORD'S THEATRE   APRIL 14, 1865

Bryan Bennett

But they that wait
upon the Lord shall
renew their strength;
they shall mount up
with wings of eagles,
they shall run, and not
be weary, they shall
walk, and not faint.

Isaiah 40:31

REKINDLED MEMORIES

Abraham Lincoln had finally acknowledged that he'd become a household word all across America because of the fierce Lincoln-Douglas debates. Yet, regardless of his stature in life, he never forgot anyone who had ever befriended him.

Early that same year he'd learned that Attorney William Walker and another lawyer named Dillsworth had agreed to defend a young man named Armstrong who was about twenty years of age. When Abe heard about the case, the name "Armstrong" brought back sole-satisfying memories of the widow Armstrong, who everyone called "Aunt Hannah." Curiosity surged through Lincoln's mind.

Could the boy accused of murder be related to the woman who had befriended him at New Salem when he'd first moved there? Abe smiled to himself as he reminisced about the widow who'd offered him so much, mending socks and darning holes in his worn clothing and offering him an open door anytime he was lonely and wanted someone to chat with. At that time Abe had been just a little older than the boy accused of murder. Yes, he had a warm spot in his heart for dear Aunt Hannah. If she or her son were in trouble, Abe wanted to help.

And so, Abraham Lincoln, at the time when he was waiting to be inaugurated as the President of the United States of America, decided he must relieve himself of his hectic schedule long enough to find out if the lad was actually an offspring of his old friend.

Upon further investigation he learned that the twenty-year-old fellow did, indeed, belong to Abe's endeared Aunt Hannah.

His inquiry of Walker's legal clerk filled in the details of the crime: "Mr. Lincoln, Armstrong and another young man had been involved in a difficulty at a camp meeting in Mason County near Salt Creek resulting in a man named Metzker being killed. Armstrong and the other fellow with him were both indicted for murder in the first degree. My employer obtained a court order allowing separate trials and his trial is to take place in Cass County, Illinois at Beardstown. Attorney Walker and Dillsworth have already checked in at the hotel there to plan their strategy to defend him."

Once he had that essential information, he made the long ride to Mrs. Armstrong's home to consult her feelings on the matter. She squealed with delight when she opened the door and saw Abraham Lincoln standing there. "Abe, Abe, you will never know how much I wanted to talk with you, but I know you are such a busy, important man now and I did not want to bother you. But you see, my son is in terrible trouble. With that her short, matronly body broke into sobs and she wailed, "Oh, Abe, what can I do?" her brokenness tore at Abe's own heart as he leaned down and scooped her up in his arms. "Aunt Hannah, Aunt Hannah, that's why I'm here. I want to help free your son."

"Oh, Abe. I would have never asked, but will you? Perhaps you've heard that I hired Walker and Dillsworth to defend him, but will you go to Beardstown to help them? I'd feel so much better if you did."

Abe patted her on the head then gave her a peck on the cheek. "You know all you have to ever do is ask and I'll help you any way I can."

"Oh, Abe, he's the most important thing in my life. They could even hang him if they find him guilty. Will you help?"

After one more hug, he whispered in a choked voice, "I'm on my way."

With that, Abe mounted his horse and headed toward Beardstown where he found the two lawyers in a hotel room planning their defense for young Armstrong's trial. Both men gaped in amazement when they responded to his knock at their hotel room door.

"Abraham Lincoln!" William Walker's voice showed his utter disbelief at seeing their visitor. "Aren't you engaged in bigger things than visiting the likes of us?"

To that question Abe grinned and replied, "That's not so, Bill. A young man's life is at stake. I'm most concerned about the Armstrong boy. I want to help clear his name. His mother's a dear friend of mine and has asked me to help."

"Welcome, welcome," Dillsworth declared as he extended his hand and then invited Abe, "Come on in, we need all the help we can get."

For the next few hours the three attorneys sat in the small hotel room on hard wooden chairs. "This is not the fanciest place to entertain you," Bill Walker said.

"Not here for entertainment, boys. A lad's life can be snuffed out, so we must get down to business," Abe declared with a stern look. For the next hour the two lawyers shared all they knew about the case as Abe paced back and forth across the tiny room, trying to digest all the facts.

Once he seated himself again, he asked, "What is your line of defense?" Before the two attorneys had time to reply, he also inquired, "What kind of jury do you think would be best?"

Without hesitation Dillsworth replied, "We're in favor of a jury of young men."

Abe cupped his chin in his hand as if in deep thought before he inquired further, "For what reasons?"

William Wallace never hesitated before answering, "Since your friend Armstrong is young, we thought the sympathies of men around the same age could be more easily aroused in his behalf."

Abraham Lincoln pondered for a moment before he answered, "I hope I don't offend you fellows, but I believe that is not the best move. Could I get you to let me challenge the jurors?"

"If that's what you want, you know we'll go along with you," Dillsworth replied. "In fact, I'll leave the decision about each juror up to you and Bill."

Thus it was agreed, but both men looked amazed at Lincoln's choices. Abe chuckled to himself as he watched the other two attorneys' faces while he picked twelve men who'd passed middle age. Whenever a prospective juror claimed he wanted to enforce obedience and desired to keep order in society, the more Lincoln showed his pleasure toward choosing such a man.

Abe realized his choices were baffling his two legal friends, but as the trial progressed, he began to sense their approval. At times he'd let his eyes drift toward Aunt Hannah who sat in a rigid position as if she were too frightened to move until Abe flashed a quick smile toward her.

The evidence against Aunt Hannah's son was presented by the state, then Abe spoke in the lad's defense.

The prosecuting attorney stated his closing arguments against the man accused of committing murder, then Attorney Abraham Lincoln gave his closing on the boy's behalf, a plea so impassioned that even he was amazed at his own words.

None of the eyes of the jurors of his choice ever left his face as he continued to give one of the most eloquent speeches of his lifetime. All twelve jurors and everyone else in the courtroom had tears in their eyes by the time Abe got through defending his client, beseeching them, "Not to indict a youthful man of such a heinous crime if you have a shadow of a doubt."

In less than an hour the jurors were back in the jury box, causing the judge to ask the foreman, "Have you reached a verdict?"

"We have, your honor."

"What say you?"

"We find Mr. Armstrong, the defendant, NOT guilty."

Bedlam broke out in the courtroom as the judge announced, "The defendant is free to go."

Aunt Hannah rushed to her son's side. Abe sauntered over to stand by, smiling as the teary eyed mother and son embraced. Then Hannah Armstrong turned to Abe and whispered, "Abe, how can I ever thank you?"

Once more he scooped her up in a hug and found himself also choked up with emotion. "Dear, dear Aunt Hannah, you already have."

As Abe made his way out of the courtroom the two attorneys who'd been hired to save the boy's life stopped him and said, "That was a fabulous piece of legal work. We'd like to compensate you somehow."

The smile that engulfed his face showed Abe's pleasure. "If you mean you'd like to pay me for my services, forget it, fellows. I wouldn't take a cent. I was paid in full by all the kindness and consideration Aunt Hannah gave me years ago!"

Upon his arrival back in Springfield, Nicolay reminded him, "Mr. Lincoln, you asked me to remind you to pay off your so called 'National Debt' before you leave for Washington."

"Now is as good a time as any. I have to pay all those dear folks. Want to ride with me?"

Nicolay agreed to go. On their way Abe brought his horse to a sudden halt, dismounted, rushed off toward a tree, retrieved a baby bird, then reached up and placed it back in its nest.

John Nicolay watched in amazement, then declared, "Mr. Lincoln, you are going to be President of the United States, but you take the time to rescue a baby bird and a lad accused of murder."

Abe grinned, "The Lord always takes time to rescue me. That mother bird would be upset if her wee one was missing and Aunt Hannah needs her son. Besides that, you know how I love all God's creatures."

It was Nicolay's turn to grin. "You are a wonder, Mr. President."

THE grand legacy of American freedom, bequeathed to us by the Father of his Country, and which a wicked rebellion would have squandered, was saved, we trust, for all coming time, by that noble martyr, *Abraham Lincoln.*

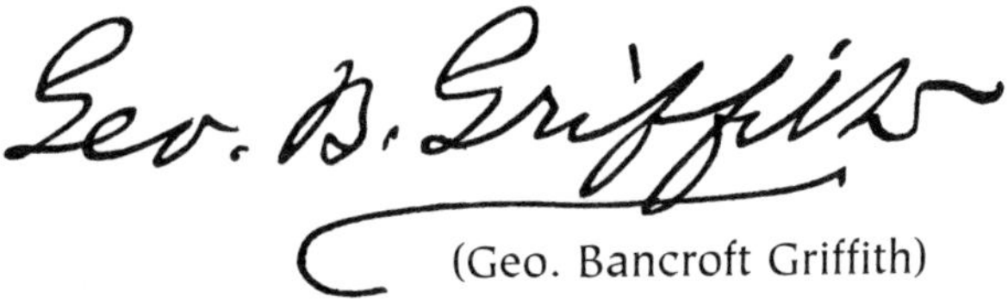

Geo. B. Griffith

(Geo. Bancroft Griffith)

EAST LEMPSTER, 1881.

ABRAHAM LINCOLN at all times impressed me as a man of native good sense, singleness of motive and integrity of purpose. His life has been of great good to this nation, because he " desired to be on the Lord's side," gave his voice for the freedom of the oppressed and his life for the Union of the States. No better legacy can be left to the youth of our land than the example of great men and women—great in goodness of heart and character.

John G. Fee

(John G. Fee)

BEREA COLLEGE, 1882.

FAREWELL SPRINGFIELD

Abraham Lincoln had obtained his goal to become President of the United States of America, on November 6, 1860. However, national political happenings did not make his determination to keep the Union intact look promising at all.

Even though he was not to take office until the next March, Nicolay and Hay worked with him at the law firm of Lincoln and Herndon while yet in Springfield. His two associates were to go with him and be his chief aides in Washington. He most appreciated Nicolay who kept him abreast of the political tide.

"Mr. President," he said one morning as he entered the office, "according to the papers, things don't look good for your main agenda."

Before his aide could speak further, Abe interrupted him with, "What's with the 'Mr. President' stuff?"

John Nicolay sported a mischievous grin, "I thought I'd best get used to addressing you that way or do you prefer 'your majesty'?"

Lincoln picked up a notebook and tossed it in John's direction, but he also grinned while his aide ducked as Abe declared, "No more of that! Now, what are you talking about?"

"It's the South. Rumor has it that they're going to leave the Union. Jefferson Davis has taken on their leadership and he claims that the Southern States are sovereign and they have the right of self-determination. The grapevine also has it that South Carolina will secede in late December."

Abe strolled out to the window to contemplate the impact of

that knowledge before he answered. Then turning, he looked as if he were about to cry. "They can't divide the Union! Our fore-fathers fought the British to get us freedom. NO!" He declared. "They CANNOT separate us because of their stand on slavery or any other issue! As grown men we need to sit down and peace-fully resolve our differences."

Yet things did not progress according to the President-to-be's wishes. On December 20th South Carolina did secede, caus-ing Lincoln to bewail the act, "Don't they know what they are doing? They're destroying the nation that God meant to stay unified."

1861 rolled around. Rumors about the South's determina-tion kept mounting.

February brought forth more ripples in his troubled waters when he read in the Chicago Tribune about the meeting of the six seceding states. "Nicolay!" he called out to his aide in the outer office, "Oh, Nicolay, they're forming the 'Confederate States of America'. Jefferson Davis is going to be their President."

The weeks before March 4th arrived the Lincolns had been occupied so much with saying good-bye to their friends in Spring-field. Mary held open house in the two-story home that she'd converted from a three-room bungalow. On a cold February 10th guests began to arrive. Many were dignitaries, but Abe was so pleased when hundreds of old friends came to bid the Lincolns farewell and wish him the best in his tenure as President.

Late that evening the last of the well-wishers left. Mary made a quick count of the names in the guest book. "Seven hundred!" she exclaimed. "Abraham Lincoln, seven hundred people came to wish you God's speed."

A weary Abraham Lincoln reached over to hold her in his arms in their bed after they finally turned the kerosene lights out. "Mary," he whispered, "I know I would not be on my way to the White House if it were not for your enthusiastic support. Your encouragement has helped me over so many of the high political hurdles."

With that they said good night. Earlier in the week Abe had told her, as they'd both been taking in the latest news about viewpoints on his election in different newspapers, "I think you should take Bobby and go on one of your shopping trips."

Mary stopped reading to eye him with suspicion, "Why would you ever suggest such a thing? You know that's something you usually frown upon."

Abe continued to read the Chicago Tribune's latest comments on him and his ambitions, but he answered her softly, "Mary, don't look for ulterior motives. You can meet the train later in Indianapolis. That'll give you time to shop and still get to enjoy some of the whistle stops."

He waited for her response, pretending to be immersed in what he was reading, but in reality he did not want her on board in case any of the many threats against his life might materialize. As her husband he was aware that the opportunity to take a shopping trip was irresistible to her, so Abe hoped she'd take the bait.

Her next words assured him that she was willing to go along with his suggested plan. She walked over and planted a kiss on his forehead, saying, "What a nice man you are, Abraham Lincoln. I'll be glad to go if you'd like me to shop."

The idea of his wife loose in a strange town and with the new title-to-be as "the wife of the U.S. President" caused Abe anguish inside. She never knew when to quit, but he deemed it necessary for her to go to keep her safe.

Later he walked to the law office of Lincoln and Herndon. He'd told his partner to meet him there, but Abe chose not to let his wife know where he was going.

Sixteen years previous he'd gone from Logan's law firm to become partners with William Herndon, but Mary and the man Lincoln cared so much about that he addressed him as 'Billy' never met with Mrs. Abraham Lincoln's approval. Abe tried to keep the two people who probably cherished him the most distanced from each other. Their's was a verbal dual, but Abe did everything he could to escape their bantering back and forth. In fact, whenever possible he never mentioned one to the other. Once Nicolay had inquired about the strange arrangement, "Mr. Lincoln, wouldn't it be better if your wife and partner made up?" To that Abe replied, simply, "Peace, I try to keep peace regardless of the inconvenience."

From her indignant remarks he knew that there was no need to tell his law partner about his own wife's feelings. Some evenings she'd snort, "HE stopped by to see you, and I don't know what he wanted because he wouldn't say. He assumes I'm an imbecile."

She always emphasized the word "He," but Abe never had to ask who "He" was. No doubt was left in his mind. Nearly a quarter of a century had passed since the Lincolns had met each other, and Abe knew when to leave well enough alone. Just because Mary claimed to detest his partner because of his vent toward alcohol and carousing, Attorney William Herndon looked up to Abe as his hero. In spite of that being a fact, Abraham Lincoln had a certain amount of respect for his partner's brains and charisma.

Abe had already quit coming to the office before leaving for Washington, but they made this appointment earlier to converse and determine their futures.

William Herndon inquired of Abe as they chatted, "Do you want me to take your name off the firm?"

Abraham Lincoln's eyes twinkled as he asked, "Don't you think I'm ever going to come back? You think I'll be too old?"

Bill Herndon shrugged his shoulders, "No, Abe, but who knows what the future will bring? I'm just a lowly lawyer and you're going to be the President of the United States." A lengthy sigh gave Abe some indication that Bill Herndon was feeling somewhat inadequate. In an effort to bolster his morale, Abe told the man he was leaving, "One of the things I have been taken with from the start of our partnership together was your ability as a lawyer. You have a vast knowledge of the law."

Bill Herndon acted surprised, "I never knew that, Abe. Quite a compliment coming from you."

Abe grinned that special smile which encompassed his face, "Besides who else would have put up with my young Trojans when they came with me on Saturdays and climbed around like monkeys and did everything but gut the place? You had to spend a good part of Mondays just to get us some degree of order again."

Both men looked around the cluttered office. Bill picked up the small pile from off Abe's desk that was tied together with string. On the top of the papers was a note in Abe's handwriting, "When you can't find it anywhere else, try here."

The two men settled back in their wooden arm chairs and had a good laugh together. Following that Abe grew serious, "I don't expect you to think so little of me that you take my name off the shingle."

"You know I'd never want to," Bill admitted in return.

It was dusk outside and a strange haze was settling on the horizon, leaving a dismal feeling in Abe's mind. He didn't mention the heaviness he felt inside, but both men sat in a contemplative mood while the sun set, yet neither made a move to turn on the kerosene lights on each of their desks.

"How long have we been together?" Abe asked.

"Sixteen years."

Abe got up and walked over to Bill Herndon's chair as he rose. The two stood in the twilight, little more than silhouettes, as Abe said, "I hope to return. You'll carry on well if you'll curtail your drinking, Billy. I need to go home and finish packing and labeling the trunks." The two men embraced and parted, leaving Abe feeling sad and melancholy. Billy was right. Who knew what the future held?

The next day Abe dreaded saying farewell to his Springfield friends at the railroad station. Yes, it would be difficult. He really didn't expect any of the threats to materialize so he had decided to keep Taddie with him, yet he didn't know how wise that was. He'd only decided to keep his most active child with him in order not to thwart Mary's decision to go to Indianapolis with Robert. Abe prayed that his small train would make it to Washington without incidence, more for the safety of his son and the others aboard than for his own.

Abe awoke in the morning he was to leave the town where his heart had been anchored for a good portion of his life. He rounded up Tad and immersed him in love, more than he had in a long time. Abe knew it was not meant to be just a selfish act, but as he hugged his youngest remaining son, a sense of love and belonging filled his body and soul.

Nicolay and Hay arrived with a wagon to pick up the steamer trunks that Abe had labeled himself. "Abraham Lincoln, Washington, D.C." A strange sense of anticipation flooded his mind. He, Abe Lincoln, was going to be the head of what he thought to be the greatest nation in the world. "Oh, God," he prayed. "Please make me worthy of this calling. I need You to give me discernment on how to keep the Union together."

The two men's arrival had brought him back to the present. He directed the loading of the trunks then went with them to the railroad station, Tad hanging out the side of the wagon hollering, "We're going to the White House! My father's going to be PRESIDENT!" It only took one such holler for Abe to stop his son. "Taddie, nobody cares but us."

Nicolay grinned. "That's what you say, Mr. President. The world wants you."

"There you go again. That's enough of that Mr. President stuff."

Nicolay stared at him for a moment. "I'm not going to stop saying that, sir. You're going to have to respond to that in Washington so you and I might as well get used to it."

As he approached the train depot Abe's eyes grew wide with dismay. A band was playing, placards spouting messages to him were everywhere. "Go, Abe,"— "God Speed." When his eyes came upon the one that declared, "Abraham Lincoln - Mr. President" his eyes twinkled as they met Nicolay's.

Tad was bouncing up and down with enthusiasm. His father chuckled, certain that the little guy really had no concept of what was taking place.

As Abe boarded the train the mob cheered with a deafening roar. He stood mesmerized for a moment, but then raised his hand to still the crowd. A tightness seemed to keep him from speaking for a moment as the emotional impact of the moment hit him full force. The throng before him came to a complete hush as Abraham Lincoln found the words to address them, that February 11th.

ADDRESS OF ABRAHAM LINCOLN

TO THE CITIZENS OF SPRINGFIELD, ON HIS DEPARTURE FOR WASHINGTON, FEBRUARY 11TH, 1861.

My Friends:

No one, not in my position, can appreciate the sadness I feel at this parting. To this people I owe all that I am. Here I have lived more than a quarter of a century; here my children were born, and here one of them lies buried. I know not how soon I shall see you again. A duty devolves upon me which is, perhaps, greater than that which has devolved upon any other man since the days of Washington. He never would have succeeded except by the aid of Divine Providence, upon which he at all times relied. I feel that I cannot succeed without the same Divine aid which sustained him, and on the same Almighty Being I place my reliance for support; and I hope you, my friends, will all pray that I may receive that Divine assistance, without which I cannot succeed, but with which success is certain. Again I bid you an affectionate farewell.

The engine began to hiss as the crowd cheered wildly at the end of the speech. As Abe scanned the many familiar faces, he saw some wiping their eyes. He tried to gain his own composure. As he wondered about the future, his son slipped his hand in Abe's while Springfield, Illinois disappeared from view.

Taddie was quiet for a short time indicating to Abe that even his small son realized he was in a contemplative mood until he smiled down at his youngest child and said, "Son, I hope you never call me Mr. President."

174

RESIDENCE OF ABRAHAM LINCOLN, SPRINGFIELD, ILL.—FROM 1846 TO 1861.

P. 142

DESTINATION WASHINGTON

Mary met the train in Indianapolis as they'd planned.. She looked fine, as did Robert. When she saw Abe standing on the rear platform of the train with Willie and Tad by the hand, she called out to them, "Thank God, you're all safe!"

As Abe reached down to help his wife up the steps he asked, "You knew?"

Mary sighed before replying, "You silly goose, did you think I was an imbecile or something? The newspapers are full of stories about your enemies trying to do away with you. How did you think I didn't know you and our babies were in danger? I didn't know before I left, but I did as soon as I saw a newspaper."

Abe smiled. "I should have known you'd be suspicious if I sent you on a shopping spree. By the way, Lamon is my self-appointed bodyguard and Seward has stood on his ear to make certain all of us arrive in Washington in one piece. I'm not certain about Lamon's great dedication to my safety after all. He's been back in another car picking ballads on his banjo."

Mary giggled. "Then I'm extra glad you didn't meet with a crisis."

The train started up again and some of the men took on the job of entertaining the Lincoln boys.

Every time they made a whistle stop, Abe complained to Mary, "I'm not giving anyone much hope that I know what I'm doing. You know that I've never been able to give a good extemporaneous speech."

During their stopover in Columbus, Ohio Abe tried to diminish the national problem by saying, "There is nothing wrong." He also declared, "Time, patience, and a reliance on a God Who has never forsaken this people will see us through."

The train later chugged into Pittsburgh during a dismal downpour. There he announced his belief, "There really is no crisis except an artificial one."

In Cleveland, Ohio he and Mary were both amazed to find an immense crowd standing in snow, rain and mud. There he chose to ask questions about the South, "Why are the Southerners so incensed? Why all these complaints?"

Abe declared to Mary afterward, "I know all the questions, but I fear I don't know the answers any more than they do." Several times he declared to an eager, waiting crowd, "It's not up to the President to save the Union. It's up to the people." Scanning their faces, he realized that they were not pleased with that remark, that they wanted HIM to unite the country again.

When his special train arrived in Westfield, New York, he gave Grace Bedell a kiss. She was that little girl who had written and convinced him that he'd have more impact on the voters if he sported a beard. To Abe, that gesture of thanks from him was a most welcome diversion from the seriousness of all his other stops.

Abraham Lincoln finally admitted to one audience, "I am so weary that I haven't the strength to address you at greater length." In truth, he felt depressed. Nicolay had informed him earlier, "Sir, I think you need to know that Jefferson Davis was sworn in as President of the Confederate States today. They say that folks were so excited that there was dancing in the streets."

Exasperated with that news, Abe moaned to Mary, "What else can happen? I'm going to Washington with the purpose of saving the Union, but the South is jubilant, dancing in the streets because they seceded. The weather isn't my problem. They are."

New York newspapers didn't help his depressed, weary mind. Mary tried to dispose of the cartoons and the descriptions depicting him as a baboon, but Abe retrieved them from the wastebasket and decided not to discuss the degrading caricatures with anyone.

Arrangements had been made for him to speak at Independence Hall, so he planned to focus on that, but the Pinkerton Detective Agency set up a secret meeting at the Continental Hotel where he was staying with the family to warn him, "Sir, you have to be careful. There's a serious plot to assassinate you in Baltimore. The place is crawling with pro-Confederates. Your schedule makes it necessary for you to change trains and those men intending to get you are planning to attack as you take a carriage from one station to another."

Abe sat, taking all this in before he spoke, "Don't you imagine this is just some more idle speculation?"

The head of the detectives, a bewhiskered little Scotsman, declared, "No, sir. No doubt that the conspiracy exists! You must catch a train for Washington this night. That will foil their plans."

"Sorry boys, I can't. I promised I'd speak at Independence Hall on Washington's birthday tomorrow and talk in Harrisburg in the afternoon. Whatever my fate might be, I will not forego my engagements for tomorrow. My word is my bond."

Later that night while he was attempting to sleep, a knock came to Abe's hotel room door. Seward's young son Frederick handed him a letter. Upon opening it he found a message from the Secretary of State and General Scott saying, "There is a definite plot to kill you in Baltimore. You must avoid that city at all costs."

Mary stirred in their bed. "Abraham, what is it?"

"Just a letter, dear. Don't worry yourself. We both need some rest." With those words he got back into bed and went to sleep.

On George Washington's birthday Abe went to Independence Hall. Surveying the crowd, he wondered if they had any thought of the maze of problems parading through his head as he addressed them:

"I have never had a feeling, politically, that did not spring from the sentiments embodied in the Declaration of Independence. I have often pondered over the dangers which were incurred by the men who assembled here and framed and adopted that Declaration. I have pondered over the toils that were endured by the officers and soldiers of the army who achieved that independence. I have often inquired of myself what great principle or idea it was that kept this Confederacy so long together. It was not the mere matter of the separation of the colonies from the motherland, but that sentiment in the Declaration of Independence which gave liberty not alone to the people of this country, but I hope to the world for all future time. It was that which gave promise that, in due time, the weight would be lifted from the shoulders of all men. This is the sentiment embodied in the Declaration of Independence. Now, my friends, can this country be saved on that basis? If it can, I shall consider myself one of the happiest men in the world if I can help to save it. If it cannot be saved upon that principle it will be truly awful. But if this country cannot be saved without giving up that principle, I was about to say I would rather be assassinated on this spot than surrender it."

That afternoon while heading toward Harrisburg a secret service man named Judd told Abe in private, "We've worked out a getaway plan with the railroad and special army officers. At twilight we'll disguise and take you back to Philly on a sleeping car where a night train will take you to Baltimore. Another will smuggle you back to Washington. Along with a military escort we'll protect the train transporting your family and friends."

Abraham Lincoln objected. "I don't like the idea of sneaking back to the capitol, but I'll go along with it if you'll let me tell my wife."

Abe realized from Jesse's next remark that the man knew of his wife's reputation for having a temper for he protested, "I can't stop you, but I'd rather you wouldn't."

When Abe tried to relate the plans to Mary later while on the train to Harrisburg, his regrets for doing so were immediate. "What?" she demanded. "They're going to take you away from me and let you loose in a hostile city where men's plans to kill you are already known?"

Panic surfaced in her eyes. Her husband was not surprised at her next words. "What if you ARE murdered? What if I lose the husband I love and depend on for everything?"

"I'm sorry, Mary. Judd and his aides are doing the best they can for all of us."

Tears streaming down her face, she cried, "Oh, Abraham, take Lamon with you. He'll protect you with his life."

The President-elect felt as though he were going to act in a ridiculous play when they tried to disguise him in a long overcoat and a Kossuth hat. When he waited in a carriage outside of Philadelphia he had chuckled as Lamon joined him. "Can you use all of those at one time?" he asked his friend and well-armed bodyguard.

A slight grin crossed Lamon's face as he looked down at the weapons he'd brought with him — two long knives, two derringers plus two revolvers.

"Reckon not, sir. I just came prepared for any eventuality."

A deep furrow formed on Abe's brow. "Everyone's taking care of me. I hope and pray that the same precautions are being taken for my wife and family."

Lamon grew uneasy as someone approached the carriage after dark, but both its passengers sighed with relief when they found out it was Pinkerton who assured them, "Everything's going as planned."

Following that Abe was taken to a sleeper on a night train to Baltimore. The President-to-be tried, but found no sleep in his train berth that night. He didn't know if word had leaked out or not, but the Baltimore assassination planners might still try to pull off their scheme while Mary and the boys were on the train. As his so-called "sleeper" pulled through Baltimore it was after three in the morning. The streets were empty so he assumed no one realized he was on board.

At Cambria Station he was transferred to another train which chugged and hissed until it finally pulled into Washington close to dawn, where congressman Washburn from Illinois was waiting to take him to the Willard Hotel.

The sun was rising. Abraham Lincoln looked around but nothing impressed him in the city he was to call home on a temporary basis. If anything, it looked worse than it did while he was a congressman. Smells were obnoxious. Open ditches ran through the streets. Dingy shanties where the Negroes lived were in sharp contrast to the Southern style mansions. Black men were already at work.

"Slaves?" he asked Washburn.

"Most likely," came the reply. "Washington is still considered to be a Southern city. At least there are no more pens or auction blocks for slaves now."

"I should be grateful for that. The first time I witnessed a ship and auction and the slaves' treatment, it was almost more than my soul could stand."

The Congressman sympathized, "I never saw one. I'm certain I never want to. On a lighter note, the Willard Hotel has running water in every room. You have suite 6, the one reserved for important people. Here we are," Washburn said as they pulled up to a fortress-like building. "You'll be safe."

Once inside, Abe found a letter waiting for him. Upon opening it, he scanned the message, "If you don't resign, we'll play the devil with you." Following the threat he read the rest of the message which contained lines of obscene language. Abraham Lincoln tore the letter, envelope and all, into shreds and tossed it in the wastebasket while thinking, *I don't think such threats are a joke.*

Because of this Abe became anxious. When Mary and their sons arrived, he welcomed them with open arms.

"Abraham, you'll never believe how they screamed for you. No one seemed friendly, they just seemed to be in a frenzy because they thought you have nerve enough to go there. They are our enemies! I have such a headache." Saying that, she laid down with a wet cloth over her forehead. Abe noted that she did seem pleased with the running water.

Her headache did not improve when she looked at the newspapers the next day. "Look!" she cried, "The newsmen must have found out about your escape. Here's a whole section of cartoons making fun of you." Then, as if aghast, she wailed, "Oh, Abraham they're even making fun of ME! Don't they know of my upbringing? I was raised to be a woman of culture, and you, you are so intelligent. We'll show them, won't we? I'll entertain like no one ever has before. No woman from the past will be a candidate for being the First Lady of the land. I will be the first one!"

Abe admitted to himself that he did not enjoy being the object of abuse in the newspapers. When they said he was a "hick" he wanted to show them his abilities, but he was not as incensed as Mary.

He thought with a smirk on his face, *I need to warn the people. Watch out Washington, my wife's in town.*

LINCOLN came so aptly to the need of his times, and was so exactly fitted for the burden of his greatness, that probably he impressed few of his casual acquaintances with his transcendent qualities. Now that he has gone from the world, which he did so much to make better, those who have a definite knowledge of the crisis in which he was the greatest actor can see and wonder at his greatness. Others were divided upon abstract questions, which, by unkindly discussion, seemed to have grown into causes of sectional hate. Even many of the leaders of the party which made Lincoln President forgot their love of country in their hatred of slavery, and would have accepted disunion even, that they might fight slavery more earnestly. They made the mistake which history shows has been made so often. They fancied that excessive philanthropy might take the place of patriotism. Lincoln first and above all loved his country. Every other love, opinion, principle was in utter subordination to his patriotism. That was his strength. That made him the representative and the worthy leader of all patriots of every sort of opinion. He was the leader of all the patriotic people; he was the leader of the war. He was the incarnation of a nation's love of country. In his grave he remains the exemplar and the idol of patriotism.

C. E. Lippincott

(C. E. Lippincott)

CHANDLERVILLE, 1881.

WAR OR PEACE?

That March 4 Abraham Lincoln was appalled by the surroundings in which he and outgoing President James Buchanan found themselves. Sharpshooters were positioned on roofs on buildings: streets were blocked off by soldiers. "General Scott and General Wool set up their safeguards," Buchanan informed Abe.

"Looks more like a military operation than a political parade," President-elect Lincoln remarked to the outgoing President as they watched from their well-guarded carriage.

As the two men were escorted through a boarded passageway, Abe shook his head. "Seems to me they've gone to extremes to protect us." Buchanan sighed and answered, "At this point they're trying to make certain no one follows through with their assassination threats against you. They want to kill you. You're being inaugurated — not me."

Abe simply shook his head in wonderment as they entered the Capitol where Vice President Hannibal Hamlin was to be sworn in. Next E. D. Baker introduced Abe. Abraham Lincoln, President-elect, fumbled with his high top hat until Douglas offered to hold it while nearly 84-year-old Justice Taney administered the oath of office, making Abe the 16th President of the United States.

"What do you say to the American people at a time when we are living through a crisis?" he'd asked some of his associates as he shared with them the speech he had composed and polished before leaving Springfield. In the final analysis, after hearing all sides, he decided to remove the words, "In YOUR hands, my dissatisfied fellow countrymen and not in MINE is the momentous issue of civil war. With YOU and not me, is the solemn question of 'shall it be peace, or a sword?'" Seward was the one who talked him out of it, claiming, "Those words are much too provocative to a South who already feels defeated, irritated and frenzied."

Abe accepted much of what Seward suggested. At the end of his address he used his own distinct wording; "I am loth to close. We are not enemies but friends. We must not be enemies — the mystic chords of memory, stretching from every battlefield and patriot giving to every living heart and hearthstone all over the broad land, will yet swell the chords of the Union when again touched as surely they will be, by the better angels of our nature."

The newspapers headlines the following day shared reactions that astounded both Mary and Abe. "Lincoln Inaugurates Civil War" headed some Southern papers. The Charleston Mercury called the new President "The Ourang-Outang at the White House." The Confederate reporters all declared war inevitable. Most Republican papers offered praise but the *Columbus Daily Capital City Fact* predicted that the speech indicated that "blood will stain and color the waters of the entire continent — brother will be arrayed in hostile front against brother."

President and Mrs. Abraham Lincoln surveyed the reports the next morning, causing Abe to sigh and shake his head as if to say, "What's the use?"

That morning he was greeted by Nicolay with an urgent request from Major Anderson about the Confederates attempt to take Fort Sumter, South Carolina. "You must send help. We have need of 20,000 qualified men to make the fort secure."

Stunned, Lincoln turned to Nicolay, "What are my options? It's my first day in office and already I have to make a major decision which could mean the difference between war or peace. If I evacuate and let the rebels take the fort, such an act would avoid bloodshed and violence. My other option is to hold, occupy and possess our government's property. That includes Fort

Sumter. I'm afraid I have no choice."

He knew better than to make such a decision in haste. On March 9 he asked his cabinet, "If Major Anderson says he needs 25,000 men and the entire Union Army is less than 16,000 who are situated at remote Indian outposts, what are we to do? Must we surrender Fort Sumter? The thought appalls me."

Yet no conclusive decision as to what positive action the Union should make came from that meeting, but when Francis Blair, Sr. forced his way in to see Lincoln the next day, the President was moved by the old man's words, "I am warning you — the surrender of the fort will be on the same plateau as the surrender of the Union itself— the equivalent of treason."

After Blair left, Abe turned to Nicolay and moaned, "I guess I've been properly told off. I need to pursue all possibilities further."

Former Navy Lieutenant Fox came to him with a plan, "Sir, I know we can use light tugboats to bring reinforcements and men under the cover of night. That's how we can bring Anderson more reinforcements."

Abe pondered and prayed. Montgomery Blair urged him; "Mr. President, send an expedition in. Southerners are sure that Northern men are deficient in the courage necessary to maintain the Government."

That was one side's opinion, but Lincoln's cabinet was so divisive as to what to do that he was perplexed. Secretary Seward was adamant when he declared, "Trying to relieve Sumter would provoke combat and probably incite a civil war."

"That, my dear friend," he answered with a wistful look, "is not my choice for our beloved Union. I do not feel that bloodshed and violence solves any problem."

Still he told Nicolay in private, "The choice for war or peace seems to be out of my hands. It is up to me to prepare for whatever problems that confront the country. I have thought and thought about who would be the most capable man to run the Northern army. The most logical source is to consider all the West Point graduates as a possibility, yet I am certain that my first choice will join the South."

The winds of war began sweeping the country. Northerners were irate that the South had fired on and captured a federal fort. With the news of the fall of Fort Sumter Abraham Lincoln declared to his cabinet, "I do believe we have reached a point of no return. We must prepare. War is imminent."

Because of this awesome reality Abe continued to seek recruits for the Union army. Men responded to the government's offer of special pay and a fierce sense of loyalty to the Union. Lincoln shook his head in despair one night as he explained to Mary, "The whole thing frightens me. I've talked to so many men who view this war as a way to show off their valor. I'm afraid, little woman, that there is no glamour in actual combat. There have been skirmishes, but I fear real battles are on the horizon."

The next day Abraham Lincoln told his aide, "Nicolay, it seems to me that it would be best to enlist a West Point graduate to run the Union Army. The best man for the job has to be Robert E. Lee."

A frown crossed Nicolay's face, "Sir, do you know where his allegiance lies? You know that he's a Virginian and his heart may be swayed by the Confederacy."

With a shrug of his shoulders Abe responded, "We won't know if we don't ask him. Contact General Lee so we can chat."

Robert E. Lee came to the White House in response to Abraham Lincoln's summons. Abe thought his guest appeared to be apprehensive as he shook hands and greeted him. "So nice to see you, Mr. President."

Lee sat down at Abe's invitation, then the President spoke, "I am of the opinion that civil war is imminent and the country needs a general who has the finest leadership qualities. I believe, sir, you are the best man to qualify to be the head of the Union Army."

Lee's expression made Abe aware that his statement had startled his visitor. "Does my suggestion make you uneasy, general?" he asked.

"Mr. President, sir, I am most flattered by your words, but I have not made up my mind for whom I will give my allegiance.

First and foremost I am a Virginian. If my beloved state goes with the South, then I will have to be a Confederate leader."

Those few words dashed Abe's hopes. He was certain the state next to the nation's capitol would side with the Confederacy, so he ended the short visit by saying, "My preference is that the Union would stay intact and there will be no war, but it seems inevitable. May the Lord direct your path, General Lee. Thank you for coming."

On top of all his war concerns and a need for readiness, the financial problems swelled. Only thirteen days after his inauguration the stock market began to plummet.

On July 21 Nicolay greeted the President with a telegram. Abe knew by the expression of his aide's face, that the Union had lost a battle. "Where was this confrontation?" he inquired.

"Bull Run, Mr. Lincoln. They whipped us soundly."

A downcast President's sigh sounded more like a moan as he wailed, "There's no turning back now. The war is here and we must win."

THE name and fame of Mr. Lincoln will live as long as the history of the republic endures, as that of a true lover of his country and of humanity—as that of a man equal to all the conditions of life, from that of the humble and lowly to that of the proud and exalted position as President of the grand republic and peer of the proudest monarch, and in every position the same plain, honest, prudent man—safe in council, wise in action and pure in purpose.

(Jno. C. New)

INDIANAPOLIS, 1880.

THRESHOLD TO CHANGE

A glimmer of joy filled Abraham Lincoln's heart as he escorted his spouse and three sons from the Willard Hotel up the walk to the White House for the first time. A strange sense of unbelief overtook him as he thought to himself with a feeling of utter amazement. *How can a man who'd been born into one of the poorest families in the land attain the right to dwell in the most famous, most prestigious home in the country?*

Glancing at his wife, reality impacted him. Mary's face glowed with anticipation. She'd been the one who'd pushed him toward this goal, always claiming, "My heart's desire is to be the wife of the President of the United States."

It was happening! A sudden thrill rushed through him and he felt much like a young bridegroom. Abe even thought about carrying his little woman across the threshold, but a mental picture of his long, scrawny frame lifting her short, rather robust body with three little boys in tow deemed the whole notion ridiculous.

Instead, Abe offered his hand to her, and each of their sons reached out and joined in the chain so that they walked up the few steps to their new home looking and feeling very much like a family until Mary made an abrupt stop.

"Look! Look, Abe, the cement is cracked! Take a good look at that paint, the White House is almost gray!"

Once Abe turned the key and opened the front door, Mary and he stood, horrified at the sights inside. Faded wall paper, worn furniture, chipped paint and plaster gave every room a worn-out look. In the living room cotton stuffing was spilling out of a worn red velvet couch. Mary cried, "Abe, look! That couch had to have been an exquisite piece of furniture once. Even in here everything's an eyesore."

By the time they reached the basement, a large rodent zoomed right in front of them, Mary jumped and screamed, "Rats!" Without taking another breath, she cried "Abe, let's get these children out of here!"

With that, they turned and hustled back upstairs. At that moment Abe decided his first official duty to God and his country was to calm his disappointed wife. Once they were back on the main floor, he reached down to hug her, trying to console Mary by saying, "Sweetheart, I've seen what you can do to renovate a house and make it so that is hardly recognizable. You've done it before." He squelched the urge to add, "You did it behind my back and at great expense."

"Oh, Abe," she wailed, "it'll take thousands and thousands of dollars to restore this huge place into the mansion it was meant to be. We can't afford to do that!"

Placing his arm across her shoulder, he tried to soothe her as he said, "Mary, restoration of the President's home isn't something we need to pay for. Congress will do that."

"Oh, that's true, isn't it?" A look of relief flooded her face so Abe realized her mental wheels were already turning. *Maybe,* he thought, *she'll get so involved in that project that she'll forget trying to run me and the country.*

The first day that Congress was back in session, he stated his impassioned plea for funds to restore the White House, assuring the Senate and House members that it was as he claimed, "In a deplorable state."

His request was granted so Abe returned home in a jubilant mood. At dinner he announced, "Mary, the men all listened to my wailing about this run-down house, and they agreed to grant us twenty thousand dollars during my four-year term for its renovation."

The announcement excited his wife so much that she couldn't finish her meal. "Wonderful!" she cried. "That's a lot to work with."

Abe listened to her plans and decided to caution his extravagant spouse. "Twenty thousand is all they offered. Remember, not a penny more."

"No problem," she consoled him. "I can make twenty thousand dollars go a long, long way."

During the next few weeks the White House resembled a beehive full of activity with plasterers and painters working on the walls of every room of the huge mansion. As soon as they were finished, carpet layers arrived with scarlet rolls of plush flooring material. Mary's eyes danced with excitement when Abe arrived on the scene, "See, dear, we're rolling out the red carpet for our guests."

Abraham Lincoln smiled and queried as he arrived from a trip out of town, "Are you expecting royalty, Mary?"

"Oh, Abraham Lincoln, of course I am. Look in the East Room, dear. A beautiful sea foam green covers the floor."

Abe sauntered over to the room and looked in at the sea foam green carpet, but resisted the urge to ask her if he was a ship's captain or the country's president. One glance at her face which glowed with pleasure assured him it was not the time to jest. He'd had to learn to live with her moods years ago.

In the ensuing weeks Abe noticed a drastic change in the White House decor. Mary bubbled with delight as she showed off the new "Solferino and gold" Haviland China emblazoned with the American coat of arms.

Not wanting to ebb her enthusiasm too much, Abe tried to be gentle as he cautioned, "Mary, Mary, please remember you are on a limited budget. Everything looks so expensive."

"Mr. President, sir," she giggled. "That's the idea! I've dickered and shopped for magnificent things at bargain prices. Aren't you proud of me?"

Abe sighed, " I am — if that's so, but, dear Mrs. President, I've been married to you for over twenty years and I know you very well. Just remember if you soar over your budget, you'll have to figure out how to pay for your extravagance yourself."

Mary giggled again. "Don't worry. You have enough to think about. Running the war and the country should consume your time."

Abe agreed, "You're right. I have enough to do just to take care of the affairs of state. I'll leave the refurbishing of this old place in your hands."

Unbeknownst to Abe, Mary had the rudest of awakenings when the bills started coming in, causing her to make certain that the total sum for her outrageous purchases be kept hidden from her husband. To her horror she learned that she'd not only spent all four years of her Congressional allotment, but all of Abe's salary for his entire term of office.

As President, Abraham Lincoln was unaware of his wife's maneuvers behind his back. John Watt, their gardener, suggested to Mary when she confided the amount of her staggering debt to him; "You have no choice but to pad the bills for the things you buy for the White House, and you owe so much you'd better submit requests for funds for items you never purchased."

Abe had no knowledge of the fact that Mary had even discharged the White House steward, then submitted bills in the name of Mrs. Watt as a replacement, but kept the salary for herself.

Early in his presidency Abraham Lincoln had told her, "You know we don't have to make this into a palace. It's better than any place we have ever lived, and we must keep funds for the poor soldiers to have blankets!" Remembering this, she must have feared going to her husband to confess her list of sins.

His words had been so adamant that, because of all these secret behind-the-scenes maneuvers, Abe was caught off guard and thrown for an emotional loop when Benjamin French, the man in charge of public buildings and White House accounts, came to him and announced, "Sir, we have a problem. Your wife has asked me to come to you on her behalf. From the stack of bills for renovating the White House, I soon realized that it is so far beyond the budget allotted, that we need to get Congress to allocate a great deal more funds. Fearful of your reaction, she begged me to come to you on her behalf."

Abe sat, stunned, that Mary had put him in such a position. How could she? He'd warned and threatened her so many times. His face clouded. Flame red color crept from his neck upwards. At last he spoke, "I do not want the government to have to foot the bills for my wife's frivolities."

Mr. Franklin cleared his throat before speaking again. Abe realized the accountant was taking his time and measuring his next words. "Sir, I want you to know that she's tried. Your wife came to me as a last resort after she'd sold off all the second-hand furniture that's been replaced. She'd even gone so far as to sell the manure out of the stable for ten cents a load."

It was Abe's turn to weigh his words prior to addressing the accountant once more, but at last he said, "Sir, I am so sorry she has put us both in such a humiliating mess. Knowing Mary as I do, I realize that she has gone to other extremes to get herself out of this dilemma — actions you and I would be humiliated to know. Somehow, some way, we shall pay off the debt from out of my salary."

That was his heart's desire, but after days of frustration he realized he had no choice. Using his entire wages would not pay off the massive expenditure that Mary had made. With deep humility he requested Congress to allocate enough funds to cover Mary's extravagance. They did, but Abe vowed to his spouse, "Never will I trust you again with any venture of this sort. You've shot me down for the very last time."

One night as Mary was getting ready for bed, Abe made up his mind to confront his wife. "Mary, sit down. We need to have a talk. No, I've worded that wrong!" His voice deepened and he emphasized the word "I" as he went on. "I need to talk to you and YOU need to listen for a change! You have lied and cheated and literally stolen money that isn't yours. Are you never humiliated by your action?

"Back in Springfield no words can convey my feelings when I found you'd gone against any sane judgment and betrayed my wishes by changing every aspect of our home so that I was so baffled and hurt that my vocabulary is not capable of describing my feelings then. There's a war on now. Boys and men are being killed, but you are only being selfish.

"Through this current extravagance of yours you have not only put us in a most embarrassing position, but you have even given the Treasury Department of the United States government a problem. You want me to keep the presidency, but my extravagant wife, remember that YOU — yes, YOU have a bearing on whether or not I keep the office. Furthermore, I vow here and now, that if you do anything so foolish ever again, you may also find your marriage will suffer. Have I made myself clear?"

A meek, "Yes, dear," came from Mary's lips, then she got in bed beside him, "I'm sorry," she whispered. Abe sighed and placed an arm around her as he answered back. "Me, too."

OLD FRIENDS

Bull Run, Manassas, battles were springing up on every front, causing more and more pressure on President Lincoln. A short while after the war began to escalate, Abe glanced down at the business cards John Hay presented him one morning. The name, "G. S. Hubbard," triggered treasured memories of a man who had made a valiant attempt to get the Illinois State Legislature to pass a bill to build a canal linking Michigan and Illinois. It failed. Undaunted, State Senator Hubbard had tried to get legislation so the railroads could provide faster, easier transportation between the two states. That bill was also voted down.

Abraham Lincoln was aware of all the Senator's efforts when he'd entered the Illinois legislature and he had assured Hubbard that the canal version would be the most beneficial of the two proposals. A glimmer of joy surfaced in Abe's mind at the remembrance of his visitor and his appreciation when Abe decided to put his influence behind the canal version and saw to it that it was finally passed. Senator Hubbard's parting words to him after the successful vote were etched in Abe's keen mind, "Abraham Lincoln, you are a man of great honesty and integrity. I also enjoy your quick wit and good humor."

As President on that busy morning when his old friend came to call, Abe could only reminisce for a minute about their former times together since he had far more pressing matters. Abe welcomed him into his office at the first opportunity, but it only took a short time before Hubbard announced, "Mr. President, I notice your usual jovial mood is missing. You have such a serious frown on your face."

Abe did not respond with a smile, instead he explained to his visitor, "I'm most anxious about this horrible conflict that has divided our nation, but I feel confident that we will squelch the rebellion. Surely, I have some reason to rejoice since such a large portion of the people are for using the resources of our country to bring the rebellious states back into the Union."

With that, the President pointed to the map on the wall and indicated spots which were the strongest in the rebel district. Next he turned to his visitor and shared with him words of praise about a man who had once played the role of Abe's adversary during the much publicized national debates. "Douglas and myself have studied the map very closely. I am indebted to him for his wise counsel. I have no better adviser and feel great obligations to him." A flicker of a smile crossed Abe's face. He realized his visitor knew about all the concerns Abraham Lincoln had once held in his heart about the man who had once been a true political adversary!

Abe also realized that Hubbard understood how he was pressed for time for he soon left the White House office and did not return until much later.

During his next visit Thomas Forrest also sat with Hubbard in the anteroom outside the President's office. The two men chatted for two hours after giving Nicolay their business cards to announce their presence, yet Abraham Lincoln was so pressured by imminent demands for decisions that he had been unable to rid himself of his duties long enough to greet his old friends.

Seated by the window opening upon the spacious grounds and the garden at the rear of the White House, Forrest and Hubbard kept conversing until a band began to play outside. Forrest glanced first at Hubbard, then at his watch, then remarked, "This is Saturday when the grounds are open to the public. The President will go out through the White House and he'll present himself on the balcony below. Let's go join the crowd."

With those words they left the room to go see the president and listen to the Navy band. Abraham Lincoln had already seated himself on the balcony where he sat and watched the citizens parade past him. A strange sense of embarrassment swept over him as men raised their hats as though they were saluting him.

Abe's face lit with recognition as he spied G. S. Hubbard. Noticing his reaction, Tom Forrest remarked, "The President seems to notice you — turn toward him."

Hubbard whispered back, "No, I don't care to be recognized."

Abe saw to it that the choice was not Hubbard's to make, for the President sprang to his feet, beckoned with his long arm over the iron railing as he called in a most undignified manner, "Hubbard! Hubbard! Come here!"

Leaving the ranks of citizens who were staring at him with wonder, the well-known politician ascended the steps to the balcony in reply to the Presidential summons, only to find the entry was locked.

General Thomas told the President as well as the invited guest, "Wait a moment. I will get the key."

Abe's face shone with pleasure, something even he realized hadn't happened much in those trying days. His eyes twinkled as he declared, "Never mind, but my friend Hubbard is used to jumping. He can scale the fence."

A red-faced Hubbard rose to the challenge, pushing his body up and over the obstacle before him. After that the two men sat together for close to an hour while watching the huge crowd below. "The greatest challenge of my career from this vantage point is not because of the milling throng, but because of the rebel flag that is in full view from here, flown in defiance of the Union in nearby Arlington Heights." His voice gained momentum and force as he declared, "I will not rest until the Confederate banner comes down and Old Glory flies from that flag pole once again!"

Having said that, Abraham Lincoln added, "I have accepted the tremendous challenge of bringing together the Rebels and the Union so they once more could become 'The United States of America,' one nation, indivisible, with liberty and justice for all."

THE name of Abraham Lincoln will stand forever, as the second in our history, following immediately that of George Washington. This one was the principal agent in emancipating the western continent from foreign domination, that one the principal agent in rescuing it from a domestic domination even more hurtful. Both were spotless apostles of human liberty.

Parke Godwin

NEW YORK, 1880.   (Parke Goodwin)

INDEPENDENCE DAY

Abraham Lincoln felt the need to discuss the war situation with Congress so much that summer of 1861 that he summoned all the members to a special meeting on the 4th of July.

As the President surveyed the joint session, he felt squeamish inside. The Senate and House seats of all the seven states that had seceded were vacant. *Look at this*, Abe thought. *The number of representatives from the South that are missing shows the gravity of the situation.*

Breckenridge, the lone pro-slavery leader left in the Senate, not only hailed from Kentucky, but Abe felt no thrill at seeing a spy sitting there amidst all the Congressmen from the North. The Senator had even been the Southern candidate for the Presidency. Other pro-slavery leaders were absent. Lincoln knew many of them were setting up the rebel government in Richmond. Others were marshalling troops in the fields. Signs of their rebellion were evident when the President of the United States had his heart torn with regret when he had looked out of the Capitol dome earlier and seen the Confederate flag flying across the Potomac and on toward Fairfax, Virginia. Besides that, Secretary Stanton had informed Abe, "Sir, you need to know that a hostile army is enmassing to the south," which was little consolation to Abraham Lincoln who detested the very thought of war.

As Congress was called to order for the special session, Abe could not help but think of the message he'd heard from General Charles Stewart after the general had visited with Senator Douglas, the same Stephen Douglas who had been Abraham

Lincoln's adversary during the bitter Lincoln-Douglas debates back in Illinois. Since then the "Little Giant" had been elected to the Senate and married a cousin of Mrs. Madison, one of the most intelligent and beautiful woman in Washington, and lived in the "Minnesota Block," one of the most magnificent areas of Washington.

The conversation between the two men kept parading through the President's mind as he stood surveying the empty chairs of the statesmen from the South.

Stewart had told him, "On that New Year's day I asked the Senator, 'What will be the result of the efforts of Jefferson Davis and his associates to divide the Union?' We were sitting on the sofa, but Douglas rose, paced rapidly around the room, then exclaimed, 'The Cotton States are making an effort to draw in the Border States to their schemes of secession, and I am too fearful that they will succeed. If they do, there will be the most fearful war the world has ever seen, lasting for years'."

Pausing a moment he looked like one inspired while he proceeded. "Virginia over yonder across the Potomac," he said as he pointed toward Arlington, "will become a channel house but in the end the Union will triumph. They will try," he continued, "to get possession of this capitol to give them prestige abroad, but in that effort they will never succeed; the North will rise enmasse to defend it. Churches will be used for the sick and wounded, this house," he said in reference to his own home, "will be devoted to that purpose by the end of the war.

"Then," still standing, and you could sense the anger building up in him, Douglas declared, "I will go as far as the Constitution will permit to maintain their just rights. But," he cried, raising his arm, "If the Southern States attempt to secede, I am in favor of their having just so many slaves, and just so much slave territory, as they can hold at the point of the bayonet, and no more!"

A sad, wistful smile crossed over Abraham Lincoln's face. The vacant seats showed the seceding part of Stephen Douglas' concern had already taken place. Abe knew that many of the southern leaders had believed there would be no war, and those in the seceding states had proclaimed that idea to the Southern people.

Abraham Lincoln also thought of how Benjamin Butler from Massachusetts who had voted for Breckenridge, the extreme Southern candidate for President, had come and asked his old associates what they meant by "threats."

He'd informed Lincoln, who had no choice on that July 4th but to ponder their words as Butler had related them to him then, "We mean separation — a Southern Confederacy. We will have our independence — a Southern government — with no discordant elements."

"Are you prepared for war?' Butler said he asked them.

"Oh, there will be NO war. The North won't fight, they informed me."

"But I protested, 'The north WILL fight. The North will send the LAST MAN and the LAST DOLLAR to maintain the Government."

"To that," Butler declared, "My Southern friends told me that the North can't fight. We have too many allies there."

"I answered them directly to the point," Butler assured Lincoln, "In the North you have friends who will stand by you so long as you fight your battles in the Union, but the moment you fire on the flag, the North will be a unit against you. You may be assured that if war comes, SLAVERY ENDS."

Those two conversations were uppermost in Abe's mind as the joint session was called to order. How he wished there would be no military confrontation, but the circumstances that Douglas and Butler had been concerned about when Senator Breckenridge stood to speak, he knew that the last holdout was viewed with distrust by men with whom he had worked alongside for years. Gloomy-looking and perhaps sorrowful, the Senator ended with, "I can only look with sadness on the melancholy drama that is being enacted."

Baker, the Senator from Oregon, stood and made a brilliant and impassioned reply to Breckenridge's speech by claiming, "You are nothing but a traitor, giving aid and encouragement to the enemy by your speeches."

Fixing his eyes along with every eye in the Senate and the crowded gallery and the President himself; Baker asked, "What would have been thought if, after the battle of Cannae, a Roman Senator had risen amidst the Conscript Fathers, and denounced the war and opposed all measures for its success?"

Silence. The President felt a tinge of compassion for the man he'd cared about and respected, for the solitary representative from the South had to feel completely alone.

After that pressure began to mount against Lincoln for the war to end. General John C. Fremont caught the nation's attention in late August. John Hay was the one who brought telegrams to Abe as he entered his office, telling Abe as he placed them on his desk early in the morning, "President Lincoln. Sir, I believe you'll want to give the news from Missouri your immediate attention."

Abe scanned the messages, then groaned, "Fremont not only went all out to defeat the rebel invasion in his territory, but he has declared martial law." His voice gained momentum and depth as he continued, "He never consulted anyone here, but declared that any civilian caught bearing arms could be court-martialed and shot if convicted and any slaves of folks aiding in the rebellion will be freed."

The President paced toward his office window and stood staring into space. "His doctrine is totally against my inaugural speech declaring that my only aim at present is restoration of the union. I promised not to interfere with the slavery situation established in any state. I have no choice but to write and tell him that he has gone far beyond his authority."

Yet his letter caused great furor. Mrs. Fremont even came to confront him about the issue, but Abe felt no need to apologize. After that Fremont continued to act so recklessly in his military campaign that even the people left in the Union began to criticize him and he lost his popularity.

Abe declared to his aides, "My own popularity has decreased to the same level as a fox in a hen house. General McClellan is hailed as the great defender. Young and handsome, he has the Senate members clamoring to shake his hand. They see him as the defender of Washington."

Although McClellan had been placed in charge of the vast Army of the Potomac, even Congress began to grumble that the war was going nowhere.

Abe shared his frustration with Mary about the war's status. "McClellan is doing nothing. I am going to compose a general war order telling all the army and naval forces to undertake a general advance on the twenty-second of February and hold all the officers accountable for neglecting to carry out my order."

And so he did, causing Union armies in the West to become victorious. January 19 Abe received a telegram saying "General Thomas' forces have routed Confederate forces at Mill Springs and broken Confederate lines in Eastern Kentucky."

Abraham Lincoln smiled. His order was working!

THE memory of Abraham Lincoln is entombed in the hearts of the American people. Their love and gratitude are the columns which support the monument of his fame, more enduring than bronze or marble. His will live forever, not only in the story of his country, but in the reverence and affection of his countrymen. The purity of his patriotism inspired him with the wisdom of a statesman and the courage of a martyr.

(Stanley Matthew)

CINCINNATI, 1880.

BY INVITATION ONLY

"Abe, we must show off our White House now that it's reached its mansion status," Mary cooed one evening at dinner.

Usually when she used that tone of voice, he trembled, but President Lincoln's mind was off in the battlefield. Grant was toying with the idea of capturing Fort Henry, so Abe was weighing the merits of such a venture and was paying little heed to Mary. He didn't listen or weigh the consequences of whatever she was chattering about, "Whatever you say, dear," he answered without realizing the gist of her conversation.

"Good!" she exclaimed. "I'll make up a list of invited guests. We'll have a shindig the likes of which this old place has never had!"

When the reality of what she was proposing penetrated his troubled mind, he cried, "Mary, Mary, how would you feel if your sons were off to war to fight for a country that has so little respect for their lives that the President has a big splash to celebrate the renovation of his residence that cost the taxpayers too much money? The State Department has requested that only events open to the public or small private dinner parties be held here during the war." After a huge sigh, he knew he best give in to her whim in order to live with his spouse, so he said, "We can, if you want, hold a limited event."

"Oh, good. Then, we shall."

Abraham Lincoln dismissed the proposed gathering from his mind, but his wife did not. It wasn't until he heard rumblings from both Democrats and Republicans that they hadn't been invited to "Your dinner party" that he knew he had to confront his wife again.

"Mary," he asked at dinner, "just how many guests do you have coming to your small, private party?"

"Not too many," she replied.

"Knowing you as I do — how many is that?"

"Oh, Abe, not more than five hundred."

"What!" his outcry was more of a shocked exclamation than a question.

"Abe, now listen to reason. How do you not include some people? Just imagine a politician who has been snubbed by not getting an invitation to a party at the White House. How would you like to be confronted by him?"

Abe rose from the table without finishing his meal. "I already have. The rumor has it that if Mrs. Lincoln doesn't like you, then your chances of being a guest 'by invitation only' is almost nil and I fear, my dear wife, the rumors are right!" After that announcement, he walked away, realizing her damage had already been done. *I cannot retrieve a half-a-thousand invitations. Will she ever listen to reason or have common sense? he wondered. What is she thinking of when we're involved in a horrendous, heart-breaking war?*

In spite of his protests, the night of February 5th came and carriages began arriving around nine o'clock.

Mary had the White House staff dressed in mulberry-shaded uniforms to match the color of the new Solferino China with the American Seal in the center of each plate. She'd purchased a black swallowtail coat for Abe and for herself she'd ordered a white silk dress with raised black silk flowers and a low neckline. The United States Marine Band provided the background music. One of the songs? "The Mary Lincoln Polka!" Members of the cabinet, generals, the politicians — both Democrat and Republican — who held Mary's favor arrived in their most elaborate, colorful dress and dined on exquisite cuisine starting at midnight. The center displayed replicas of the Ship of State. Fort Sumter and Fort Pickens made from a sugar concoction which were surrounded by slices of ham, turkey, duck, pheasant and even turtle graced the center of the elaborate table. The food had been prepared by New York's most expensive caterer.

The evening's festivities were dampened for the Lincolns by only one source. Little Willie had come down with a high fever which the doctor declared, "He has to have a form of typhoid. The White House must have a contaminated water supply."

"Oh, Abe, with all the work I've put into restoring the looks of this place, I never thought to check out the water;" Mary wailed at the hurtful words she'd heard before when Eddie had contacted the same malady.

Abe stood like a mummy with an ashen-white face as he heard the White House physician's diagnosis. The word "fever" had impacted his life with sorrow too often. Too many of those he'd held closest and dearest to his heart had been lost from his life forever by the word "fever." "We must call the party off!" he'd insisted. Thoughts of his mother, Ann, his great aunt and uncle and little Eddie and how they'd all lost their lives flashed through his mind.

Mary's face darkened like a storm cloud in the summer sky which was about to burst open with rain. "Oh, Abe, how can we? We'll just have to act as though nothing is wrong. Both of us can take turns taking care of our baby." The tone in her words was not that of the great hostess, but that of a mother who was devastated by her child's sudden, serious illness.

"Typhoid fever," Abe mused, "is not on the invitation list, but yes, dear, you've got food and people and all the trimmings, so we have no choice we must go on with your show." He never thought of her extravagant endeavors as being his in any way.

All evening Abe excused himself to go up the stairs to hold and try to comfort his sick son until Mary would come to relieve him. Then he would stand and watch for a moment as she cooed, "It's all right, Willie, Mommy's here." At moments such as that when he saw her caring heart, Abraham Lincoln respected and cherished his spouse.

After the last of the guests were gone at the break of day, the uninvited guest lingered. In fact the little lad with the fever became the focal point of their lives, both of his parents taking turns staying with him. Terror tore at Abe Lincolns' heart. Mary and he had lived a similar experience before, but he hoped the outcome would not be the same. Dr. Stone came daily to check on the boy, give his advice, but finally told them, "I've done everything I know to do for your son medically, but I'm sorry to say, his lack of improvement not only baffles me, but it also worries me."

By the 19th of the month Dr. Stone checked the boy's forehead, then turned to face the anguished faces of both his father and mother. "Mr. President and Mrs. Lincoln, there is nothing more I know to do. His recovery is in hands Higher than mine. All I know to do now is pray."

Yet, on February 20th, fifteen days following the party after Mary Lincoln had been dubbed, "The First Lady of the Land," she became once more the grief-stricken mother who had lost another little boy. To Abe's horror, his Taddie had also come down with the disease, but to his relief and Mary's, his illness did not seem to be as acute as Willie's. Their middle son began to show signs of getting well again.

Rumors flew around Washington about Abe's wife, most of them classifying her as an "arrogant shrew," mainly because of the people she had shunned at her great party.

Abe had a strange sense of loyalty to her at that time. He saw her so devastated by the death of a second son, that he empathized with and pitied her. So overcome with grief, she could not get out of bed for three weeks, not even to attend Willie's funeral. When she finally emerged from her room she was draped in black with a heavy veil, which she wore for months afterward.

Abe had no recourse but to take over the demands of the White House, try to hold and comfort Taddie, yet still attempt to run the country in the middle of its most trying era since the Revolutionary War. During that time he spent hours delving into the scriptures for answers. Willie's death caused him to look for more meaning in life.

At times Abraham Lincoln could not contain his grief, but would break out in tears and weep openly. It was during this devastating part of his life that he sought out Dr. Andrew Gurley, the pastor of the New York Avenue Presbyterian Church for solace. "Surely Divine Providence has an answer for our broken hearts," he told the pastor, to which Dr. Gurley tried to console the man who was the leader of the nation by praying with him and reading scriptures. Abe was most grateful for his words at such a trying time for both the nation and his family.

WHEN I began, a few weeks after his death, to write the life of Abraham Lincoln, I entertained a profound respect for his strong mind, his tender heart, and the memory of his beneficent life. When I wrote the last page of the book, I had become his affectionate admirer and enthusiastic partisan.

L. G. Holland

(J. G. Holland)

NEW YORK, 1880.

WAR MANEUVERS

Following Willie's death, as President, Lincoln was forced to continue making grave decisions. One of them was to plan to promote U. S. Grant.

Mary, still enveloped in grief, confronted him, "Abraham Lincoln how can you dismiss the death of our son so lightly?"

Abe was standing in the doorway of the East Room when she asked him this question. Tears surfaced in his eyes. "Mary, Mary, there is no time to grieve. We have lost two sons and we both know about the agony of being separated from them. I have been studying the scriptures to see if there is real hope that we may see them again in heaven. In my talks with Dr. Gurley I have had to consider the resurrection power of the death of Jesus Christ, but I have not yet made up my mind as to whether or not to accept what the Bible says.

"In the meantime we both need to consider the hurts of every one in this nation. Many, oh so many, have lost several members of their families. Oh, little woman, I understand your hurting heart, but we are at a time in the history of the United States of America that we MUST be concerned with others more than ourselves. My prayer is that I can be a part of leading this great nation on to victory and the war will soon be past."

Yet in his office he bemoaned the fact that little was going on. "McClellan seems to be sitting on his hands," he declared to his two aides. "That is why I gave my Presidential order. We must get this miserable conflict over."

Telegrams began to filter in. Nicolay greeted him with this greeting and a grin one morning, "Your belief in Grant has proven to be well founded. This wire says that he not only took Fort Henry on February 6 but Fort Donelson on February 16. President Lincoln, sir, you must be thrilled."

Abe flashed a half smile Nicolay's direction. "I am. He's a mover. The Union has hope at last."

On April 8th another telegram arrived, "He did it again! For two days they battled the Rebs at Corinth. We won, but Grant says that casualties were enormous."

Abe hung his head as if the last segment of the message had pained him. "I pray to God that it will end soon. So many boys!"

John Hay shared upsetting news with him on July 3rd. "We'd like to celebrate Independence Day with a big bang, but after seven days of fighting, McClellan's Army of the Potomac was pushed back." What became known as the 'Seven Days Battle' dealt a blow to the President's hopes.

Lincoln never left the battlefields in his mind, consulting always with his Secretary of War. The two of them spent hours each day pouring over the maps which showed the location of the troops.

At times, when he was able, he went to review the troops and as he told Mary, "When things are too horrendous I choose not to visit the hospital tents but often I feel compelled to go. After part of the Army of the Potomac battled at Malvern Hill I visited there and to my amazement a Chaplain Stewart from Pennsylvania's 102nd Regiment asked me to look in on a young Negro soldier."

"To my surprise I found the lad in the tent with their battered mascot that the young man introduced as 'Dog Jack'. I've seen a lot of wounded soldiers that have amazed me, but this dog struggled to his feet when the former slave boy told him I was there. Still wrapped in bandages from wounds he suffered in battle, he overwhelmed me by standing at attention as if he understood that I was somehow important. Mary, you know how I've always loved animals so I was most taken by the boy and his dog."

Another bit of disheartening news came from Hay. "Mr. Lincoln, we must be jinxed at Bull Run. For the second time they made us run."

Abe realized that his aide was trying to throw a bit of humor into the situation, but he got no delight in hearing such news. His heart felt so heavy, his spirits so downcast. He felt emotionally ill.

Prospects for the war ending again became hopeful when Nicolay said, "Sir, this news should cheer you. Lee has been forced to flee across the Potomac after the battle at Antietam."

"Did many men lose their lives?"

"I understand the casualties were horrendous on both sides."

Abe hung his head. "Not much to celebrate then, is there?"

"I guess not, sir."

That night Mary asked Abe, "Why are you so glum? I'm trying to revive our spirits but you are NO help."

"Mary, how can I be gleeful? We just lost not only the battle, but many more men at Fredricksburg."

"Things look bleak to me," Abe admitted to Secretary Stanton. "Nothing has happened to accelerate my hopes for some time."

May 5th, 1863 he sunk into a deep depression after learning that Union forces had lost at Chancellorsville. "Is this war dividing our great country ever going to end? Is slavery going to keep on existing forever? More and more I have decided that Divine Providence is not going to let the war end until slavery is eradicated. That's my desire, too," he told his aides.

As President he made a point of avoiding the streets where he knew the wounded were being transported. After his initial shock of seeing maimed men being hauled like wagonloads of cattle, he'd felt he simply could not bear to see them struggling in their hopelessness. Knowing that thousands of men were being wounded each day in battlefields across the country was enough to think about in his mind's eye, but seeing their sufferings in person tore at the depths of his soul. *How*, he prayed, *as the leader of this divided nation, am I to stop this horrible carnage?*

One morning he decided he had to get over his cowardice, to go and look into their faces, and to accept the fact he was responsible in part for their broken bodies, their broken lives.

As they reached the street where most of the wounded were being transported he ordered his driver, "Turn here and please park where we can watch the ambulances as they pass by."

Abe and his carriage driver sat in silence, watching the seemingly endless carriages and wagons loaded with men swathed in bloody bandages. From his lofty perch he could look down into the wagons.

A single towheaded lad, not much older than Taddie, met the eyes of his commander-in-chief, but there was no recognition in them. No spark. No hope.

Surveying the boy's body, Abe realized that not only the lower part of his right arm, but his right foot was also missing. A wave of nausea swept over him. Putting his hand to his mouth, he tried to control his emotions and his repulsions.

Once the wagon passed, his driver inquired in little more than a whisper, "Need to leave now, Mr. President?"

Abe could barely nod his assent. His driver reached out and clasped his hand over Abe's in a gesture the President knew was filled with compassion. The pair journeyed back to the White House in ghostly silence, making Abe certain that his driver had also been overwhelmed with emotion by the boy's plight.

That vision of the boy's despair and hopelessness stayed imprinted in his mind. *How many more,* he asked himself, *have been left in such a sorrowful state?* That night he kept brooding about the personal lives of the men who were being forced to fight. Abe could not respond to Mary's efforts to lighten his mood at the dinner table, so his wife finally asked, "Abraham Lincoln, what is plaguing you?"

A short wile later he attempted to convey to her how the young Union soldier's plight had torn him. "Mary, he's missing his right arm and foot. What chance does he have? Will he even survive? I've asked myself a thousand questions since I saw him. His eyes and the eyes of all the suffering lads will haunt me forever. I pray and I pray, but I do not know how to stop the bloodshed and the heartache that has effected every family in this nation."

TURMOIL IN THE WHITE HOUSE

As a lawyer Abraham Lincoln prided himself in always getting the exact facts in using his analytical mind to understand any problem. Ever since his childhood he had no doubt about there being a God whenever he watched the awesome miracle of the little bull being born, then of watching the dead-looking seeds germinate and see the stems burst forth through the soil and grow into living, vibrant plants. *How could anyone dispute the existence of the Creator?* Abe often asked himself.

Yes, he'd studied the Bible. Abe knew it so well that he'd memorized nearly every verse of Scripture. In his political speeches, in his anecdotes, he nearly always used some reference to the Bible to prove his point. Friends said Abe had the Word of God set in his mind so well that he would take a pen and punctuate any portion if someone wrote it down wrong.

At Hodgenville as a young child he'd attended the Baptist church where he drank in the sermons. As his mother said, "You memorized them." And he did. He had such a thirst for knowledge.

As he grew older he never placed much emphasis on church attendance, yet he never failed to pray, read the scriptures and ask for Divine Guidance in everything he did.

As President, Abe told Mary while they sat in the White House living room after dinner was over one evening, "There's nothing more important in these critical times than to ask our Maker for direction. Sometimes I'm in a quandary and I can not discern the course of action we need to take to free the slaves and unite the Union. But later it's as if God opens my mind and I KNOW His direction and I get the answers to the country's most perplexing problems. Mary, I would never have had the courage to announce the Emancipation Proclamation if I hadn't been positive it was the Will of God.

"I know folks question my Christianity and I sometimes do myself," he said softly as he walked to the window and looked out.

Mary stared at her husband, "Abe, that last statement amazes me. You have more compassion in your little finger than most men do in their whole body. I have never known a more kind, considerate person."

Abe's half-smile in return made his answer seem almost wistful, "Thank you, dear, but I'm serious about calling myself a Christian. Christ's resurrection and ascension have always been a concern for me. Most of His teaching I've taken to heart, but some things they claim He did bothers my rational mind."

Mary shrugged her shoulders. "There's no way for me to help you, because I don't understand myself. Perhaps Pastor Gurley can help clear up your questions."

Abe sighed and said in such a soft voice that it was little more than a whisper. "I can go down to the big Presbyterian Church where we've gone ever since we came here, but I doubt that any mortal man can clear up my doubts."

That conversation had taken place early in the spring and then came that July day when Abraham Lincoln felt the pressure of the war more than he had at any time.

While Abe was seated in his office Nicolay rushed in with dispatches that he'd received from the telegraph office. "Excuse me, sir, if I'm interrupting anything important but I have messages here that I know you'll want to know about."

Abe raised his eyebrows. "Let me see what's going on," he said as he reached over with his long, bony right hand to retrieve the papers from his aide.

"You are right," he exclaimed. "McClellan is about to embark on a huge encounter with Lee's forces in farm country in the middle of Pennsylvania. Nicolay, I somehow believe that this battle is going to be one that could change the fate of the war. There's a little town near where they're about to meet."

Nicolay stared at him before he spoke and Abe realized the years he and his aide had spent working together had made it possible for them to have a depth of understanding far beyond employer and employee status for he spoke in a concerned voice, "President Lincoln, sir, I am most concerned about you. In all the years I have known you, I have never seen you looking so desolate for so long a time. Sir, I really believe this battle between us and the Rebs in that little town WILL have some bearing on the outcome of the war. By the way, I've looked at the map and believe this small town is named Gettysburg."

After his speech he picked up the communiques he'd brought in. Then as he turned to leave the office, he spoke, "Sir, please forgive my candor. I have seen how this war has torn you down and I want you to know I care. You are so much more to me than a boss. I see you as a great, dedicated Godly man who loves his country with a passion, but even more than that, to me you are a beloved friend."

Tears surfaced in Abraham Lincoln's eyes as he answered, "Nicolay, you are so dear to my heart. You knew me when I began my political struggle and I hope that my current position has not put me on any different footing than that of being a 'friend'." After a pause as if to measure his next words, he said. "I also have great regard for John Hay, but he is more like a son to me than a close confidant. You and Speed both qualify much like my brothers in my mind."

At that very moment a breathless John Hay rushed through the door, a look of terror had taken over his usual placid face. "Mr. Lincoln, Mr. Lincoln!" he cried. "Mrs. Lincoln's been hurt!"

Abe bolted for the door, "Where is she?" he demanded without asking any particulars. As he raced down the hallway, he called back, "Stay there and watch the fort, will you?" His words came more as a request than an order.

The two men stood, mystified as to what to do for the head of the country who both of them loved and respected so much.

"That's all he needed," Nicolay said, in a sarcastic tone.

John Hay nodded in agreement. He knew that the other aide to President Abraham Lincoln was as concerned as he was about Abe's health and well-being. "I'd already been aware that he's been forced to bear too much hurt and responsibility over the war. This might be his breaking point."

John Hay's face twisted with emotion as he replied, "I hope not."

RECOGNITION

Upon reaching his wife's bedside, he stared down at her still body. "What happened?" he demanded of a young man, a stranger, who stood nearby with Watts the gardener.

"I'm not certain, sir. I found her lying on the road just a few yards from the Sailor's Home. See the nasty gash on the one side of her head? She must have hit the rock that was there beside her. I assume that was what she hit. When I found her she was unconscious just as she is now. Because I recognized her I brought her directly to you as soon as I tended to her wound a bit."

Abe was not satisfied with that answer so he decided to query the young man further, "I do thank you, sir, but what about the carriage? When it left here it was in perfect condition. The poor woman just wanted to escape some of the city's heat."

At that moment the door burst open to the downstairs bed-room where Mary had been placed on a bed. Dr. Stone, the White House physician rushed in. "She's had quite a blow to the head," the doctor declared as soon as he examined her, "but I'm sure she'll gain consciousness soon. She should have some-one with her for at least twenty-four hours after she comes to for signs of nausea and other complications."

"We'll get her friend Elizabeth to do that." Those words caused Mr. Watts to fly out the door in search of Lizzie without Abe even asking him to do so. Abe turned to Dr. Stone and asked, "Mary has suffered from violent headaches for as long as I can remember. They seem to be even worse since our Willie's death.

My concern — will it have any lasting effects?"

"Unless some other complication shows up in the next day, I wouldn't think so."

"Good," he answered to the doctor's reassurance, then Abe turned once more to the young man, "Sir, I still have a lot of unanswered questions. She wasn't riding a horse, can you tell me why she fell out of a carriage?"

The young man frowned as if reluctant to give him a reply, "Sir, I hate to tell you, but the carriage had toppled over. Two of the wheels were off. One might assume someone wanted her to wreck. They must have loosened the bolts so that she couldn't get very far before she'd meet with an accident."

The color drained from Abraham Lincoln's face. "One would also assume that the culprit wasn't really after my wife. I had to be the victim he wanted. He undoubtedly thought I was there with her!" Anger flashed through his grey eyes as he cried, "If my enemies want me, they can have me. BUT I WISH THEY'D LEAVE MY FAMILY ALONE!" His last words carried such force and volume that Mary stirred and moaned a bit.

Elizabeth hustled through the doorway. Wide-eyed, she cried, "Mr. Lincoln, what in the world happened NOW?"

As soon as Abe shared the events of the day, Mary's beloved Lizzy exclaimed "Mercy Me! You need not stay. You know I will take care of her as if she was my own child."

Abe leaned down and gave his hurting wife a kiss on the forehead. "Just rest, dear," he whispered. "Your Lizzy is here to take care of you. I'll be in my office. If you need me, just have her call." Then he turned to Mary's seamstress. "Thank you, Elizabeth. You are a dear friend."

On the way down the hallway his pent-up emotions that he'd let build up behind an invisible dam wall in his mind, began to seep out.

By the time he reached his office that wall had collapsed and tears had broken through like a flood. Flinging himself in his chair, he leaned against his desk and sobbed, "Father, Father, what can I — a mere mortal do? More boys and fathers are being brought down on a bloody battle in the middle of a little country field this very moment. My wife and children's lives are in jeopardy, too. Oh, God, help me!" Unable to speak or pray further, his body heaved with sorrow.

A hand caressing his back and the words of a soothing familiar voice whispering "Oh, Abe, dear honest Abe," brought him back to reality. He spun around in his swivel chair in amazement as he spoke to his ardent confidant, Nicolay. He cried, "I thought I was alone!" In all the years they had worked together his aide had never before addressed him in such familiar terms.

"I'm sorry, sir. You have so many burdens right now, I took the liberty to stay here to make certain you would be all right." And then, as if his mind went off into a totally different avenue of thought, he asked, "Sir, I know you pray with all your heart and soul to your Heavenly Father, but do you ever pray in the name of Jesus?"

"No," Abe admitted. "I don't."

For a moment Nicolay pondered before asking his next question, but then he said, "Sir, it says in the Bible that 'no one comes to the Father, except through Me,' that's what Jesus said. Do you mind if I pray for the country and you and all your family woes? I'd like to do that, sir." A look of pleading formed in John K. Nicolay's eyes.

Abe responded with a glance that showed his appreciation for his aide's concern as he told him, "I would never turn down such an offer. It is my hope that the whole country is praying for the same concerns. Please, John, I would be thrilled to have you express your concerns in your way." In a moment he was stunned by Abe's use of his first name — something Abraham Lincoln had never spoken before either. After a nod acknowledging the President's comment his aide began to pray.

"Heavenly Father, I come to You in the name of Jesus, seeking your favor for this nation which is in terrible turmoil. Boys and men are dying as we seek Your Divine Guidance at this critical time.

Dear Abraham Lincoln has to guide and direct all facets of this country — including his own family life and, Lord, I don't need to tell you that he has a tremendous burden on his shoulders. All I can do is ask you to help him through these trying days. You say in Your Word that if two or more are gathered in YOUR NAME You will answer their prayer so I am praying in the blessed Name of Jesus. Amen."

For awhile Abraham Lincoln sat as if he was stunned by the words, but then he spoke in a choked voice as if his emotions were too much for him. "Bless you and thank you, John Nicolay."

Nicolay reached over and patted the shoulder of the President, then left the room as Abe sat in the stillness, pondering his thoughts of Nicolay's words and how powerful they seemed. He fought back a sudden urge to call after him, "You do believe the Lord will answer your prayer, don't you?"

Abe didn't follow that urging, but Nicolay appeared back in the doorway. His next words startled Abe. His aide spoke them as if he read the President's thoughts, "Yes, sir, I believe He will. The Bible says that with faith you can move mountains, and I believe it." With that Nicolay turned and was gone again.

In the following days and weeks new problems arose on the horizon. A tremendous event took place during the first days of July. The Union troops won the battle and sent Lee's forces on a swift retreat into Virginia. As the President, Abraham Lincoln was thrilled with the victory, yet the tremendous loss of men's lives made the taste of victory very short-lived. As the commander-in-chief he also was disheartened because Lee and a segment of his forces escaped, meaning that they would fight again.

A telegraph from the Governor of New York arrived with his cry for help. "The Irish are rioting in the streets. They are rebelling because of the draft. A hundred men have been killed."

President Abe felt he had no recourse but to squelch the riot by sending troops who'd just finished the horrific battle in Gettysburg to go to New York to put down the Union draft dodgers. No other recourse seemed advisable.

Next the miners in Eastern Pennsylvania plus men in several other states were rioting against the draft so Abe had to contend with inner Union turmoil as well as battle against the South. He sent fervent prayers to his Heavenly Father every day on behalf of his beloved country.

ACCEPTANCE

That July of 1863 President Abraham Lincoln had been so elated over the Confederates defeat at Gettysburg that he'd gone to the War Department to give them a press release sharing his feelings about "This great success to the cause of Union" and then he requested, "That on this day, He whose will not ours, shall ever be done, be everywhere remembered and reverenced with profoundest gratitude."

Only three days later the Secretary of the Navy had come to him with the news that Vicksburg had fallen into Union hands. Abe could hardly contain his jubilance over another victory for his army and navy. "It is great, Mr. Wells, it is great!" he cried to the bearer of the good news.

Because of these summer Union victories Abraham Lincoln felt that September held great promise. The entire North showed signs of hope that the war might come to an end at last. Abe was quite pleased when his self-appointed protector, Ward Lamon, came to him with a proposal. "Sir, the Gettysburg Cemetery Commission would like you to speak at the dedication there on November 19. I am deeply honored to have been asked to be the grand marshal of the procession. The planners have told me that it is of great importance to them that you also be there. I do believe because of our close relationship that they chose me to ask this of you."

Abe's affirmative answer was immediate, "Tell them I also would be honored to be a part of their ceremony. What is the date?"

"November 19, sir. I will let them know."

Later that same afternoon Abe had Nicolay summon William Saunders to the White House since he was the one who had been hired to be the landscape architect to lay out the cemetery. He had maps of the topography of Gettysburg. Abraham Lincoln gave much thought as to what he would say, even consulting his military leaders about the particulars of the great battle.

He told his friend Speed when he dropped in to see him, "They tell me I'm to follow Edward Everett who is known as a great orator, but he is also one of the lengthiest speakers I know. I've drafted most of what I have to say, but I'm not certain how to end my speech. I have weighed the merit of each word."

November 18, on the morning of his scheduled departure, Mary rushed into his office. Hysterical, she cried, "Taddie is so sick! He couldn't even eat breakfast! You can't leave me alone with another sick child."

"Mary, Mary, I have to go. Tad will get better. You are hyper now when one of the children sneezes." He finally shrugged his shoulders and walked away, then drove by carriage to the special four-car train which would take him, Nicolay and two members of his cabinet to their destination. On the trip to Gettysburg Lincoln laughed and felt in good spirits, only for a brief time laboring over his speech.

Once they reached the town where the battlefield was to be consecrated, he was given quarters at the Wills household. The following day he stayed in his room until he finished writing his final remarks, then made a clean copy before he joined the parade where he was given a horse which was much too small for his long frame. Abe felt ridiculous in his new black suit and the stovetop hat with the black band that Mary insisted he wear to show that he was still grieving over losing Willie. His lanky legs nearly dragged on the ground, making him feel more conspicuous than Presidential.

The slow, tedious three-quarter mile procession to the burial ground gave Abe time to imagine what it must have been like on those same grounds back on those scorching days in early July. One of the captains who had been fortunate enough to escape musket and cannonball fire and the piercing of the swords had earlier tried to share the horrifying experience with Abe while he was still back in Washington. "It is most difficult to attempt to explain the terror of men coming at you with their swords aimed your direction. The smell of gunpowder was so powerful it made breathing next to impossible. Pungent, sulfurous smoke fumes filled the air. The roar of cannons was deafening. The percussion caused by all the blasts and explosions made the earth tremble beneath us. No words in my vocabulary can aptly describe watching men dropping like flies around you, many of whom were close friends, but you dared not stop to help without endangering your own life. After the first day of combat the stench of the men sweating profusely in their wool uniforms and the men who still lay in the fields being baked in the July sun was unbearable. Just thank God that you were not present at the unholy massacre."

Abraham Lincoln kept dwelling on those mind-blowing descriptions as the parade made its way at such a slow pace. In his mind's eye he could envision the battle. Looking across the fields, he imagined hoards of men in blue and grey uniforms locked in combat during those hot and humid days, *"OH, GOD, LET SOME FEEBLE WORD OF MINE HELP THOSE WHO ARE HERE FIND SOME RELIEF FROM THEIR GRIEF. BRING AN END TO THE MASSACRES SOON,"* he cried inside. His exhilaration during the train ride had turned to anguish and despair.

He listened to Edward Everett's speech which he began to think would never wind down. At last it was his turn to try to give some sense to the slaughter. When he rose to be introduced he prayed inside, *"FATHER, LET MY WORDS HAVE MEANING,"* and then he began:

"Fourscore and seven years ago our fathers brought forth upon this continent a new nation, conceived in Liberty, and dedicated to the proposition that all men are created equal. Now we are engaged in a great civil war, testing whether that nation, or any nation so conceived and so dedicated, can long endure. We are met on a great battlefield of that war. We are met to dedicate a portion of it as the final resting-place of those who here gave their lives that that nation might live. It is altogether fitting and proper that we should do this.

"But, in a larger sense, we cannot dedicate, we cannot consecrate, we cannot hallow this ground. The brave men, living and dead, who struggled here, have consecrated it far above our power to add or detract. The world will little note, nor long remember, what we say here, but it can never forget what they did here. It is for us, the living, rather, to be dedicated here to the unfinished work that they have thus far so nobly carried on. It is rather for us to be here dedicated to the great task remaining before us — that from these honored dead we take increased devotion to the cause for which they here gave the last full measure of devotion — that we here highly resolve that the dead shall not have died in vain — that the nation shall, under God, have a new birth of freedom, and that the government of the people, by the people, and for the people, shall not perish from the earth."

When he finished his speech, Abraham Lincoln, as President of the United States, rationalized that he'd had no choice except to bear the huge emotional knot that had kept churning inside him as he'd reenacted the horrendous battle in his mind.

As Commander-in-Chief of the Union forces he felt such a tremendous sense of responsibility that he deemed it necessary to keep up a good front. How could he let the upheaval of grief that swelled up inside him cause him to break down and weep before the throng? The expressions on faces of those who had listened to him conveyed the fact that most of the folks standing there were also experiencing thoughts of their own personal loss.

His eyes swept over the multitude of people, yet Abe could not help but wonder. *How many are here because of the loss of a son, a husband, even a father?* A few children played on the outskirts of the crowd. He was somehow relieved that he hadn't shown any outward display of feelings to the grieving observers concerning the gravity of the remembrance of their kinfolks' blood that had been spilled on the ground where they were standing with their children playing nearby.

As he finished a splattering of applause brought Abe back to reality. He walked down from the platform. For the next few minutes he went through all the formalities of shaking hands and acknowledging folks who spoke to him. Yet as he boarded his railroad private car and shut the door, the flood of tears came. He wept as he had when his beloved Willie died. "Oh, Lord," he cried aloud, "am I responsible for all the horror that is going on? I can't bear the burden any longer."

His emotional outburst brought some relief, but he was gratified when the wheels of the train began to turn. Scenes of Pennsylvania farms gave him some consolation. Smoke curled from many chimneys, pleasing him. It indicated life was still going on inside.

As his car swayed back and forth on his journey back to Washington, thoughts of his own life paraded through his mind, when a knock on his door brought his attention back to the moment. "Yes?" he asked his unseen visitor.

"It's Nicolay, sir. May I come in?"

"You know you don't have to ask. You're always welcome."

Abe thought, *That 's true. It seems that fellow has always been around whenever I needed a friend.*

He decided to share his feelings with his long-time companion. "John," he said as Nicolay seated himself across from him, "you have somehow been a mainstay in my life. How often I've stopped in your room early in the morning on my way to the office because something was terribly amiss and I felt I had to share it with you. How grateful I am that you never seemed to resent the intrusion."

His aide smiled, "Why would I, sir? I've been in the same house with your missus long enough to know that it is most difficult to have her understand some situations. You needed somebody to talk to."

Abe sighed, "John Nicolay, you have great perception, but sometimes Mary is a great asset. I would not be President without her."

Nicolay seemed to ignore Abe's last comment as he sighed and declared, "Yes, but she creates so many horrendous problems — like the time she eliminated Secretary Chase and his family from the list of guests I'd made up for one of her big parties. I know she didn't want him because he was a possible candidate for winning against you for the Presidency, Sir, she didn't use her head. Why would she not consider the snobbery of leaving out a member of your cabinet just because she viewed him as competition?"

For a few moments Abe pondered his answer before asking, "Don't you think she was just being loyal to me?"

Nicolay took only a second to reply, "No, sir. I don't. I can't remember a time when she displayed any actions but selfish ones. Look what she did to you when she so splendidly redecorated the White House! I have to admit one thing to you, sir. If ever I thought of leaving my job, it was never because of you. She was always the culprit. After trying to eliminate Secretary Chase, I got so furious that I told Hay she was evil."

"Nicolay! What a horrible thing to call her!" Abe cried in shock and furor.

"I even surprised myself," John Nicolay admitted. "I had to go to the Lord and ask His forgiveness for describing her in such a way, but that time I felt she'd gone just too far."

Abe's ire subsided. "John, you are too hard on her! She has some very good points."

"I hope so, sir. Can you tell me one?"

"You have to know my wife Mary is most dedicated to me and the children." Abe smiled.

Nicolay nodded. "That's true, but can you honestly tell me that she helps you understand Godly things, and that she is a spiritual comfort when things in the country go out of control? I know that you didn't approve of her crazy seances in her attempt to see Willie."

Abe let out a small groan. "You must realize the poor dear was on the brink of losing her mind. I know how distraught she was because his death was almost more than either of us could bear. I even went along to humor her but the whole idea gave me the creeps. I searched in the Bible and it doesn't say you should commune with the dead so I tried to dissuade her, but you know how useless that is once she sets her mind to something. She does go with me to Dr. Gurley's church these days."

Nicolay nodded again. "But, sir, doesn't she only do that for show? If I wasn't so concerned about you, I would have given up because of her a long time ago. Yet to me you are a giant of a man and I consider myself not only your assistant, but I value you as my treasured friend. I have prayed for a long time for you to accept Jesus as your Lord and Savior so that I know in my heart that you will go to heaven."

Overwhelmed by the sense of John Nicolay's devotion caused another flood of tears to run down Abe's cheeks.

Next Nicolay asked a question that puzzled him. Why would he ask, "Do you know the shortest verse in the Bible, sir?" Before Abe could reply, Nicolay gave the answer. "Jesus wept. I want you to know the good Lord Himself cried when everything was going against Him. You need not be ashamed of your tears."

In all their years of acquaintance the two men had discussed very little pertaining to religion so Abe asked out of sudden curiosity, "Do you profess to be a Christian, Nicolay?"

"Yes, sir. I not only profess to be one, I am one. Every day I pray that you will become one, too. I know enough about your beliefs to understand that you have great faith in your Heavenly Father, but to my knowledge you have never professed His Son as your Savior. You need to do that, sir."

"For what reason?" Abe queried him.

That question gave Nicolay an opportunity to show the depths of his feelings for Abe by also shedding tears, as he spoke softly. "Oh, dear, dear beloved son of your Heavenly Father, I have watched you for so many years and have been grieved so often by your grief. I have seen your heart broken by the loss of two sons. Even yet you speak of your mother's death at a young age. Each day you are in the forefront of my prayers because I believe with all my heart that you were destined by your Heavenly Father to lead this nation at this, it's most trying hour.

"You see, dear friend, your Heavenly Father loves each of us so much that He sent His beloved Son to die so that we can have everlasting life."

"I know your knowledge of the scriptures is so vast and detailed that you can punctuate whole portions exactly as they are printed, yet you have missed the greatest message, the message of salvation offered free to you by the blood of Jesus Christ."

After a pause he went on to say, "Your life has been built on truth. You never lost the nickname of 'Honest Abe' because truth has been so vital to your existence, yet you have neglected the greatest truth -- the one that gives you greater life now and then life eternal. It says in the Bible, 'I am the Truth, the Way and the Life, no man comes to the Father except by me.' Those are words of invitation from Jesus to come to Him. It also says, 'Ye must be born again.'"

Abe pondered awhile before saying any more, but then he declared in a solemn tone, "I guess you know people call me a 'Diest' because I have always believed in Divine Providence. That is true, but you'll have to explain the meaning of born again. I don't understand the terminology. I can not get back into my mother's womb, I am too sizable. Besides that, I lost my beloved mama years ago."

Abe's request did not deter Nicolay who simply answered, "Your Heavenly Father knows all that. You see, every man is born with a sinful nature ever since the fall of Adam. In the old Testament animal sacrifices were made to atone for man's sins. The sacrifice of Jesus' blood on the cross at Calvary changed all of that. Since his death and resurrection there is no need for blood sacrifices. Jesus took all the sins of the world on His body so that the Heavenly Father will accept us if we accept Jesus Christ as our Savior, and ask His forgiveness for our sins which assures us life eternal. He let His Son come and suffer and die for you, for me. He wants you to acknowledge His beloved Jesus Christ as your Savior."

Abe shook his head in bewilderment. "I don't know how to do that."

"Do you want to?"

"Something, Someone has to help my dilemma. Dear friend, I am at the breaking point. I have to know there is some future hope for all those dear souls who died on the battlefields." Tears amassed in his eyes. "You know Jesus on a personal basis, don't you?"

A faint wistful smile crossed his aide's face. "Oh, yes, sir, and He knows how I care about you. Every day I talk to Him and ask Him to help you. When I pray I get His blessed assurance that He is listening and wants to answer my prayers. But more than that, I know what He wants for you is to have a personal relationship between you and Him."

President Abraham Lincoln acknowledged his need by saying, "I wish I had one, dear friend, from the depths of my heart. I want to know Him as you say you do and to have the assurance that He loves me."

"Oh, Abe," Nicolay answered, again using his nickname, "He already loves you. Jesus wants you to tell Him you want to repent of your sins and ask Him into your heart. Do you want to do that?"

"Heavens, yes," Abe sighed. "I need Him to guide me through these trying times. NO mortal man can take all the anguish of this horrendous war without Divine help. Please tell me what to do."

"Come on," Nicolay invited, "Let's bow our heads and ask the Lord to give you insight into what to say."

Abraham Lincoln declared, acknowledging his need to be humble, "I think in reverence to Him that we should kneel." So there in his private railroad car Abe lowered his long frame down to the floor and knelt in front of the sofa. A welcome sense of reverence surged through him.

Nicolay, showing his love and concern, knelt on the floor beside him. He told Abe, "Just let your lips share as you open your heart to Jesus. He will guide you as to what you need to say. In Romans 10:9 it tells you that, 'If thou shalt confess with thy mouth the Lord Jesus and shalt believe in thine heart that God hath raised Him from the dead, thou shalt be saved.'"

Silent tears flooded President Abraham Lincoln's face as he let go of all the doubts he had built up in his mind about the resurrected Savior that he had read and heard about for so long. As he spoke in little more than a whisper, "Lord Jesus, I come to You as a sinner who asks You to forgive all the words and thoughts that have ever come out of my lips or harbored in my mind that would have offended You. Please forgive any deed that I have done that has hurt anyone and any actions that might have caused them pain. I ask You to come into my heart and dwell in my body and soul that I might become Your child from this day forth and forever more. Amen."

The two men stayed kneeling together in silence, each basking in the presence of the Lord's Holy Spirit for several minutes. When they rose from their knees, Abe reached out with his long, gnarled hand and whispered, "Thank you, dear friend. You are closer than a brother. Thank you for sharing life's greatest Gift."

Nicolay's face shone as he continued to grip the hand of the man for whom he cared so much as he whispered in return. "Sir, it is not just a pleasure. The fact that I had the privilege of leading the greatest President the United States of America has ever known to the Lord and Savior Jesus Christ has been my greatest privilege; one I will treasure for the rest of my life."

Abe nodded, "Those are great accolades you are giving a humble boy born in the prairie."

Nicolay smiled, "Where you were born doesn't measure your worth, sir. Now you know personally the Man who, as a baby, was born in a stable."

As the train's wheels spun back toward the nation's capital, a slow smile spread across Abe's face. He began to wonder what his commitment to Jesus would mean. Since the Union forces were victorious at Gettysburg, Abe had a deepening sense that the Lord had truly taken over the helm and the states would soon be united again and slavery could and would be abolished at last.

He received many inquiries about his Christianity over his years as President, yet it was several months after the Pennsylvania countryside had been bloodied so horrifically by both Northern and Southern soldiers, that he dictated a letter to Nicolay directed to a clergyman back in his hometown who had questioned his Christianity:

"When I left Springfield I asked the people to pray for me. I was not a Christian. When I buried my son, the severest trial of my life, I was not a Christian. But when I went to Gettysburg, and saw the graves of thousands of our soldiers, I then and there consecrated myself to Christ. Yes, I DO love Jesus."

As he signed his name to the document, he felt a surge of satisfaction that he had publicly acknowledged and proclaimed that Jesus had indeed become His Lord and Savior.

234

INFANTRY GROUP OF STATUARY. NATIONAL LINCOLN
MONUMENT.

Representing a body of infantry soldiers on the march. They are fired
upon from some covert place, and the color-bearer killed. The captain
raises the colors with one hand, and with the other points to the enemy
and orders a bayonet charge, which the private on his right is in the act of
executing. The drummer-boy becomes excited, loses his cap, throws
away his haversack, puts one drumstick in his belt, draws a revolver and
engages in the conflict. The exploded shell indicates that they are on
ground that has been fought over before.

REBEL IN THE CAMP

After his trip to Gettysburg he became physically ill. "You did yourself in on your battlefield adventure." Dr. Stone declared as he looked down on the ailing Lincoln. "Mr. President, you have a mild case of smallpox."

Lincoln looked up from his bed and smiled. "Well, well. Everyone has wanted everything from me from pardons to office seekers, now I have something I can give everybody."

From his sick bed he attempted to work on his annual message to Congress, but as he put it later, "I did not do that job well." He never mentioned that he composed it while suffering from a high fever, but admitted to Nicolay later, "I botched most of the speech, never even mentioning the more than 100,000 black troops who are serving their country beyond the call of duty. I had to call Frederick Douglas to the White House in August to calm his fears that I was vacillating about the value of his Negro troops."

Nicolay smiled and asked, "That didn't help?"

"Yes, but I should have given those faithful troops assurance in my address, too. I needed to let it be known that once I take a position, I do not back down from it. The only worthwhile thing I did was to offer the South a full pardon with restoration of all rights of property to all rebels excepting high-ranking Confederate officials who would have to take an oath of future loyalty to the Constitution and pledge to obey Acts of Congress and Presidential Proclamations relating to slavery."

On December 9th Lincoln literally "rose to the occasion" by

leaving his rest and read his annual message to Congress.

He was pleased when John Hay patted him on the back and proclaimed. "That speech was something wonderful."

Not everyone felt the same. When Abraham Lincoln read the demeaning words in the *New York Journal of Congress* and the *Chicago Times'* barbs declaring him either "insane with fanaticism, or a traitor who glories in his country's shame," Abe quipped, "You can't be all things to all people. I have to think of the courage of the Negro. No one could rationalize re-enslaving them once they have been free. Reconstruction of a post war south has to be a top priority."

Soon after that things took a strange twist when Mary came to him with a concerned look on her face.

Mary had often bemoaned the fact that her kinfolks all sided with the Confederacy. "Abraham, I feel like an orphan sometimes. I know all my relatives think of me as a traitor, but how could they expect me to be your wife and not support the Union? Still, I have to admit it breaks my heart if I think about it very much."

Abe had tried to console her, "You have me and your boys, and I most appreciate your wholehearted support!"

Tears sprang up in Mary's eyes. "Oh, Abraham, I have you and Robert and Taddie, but the other two being gone is sometimes too much for me to bear. Oh, Abe, I do so miss my Willie."

Abe kept back the urge to say, "He was my Willie, too." Instead he placed his arm around her shoulders in a consoling manner.

In December he feared their Christmas would be bleak. How could they celebrate with the war taking such a tremendous toll and their precious Willie was not there?"

A telegram came from Fort Monroe, "Emilie Helm is here. We understand she is a relative of Mrs. Lincoln, but she refuses to take the oath of allegiance to the Union. She says her husband was killed by the Yankees and she'd die before she'd support the Union cause. She has a little girl with her and she is pregnant with what she says is her third child. What are we to do with her?"

Abe mused only a minute about his wife's sister's dilemma before dispatching his reply, "Send her to me." Along with those words he also included a pass giving her the right to come to Washington.

Mary was ecstatic, "Abe, just imagine, one of my Southern relatives is coming to be with me in the White House!" Both she and Abe ran out the door to embrace Emilie when her carriage arrived. "Oh, Em," she cried, as she hugged her half-sister, "we are so glad to see you! You must stay with us and let us comfort you over your great loss." Tears spilled from her cheeks as she claimed, "I don't know how I'd survive if I lost my beloved Abraham."

Once inside, Abe turned to the distraught young woman and declared, "We'll help you in whatever you need to do. Please tell us what you need."

The entire evening Mary spent acting like a mother hen, settling her half-sister and Emilie's daughter into a huge bedroom.

That night before bedtime Mary ushered her into the room where Abe was reading. After pouring tea for each of them, she asked Emilie to describe her ordeal.

Emilie sat transfixed for a while, before she could seem to find the courage to talk about what had taken place. "Oh, Brother Lincoln, the whole thing was an unbelievable nightmare. Union troops surrounded Atlanta. The next thing we knew was the streets around us were alive with gunfire. My Ben, in a valiant effort to save his troops and his family, was shot down before my eyes."

Mary and Abe became transfixed themselves, staring at the relative that was attempting to share her horrendous ordeal with them. She paused at long intervals while she tried to share the rest of her story, "I stayed to see him buried in Atlanta, then decided to make my way to the Federal lines in Virginia, with the high hopes that you might help me back to the home in Kentucky that Mary and I had shared together in our childhood."

Abraham Lincoln, touched by her story, asked, "Dear Emilie, what are your feelings about the Confederacy now?"

"Brother Lincoln, I am surprised that you should ask such a question. My husband lost his life for our cause. As his wife that only reinforced my feelings about the South's desire to have their own government."

After her sister declaring her negative convictions about the Union, Mary added her own thoughts, "I think we best all get some rest. Emilie, you certainly must be exhausted."

"You are right, and I do so appreciate your hospitality. I'm certain you must feel I am a rebel in your camp, but let me assure both of you, I am not here to cause you any harm, but simply to somehow get back to Kentucky to have the baby that was conceived before dear Ben lost his life."

One glance at Mary's face proved to Abe that his wife was close to tears again. He was fighting back the inclination to cry himself so he spoke softly, "Let's all get some rest. We can decide what to do in the morning."

However, once he sprawled out in his bed, sleep did not come easily. He tried to reason how the Northern section of the United States was going to look upon the Lincoln visitor.

The next morning he rose early before the rest of the household got moving. His desire was to contemplate and pray about what to do next. To his surprise, he found Nicolay already in his office, so he quipped, "Did you get up before sunrise, son?"

Nicolay's slow grin acknowledged Abe's attempt at humor. "Guess I did, sir. Wondered what you were going to do about your wife's visitor."

Abraham Lincoln was startled. "She's really our company, both Mary's and mine."

To this Nicolay replied, "But, sir, everyone knows she wouldn't be here without Mary. I understand the charming rebel is her relative."

Abe stared at his aide. "How do you know all this?" he inquired.

"Your staff is like a telegraph system. When someone comes or something happens, the busy-bodies all share the gossip."

Abraham Lincoln took in that spattering of knowledge. "That's too bad. I was hoping to keep her for a while without the world knowing about her presence here."

Nicolay stared, "Sir, that will be difficult to do, but I will call the house staff together and ask their cooperation."

Nicolay turned to attempt to hush the rumor, leaving Abe frustrated with his desire to help a pregnant, frightened widow and keeping the nation unconcerned about the fact that he and Mary were housing an avowed Confederate in the executive mansion which also housed the Union's Commander-in-Chief. "Quite a dilemma, Father," he prayed, hoping to get some answers as to what to do.

Later in the day his friend Browning came to call so he confided in him, "Mary's pregnant sister is here. That's all fine, except for the fact that she is the widow of a Confederate officer. I'm telling you this in confidence because I know you will keep her presence here under wraps."

Since Abe had decided to let Mary and her sister dine alone in the evening so they could reminisce about old times, he chose to ask Nicolay to dine with him. Lonely Nicolay was glad to oblige. Besides being in the President's company, Abe decided his aide enjoyed giving him tidbits of information that Abe would not have known otherwise.

That first night Nicolay informed Abe, "You know, sir, it's already in the rumor mill here in town that your confederate sister-in-law is being given access to important information to pass on to the enemy."

Such news horrified Abe. "Nicolay, I asked you to get the staff to suppress any gossip about Emilie being here."

To this his aide replied, "You know I did, sir. They all agreed to hushing up the fact you're housing her because they all love and respect you, but sir, I might say you brought this problem on yourself. I heard you tell your friend about it."

"I also told him to be discreet about it. You don't think he did?" Abe queried his aide.

"So discreet I'll bet he told the newspaper."

Abraham Lincoln felt as though he'd been physically hit, "I can't believe he'd go beyond my request."

Nicolay's mouth twisted into a smug smile. "Someone did,

sir. The whole town is buzzing with wild stories about your guest."

Abe could feel his heart racing, "Let them talk!" he cried. "All we're trying to do is help a pregnant widow who happens to be my wife's sister."

Nicolay replied in almost a whisper, "Who also happens to be the widow of a Confederate officer. In short, folks feel you are housing the enemy."

"That's their problem. I've invited her to stay indefinitely. Mary is so pleased to have one of her own family here with us."

And so, Emilie stayed. The rumors worsened. Nicolay told Abe one night, "Gossips have now thrown your wife into the tales. They say she is a traitor who is feeding the enemy with information."

"What?" Abe cried with indignation. "They'd better leave my family alone."

Yet Nicolay kept right on talking. "Sir, we're in a terrible war, one the likes of which this country has never experienced. There's much interest because other families have lost many sons, but yours is left in college out of harm's way."

Lincoln moaned, "Oh, dear friend, what am I to do? Poor Mary has lost two sons and says she will die if she loses another."

The two men sat in silence for a while, deep in their thoughts until Abe spoke again as he rose to go and look out the window. "Mine is an awesome job, one that only Divine Providence can get us through. Trying to keep the nation and this family intact has been my goal and my purpose."

Rumors persisted after that. Even Mary got wind of them, but kept them away from her sister.

Christmas came and Emilie's presence did much to bolster Mary's morale. In private Abe admitted to Emilie, "Your sister's well-being has me concerned. I'm not sure of her health or her emotional state. I'm so grateful that you came. Just having you here is good for her. She doesn't even dwell on losing Willie so much."

Emilie lifted her charming face. A glimmer came to her eye.

"Brother Lincoln, that speech you just gave about her is the same one she gave about you."

After Christmas Emilie came to him, "Would you please give me a pass to go to Kentucky? I'm getting homesick for mother and home and I want to have this new baby there. I'm ever so grateful for you having me here so long. You are a gracious host to take in a Rebel who does not, cannot agree with your cause."

As President Abe wrote out her pass. As her brother-in-law he scooped her into his arms and declared, "We will miss you. You're the kind of Rebel we like to have here. It is my prayer that for all of our sakes, this horrible war will soon be over."

The following blustery day Emilie and her little girl kissed them all good-bye. Tears flowed from all their eyes as Abe himself hoisted the rebels into the carriage.

He stood with his arm around his wife, both sharing the sorrow at seeing someone they both loved go away from them.

Mary looked up at him with misted eyes, "Abe, the rumors can quit now, can't they?"

He looked at her in dismay. "You knew?"

"Of course I knew, but the world doesn't seem to understand that I am loyal to the Union if for no other reason than I never thought of being disloyal to you. Besides that, an auction block wasn't far from our home in Kentucky. As I watched, I vowed that somehow, someway I'd help those abused slaves. My answer came. I found the way when I married you."

Abe reached down and kissed her on the forehead then the two of them walked back up the steps to their home. The White House seemed so warm to him on that cold, blustery morning.

ARTILLERY GROUP OF STATUARY. NATIONAL LINCOLN MONUMENT.

Representing three artillerymen, one, an officer standing on a dismounted cannon in an attitude of defiance, while below him is a prostrate soldier, wounded by the same shot that disabled his gun, and a boy in an attitude of sympathy and horror, springing forward as if to succor his wounded comrade.

WAR MUST CEASE

The battle was being waged in the political arena over the upcoming election as well as in the battlefield. Lincoln knew his future as President would be dependent on the Union Army's success that winter of 1863-64. If victorious he knew he would be re-elected. After the battle of Gettysburg the Army of the Potomac and the Army of Northern Virginia had not made any major headway.

Abe shook his head while talking over the situation with his Secretary of War who had given him many disastrous sounding statistics and things claiming, "We are losing so many through death and desertion that the army is in crisis. Besides, new volunteers are almost non existent."

Abraham Lincoln sat in his chair with his head cupped in his hand before he answered. A frown furrowed his brow as he announced, "By the first of February we will be forced to order a draft of 300,000 more men. On March 14 we will have to demand 200,000 more. May the Almighty end this bloodshed soon. The citizens of this country, both North and South, have endured so much anguish too long."

During the next few months he acknowledged that he was softening to the "men who run away because God gave them a cowardly pair of legs."

"Too often," he shared with Mary, "I find myself betraying my inner feelings. I, too, agree with the populace. This war has torn the country apart and has gone on for an eternity. War must cease."

Rumors came that infuriated him. "The Confederacy threatens to shoot any Negro soldier they capture!" he cried in a Cabinet meeting. "I am today issuing my order for retaliation. For every soldier of the United States killed in violation of the laws of war, a rebel soldier shall be executed, and for every one enslaved by the enemy a rebel soldier shall be placed at hard labor in the public works."

Many in the North acclaimed that order of retaliation. Letters from folks reassured him about his firm stand. Among them one from an admirer, "President Lincoln, Sir, we are most grateful for your decision to punish the South for their atrocities. Many of us have been heartsick over their treatment of the Union boys."

"Something has to be done to break this military stalemate," he told Grant. During his talks with other military men he was most impressed with the plans devised by Colonel Ulric Dahlgren, who had lost a leg in an early battle, but was determined to defeat the South. "My plan is to get General Kilpatrick's and my men to attack Richmond from the east and west and reach the monstrous Belle Isle Prison, free our prisoners, and take Richmond."

Lincoln agreed. "We need action now so I'll back your plans." On February 29th the action began, but most disheartening to Abraham Lincoln was the defeat of the Union forces and the loss of the life of the young colonel.

So little had happened to give the Union hope on the eastern front that Lincoln decided to bring Ulysses Grant in from the West. Abe told Nicolay, "I do not know what Grant's political aspirations are, but I know the forces against my next term and the Democrats are trying to get him to run against me, but I don't want to appoint a General-in-Chief to a position if he intends to run for President too. I am going to ask Washburne who represents Grant's home district what the warrior's political intentions are."

Washburne returned with a letter reassuring the President about the general he held in such high esteem, "Grant says nothing could get him to be a candidate, especially if you are running."

Abraham Lincoln declared, "I am most gratified for that news. I want to ask Congress to create a new rank of Lieutenant General, and I will appoint Grant to that rank."

Grant came to the White House on March 8, 1864 in a disheveled looking uniform. He apologized by saying when he came close to Lincoln, "I lost the key to my trunk, sir, but I hope I do not embarrass you."

Abe grasped the shorter, stockier man's hand in a warm grasp. After introducing him to Secretary Seward and Mrs. Lincoln, he led him to the East Room where so many people swarmed around him that Grant had to stand on the sofa to shake their hands.

Abe didn't want to take the general down from his lofty position in the public's eyes, so he took Grant aside and gave him a copy of the speech he was going to give the next day and suggested, "You might want to write out your own response to make certain to put you on good terms with the Army of the Potomac and stop any jealousy of any of the other commanders."

Abe invited all his cabinet members to the White House for the short ceremony scheduled in the President's office. After Abraham Lincoln gave him his commission and made a short speech ending with, "As the country herein trusts you, so, under God it will sustain you."

Grant took out his own short speech and began to read, but found he couldn't speak any further. Embarrassed, he pulled his broad shoulders back, composed himself and started to read again. His new Lieutenant General's ending was most pleasing to the Commander-in-Chief, as he used Lincoln's suggestions and declared, "The noble armies that have fought on so many fields for our common country," Abe realized these words were to help keep other commanders from feeling less needed.

"The New York Herald says you appointed Grant as General-in-Chief to keep him from being an opponent in the election," Mary commented.

Abe said nothing in reply. He received a note from Ohio's ex-governor who said. "The canvass for the nomination is practically closed."

When Abe read those words to Nicolay, his aide smiled, "I guess that makes it a sure thing. You will be the Republican candidate for President for the second time."

DECISIONS, DECISIONS

During the seemingly endless conflict between the North and the South, Abraham Lincoln wondered why he had tried his best to become President. On more than one occasion he complained to Mary, "There are millions of people in these United States plus four million slaves. I've come to the conclusion that each one of them holds me personally responsible for his well-being."

"President Lincoln, President Lincoln," that's all I hear. I have a horrible war on my hands, yet every day I get requests for pardons from jails, other folks are seeking favors for jobs and the soldiers all think I should be responsible for their hides whenever they've done what they ought not to do. Even small lads think I'm in charge of all the hiring and firing that goes on."

A friend of his, a politician from Massachusetts named Alexander Rice, seemed to Abe to take too much advantage of their friendship for he showed up often in Abe's waiting room, expecting not only an audience with the President, but also a large favor for someone from Rice's home state of Massachusetts.

One day when he managed to corner Abe, he began a sad tale, "I've come on behalf of a captain, a brave man in one of Massachusetts's regiments. Abe, I'm sorry to tell you but he was captured by the Rebels and is being held prisoner in Richmond. Is it not possible for him to be exchanged for one of their men?"

Abe's long face grew even more sorrowful as he replied, "I'm sorry, but you must realize we have numerous men who would like such consideration. I cannot deal with them individually, but must classify and decide them in considerable numbers."

The President waited, but he could see Alexander Rice was not going to give up on his mission, for he kept on speaking with determination to obtain his goal, "If you will just hear his case, I feel you will be glad to make an exception."

"Well, state it." Abe said, then sighed with a tone of resignation.

Alexander Rice droned on and on, about the valor and value of the captain with such fervor that Abe decided he should give his negative decision more consideration. After Rice's closing statement, he directed his visitor, "I wish you would go to the War Department and tell the general in charge that story, just as you told it to me. Say for me that if it is possible for him to effect the exchange of that captain without compromising the case of the other prisoners of his rank, I wish him to do so."

Alexander Rice's face grew grave, making Abe realize he hadn't heard the whole story. "But," the politician added, "for a technical misdemeanor the captain has, since his capture, been deprived of his commission and returned to the ranks, and probably the Rebels will not exchange him for a private soldier."

For a moment Abe rubbed the side of his face and closed his eyes before answering, "Well, if the general raises that point, say to him that if he can arrange the exchange part, I can take care of the rank part, and I will do so."

Since Abe never backed out on his word, he knew that Alexander Rice would expect to welcome the captain in Washington only ten days later.

As President he wondered if it was a good idea to grant Mr. Rice favors for he found him seated in his anteroom only a short time later. A man sat beside Alexander, causing Abe to assume that the politician was going to ask for someone else to be pardoned.

After a heavy sigh of resignation Abe welcomed the pair. The stranger wasted no time in stating his case, explaining, "I am the father of a boy who is in jail and is in a terrible state."

He went on to say, "My boy went from one country town to

work for a store in Boston and became dazzled by the apparent universal distribution of wealth there. He had no idea how such funds were acquired, so he fell into the fault of robbing his employer's letters as he took them to and from the post office. He was caught and convicted of the offense so he is serving his sentence in jail."

"I have here a petition signed by a large number of respectable citizens stating their concerns about the matter."

Abraham Lincoln put on his spectacles, stretched out in his arm chair where he deliberated as he read the document. Once finished, he turned to Alexander Rice and inquired, "Did you meet a man on the stairs as you came up?"

Rice said, "Yes, sir."

"Well," said the President, "he was the last person in this room before you came, and his errand was to get a man pardoned out of the penitentiary, now you have come to get a boy out of jail!"

The total ridiculousness of the requests tickled Abe's funny bone, so much that he declared, "I'll tell you what it is. We must abolish those courts or they will be the death of us. I thought it bad enough that they put so many men in the penitentiaries for me to get out, but if they have now begun on the boys and the jails, and have roped you into the delivery, let's go after them!" Abe sat and chuckled at the ridiculousness of his own statement.

After his burst of laughter he continued, "The courts deserve the worst fate because, according to the evidence that comes to me, they pick out the very best men and send them to penitentiary; and this present petition shows they are playing the same game on the good boys, and sending them all to jail.

"The man you met on the stairs affirmed that his friend in the penitentiary is a most exemplary citizen, and Massachusetts must be a happy state if her boys out of jail are as virtuous as this one appears to be who is in. Yes, down with the courts and deliverance to their victims, and then we can have some peace!"

During his speech Abe's expression showed that he was in a

merry mood, but then his face took on a sad and thoughtful look and added, "I can quite understand how a boy from a simple country life might be overcome by the sight of abundance in the large city." He paused and thought of himself and how awe-struck he'd been when he'd taken his first trip to New Orleans and seen business bustling all around the wharves.

"Yes," he went on with his jaw cupped in his hand, "I can see how such a lad would be overwhelmed to see that almost everyone had a pocketful of money and be led to commit such an offense as this boy had done. How can I justly put him into the class of hopeless criminals? If the boy could be placed under proper influences, he can probably be saved from a bad career and I would be glad to extend him clemency."

After Alexander Rice, as Congressman from Massachusetts signed the petition, the boy was pardoned. As Abraham Lincoln placed his name on the document he admonished the father, "The fate of that young boy's future is now in your hands. I do not expect to hear about him being in a detrimental way ever again."

Abraham Lincoln wasn't the only one in his office that had to make decisions. Nicolay and Hay had to determine in what order men waiting to see the President should be received.

Protocol demanded that Cabinet ministers, Diplomatic Corps Members, Senators or Justices of the Supreme Court and then members of the House of Representatives be admitted first. Any alteration from this order could cause one of the dignitaries to be offended. Following those on that top priority list, officers in the Army and Navy and Civil service had their turns. Civilians were received last.

Alexander Rice could expect admittance sooner than usual because he had an appointment with Senator Wilson which brought him up on the waiting list.

When the door opened to admit the two members of Congress, a small lad slipped in between them.

Lincoln greeted the Congressman briefly, but the little boy who he judged to be around twelve years old drew his attention away from them. "And who is this little boy?" he asked the lad.

"Sir, I'm sorry to just break in like this, but I've been waiting outside for several days and was desperate to see you. I thought it was never going to happen, so I decided to force my way in."

A slight grin formed around Abe's mouth as he declared, "Well, you have my attention now. What can I do for you?"

The boy's eyes grew wide as he began in earnest, "Sir, Mr. President Abraham Lincoln, I have come to Washington for employment as a page in the House of Representatives. I wish you would give me such an appointment."

Abe's face grew woeful. "I'm sorry, son. I don't make such appointments. You have to get them through the doorkeeper of the House at the Capitol."

The employment-seeker was undaunted by the President's words and Abe began to get pleasure at the young man's spunk as he protested, "But, Sir, I am a good boy and have a letter from my mother and one from my Sunday School teacher. They told me that I could earn enough in one session of Congress to keep my mother and the rest of us comfortable all the remainder of the year."

Abraham Lincoln took the lad's papers, scanned them over with his penetrating and absorbed look, then took his pen, dipped it into the ink well, and wrote on the back of one of them. "If Captain Goodnow can give a place to this good little boy, I shall be grateful," and then he signed it, "A. Lincoln."

"Thank you, sir. Thank you. I promise I'll do my job well so that you can be proud of me." With that the boy's face beamed as he turned and made his way out the door.

As President, Abe could only stand and feel great satisfaction at watching the one office-seeker he had so enjoyed helping. A sudden realization hit him moments later. He turned to the two Congressman, apologized and smiled a sheepish grin. "Sorry, gentlemen. I broke protocol, but I'm certain neither of you cared. Now what can I do for you?" he asked, but before they answered, he interjected, "My life is full of decisions of all kinds. Sometimes I get more satisfaction out of making them out of the little things rather than the big ones. You just witnessed one where I didn't mind being President at all."

NATIONAL LINCOLN MONUMENT AT SPRINGFIELD, ILLINOIS.

Unvelled and dedicated, October 15, 1874.   Dimensions 72½ by 119½ feet square, and 100 feet high.   Designed and modeled by Larkin G. Mead.   Cost, $212,000.
 Emblematical of the Constitution of the United States.   President Lincoln standing above the coat of
arms, with the Infantry, Navy, Artillery, and Cavalry marshalled around him, wields all for holding the States
together in a perpetual bond of Union, without which he could never hope to effect the great enemy of human
freedom.   The grand climax is indicated by President Lincoln with his left hand holding out as a golden
sceptre, the Emancipation Proclamation, while in his right he holds the pen with which he had just
written it.   The right hand is resting on another badge of authority, the American Flag, thrown over the
fasces.   At the foot of the *fasces* lies a wreath of laurel with which to crown the President as the victor over
slavery and rebellion.

ANTICIPATION OF EMANCIPATION

As President Abraham Lincoln felt a surge of anguish swelling up in him concerning the issue of slavery. After several sleepless nights he informed Nicolay as he entered the office early one morning, "It is of no use going on with the pretense that slavery can exist in this nation. We have one hundred thousand black soldiers who have willingly volunteered to help keep the nation intact. I am going to declare my intention to free all slaves in all states."

Nicolay's mouth gaped open, "Sir, do you realize an emancipation proclamation freeing all the black folks would mean political suicide for you?"

Abraham Lincoln sighed, "Of course I have weighed that probability. However, my career in the national political arena cannot be of any significance compared to the freedom of nearly a million slaves. When I declared at home in Springfield clear back in June of 58 that the government cannot endure permanently half slave and half free, I had not anticipated that there would be such a civil strife over the matter. When I declared that we would not fail if we stood firm I expected wise councils would accelerate the matter, but that sooner or later, victory was sure to come."

Silence reigned as both men thought over the weighty matter until Abe spoke again. "I did not foresee or even dream that the people would put me at the helm of the ship when the storm hit with such power. I've considered and prayed over the merits and I will announce that an emancipation proclamation is forthcoming."

Later in the day he was not surprised to find that some of the members of the Senate had asked John Crittenden to appeal to him to withhold the proclamation he had proposed to them.

The eloquent Kentuckian had even held the office of Attorney-General of the United States. Even though President Lincoln knew this Senator was a sincere Union man, he had told him that it would be unwise to disturb slavery.

Abe listened as that elder statesman spoke to him "from the heart of one Kentuckian to another." After stating his case he added, "There is a niche near to that of Washington, to him who shall save his country. If Mr. Lincoln will step into that niche the *founder and preserver* of the Republic shall stand side by side."

As Abe surveyed the faces of the men in the Congress, he sensed that all the congressmen were acutely aware of the seriousness of the question at hand. Would it be possible to free all the slaves as he intended to do?

The next to speak was Owen Lovejoy, a patriot who sympathized with Abe. When Elijah, his brother, would not surrender his freedom of the press, he had been mobbed and then murdered.

Owen Lovejoy's voice cracked with emotion as he announced, "After my brother's murder, while kneeling upon the green sod that covered my brother's grave, I took a solemn vow of eternal war upon slavery. Like Peter the Hermit I have since gone forth with a heart of fire and a tongue of lightning, preaching my crusade against slavery." Upon ending his speech he turned to Crittenden and asked, "The gentlemen from Kentucky says he has a niche for Abraham Lincoln — where is it?"

Crittenden pointed toward heaven.

Upon seeing the Senator's gesture, Lovejoy protested, "He points upward, but, sir, if the President follows the counsel of that gentlemen, and becomes the perpetuator of slavery, he should point downward, to some dungeon in the temple of Moloch, who feeds on human blood, and where are forged chains for human limbs; in the recesses of whose temple woman is scourged and man tortured, and outside the walls are lying dogs, gorged with human flesh, as Byron describes them, lying around the walls of Stamboul. This is a suitable place for the statue of him who would perpetuate slavery."

"I, too," Lovejoy added, "Have a temple for Abraham Lincoln, but it is in Freedom's holy fane — not surrounded by slave fetters and chains, but with the symbols of freedom — not dark with bondage, but radiant with the light of Liberty. In that niche he shall stand proudly, nobly, gloriously, with broken chains and slave's whips beneath his feet. — That is a fane worth dying for, though that death led through Gethsemane and the agony of the accursed tree.

"It is said that Wilbeforce went up to the judgment seat with the broken chains of eight hundred thousand slaves! Let Lincoln make himself the Liberator, and his name shall be enrolled not only in this earthly temple, but it shall be traced on the living stones of that temple which is reared amid the thrones of Heaven."

Owen Lovejoy's words stirred the President's heart. *Oh, God,* he cried inside, *help me with this momentous decision. I have heard from men, but I earnestly desire an answer from You. Am I just to try to preserve the Union or am I to free all men? Because of my close relationships with so many of the black race, I have come to realize that they are no different than us — that they love, and laugh and have great depths of feelings the same as we do. Oh, Father, it will be a tremendous task, but I now realize the Constitution 's words are real — 'that all men are created equal'.*"

President Abraham Lincoln left the Congress that day with a new resolve. He would draw up the Emancipation Proclamation and present it to the House of Representatives and the Senate.

He made a speech forewarning them of the pending proclamation, then he told them, "I have listened to all your ideas, but I have become determined to free all the slaves!" Objections came from all corners.

Nevertheless, he told Mary one evening, "I've thought and thought about the pros and cons, but I have resolved in my heart and mind that the only just thing to do is to bring it before the cabinet. And so, with all members in attendance, and Abe feeling certain that they had arrived at the meeting with more interest than usual, he began to read on that September 22, 1862 - "Gentlemen: — I have, as you are aware, thought a great deal about the relation of this war to slavery, and you all remember that several weeks ago I read to you an order I had prepared upon the subject, which, on account of objections made by some of you, was not issued. Ever since then my mind had been much occupied with this subject, and I have thought all along that the time for acting on it might probably come. I think the time has come now: I wish it was a better time. I wish that we were in a better condition. The action of the army against the rebels has not been quite what I should have best liked, but they have been driven out of Maryland, and Pennsylvania is no longer in danger of invasion.

"When the rebel army was at Frederick, I determined, as soon as it should be driven out of Maryland, to issue a Proclamation of Emancipation, such as I thought most likely to be useful. I said nothing to any one, but I made a promise to myself and (hesitating a little), to my Maker. The rebel army is now driven out, and I am going to fulfill that promise. I have got you together to hear what I have written down. I do not wish your advice about the main matter, for that I have determined for myself. This I say without intending anything but respect for any one of you. But I already know the views of each on this question. They have been heretofore expressed, and I have considered them as thoroughly and carefully as I can. What I have written is that which my reflections have determined me to say. If there is anything in the expressions I use, or in any minor matter which any one of you think had best be changed, I shall be glad to receive your suggestions. One other observation I will make. I know very well that many others might in, this matter as in others, do better that I can; and if I was satisfied that the public confidence was more fully possessed by any one of them than by me, and knew of any constitutional way in which he could be put in my place, he should have it. I would gladly yield it to him. But though I believe I have not so much of the confidence of the people as I had some time since, I do not know that, all things considered, any other person has more; and, however this may be, there is no way in which I can have any other man put where I am. I am here; I must do the best I can and bear the responsibility of taking the course which I feel I ought to take."

Anticipating a verbal response, Abraham Lincoln was surprised that very little was said except to warn him, "You had best wait until the first of the year before making this message public." He agreed.

On the first day of January, 1863 as he prayed about the consequences of his words that day, Nicolay tiptoed in earlier than his usual appearance for a day's work.

Abraham Lincoln nodded, as if in approval that his aide was there to back him.

Nicolay spoke first, "I came because I knew you would have some concerns about the decision you made."

"That was true, but it is no longer so. I have a peace and a great resolve about bringing this proclamation before the Congress. Dear Nicolay, I truly believe that my intentions and beliefs on the matter of slavery are, in the long run, for the good of the nation."

With that he rose to go to his self-assigned task for the day, knowing that his Emancipation Proclamation would stir up more controversy. His voice was calm and assured when he rose to speak:

"Whereas, on the 22nd day of September, in the year of our Lord, 1862, a proclamation was issued by the President of the United States, containing, among other things, the following, to wit: That on the first day of January, in the year of our Lord, 1863, all persons held as slaves, within any State or designated part of a State, the people whereof shall then be in rebellion against the United States, shall be thenceforth and forever free, and the Executive Government of the United States, including the military and naval authority thereof, will recognize and maintain the freedom of such persons, and will do no act or acts to repress such persons, or any of them, in any effort they may make for their actual freedom; that the Executive will, on the first day of January aforesaid, issue a proclamation, designating the States and parts of states, if any, in which the people therein, respectively, shall then be in rebellion against the United States, and the fact that any State or the people thereof, shall, on that day, be in good faith represented in the Congress of the United States by members chosen thereto at elections wherein a majority of the qualified voters of such States shall have participated, shall, in the absence of strong countervailing testimony, be deemed conclusive evidence that such State and the people thereof are not in rebellion against the United States.

"Now therefore, I, Abraham Lincoln, President of the United States, by virtue of the power vested in me as Commander-in-Chief of the Army and Navy, in a time of actual armed rebellion against the authority of the Government of the United States, as a fit and necessary war measure for suppressing said rebellion, do, on this first day of January, in the year of our Lord, 1863, and in accordance with my purpose so to do, publicly proclaimed for the full period of one hundred days from the date of the first above-mentioned order, designate as the States and parts of States therein, the people whereof, respectively, are this day in rebellion against the United States, the following, to wit: Arkansas, Texas and Louisiana (except the parishes of St. Bernard, Plaquemine, Jefferson, St. John, St. Charles, St. James, Ascension, Assumption, Terrebonne, La Fourche, St. Mary, St. Martin and Orleans, including the city of New Orleans), Mississippi, Alabama, Florida, Georgia, South Carolina, North Carolina and Virginia (except the forty-eight counties designated as West Virginia, and also the counties of Berkley, Accomac, Northampton, Elizabeth City, York, Princess Anne and Norfolk, including the cities of Norfolk and Portsmouth), which excepted parts are for the present left precisely as if this proclamation were not issued; I do order and declare that all persons held as slaves within designated States, or parts of States, are, and henceforward shall be free, and that the Executive Government of the United States, including the military and naval authorities thereof, will recognize and maintain the freedom of the said persons; and I hereby enjoin upon the people so declared to be free, to abstain from all violence unless in necessary self-defense, and recommend to them that in all cases where allowed, they labor faithfully for reasonable wages; and I further declare and make known that such persons of suitable condition will be received into the armed service of the United States, to garrison forts, positions, stations and other places, and to man vessels of all sorts in said service. And upon this, sincerely believed to be an act of justice, warranted by the Constitution upon military necessity, I invoke the considerate judgment of mankind, and the gracious favor of Almighty God.

In witness whereof, I have hereunto set my hand and caused the seal of the United States to be affixed.

Done at the City of Washington, this first day of January, in the year of our Lord, 1863, and of the Independence of the United States of America, the eighty-seventh."

Abraham Lincoln

U NABLE to do more than wish the undertaking
great success.

Henry W. Longfellow.
1882.

CAMBRIDGE, MARCH 13, 1882.

(Henry W. Longfellow)

CLOSE ENCOUNTER

In August of 1864 Abe had become so wearied and pressured that he rose early in the morning and quietly made his way out to the stable. Saddling his own horse gave him a feeling of satisfaction. He became so tired of everyone jumping to do his bidding plus the nuisance of always having bodyguards breathing down his neck. A sense of freedom enveloped him as he turned his favorite gelding toward the outskirts of the city to the Soldiers Home where he went "to get away from it all". The early morning air, the warmth of the rising sun invigorated him. "We're alone at last," he spoke aloud to the horse. "No bodyguards, no office seekers trying to corner me. This is as close to heaven as I can get right now," he declared. "Come on boy, let her go." After giving his mount a nudge, they were off.

When he was a child he'd often heard kids that went to school each day declare that they got a thrill out of playing hookey. Abe couldn't understand that — he had such a thirst for knowledge that any bit of learning he could get gave him such pleasure, but as he rode he felt as though he at last understood the other boys' feelings. The freedom he experienced that day must have been similar to how his friends must have felt when they managed to get away from authority for a day. Abe chuckled. He was playing hookey from the government!

Once he was out in the country, he slowed his horse down to a trot, and decided he was free of any bothersome person. "No one needs to know I'm missing. We'll be back in time for lunch so Mary won't even realize I'm not around. Last night I told John Hay and Nicolay I had an appointment. Wouldn't they be surprised to find it was with a horse?" He giggled.

The sounds and smells of nature calmed his troubled soul. A humming bird neared him and he watched the tiny bird with special interest. *How does such a little thing move through the air? Will men ever be able to fly like that?* he wondered.

At that moment the humming bird flew in front of his face, causing Abe to turn his head to watch it in flight. The only noise was the perpetual movements of the miniature bird's wings and the sound of the horse's hooves hitting the dirt road, until suddenly from out of nowhere a loud crack shattered the scene's tranquility.

Abe's high top hat toppled to the ground. His heart beat faster. It had to be a shot! The pungent smell of gunpowder reached his nostrils. Dismounting, he retrieved his hat from the ground, then looked around. Everything was still. Not even a leaf seemed to be moving. *How,* he wondered, *could the culprit get away without any noise? Maybe I do need to have a bodyguard with me"* Lamon and Mary *have tried to warn me that my enemies want to do me in. How could anyone know I was out here in no-man's land so early in the morning without me knowing they were behind me?*

With that, he mounted the horse and wasted no time heading back to Washington and home, arriving at the White House just as Tad was opening the door to go outside. For a moment Abe embraced his young son. Realizing the frightening impact that Mary and his two remaining children could also become the targets of any of his own enemy's vengeance hit his mind full force. Walking into the foyer, Mary came to greet him just as he was examining his hat to see if the bullet had damaged any of his important papers or the bills he kept in a section Elizabeth had designed in its crown so he could keep them with him.

Mary Todd had been Mrs. Abraham Lincoln for more than a quarter of a century by 1864, so Lincoln knew she had come to understand his moods and sometimes seemed to read his mind. How he wished she could get out of her self-centeredness oftener than she did, but that day his wife amazed him by saying, "Abraham, what's wrong? What happened to your hat?"

"Oh, something hit it while I was out on the road."

Grabbing his black top hat from him she demanded, "What on earth are you talking about? Are you suggesting a stone flew up and knocked your hat off your head?" At that moment she found the two bullet holes. "Abraham Lincoln, someone shot at you!" she cried.

Tad, who had been standing by, became wide-eyed as he exclaimed, "There should be a law against shooting the President."

A slow grin passed over Lincoln's face as he patted his offspring on the head. "Don't worry; Tad. It IS against the law to shoot me."

Mary's face turned into the kind of scowl that usually indicated a storm was brewing inside of her. "Abraham Lincoln, you might have been killed! This is no laughing matter!" she cried as she stomped her feet. For a moment a surge of delight flooded Abe's body. His wife actually was showing concern about him and his well-being! Yet it only took a second for her to add in a frantic high pitched voice, "What would we do without you?"

Lincoln sighed. How he wished his wife Mary could get outside of herself, but she added, "Abraham Lincoln, you're going to have to watch out for your enemies. You have a wife and two children to support."

However, he was in for a surprise later in the fall when Mary announced at the dinner table one evening, "Elizabeth and I have been talking and we are both concerned about the Black troops. Abe, you must do something for them. Elizabeth claims they are lying on the ground with no blankets beneath them and the dirt to cover them. Winter is coming. Are you going to let them freeze to death? Abraham Lincoln, those men are fighting for freedom just as hard as the white soldiers are, maybe more because they have so much at stake. You need to see to it that they get better treatment! But for now," she declared, with a prideful look, "Elizabeth and I have rounded up $200 to buy blankets until the Union gets around to taking care of its own."

A smile again crossed over the Presidents' face. His eyes wrinkled at the corners, as he spoke, "Mary, that makes me so proud of you." He thought of all the times he could not find a reason for such a statement.

That weekend Elizabeth and Mary filled a buggy with blankets and started off to deliver their first load to the Black Union soldiers. Abe watched from the window as they started off. The determined look on his wife's face made her appear as though she were a general who was out to attack and conquer the entire Rebel army on her own — not quite on her own because Elizabeth, her side kick, wore a similar expression.

Lincoln chortled to himself, "Watch out, you Confederates, those women won't give you a fighting chance! Best you stay out of their way." Even though the scene hit his funny bone, a sense of pride encompassed him. His Mary was on an errand of mercy. Elizabeth, who'd been hired as a seamstress and then became Mary's close friend, could stir up the best in his wife.

During the next few weeks the two women drove out time after time taking additional blankets and supplies on their errands of mercy to the Black Union soldiers. In the meantime President Lincoln argued the plight of the uniformed Blacks who chose to fight for the cause of freedom to Congress, "These valiant soldiers need the same pay, uniforms and privileges as our white fighting men."

Battles were being fought where thousands of troops on both sides were being slaughtered. Men were vacating their posts! The heavier the fighting, the more the President felt weighted down by the war. "My personal responsibility is sometimes more than I can bear" he told his old friend Speed one day. "The fate of the Union rests in my hands."

He spent a good deal of time reading Job during this period after the North lost at Chancellorsville. He asked his aide John Hay, "How can one man bear the burden and responsibility of such bloodshed, of so many men losing their lives to a cause?"

His appearance changed. The merry twinkle, the amusing stories that had caught so many people's interest became less and less frequent. The lines in his face deepened, the hollow eyes, the dark circles changed his appearance from the look of a victorious man to that of an exhausted, worried soul. He prayed. He wept.

Men who hadn't seen him in months showed alarm as they came into his presence. Abe Lincoln exhibited few of his former traits as the war casualties mounted. He thought he could not bear the news when he was told by the war department Mrs. Bixby of Boston had lost her fifth boy in the war. *Oh, God* he cried inside. *What can I say to her? I know too-well the meaning of the loss of a loved one. Father, we've lost two small sons and the hurt was almost more than we could bear. What do I say to a mother who has lost five of her boys in this terrible war? You will have to give me the words. I do not know what to say that could help her weeping heart.* He prayed and pondered what to say to a mother who had been told that so many sons had gone down in battle. He finally picked up his pen and wrote,

Dear Mrs.Bixby,

I have been shown on the file of the War Department a statement of the Adjutant-General of Massachusetts, that you are the mother of five sons who have died gloriously on the field of battle. I feel how weak and fruitless must be any word of mine which should attempt to beguile you from the grief of a loss so overwhelming; but I cannot refrain from tendering to you the consolation that may be found in the thanks of the republic they died to save. I pray that our Heavenly Father may assuage the anguish of your bereavements, and leave only the cherished memory of the loved and lost, and the solemn pride that must be yours to have laid so costly a sacrifice upon the altar of freedom.

Abraham Lincoln
November 21, 1864

After hand addressing the envelope, he placed the letter inside and added another prayer for the dear lady that he doubted he would ever meet.

CAVALRY GROUP OF STATUARY.   NATIONAL LINCOLN MONUMENT.

Representing the rearing figure of a horse, from whose back his rider has just been thrown, and the wounded trumpeter, who is supported by a companion.

ATLANTA BRINGS HOPE

Abraham Lincoln's personal campaign for reelection was running into tremendous pressure. When the Democrats placed McClellan on the ticket to run against him, the former general declared he would have "peace at all cost."

On August 30 a group of unhappy Republicans called for another National Convention in Cincinnati, Ohio with the hopes of forcing Lincoln out, causing uneasiness in Lincoln's heart. "Even men in my own party are plotting against me," he told Mary at dinner the night he heard of the rebellion against his candidacy.

Abraham Lincoln met a jubilant Nicolay on his way to the office on September 2. "Atlanta's fallen!" his aide cried. "Sherman defeated Hood."

"Good News!" Abe exclaimed back. "It's the South's main rail center."

After a summer of bad messages Abe was elated, so he declared; "We have a gift from God. Sunday will be a national day to offer thanks and sound one hundred gun salutes in all the major cities. Our armies are winning again!"

Secretary Stanton greeted him later with a grin across his face and the message. "Good news came from Shenandoah, too. Sheridan won three battles over Jubal Early's troops in Virginia." When the President received that word his own face beamed. After hearing later about the Union's triumph in Mobile Bay, his joy soared even higher.

More than the war was at stake. McClellan was a formidable foe against him for his second term as President. He informed both Nicolay and Hay, "My hope is that an armistice will end the struggle."

He told fellow Republicans, "Keep my policy and you can save the Union. Throw it away and the Union goes with it. If my policy on Negroes is abandoned, it would mean the loss of tens of thousands of black soldiers. That would be catastrophic to the Union's cause."

The battles continued to be waged. October 19 both Sherman and Sheridan dealt crushing blows to the Confederacy in the Shenandoah Valley. Abe continued his personal battle for the upcoming election with McClellan campaigning with a "peace-at-any-price" motto in a war-weary country so Abraham Lincoln remained concerned about the outcome.

On November 8, election day, he told Mary, "You seem so uneasy about this election. If we lose, we'll still go on as a family. You seem more worried about it than I am."

He had no way of knowing that she'd enmassed some $27,000 worth of debts and frantically asked Republican politicians to help her pay them off, saying, "Poor Mr. L is almost a monomaniac on the subject of honesty. Won't you help me? He has always helped you."

All Mary's treachery had been going on behind the President's back, and the evening of the election Abe joined Hay and Brooks who made their way through the dark, soggy night to the telegraph office where one of Stanton's clerks handed him a stack of returns. Abe read them aloud, "10,000 in our favor in Philadelphia." Elation surfaced in his voice as he read the next tally, "We're even running ahead in Baltimore."

The telegraph kept ticking good news. "Pennsylvania seems to be ours, Indiana's on our band wagon, so are other crucial states."

At midnight the re-elected President went home to tell Mary, "You can relax now. We won!"

Unbeknownst to him other secret happenings were taking place. He did not know about them until Hay told him the next day, "Lamon came armed with pistols and knives and borrowed blankets from me. He kept guard all night outside your door. He was certain someone would try to assassinate you if you were re-elected."

After the election Abraham Lincoln looked in the mirror and declared to Mary, "I'm fifty-five but I look 105. The war and the election have taken their toll."

Tired, worn, he listened to Sherman's plan to march through Georgia. Nicolay told him, "He says he is planning to burn his way across the state and destroy the fields and railroads."

The plan did not meet Lincoln's approval. "My concern for the people is not all that worries me. 'Sherman's march to the sea,' the general's troops might be cut off by the enemy somewhere in the state of Georgia."

The troops lost contact with the War Department so the President didn't know their status for several weeks, causing Abe to be on edge. The problems in Tennessee where Hood's weary army were holed up outside of Nashville, also gave him reason for concern.

On December 15 Abe was so exasperated and sick at heart that he went home to bed. Hay came before midnight and roused his sleeping boss, "Mr. President, Secretary Stanton has great news."

Making his way to the top of the stairs, he heard from Stanton, "'Old Pap Thomas' dealt a great blow against Hood in Tennessee and expects to be victorious tomorrow."

The following day a surge of relief flooded Abe's tall frame when the word came, "Old Pap has done his job."

Sherman telegraphed Lincoln with his Christmas present to his commander-in-chief. "We have captured Savannah!" Abe's heart swelled with delight. Sherman also announced his next plan. "We'll march through the Carolinas and smash all the railroads that supply Lee's army."

All of the December happenings on the war front gave Abe reason to assure his spouse, "We can celebrate Christmas. Our prayers are being answered. It looks as though this horrendous conflict is coming to an end soon."

ABRAHAM LINCOLN RAISING THE AMERICAN FLAG, AT INDEPENDENCE HALL, PHILA., FEB. 1861.

STORM WARNING

In January of 1865 Abraham Lincoln was making his plans to be inaugurated for his second term of office as President when James S. Rollins came to visit him in the White House. Abe was feeling cheerful and of good humor, but it only took a few minutes for him to realize that Mr. Rollins was not. His visitor wore a very troubled look.

"What," Abe queried of Rollins, "makes you so stern and sad looking?"

James Rollins' face wore a look of exasperation as he replied. "Sir, I feel very badly about not communicating what I have to say to you earlier in the year. You see, a gentleman by the name of Colonel Lane came with me then to warn you that your life is in danger. We waited and waited in your anteroom, but we couldn't get an audience with you. There were too many people that day."

Abe sat back in his chair. With a twinkle in his eyes, he asked, "What dire news do you have that it should have been told to me before this?"

Rollins drew a deep breath, then declared, "Mr. President, Colonel Lane had been working with the United States detective force on the Mississippi when he left the boat and in town there he heard some young men and warlike fellows tell of how they were going to dispose of the President!"

Abe chuckled. "You say that he heard that earlier in the winter? I must say, dear James Rollins, that they've taken their good time in carrying out their plans." Try as he might, Abraham

Lincoln could not keep the mirth from his eyes as he asked, "Please tell me what method they intended to use for my demise so I will know what to look out for."

His light response must have been causing his visitor anguish for his brow furrowed as he replied, "It's a box, sir. Colonel Lane said he held it in his own hands. They plan to arm this six or seven inch square box with explosives and if you open it, the fool thing will explode and kill you.

"Mr. Lincoln," he went on, "I am most concerned with your well-being. They propose to send it to the White House where you would most likely get it and open it. Colonel Lane was planning to come with me to share this information with you the following day after our first attempt to visit, but he received a telegram calling him to Wheeling, West Virginia. I did not see him again until lately when he reminded me that it was my duty to warn you." In a tone and a look of total exasperation he added, "Nothing but a sense of duty and the interest I feel in you and the country would have prompted me to have mentioned a matter of this kind to you."

Abe pondered his own reply before saying, "I appreciate your consideration, but I don't pay much attention to such things, having received a number of threatening letters since I have been President. Nobody has killed me yet. The truth is, I give very little consideration to such threats."

Rollins next words made him appear almost apologetic, "I do not know Colonel Lane very well, but I hardly see why a man should make up a story of this dimension unless there was some foundation for it. I believe he witnessed what he related to me."

With that Abe's visitor rose to leave, extending his hand and saying pleasantly, "Mr. President, I feel relieved in having unburdened myself in telling you what I have. I've acted from a sense of duty and I leave you with one plea, if you should come into your office one of these mornings and find a box about six inches square sitting on your table, I beg of you, do not open it; let someone else attend to that. If you attempt to open it, and the nation loses it's President, I want it understood that I have cleared my skirts."

His finishing statement aroused Abe's sense of humor so much that he laughed heartily, but then he said, "Now, I will tell you. I will promise that if I find any boxes on my table directed to me, I won't open them."

As his visitor went to leave the room Abe felt a twinge of apprehension so he declared the way he really felt, while his face took on a melancholy look. "Rollins, I don't know what in God's world any man would want to kill me for, for their is not a human being living to whom I would not extend a favor, and make them happy if it were in my power to do so."

After that Rollins bid the President good night but Abe saw him several times in the next months on visits to his office. On one occasion he couldn't help but tease his friend in a jocular manner. "Well Rollins, I haven't received the box YET."

James Rollins simply responded, "I'm grateful for that, but, sir, please don't open any left on your table." After that he closed Abe's office door.

The two men didn't meet again until the end of the thirty-eighth Congress when Rollins visited him once more at the White House and had a conversation. "It is my hope and prayer that the war will soon come to an end. When they do, I will rejoice," Abe told his visitor.

After a bit more small talk Rollins rose to leave. Abe knew his friend's term in Congress had ended, so he willingly shook hands and bid him a cordial good bye, but then added with mirth dancing in his eyes, "Rollins, the box has not come yet"

James Rollins heaved a huge sigh before answering, "That is well, Mr. President. I am glad to hear it. I hope it never comes, but if it does, I charge you not to open it."

To which Abe Lincoln replied, "I promise, Rollins. Thank you for your care. I appreciate knowing in advance when a storm is coming."

The last day of January Lincoln walked into the Capitol and stared at the masses of people. Not only the seats, but the galleries were jammed to overflowing. The sight brought a feeling of joy to Abe's heart. He'd coaxed, even coerced some of the House members and Senators to enact his greatest political goal to totally free all the slaves, to guarantee permanent emancipation.

The amendment had gone down to defeat in May, but Abe had protested after he was re-elected, "A national election has taken place since our first attempt to get the thirteenth amendment passed and I again received the country's approval, so one must believe that the voters of this country back this desperately needed legislation."

Even so, he was apprehensive as the roll call began. To Abe's delight every Republican answered "yes". Several of the Democrats joined them. The end result? To the President's joy he heard the tally, 119 voted for the amendment, 58 against. *3 votes over the needed two-thirds*, he mentally calculated.

The vote pleased him, but the reaction of those in the Capitol that day thrilled his very soul. He felt almost giddy as cheers filled the huge room and normally distinguished statesmen threw their hats and canes in the air. Hankies fluttered from the gallery. Newsmen rushed to telegraph the news across the country.

Abraham Lincoln could hardly contain his exuberance as he embraced his wife and exclaimed with delight, "We've a great moral victory!" An all-encompassing grin passed over his face as he proclaimed, "Maryland and Missouri have already abolished slavery by state action. So have my reconstructed governments in Louisiana and Arkansas."

As he stood looking out the White House window he pointed to the Potomac and cried with excitement. "If the people over the river had behaved themselves, I could not have done what I have."

President Abraham Lincoln soon found out his victory was short-lived. His friend Sumner opposed the military government that Lincoln had set up in Louisiana. On a visit to the White House he tried to convince Lincoln about his viewpoint by saying, "Congress should control reconstruction throughout the South."

Abe objected, "We need the military to establish government there." To this Sumner retaliated by crying, "The eggs of crocodiles can produce only crocodiles." It is not easy to see how eggs laid by military power can be hatched into an American state."

Because of the battle in Congress which went on over the question of restoring the South, political friction also continued between Stanton and Lincoln, but they remained friends although Abe had withdrawn from confidences between them. He'd even told Nicolay one morning, "I have no one I can trust except you. Mary has let me down in so many ways. She is not good at hiding things from me. For some time now I've felt I could not trust her."

Nicolay nodded, "Is it because of Stanton? She seems to come alive when he arrives with his ridiculous attire of a brown coat, maroon vest, and lavender pants and a gold cane."

Abe chuckled, "If you're worried about him being a bachelor, I am not. Mary is taken with his attention and I know the busybodies are carried away with the attention he gives her, but not me. He makes her happy. I'm too busy to indulge her, so it pleases me too. I am not worried about her being unfaithful. She is not capable of that, but I am concerned about her being up to something in our financial realm. She is capable of deceiving me on that. My wife is also busy telling more than she should about politics, so for the most part I steer away from telling her anything of importance anymore."

Nicolay shook his head, "You have enough to contend with in the government without contending with her."

Abe turned and stood looking at his long-time aide, "Nicolay, I know I can tell you anything. It is such a relief to have a trusted confident. There's something else that has driven a wedge between Mary and me. It is Robert. He's her pride and joy, and I feel I have let him down as a father. When he was little I never had time to tussle with him—too busy making a living, and now I'm faced with the problem that MY son has NOT gone off to war and a wife that screams that she is NOT going to lose another son. In truth, I don't know what to do."

Nicolay nodded in agreement. "You really do need to let him go. The entire country is complaining because your boy is at Harvard while theirs are all in the military. Why don't you ask

Grant to give him a desk job? I know your son himself has been pressuring you to let him go."

Abe's face lit up with a glow, "I'll do that! Even Mary can't protest!"

And so, that February Robert left to go to Petersburg with the rank of Captain. His mother and father stood on the White House steps bidding him a fond farewell.

HOPE RISES

Joshua Speed dropped by before the inauguration. Abe acknowledged the alarmed look on his friend's face, by saying, "I am very unwell. My hands and feet are always cold. I suppose I ought to be in bed."

A pair of women came in. One cried, "Mr. President, we plead with you to release our sons who are in prison because of resisting the draft." Tears flowed. One tried to kneel before him, causing Abe to order, "Get up. Don't kneel to me. Thank God and go."

Speed stood amazed. "With my knowledge of your nervous sensibility, it is a wonder such scenes don't kill you."

"Speed, it is the only thing today that has given me pleasure. Long ago I gave up having to make decisions concerning the men who ran from duty. I left it up to their commanding officers. I hate anyone to have to make negative decisions, but I am still most unpopular with so many."

He knew Stanton was doing his best before the inauguration to keep bedlam out of Washington, that threats came in the mail each day threatening his life, yet he was too sick and tired to give much thought to danger. As the re-elected President, he knew many were unhappy with his views, so he prayed that his speech would make a favorable impression on the citizenry.

March 3 brought a dreary, dismal day to the nation's capitol. Rain came, threatening to drench the bands, the cavalry parade and the spectators. At twelve o'clock Abe sat in his carriage and watched the throngs. As he got up to speak suddenly the sun burst through with brilliant rays lighting up the platform. The clouds gathered again just before he began to speak:

"Fellow Countrymen: At this second appearing to take the oath of the presidential office, there is less occasion for an extended address than there was at the first. Then a statement somewhat in detail of a course to be pursued seemed fitting and proper. Now, at the expiration of four years, during which public declarations have been constantly called forth on every point and phase of the great contest which still absorbs the attention and engrosses the energies of the nation, little that is new could be presented. The progress of our arms, upon which all else chiefly depends, is as well known to the public as to myself and it is, I trust, reasonably satisfactory and encouraging to all. With high hope for the future, no prediction in regard to it is ventured.

"On the occasion corresponding to this four years ago, all thoughts were anxiously directed to an impending civil war. All dreaded it; all sought to avert it. While the inaugural address was being delivered from this place, devoted altogether to saving the Union without war, insurgent agents were in the city seeking to destroy it without war —seeking to dissolve the Union and divide its effects by negotiation. Both parties deprecated war; but one of them would make war rather than let the nation survive, and the other would accept war rather then let it perish. And the war came.

"The prayer of both could not be answered — those of neither have been answered fully. The Almighty has his own purposes. Woe unto the world because of offenses! For it must needs be that offenses come; but woe to that man by whom the offense cometh.

"If we shall suppose that American slavery is one of those offenses which, in the providence of God, must needs come, but which, having continued through his appointed time, He now wills to remove, and that He gives to North and South this terrible war, as the woe due to those by whom the offense came, shall we discern therein any departure from those Divine attributes which the believers in a living God always ascribe to Him? Fondly do we hope, fervently do we pray, that this mighty scourge of war may soon pass away. Yet, if God wills that it continue until all the wealth piled by the bondsman's two hundred and fifty years of unrequited toil shall be sunk and until every drop of blood drawn by the lash shall be paid by another drawn with the sword, as was said three thousand years ago, so still it must be said: 'The judgments of the Lord are true and righteous altogether.'

"With malice toward none, with charity for all, with firmness in the right, as God gives us to see the right, let us strive on to finish the work we are in; to bind up the nation's wounds; to care for him who shall have borne the battle, and for his widow and for his orphan; to do all which may achieve and cherish a just and lasting peace among ourselves, and with all nations."

After his address he took the oath of office putting his hand on the Bible which Chief Justice William Chase had opened to Isaiah 5:27 and 28.

Back at the White House Noah Brooks asked, "Did you notice the sunburst?"

Abe smiled. "It made my heart jump."

Later, at the evening reception Nicolay informed him, "Your old friend Frederick Douglas, the Negro reporter, has been trying to gain access to see you, but the police won't let him in."

Indignant, Lincoln ordered, "Show him in at once."

When the reporter entered the room, Lincoln declared, "Here comes my friend Douglas." While shaking his hand, Lincoln added, "I saw you in the crowd today, listening to my address. There is no man in the country whose opinion I value more than yours. I want to know what you think of it."

"I was impressed. It was a sacred effort."

"Glad you liked it," Abe responded, then stood with delight as Douglas passed down the line and Abraham Lincoln thought, *How wonderful it is that a Negro has been a part of the inaugural and reception for the very first time in history.*

Following the inauguration, Abe was gratified to learn from Nicolay, "Sherman is winning. The South Carolina state capitol was gone up in smoke."

"So many innocent lives," Abe moaned, as he listened to the

latter part of Nicolay's announcement.

Abraham Lincoln's long-time aide went on to give him the rest of the war details, "Sheridan is also winning in the Shenandoah Valley where rebel cities and fields were set aflame." Later the President felt a surge of relief when some of the Confederate hierarchy agreed to meet with him aboard a ship near Hampton Roads, Virginia.

At that meeting Abraham Lincoln set his definite terms to them. "You from the Confederate states must recognize the national supremacy and accept the complete eradication of slavery before hostilities can end. However, I do favor some sort of compensation for slave holders."

Regardless, Abe was disheartened when the meeting came to an end and nothing was resolved. Back in Congress he could get little or no endorsement of his plan to reimburse the slave holders, so he was disappointed again and abandoned the plan.

Secretary Stanton came to him at the White House, sharing with him, "Grant says Lee had contacted him and suggested those two generals settle the war."

Lincoln's reply even surprised Abe himself, sending a telegram to the general, "I will deal with political questions and negotiate for peace. Your job is to fight."

As Sheridan and Sherman drove their forces through the South, Lamon, Abe's bodyguard, had concerns about his safety. Even though President Abraham Lincoln knew his life could be in danger, he told Hay, "Lamon is a monomaniac about my safety. As to crazy folks," he added, "I must take my chances." Still he knew that Stanton and Lamon worried endlessly about his life being in jeopardy.

Abe felt wearier each day. By March 14 he felt a desperate need for a meeting of his cabinet, but was too weak to get out of bed so his secretaries gathered around his bedside.

A few days later Abe rallied when he received an invitation from Grant, "We need to meet. Is it possible for you to come to my headquarters at City Point?"

Mary also met the request with enthusiasm. "We could get on the River Queen and go there since it's only about 20 miles south of Richmond. The fresh air will invigorate you and you'll have a much needed rest."

Taking Tad and a bodyguard along with them, Mary looked quite pleased when Grant brought some of his men to greet them at the wharf that night so they could escort the Lincolns to the general's headquarters for a good time. Grant's wife, Julia, acted as hostess. Abraham Lincoln glanced around the room and noticed that Generals Meade and Ord were there.

A thrill for Lincoln was keeping in secret who was going to be their special guest at breakfast the next morning. "Who is this unknown visitor?" Mary asked, when Abe told her someone important was going to join them.

Abe grinned. "You've heard of him. His name is Captain Robert Todd Lincoln."

Their son told him after they'd met and hugged each other, "Lee attempted to break through the Union lines at dawn today, but was defeated in a counterattack."

As President, Abe felt as though he had to survey the damage so he boarded a train that took him past battlefields with wounded and dead men's bodies still on the ground. Heartsick, he announced, "I have seen enough of the horrors of war, but I hope this is the beginning of the end."

Meeting with Grant back at his headquarters Abe bemoaned the problems he'd encountered during his Presidency. "The human loss is heart-shattering. No home in this entire republic has not been devastated by some loss; the country's financial debts are beyond human imagination."

Having said that, he declared, "The day's sights have done me in. Will you please excuse us?" Then he and Mary rode back to the River Queen to go to bed.

The next day after meeting with Sheridan, Abe rode out to review Grant's troops. Mrs. Lincoln and Mrs. Grant followed in an ambulance carriage, with Mary complaining, "This rough road has given me a terrible headache."

Mrs. Grant walking ahead exclaimed, "Oh, Mary, look! The troops with their banners make an awesome sight," but all Mary Todd Lincoln must have seen at that moment was the pretty

Mrs. Ord riding at Abraham Lincoln's side while he reviewed the troops.

As Mrs. Ord trotted over to greet the ladies, Abe knew from the look on Mary's face that she was not going to act like a lady. She proved him right. The President's heart sank as he heard his wife scream at the lovely woman in a jealous rage until poor Mrs. Ord burst into tears.

Humiliated, Abe tried to calm his wife and then attempted to find fitting words to apologize to the target of Mary's tongue-lashing and the embarrassed generals. His hope was that his wife would settle down, but instead she turned on him. With tears rushing down her face she wailed, "How could you do this to me? All the soldiers will think that SHE'S your wife."

Abe did not bother to respond. Turning, he walked away. Mary's regret for her actions kept her holed up on the River Queen for several days until she left Tad with his father and went back to Washington.

Her husband had more important things to do than to dwell on her emotional outbreak even though it tore at his soul. Abe knew that Sherman had met with Grant to discuss their plans for ending the war, but they didn't share much of their strategy with him which caused Lincoln concern.

Late in March Abe was still on the River Queen when the roar of cannons and the flashing from the artillery lit up the night sky. Abraham Lincoln's heart raced. Was this the beginning of the end? Petersburg was bombarded while the President watched from the River Queen where he continued to communicate with Washington. Stanton wired back for him to stay put, so Abraham Lincoln watched the horrific scene and prayed, "Lord, bring this bloody mess to an end."

"I'm going to City Point and Grant's Headquarters," he wired Stanton. As he rode into Petersburg where he met an excited General Grant, "Lee's gone! Meade and Sheridan are rushing to cut him off! It's coming! The end is coming soon! I feel it in my bones!" he cried.

At City Point Abe was given dispatches with other important news. Gratitude filled his body as he read aloud, "Richmond has fallen. Davis and his cronies have fled."

"I'm going to Richmond," he announced. Taking Tad, Captain Pierson and his bodyguard, Abe boarded a gunboat and headed up the James River. A smoke screen nearly cut off his view of the Confederate Capitol.

When he stepped off the dock followed by armed sailors, he knew from his reception by black workers that they recognized him because of his stovepipe hat. "Father Abraham!"—"Glory!" filled the air as Negroes rushed to see their hero. Abraham Lincoln, appalled as they bowed to him, cried out, "Don't kneel to me! Only God deserves such allegiance!"

The men assigned to protect him went wild with fear when the President traveled back through Richmond. "Sir," he cried, "there is no way to keep you safe." As their entourage left the Virginian capital one of the protectors glanced up and saw a Confederate soldier standing in an upstairs window with a rifle aimed straight at Lincoln.

"Mr. President," he screamed, "watch out!"

Expressions on their faces showed their great relief when no shot was fired. Abe made light of the danger he was in, jesting, "Who would want this tired old hide?"

Back on the Malvern which had brought him there, two strangers attempted to board the ship at dusk, but were stopped since the officers thought they both looked suspicious. Panic again encompassed those around Lincoln the next morning as General Edward H. Ripley came on board with this threatening message: "A Confederate soldier told me that the President is in danger and best take care if he goes ashore again."

Abe moaned, "Why won't they let me rest? I'm worn out. My hope was to help restore peace and I have invited John Campbell to bring a delegation and meet with us here tomorrow."

Abraham Lincoln was not surprised when Campbell arrived with just one other man who he told the President, "Sir, this is Gustavers Myers, a prominent attorney from Richmond." Abe's friend General Wetzal was on hand to back his commander-in-chief.

During their conversation John Campbell declared, "Sir, slavery is no longer an issue between the North and South as it is now defunct. The problem now is that Jefferson Davis has declared that only a convention of the Southern States can end the Confederacy and the Confederate Congress refuses to overrule the President."

Lincoln answered. "It is as I feared. The war is not over, and I can see more bloodshed ahead. All those rebel soldiers who are loose will probably take up guerrilla warfare. Society will be broken up; anarchy will be next. It is my hope that I can meet with the officials of the existing government."

One group of cavalry soldiers met him and escorted him again through the streets of Richmond past windows filled with silent faces. At the Confederate executive mansion he sat down in Jefferson Davis' chair. Victorious cheers — "Hurrah! Hurrah!" — rose from the Union men, but the thrill Abe had anticipated did not materialize as he looked at the scattered papers, the shambles of the offices. Broken furniture was strewn about. "Good heavens," he muttered under his breath.

The rebel Assistant Secretary of War was ushered in. In his most Presidential manner Abraham Lincoln announced, "We expect an unconditional and complete surrender."

To the secretary's inquiry, "Will you give our men amnesty?" he replied, "I can not promise amnesty but it is within my power to pardon and I will save any repentant sinner from hanging." After that he took a ride in a carriage through Richmond. Upon seeing the infamous Libby Prison he declared, "So that's the hole where they kept our troops and let many of them die from disease and starvation."

Returning to Grant at headquarters he read recent telegrams, "Sheridan has seized the Danville railroad, cutting off Lee's escape into North Carolina." As he picked up the wire from Sheridan to Grant, he read: "If the thing is pressed I think that Lee will surrender."

Putting the telegraph down, he exclaimed, "I want this holocaust over! Send Grant a wire from me, "Let the thing be pressed."

Back at City Point two wires came from Washington. The

first, from Mary said, "I am quite well now. I will arrive at City Point with a party." The second declared, "Secretary of State Seward was injured severely in a carriage accident."

The news upset Lincoln. "I need to return to Washington," he told Grant's staff. "However, I have some unfinished business." With those words he went to tour the hospital camps. Abe was thrilled at the response of the soldiers as he stopped to encourage each one, shaking hands with everyone that physically could lift an arm to respond. Others, too injured, he tried to encourage. One battered body had only his two eyes staring out from the bandages. Abraham Lincoln leaned down and whispered, "I will pray for you, son." When tears surfaced in the boy's eyes, Abe's mission came to a halt until he could control his own emotions.

As they left the hospitals Abe inquired of Grant's aide who was with him, "How many are there here?"

"Seven thousand, sir."

"Seven thousand," Abe repeated. "That's incredulous."

"That's a lot of hands to shake, sir." the aide declared.

Abe's eyes misted. "That's seven thousand lives, young man. Only time will tell if their sacrifices were worth giving."

Mary returned to City Point to accompany him on the River Queen back to Washington on April 9. Secretary Stanton met him there with a telegram from General Grant, "General Lee surrendered the Army of Northern Virginia this morning at a place called Appomattox Courthouse."

"Hallelujah!" After Lincoln gave out a shout of jubilation, he threw his arms around Stanton and danced. Yet, as all of Washington cheered in the streets during the next few days, President Abraham Lincoln became apprehensive about how the South was going to be rehabilitated.

On April 8 he decided to head home since word had not come that the South had signed a peace treaty. Before heading up the James River he ordered the band to play "Dixie", declaring: "It is one of my favorite tunes."

The ride up the river was slow and tedious. The President showed some surprise when the boat anchored and he could see the nation's capitol was lit up and Washingtonians were dancing in the street over the capture of Richmond, but Abe had another concern — his friend Seward had broken both arms and his jaw. On a visit so that his dear cabinet member wouldn't have to move his head, the President of the United States sprawled across Seward's bed to talk with him telling him about the Northern victories.

Nicolay met him at the White House, "President Lincoln, Sir, Lee surrendered to Grant at Appomattox!" Even though he already knew the news Abe smiled at his aide who looked as though he couldn't contain himself. President Lincoln couldn't wait to share the news with Mary. On his way to see her he realized that he must look as enthused as Nicolay.

The next morning they awoke to the roar of five hundred cannons. Abe looked outside. Men were laughing, children cheering, flags flying, guns firing. "They're as pleased as we are. The battle's won!"

He had much paper work to do after being away for two weeks, but he did take a moment so speak to the throng who had gathered outside the White House after they chanted over and over, "We want our President." Again he asked the band to play "Dixie." After that he went back to composing his message for the next day.

On April 11 the nation's capitol was illuminated. The people had suppressed joyful feelings for those four long years, but with the war's end they suddenly had reason for a shine on their faces to match that of the city.

After cheers and applause from the crowd again demanding his appearance, Abe stepped to the window to speak: "We meet this evening, not in sorrow but in gladness of heart. The recent victories will give hope of a righteous and speedy peace."

After promising a day of national thanksgiving and commending General Grant, his skillful officers and brave men, he began talking about reconstruction of the South and the problems confronting the nation. The throng outside began to thin as he laid out his plan for reorganizing the government. As President he publicly announced, "I am in favor of Negro suffrage."

He knew no other leader in the history of the country had ever stated such a brash statement. He'd made some concessions to the radicals, but he'd been most sincere in his desire to spell out what was in store for the United States of America. The negative reaction of the public disheartened him.

At the end of his delivery, Abe turned to Mary. With a shrug of his shoulders he sighed, "I gave them my all, but I let them down."

Mary patted his back. "Dear, I'm afraid they weren't wanting to hear more troubles right now. They wanted so to have you share their joy and jubilation with them. They wanted you to shout with joy because the war is over. Abraham, dear, be happy! The war is over!"

Abe smiled for the first time and encircled his wife in his arms. "So it is, Mary! Thank the Lord!" Yet he could not stay happy.

After sitting silent in a chair, he sighed, "I'm so tired, but even when I go to bed dreams and nightmares haunt me." After adding a "good night" he went off to his room.

The commander-in-chief had experienced many nights of restless sleep. One dream had bothered him immensely. Before when he shared it with Mary, she told him, "You have been dreadfully solemn," but after he told her the contents she reacted in her usual emotional manner, "I wish you wouldn't have told me."

Abe just nodded his head. He wished he hadn't either, but later he talked with his bodyguard about what he considered to be a nightmare, "I dreamed that there was a corpse and a throng of people stood around weeping with such grief that I asked a soldier who was standing nearby, 'Who is dead in the White House?' To my question he replied, "The President. He was killed by an assassin's bullet."

From Lamon's look of horror, Abe realized the news impacted the man who had even slept outside his bedroom door armed with a pistol and knives when he thought Abe's life was in jeopardy. His bodyguard seemed overwhelmed by the President's dream.

288

"Lamon, don't take it so seriously. How long have you been determined that someone was going to kill me? The ghostly assassin must have been after someone else. The Lord will work this out in his own good time." he added with a sigh. "As I told Mary, 'Let it go'."

FORD'S THEATRE,
TENTH STREET, WASHINGTON, D. C.

FRIDAY EVENING, APRIL 14th, 1865.

THIS EVENING
the performance will be honored by the presence of
PRESIDENT LINCOLN.

Benefit and last night of MISS

LAURA KEENE,

The distinguished Manageress, Authoress and Actress, supported by
Mr. JOHN DYOTT and Mr. HARRY HAWK.

Tom Taylor's celebrated Eccentric Comedy as originally produced in
America by Miss Keene, and performed by her upwards of
ONE THOUSAND NIGHTS

ENTITLED

OUR AMERICAN COUSIN.

FLORENCE TRENCHARD	Miss LAURA KEENE.
Abel Murcott	John Dyott.
Asa Trenchard	Harry Hawk.
Sir Edward Trenchard	T. C. Gourlay.
Lord Dundreary	E. A. Emerson.
Mr. Coyle, Attorney	J. Mathews.
Lieut. Vernon, R. N	W. J. Ferguson.
Captain De Boots	C. Byrnes.
Binney	G. G. Spear.
Buddicomb. a valet	J. H. Evans.
John Whicker, a gardner	J. L. De Bonay.
Rasper, a groom	
Bailiffs	G. A. Parkhurst and L Johnson.
Mary Trenchard	Miss J. Gourlay.
Mrs. Mountchessington	Mrs. H. Muzzey.
Augusta	Miss H. Truman.
Georgiana	Miss M. Hart.
Sharpe	Mrs. J. H. Evans.
Skillet	Miss M. Gourlay.

THE PRICES OF ADMISSION:

Orchestra,	$1 00	Dress Circle and Parquette.	$ 75
Family Circle,	25	Private Boxes,	$6 00 and $10 00

J. R. FORD, Business Manager.

THEATRICAL ADVENTURE

As President, Abraham Lincoln felt he should have more exuberance. The war was over! Why couldn't he savor that fact? During a chat with his friend Speed, he admitted his own downtrodden spirit had not left him at the war's end. "I know that great animosity still exists towards me down in the South. After looking at the casualty list and being impacted with the unbelievable fact that over SIX HUNDRED THOUSAND men died in our terrible holocaust, how can I not feel burdened? The army has asked me to go to Fort Sumter down in Charleston and have a ceremony and install Old Glory over the post once more, but I feel I cannot go. That was where the first shot was fired, and I should be enamored by the idea of seeing the stars and stripes flying there again, but I do not think my soul could tolerate looking at the battered remains of a place that started a conflict where so many died. No matter what people think of that decision, I have to abide by it. It seems to me that the only thing that will help change my distressed feeling is to do something to lighten my heart. I'm going to take Mary to the theatre."

Abe had made the pronouncement while Speed was on a visit to his office. His friend had just left when he heard a knock. Lamon, his bodyguard, stood before him when he opened the door.

"I'm on my way to finish a mission in Richmond. Promise me you will not go out at night, particularly to the theatre."

During the war when so much controversy had arisen over his decisions, Abe had heard such warnings over and over and over again from several outsiders plus Lamon and Stanton. "Surely folks are getting over wanting to take my hide," the President quipped, but then added with a grin, "Well, I promise to do the best I can toward it, too."

Back with Mary, she even echoed the others with her own warning, "Everyone knows that General Grant is expected to join us tonight. The two of you would make great targets for the Rebels. You must be extra careful."

Abe smiled. How well he remembered the time when he was traveling that his advisors convinced him his life was in jeopardy and that he had to attempt to hide himself in disguise. He'd gone along with their wishes, but no attempt was made on his life then. The only time anyone had come near succeeding was that single shot that toppled his hat when he was out for a country ride. That was when the war was at its peak, but why would anyone try to take it now? Besides, he deemed any disguise was ridiculous. What could he do to attempt to hide his lanky, lean frame?

On that Good Friday, April 14, Abe had trouble getting anyone else to agree to accompany the Lincolns to Ford Theatre. Even Stanton refused, but added his concerns, "Mr. Lincoln, you ought not to go. It is too great an exposure."

Earlier Abe had received a verbal acceptance from U. S. Grant, but when Ulysses later declined, the President wondered if it didn't have something to do with the general's wife's disdain for Abe's own spouse.

Wanting to feel exhilarated about something and somehow desiring to still make a party of the evening, Abe continued to ask several others to accompany him and his wife, but received one refusal after another. He finally declared to Mary, "I'd have had a greater reception trying to round up a group of Confederates than the ones I've received from the group we call 'friends'. You'd think they'd be honored to be asked by the President," he said jokingly. "I'm looking forward to this evening even if John Wilkes Booth is not acting tonight. He puts on a brilliant performance."

Abe's wife gave him a look of disdain. "Abraham Lincoln,

why are you so taken with that man? He's deluded himself into thinking he is Southern aristocracy. That's a joke! I read where his father abandoned his wife in England and then came here and had a passel of children to another woman. He's one of ten, and there's no record of his parents ever getting married. That makes him illegitimate!"

The President frowned at his wife. Thoughts of the rumors he'd heard in his youth that his precious Mama was likely an illegitimate child of a Southern gentlemen had always bothered him, but folks ridiculing his cousin Dennis because he had no known father had always infuriated him even more, so he scowled deeper and chastised his spouse, "Mary, you should not spread such gossip. You do not know any of that nonsense for sure, and even if it's so, you must not repeat things that tear people down. You protest violently anything that someone says that demeans your character! Now, we're planning a special evening and I need to know who else you can think of who might like to share it with us."

Mary pondered for a moment before she suggested, "Why not ask Clara Harris, the daughter of the Senator from New York? She could bring her Major fiancé."

Abe agreed, and with delight, he was able to later announce to his wife, "Clara and her beau seemed to want to come along."

Upon hearing the news, Mary showed her own pleasure by smiling and answering, "We won't have to worry so about your safety. Henry Rathbone is such a strong, capable officer."

Once inside their carriage, Abe directed the driver to go to the Harris home, then to take them to the Ford Theatre on Tenth Street. As he looked out on the cobblestone streets of Washington a feeling of satisfaction began to germinate, then to grow inside his tall, lean body. The banners, the lights still reflected the capital's jubilation of the recent war victory, Abe sighed, and decided he should be able to breathe easier. The horrible conflict was finished! Over!

During the ride Mary began to extol the virtues of the performer that was not to be on stage that night, "The President has been taken by John Wilkes Booth's performances. He gets delight in watching the actor's antics. His audiences gasp with pleasure when Mr. Booth often leaps from a spectator's box some twelve feet in the air before the beginning of the show. Besides that, many women admire his looks. His black, curly hair, his pale skin and heavy eyelids gives him a sort of Oriental look. As for me, I am more impressed with tall, thin, distinguished men." She smiled coquettishly at her husband who grinned in return.

Clara Harris shook her head in agreement as she moved closer to her groom-to-be. "John Wilkes Booth isn't my type either. I prefer handsome, well-built men like my major. Besides, Mr. Booth is only about five-foot-seven. He's too fragile to impress me."

Mary laughed and agreed, "Me, too."

Abe, pleased with the gist of the conversation, reached over to clasp Mary's hand in his. "This is a good night. We have a reason and a right to celebrate. All of America does," he told her, then added with a chuckle, "I hear the scalpers are getting more than double the ticket money because Grant is supposed to be with us tonight. Won't the high-paying audience be shocked when they only get to see the President, but not the General?"

The show had already begun when the Lincoln party entered the theatre, but Abe was noticed by William Withers, the orchestra director, who stopped the performance, and at his signal, all the musicians filled the hall with the music "Hail to the Chief." The audience rose to their feet. The music was nearly drowned out by their enthusiastic cheering and applause.

As Abe climbed the circular stairs to his private box, he carried his high silk hat in one hand, keeping it there while they made their way down the corridor to the double box that had been separated so that any large Presidential party could be accommodated. As they opened the door, Mary gasped in wonder, "Look, dear, they even put a rocking chair in here. Someone must have told them that you like to rock."

Her comment tickled Abe's funny bone so much that he quipped in return, "Lots of folks think I'm already off my rocker."

Since the noise and applause of the audience hadn't subsided, Abe decided to please them by going to the railing, bowing, then giving the throng below one of his broad smiles which he knew from experience could, and most often did, melt hearts.

After that he sat down to enjoy the show, knowing the people down below could not see inside unless the occupants chose to somehow look over the top of the banister which had been decorated with red, white and blue banners. Someone had told him his box was about eleven and a half feet from the stage and it was doubtful that anyone was going to jump either up or down from there. He sat back and relaxed, feeling quite safe.

As the comedy farce progressed Abraham Lincoln began to forget all the miseries of his war years and enjoyed one hearty laugh after another. While Mary snuggled close to her husband she whispered a question which Abe deemed to be ridiculous, "What will Miss Harris think of my hanging on you so?"

Abe just grinned and shrugged as he answered, "She won't think a thing of it." He wasn't certain which he enjoyed more — the play or Mary's reaction to it. To his great pleasure she seemed to be having a delightful time, applauding at every humorous spot so Abe just sat back and laughed with great gusto.

At one point a little after ten o'clock while the third act was going on the Great Emancipator was so engrossed with the performance that he sat with his chin cupped in his hand, and did not notice that the Metropolitan policeman assigned to watch over him had left the booth. Only the White House footman, Charles Forbes, was left standing guard over the Presidential party.

Unbeknownst to Abe also was the presence of one of his favorite actors who had also made his way down the long corridor, then stopped to offer Forbes his calling card. The footman knew the actor from all of the posters bearing his image, so he was not reluctant to letting the celebrity enter the box. When John Wilkes Booth maneuvered himself up to about two feet of the President, he pulled a derringer from beneath his cloak and aimed it at the back of Lincoln's head. He squeezed the trigger. A shot rang out.

Major Rathbone sprang to his feet and began to struggle with the invader, but Booth lunged at him with a wide, razor-sharp hunting knife, tearing the major's shoulder open. Blood spurted out. While the major was occupied in trying to stop his profuse bleeding, the actor-attacker leaped from the Presidential party's presence over the railing. In his haste his foot caught in one of the patriotic banners fastened to the outside of the box. Not part of his plan, the error caused him to misjudge his fall. His leg was damaged when he landed on the stage.

Booth's shout of "Sic semper tyrannis" (Thus always to tyrants) caught the audience's attention as the actor looked as though he was trying to imitate a wounded frog as he made a desperate attempt to hurry off the stage.

Mary's terrifying shriek, "They have shot the President!" came out so shrill that it pierced the air. Blue-white smoke caused by the pistol firing began drifting across the top of the theater. The pungent smell of gun powder filled the air, letting the people know that the drama that was unfolding was not rehearsed and not a part of the play.

LAST STAND

All bedlam broke loose upstairs in the balcony of Ford Theatre following the shot that felled the President. Mary's screams subsided somewhat when Dr. Charles A. Leale rushed to Lincoln's side, only to find Mary holding her husband up in the rocking chair. Abraham Lincoln's closed eyes, his slumped head made the physician recoil.

Feeling Abe's arm, Dr. Leale found a slight pulse. "He is alive!" The doctor's face mirrored his amazement that he found signs of life in the wounded leader's body. "His pulse is weak — very weak, but he has one! Let's stretch him out on the floor so we can determine the extent of his injuries."

Next the physician examined the wound at the base of his skull until he found and removed a clot that had accumulated there. He told the onlookers, "That'll relieve the pressure on his brain."

After that he began giving the President artificial respiration. Mary no longer wept, but just stood wide-eyed as Dr. Leale labored to get her husband breathing again. "It's working! I hear a feeble heartbeat!" Everyone watched in wonder as the long, thin chest began to heave up and down. "He's breathing!" the physician cried. "It's irregular, but he's breathing."

Some of Abe's Cabinet had gathered. Stanton suggested. "Let's take him to the White House."

"No! We can't jostle him down the streets of Washington. That would finish him for sure." Dr. Leale exclaimed.

"Well, my tailor lives across the street. I'm certain William

Peterson would be honored to have him taken care of there."

In the small back room of the tailor's home on Tenth Street Lincoln's body was so long that he had to be placed at an angle across the bed. "Put that army blanket on him and that wool afghan. He's getting very cold. Someone get some hot water bottles. We can't let him get any colder."

In the meantime Dr. Gurley, the Presbyterian minister who had tried to console the Lincolns when Willie died, arrived on the scene. Mary had only quit her sobbing when the doctor arrived. She'd continued her woeful wailing as soon as she heard her husband was alive, so Dr. Gurley went over to her as she sobbed by the side of the bed and tried to console her.

Nearly every medical man in Washington made an appearance when they heard the news. Dr. Charles S. Taft was one of the first. He, too, had been attending "Our American Cousin" so he and Dr. Leale were in charge until Dr. Stone, Lincoln's physician, arrived and took over. After consulting with Joseph K. Barnes, the surgeon general, they agreed that the President had no chance to live even though Dr. Stone declared, "The average man could not live more than two hours with such a wound."

When Robert came in he looked as though someone had hit him, but he immediately announced when he saw his mother's distraught shape, "Someone needs to get Elizabeth Dixon. She's mother's close friend and she'll help calm her down."

Mrs. Dixon hustled in the door, took Mary by the arm and escorted her to the front room of the tailor's home, but Mary returned every hour to check on Abe's status.

On one of her hourly visits the President's breathing became very labored. His frightened wife screamed, fainted, then fell to the floor. Upon hearing her, Secretary Stanton rushed in and ordered, "Take that woman out and don't let her in again."

Word spread around Washington. Crowds gathered. All the cabinet members except the wounded Seward came to share in the President's physical crisis.

Vice President Johnson came, but Stanton advised him, "Don't stay too long. You know how Mrs. Lincoln feels about you and we certainly don't need to have her put on one of her scenes."

The man who was next in line for the Presidency took the advice and left shortly after his arrival. Secretary Stanton took over the leadership instead, making certain that all the wheels of the government kept turning. He ordered his assistant secretary of war, "Go after that culprit. Blockade all the roads. He must NOT get away. By morning I want all the roads cut off!"

The night wore on. Mary kept visiting her husband's side, crying over and over, "Don't leave me, my darling. What will I ever do without you? — Oh, Abraham, speak to me. Tell me that you love me."

Most of the crowd stood outside in silence, waiting for some word about their President's condition. Tears streamed down the women's cheeks as they heard the report close to dawn, "He has never regained consciousness."

Robert, always the stalwart Lincoln, stood like a stoic statue until he heard the words, "His breathing is so much more labored. He cannot last much longer."

When Lincoln gave out a low guttural sound Dr. Stone sighed, "It'll be soon. That's the death rattle."

Those words sent Abe's eldest son into a frenzy. Sobbing uncontrollably, he leaned on Secretary Sumner for comfort for a moment, but then he straightened himself up.

At seven twenty-two — nine hours after being shot — the Great Emancipator drew his last breath on that April 15th morning, as the doctors announced, "It's all over! The President is no more."

Dr. Gurley spoke words of consolation to the grieving folks in the tiny back room. Stanton, with tears streaming down his cheeks, stood at the edge of the bed where Abraham Lincoln still lay. The secretary placed his hat on his head, then removed it in a tribute to his beloved friend. "Now," he declared, "He belongs to the ages."

Abraham Lincoln's eldest son felt as though he'd also been hit. He'd never considered what would happen if the man who he thought held the family, the country, even the universe together met his demise. As he stared at his father's lifeless form reality set in. Abraham Lincoln could no longer cure the world's ills. *Let's face it, Robert,* he told himself, *you've become the man of the family. Tad and your mother are your responsibility. What now?* Robert Todd Lincoln was certain that assuming any of his father's responsibilities would not be easy.

AFTERMATH

The nation had been stunned by Lincoln's assassination. They'd been in mourning for three days. The morning the funeral was to be held everyone at the White House was somber except for the President's wife who had secluded herself in the bedroom and wailed aloud. When Elizabeth, Mary Lincoln's dressmaker and confidant, who she'd come to fondly address as "Lizzy," came to Mary's room over to the other side of the White House, Robert knew she'd come to check on him and Tad. He was certain that she had no doubt that Abraham's oldest son would be dressed well and look quite handsome. but one never knew what weird combination of clothing Tad might be wearing. She appeared to heave a sigh of relief when she saw that he actually had appropriate attire for such a solemn occasion.

Robert realized that she wanted to help Abraham and Mary's two sons. What could she say or do? As was her custom, she reached out and gave Abraham Lincoln's youngest son a quick hug, then opted not to give one to his brother because he'd informed her years before that he'd outgrown such gestures. At that moment he wished he'd never issued such an ultimatum. He certainly could use a hug. Instead she turned and gave Tad another quick squeeze as she told them the message she obviously dreaded to give, "Your mama can't be with you today. She says she's not up to it. This whole terrible thing is more than she can bear."

Abe Lincoln's oldest son frowned as he answered, "Doesn't

she know the government is sending a special private carriage draped in black for Papa's family? Doesn't she care enough to do this one last thing for him? Everyone will expect her to be part of the procession."

With a shrug of her shoulders, Elizabeth answered, "You know your mama. If she says she won't do something, nothing in heaven or earth will change her mind."

Robert's scowl deepened as he declared in an emphatic tone of voice, "Elizabeth, won't you please plead with her to do her part? Assure her that Tad and I will never leave her side. We'll sit beside her in the carriage, but PLEASE," he pleaded, "tell her we do not want to go through this alone. Tell her that if you lose one parent, you need the other one with you."

It was obvious that Mary Todd's friend tried to hold back the involuntary tears that began misting in her own eyes. "Master Tad and Master Robert, I cannot work miracles. She has gone into her bedroom and locked her door as you both know. Nothing I have tried to say has made any difference thus far, but I'll give her your message."

Tad broke the silence by begging, "Elizabeth, PLEASE, PLEASE let her know we NEED her. His twelve-year-old changing voice cracked with emotion in his effort to keep from crying as he added, "PLEASE tell Mama her baby needs her."

Elizabeth turned and left the two boys in the alcove standing beside each other. Robert at age 22 had never been excited about his younger brother because he understood why Tad had become the favorite son of both their parents since they had lost both Eddie and Willie, but that hadn't made it any easier for the older son to deal with the situation.

Since Tad's arrival had come a year after Willie's death, Abe and Mary had consoled their grief by coddling the new baby, making Robert's resentment toward his younger brother grow over the years. Tad had become spoiled from all the concessions and indulgences his parents had bestowed on him as well as the numerous gifts and toys. No love had ever been lost between the two brothers for their sibling rivalry had kept them apart as much as the ten-year span of their ages.

At the time of Lincoln's death Robert had become quite a young man. Tad, on the other hand was, as his brother so aptly put it, "quite spoiled." Other than the fact that they both had been born to the same parents, they had little in common. Robert excelled in anything he attempted to do, Tad had a difficult time learning or doing anything of any consequence which frustrated both of them even further. In truth, they often went to great pains just to avoid each other.

Yet, that day in April the two boys found a strange new bond beginning to form between them. Both of them loved their parents and were just beginning to accept the untimely death of the man who each considered to be the greatest man in the universe. They yearned to have their mother share their sorrow, but they'd been told that she was too wrapped up in her own grief to consider theirs.

After waiting a while longer in the alcove, Robert suggested: "Let's go and see if we can get Mama to come along." Being the older son, he never called Mary anything but Mother, but on this occasion he was willing to say anything that might lessen his younger brother's heartbreak.

Before they even mounted the steps to go to the second floor, they could hear their mother's wails. Dear Elizabeth, looking most distraught, turned to them and declared, "It's no use trying, boys. Your mama has too much anguish and pain to do anything sensible this day. Since your papa always tried to humor her and give her everything she demanded, she is feeling sorry for herself because he won't be able to do that anymore."

Robert and Tad stood there, horrified at the soul-shattering sounds coming from the other side of the huge wooden door which loomed as a great barrier between them and their mother. The older brother took the younger one's arm and spoke in a far more patient tone than usual, "Come on, Tad. We have to grow up ourselves today. Someone needs to represent the family at Papa's funeral. After all, he was the President of the United States of America." The word "was" impacted his own mind, but he acknowledged mentally that he himself had not yet accepted the fact that Abraham Lincoln was no longer the country's leader.

Robert could not help but wonder how one single bullet could change the course of so many lives.

Tad and Robert walked down the steps to the carriage that stood outside awaiting their arrival. To the driver's inquiry, "Is your mother not coming?" Robert answered simply, "No, our mother is unable to come." Yet he thought to himself, *Mother has had four days to prepare herself emotionally for this event.* Their father had been lying in state in the Rotunda ever since they prepared him for his burial. Robert had heard thousands had passed by their father's body, weeping over the nation's loss.

That April 19, the horse-drawn carriage left the White House and followed behind the huge, flag-draped hearse carrying President Lincoln down Pennsylvania Avenue toward the Capitol Building where Abraham Lincoln would be eulogized amid all the other great American heroes. Robert spoke softly to Tad, "You do know that Papa's body is going to be sent to Springfield by train to be buried there, don't you? He said he loved Illinois and its people and he wanted to 'go home to rest' when he died." Tad could only nod that he understood.

Throngs of distraught citizens crowded both sides of the avenue near the Capitol. Women wept openly. Grim-faced men fought to keep their composure as the body of the head of the nation passed by them. Signs and placards, displaying the depth of the people's emotions following the tragic demise of their great American hero hung from store fronts, flag poles and street signs. Many folks stood with handmade placards announcing their feelings, "We love you, Abe" and "Hail to the Great Emancipator."

Upon their carriage's arrival at the great hall, the two Lincoln sons were escorted from their carriage to special seats where they watched and listened with a sense of awe as dignitary after dignitary rose to share their feelings about the departed President.

After what they were certain was an eternity later, Tad and Robert watched some soldiers carefully remove the American flag from on top of their father's coffin and then fold it with care into a neat triangle. Then, to their surprise, a military officer came and offered it to Robert with a salute. Abraham Lincoln's eldest child had great difficulty keeping his composure as he stood and saluted in return. Flowers were strewn along the roadway which the hearse would take the President back down the road to the railroad station. Soldiers began playing taps, indicating the service was over at last.

Mourners who'd come dressed in dark clothing for the solemn occasion, turned to leave. Women approached the two boys with their arms outstretched, sobbing and crying, "We all loved your father." "You will miss him, I'm sure, but it is so sad that he won't be here to help America after this terrible war," one older lady declared. Stone-faced men stood like stoic statues, assuring Robert that they were also having a struggle keeping their emotions intact. A few women finally broke through the crowd, flinging themselves at the boys, sobbing uncontrollably until policemen pulled them away.

Both Tad and Robert stood straight and tall as they thought Abraham Lincoln's sons should during the trying ordeal. When the crowd finally dispersed, their driver helped each of them back into their carriage. On their trip to the railroad station they both remained silent, haunted by all the sobering events. Robert thought the clip-clopping sound the horse's hooves made as they hit the cobblestone streets had the impact of the percussion of a big bass drum hitting his head. His emotions for the past two days had been so draining that any noise made it ache more.

The streets of Washington showed signs of new life. Spring had arrived at the nation's capital, but the orchid crocuses and waving daffodils were not helping the mood of the two young men sitting inside the carriage. A stabbing pain, the kind that Robert had never experienced before, took place when the procession stopped beside a flag-draped railroad car. The military band played. The coffin carrying their father's body was carried by soldiers and lifted up into the train. More speeches. Robert looked at his younger brother and acknowledged mentally that the hurt he was experiencing at being near his father for the last time was not uniquely his. Tad was being torn apart, too.

At last their driver turned onto Pennsylvania Avenue. When the home the boys had become so accustomed to came into view, Robert finally broke the silence between them. "Don't you wonder how long will we stay in the Lincoln residence? Andrew Johnson and his family will surely want to move in soon."

Tad's face expressed sudden panic. After pondering his brother's question for a while, he finally answered, "I hadn't thought of losing our home!" With tears welling up in his eyes, he declared in such a high-pitched voice that his brother realized how desperate his younger sibling's emotional status had become. "Doesn't anyone care that we've lost our father and our mother seems to have lost her mind?"

Robert shrugged. He didn't answer until they'd walked from the carriage into the huge white mansion they'd called "home" for several years. "Tad, we knew from the start that the White House was only ours to use while Papa was President. Now that he's gone, we WILL have to move on."

After hearing such news, Tad's face twisted into what Robert knew was an emotional knot. As the older brother, he realized the younger one was fighting to keep his own composure. Surely no one would criticize them if Tad broke down and sobbed aloud and Robert wept with him. Yet neither did. The entire country appeared to be in the same state of distress. Why would anyone criticize the President's sons for their own grief?"

After a few minutes Robert suggested, "Come on, let's go check on mother." With those words, he began to steer his sibling in the direction of the stairs.

The two boys mounted the steps to begin their climb to the second floor. Mary Todd Lincoln's sobs were just as loud as they were when they left. Their mother's cherished Lizzy sat on the sofa across from their mother's doorway. Upon seeing the boys, she gave a shrug of despair as the wails grew in decibels.

Next she stood and declared to the Lincoln sons, "She has to wear out sometime. A body can only go through so much stress before it is forced to rest! Your mama has surely reached that point."

Tad's face looked as though another emotional storm cloud

was brewing inside of him, so Robert took his arm again and encouraged him, "Come on, let's go out on the balcony." Turning to Elizabeth, he asked, "You will call us if we can do anything for you or mother, won't you?"

After a nod of agreement from Elizabeth, both the youngest and the oldest of Abraham Lincoln's living sons went outside to look at the city from that high vantage point their father had enjoyed so much.

Dusk was setting in. Over toward Arlington, Old Glory, the flag that had been flown again with victorious flare at the war's end, was sharing its colors at half-mast as a tribute to the President who had told his family how deeply troubled he had been when the Rebel's banner had been flown there so close to the nation's capital. That day the country's red, white and blue symbol drooped as if in mourning with the rest of the nation.

Robert tried to think of words to console his younger brother, "Tad, you had to become a man today. I'm so sorry you had to do it in such a short time, but both your mother and father would be proud of you." To his own surprise, he reached out and drew Tad's lean body toward him. The impact of their father's murder, the traumatic time with their own loss and then their mother's soul-wrenching reaction caused a volcano of emotions to erupt. They wept in each other's arms.

Once they regained their composure, Robert gave a wistful look and then announced to his only living sibling, "I think Papa would be pleased, but it certainly took a terrible tragedy for us to act like brothers."

The sun was radiating its last golden rays when their eyes turned toward Arlington once again. Someone was lowering the flag which displayed the stars and stripes. Darkness was descending on Washington on that memorable day in April.

Tad looked at his brother, "It is real, isn't it? Papa being shot and everything that's happened since seems like a horrible dream."

"I wish that it was, little brother."

Do you remember when Papa told us about his grandfather being shot by an Indian who grabbed our grandfather Tom? The

Indian was kidnapping him until his brother Mordecai managed to shoot the Indian, and our grandfather escaped."

Tad's question amazed Robert. Too often Tad's involved thoughts didn't come out right, but this time he had all the facts straight. "Of course I remember. Don't you wonder what they might have done with Grandpa and what if we'd have never been born? Even more important than that, would Papa have ever existed? What do you suppose would have happened if our father hadn't led the fight between the North and the South?"

"Do you think the Lord would have raised up someone to save the Union if Abraham Lincoln hadn't been President?" Tad asked.

The two boys stood looking out on the nation's capital which became strangely quiet as the dark night shrouded its streets.

Robert sighed, "Who knows, Tad? Maybe our father's father was saved from disaster so the younger Abraham Lincoln could free the slaves and reunite the North and South so they could once again become the United States of America."

Tad declared, "From all his accomplishments, we should be proud to be his sons."

Robert smiled for the first time in the last three days, "Sometimes I get disgusted with what I made him put up with because of my own ridiculous actions. Remember the time he was playing chess with a Supreme Court Judge and Mama sent me three times to summon them to supper, but the third time I showed my Mary Todd temper and kicked the game board over his head? The chess pieces went flying everywhere, but Papa simply said, 'I guess we'll have to finish playing some other time.' He should have beaten me soundly, but he never even raised his voice.'"

Tad shrugged. "Guess he should have been more forceful with all of us, but he never gave up his determination to do what he felt he must do during the war. I can't help but wonder if Papa wasn't intended by God to do what he felt he must do to free the slaves and keep this country together."

The night air brought a chill once the sun went down in the west, so Robert suggested, "Maybe we need to go inside to check on Mama. As for the question about our father being born to keep America from being divided into two nations, I guess our Father in Heaven is the only One who knows."

For a moment the two brothers stood immersed in their thoughts until Robert spoke again, "We know how much he meant to us and how we will have a difficult time getting over our personal loss, but think how much our country's history would have been altered if our Papa had never existed. Like I said, Tad, I don't know the answer to our questions. As Papa would say, 'There's some things that only God knows'."

"It is better to be quiet
And be thought as a fool
Than to speak and
Remove all doubt."

Abraham Lincoln

AUTHOR'S MUSINGS

Ever try to put together an involved puzzle — especially one where you can't look at the total picture to get a hint of where the pieces should go? Sometimes the shading amazes you because you're not certain if the color of the section that you are trying to fit into place is really meant for the portion you are attempting to construct. At times an off-shaped piece fits into a spot where it seems it could never be a possibility.

That's a little like trying to construct this novel. At first I thought the writings in *Lincoln Memorial: Album Immortelles — Original Life Picture with Autographs —Together with extracts from his speeches, letters and sayings* would suffice to create *Love and Loyalty — The Traits That Made Lincoln Great*, but I soon found that was not so. Too many gaps in the puzzle.

To complete the project I went scurrying to the local libraries. In New Castle, Pennsylvania where willing helpers offered me a copy of the *Lincoln Reader* — an old book published in 1947 by Rutgers University Press.

From that I gleaned a run-down of the chronological happenings in our 16th President's life and other pertinent information. I also visited Shenango Valley Community Library in Sharon, Pennsylvania and scanned their data on Lincoln.

However, the greatest wealth of knowledge, the bulk of the puzzle's first pieces, were fit together from the vast information in the book *Lincoln,* by David Herbert Donald and published by Simon and Schuster in 1995. For anyone who has whetted their appetite by reading this novel, I recommend you get yourself a copy of this intricate work by the man who acknowledges in his dedication that he'd become so immersed in his search into the complexity of Abe's life that he wanted to give his family credit for their patience— "For Aida and Bruce who have had to live with Lincoln for most of their lives." Several chapters in this novel could not have been written without David Herbert Donald's intricate details in putting my puzzle together, especially the two relating the night at Ford Theatre and then the events of subsequent days when Abraham Lincoln's life came to a close.

Another book which became a tremendous resource in constructing many of the gaps in my puzzle is *Lincoln's New Salem* by Benjamin P. Thomas, published by Alfred a Knopf, Inc. in 1954. In his epistle about that portion of Abe's younger years, he assessed Lincoln's life in depth as he struggled to find a life of his own. These resource books came from Greenville, Pennsylvania's public library where dear friends gave me favors and access to everything on their shelves about the Great Emancipator, but the two books from there became my greatest resource until I discovered the tremendous work of Stephen B. Oates, *With Malice Toward None*, published in 1977 by Harper and Row. Both histories offered a tremendous insight into Lincoln's life and would prove invaluable to anyone who enjoys delving into America's roots. *Love and Loyalty* would never have happened without the great works of these three authors plus the anecdotes and stories about our sixteenth President by people who knew and loved him and placed them in *Lincoln Album of Immortelles*.

The date for the sequence of events in the Civil War came from *The American Bicentennial Edition of the Holy Bible, July 4, 1975*, published by Jerry Falwell Ministries, Lynchburg, Virginia.

Some controversy arose in my mind as to Abe's first romance. Being a romantic, I felt the depth of his emotions toward Ann Rutledge when he was still young, and was quite taken with his despair at losing her as it was so aptly portrayed in *Lincoln's New Salem*.

Differences in many of the references I read caused me to

ponder if my finished product would present an accurate picture. Abe's own signed declaration "I was not a Christian until after the battle of Gettysburg" — astounded me so that it took weeks of contemplating what might have taken place in President Abraham Lincoln's mind to finally come to understand why he made such a step so late in life and not before. The details of his actual acceptance of Jesus as his Lord are for the most part fictionalized except for the exact wording of the letter in which he claimed for the first time, "Yes, I DO love Jesus." At other times, in other speeches, he made reference to a Savior, but that letter to a clergyman after his speech at Gettysburg is the first reference I could find about the Lord Jesus in his speeches or writings although he made many tributes to "Divine Providence," "The Creator," plus other references to God all during his political career.

I believe he accepted the message of the resurrection power of Jesus at that point because he encountered the Holy Spirit as he felt a desperate need to believe that the soldiers who died in that horrific battle would meet their Lord and have eternal life.

Friends sent clippings, and brought books. Many statistics were gleaned from Ken Burn's specials about the Civil War on PBS. Don and Fran Pratt even brought their antique song books and compilations of anecdotes about Lincoln and shared the story of Lincoln's purchase of a slave girl published in a devotional, *The Word for You Today* by Bob Gass published in a 2001 issue. They willingly proofread. Ron Rotunno scanned the Internet and brought me pictures and films about the Civil War.

However, this novel could not have been put together without the first five books mentioned. It definitely would not have come to fruition without Delores Cox's endless hours of typing on a computer to make it possible to get to the completion of the puzzle. Once I'd put my hand to the plow, how often I wished I could turn back.

One of my talented granddaughters, Ashley Ceremuga, went to work immediately when I asked her to paint the cover picture of Lincoln on a horse. The next July I asked her to do some changes after I'd had her painting for several months. She just entered her last year in high school so she asked me, "Are you ever going to get that book done? Grammy, I want to use it for my senior project."

Jim Jackson, my friend and great graphic designer, took Ashley's beautiful portrait and added part of the Gettysburg address, an American flag and a photo of the Capitol from 1864. He also set up and paginated the entire book. Once he added the lettering we had another finished puzzle.

When my sister Betty Jean announced, "I'm planning to use the book for gifts," I moaned and said, "I don't know if I can put the puzzle all together."

To which she replied, "Of course you can. You know I think you can do anything." This book would probably never have come to fruition without the loving prodding of my sister and my dear husband Jim and our devoted staff and writer friends at the Mercer, PA Roundtable.

And so, it is close to the end as I write this bit of musing. As I wrote this we remembered the first anniversary of the bombing of the World Trade Center.

This September 11, 2002 we sat transfixed as the Mayor Rudy Giuliani read the Gettysburg address. I pondered those words again. Tears formed in my eyes as I realized the man who, as a child had survived part of a frigid Indiana winter on a mattress of leaves under a bearskin rug, had become a states-man who made such a mark on world history that his words had a tremendous impact on another battlefield one hundred and thirty-nine years later. This one was not Gettysburg, but a place where the Twin Towers toppled and thousands died. Abraham Lincoln's words to the nation still hold significance today. "It is for us, the living, rather, to be dedicated here to the unfinished work which they have thus so far nobly carried on. It is rather for us to be here dedicated to the great task remaining before us that from these honored dead we take increased devotion to the cause for which they here the last full measure of devotion that we here highly resolve that the dead shall not have died in vain — that this nation, under God shall have a new birth of freedom, and that the government of the people, by the people and for the people shall not perish from the earth."

It is ironic that he also said, "The world will little note, nor long remember, what we say here," yet his words have become a cornerstone of freedom and hope.

It is my hope and prayer that this book about the life of one of the most honored Presidents in American history will instill some of the Godly faith of our forefathers in your heart; that you will strive to reach for greater plateaus in your life as Abraham Lincoln proved you can reach regardless of your roots.

Failure or disappointment never stopped his determination for long. My friend Scott sent me a list of Lincoln's defeats and triumphs, showing how he failed in business at the age of 22. After many ups and downs, he persisted until, at the age of 51, he became the President of the United States of America.

Other sources for Abe's background also came from personal visits to sites where Lincoln's life is remembered. My husband, his partner Ron and I stopped by the Lincoln Museum on the town square in Hodgenville, Kentucky where I gleaned many of the facts about Lincoln's birthplace. There I learned many details from a most intriguing film depicting Abe's life. The pictures used in the color section are the actual photos of the awesome scenes displayed in the wax museum, each depicting twelve stages from the great President's life taken by W. L. McCoy of Elizabethtown, Kentucky.

We also rode past the Sarah Bush Johnston Lincoln Memorial in Elizabethtown, Kentucky which was built to resemble the one where Sarah Lincoln had lived, including furnishings as they were created and used in that era.

My own initial visit to Gettysburg years ago while I was researching facts about my novel *Dog Jack* impacted me so much that I, too, wept at some of the monuments declaring that thousands of American boys, both Union and Confederate, had given their lives on that spot in 1863's hot, humid July when the nation should have been celebrating Independence Day. Instead men from the North and South were engaged in a bloody Civil War conflict. Seeing the markers which shared the loss of thousands of lives made a permanent impact on my mind and heart.

During that encounter with America's past, the life and struggles of the boy who was so determined to later make his mark on history became real.

This book was not meant to be a synopsis of the Civil War, but rather to show the traits — Love and Loyalty — that made the person, Abraham Lincoln, such a great giant in the history of America.

On the wall of the Ralph Watson farm in Mercer, Pennsylvania is an old calendar. There, beneath a small picture of Abraham Lincoln are the words, "I will study and prepare and perhaps my chance will come." His did — yours will too!

Appendix

Description of Photo Inserts

SCENE 1: THE CABIN YEARS 1809-1816

This slave-era cabin was removed from a farm in north eastern LaRue County and reconstructed here in the museum. The chinking and the mud floor were made according to pioneer recipes. Note the creek stone fireplace which was the hub of household activities.

This scene depicts the Lincoln family on a typical evening at their Knob Creek home. We see Thomas and Nancy Hawks Lincoln, and young Abe enjoying his favorite pastime - reading.

As President, Lincoln wrote "My earliest recollection is of the Knob Creek place." It was here that he first witnessed the slaves being driven south along the toll road to be sold. It was also here that he was saved from drowning in Knob Creek by his playmate, Austin Gollaher.

SCENE 2: THE BERRY-LINCOLN STORE 1831

This small frontier store, located on a bluff above the Sangamon River in New Salem, Illinois, was stocked with food stuffs, dry goods, furs, hides, pots, plates, glassware and medicines. The store carried sugar, salt and coffee imported through St. Louis. In addition firearms, ox yokes, and tools were available. During quiet times at the store, Lincoln read and studied grammar, mathematics, and even Shakespeare. It was during his six-year stay in New Salem that Lincoln began his fledgling efforts at speechmaking and politics. Here we see young Ann Rutledge whom legend calls his first sweetheart.

SCENE 3: THE RAILSPLITTER 1825

In 1816, the Lincoln Family moved from Knob Creek farm and settled on Pigeon Creek, Spencer County, Indiana. Abe was seventeen, standing 6'2" and weighing 160 pounds. A neighbor said, "He was a strong man, physically powerful, and could strike with a maul a heavier blow than any man, as well as sink one deeper." His political supporters later used the image of "The Railsplitter" and "Honest Abe from the Backwoods of Kentucky and Indiana" as effective campaign slogans.

SCENE 4: THE MARY TODD HOME   1849

This spacious two-story red brick residence of Georgian Colonial design, located at 574-576 West Main Street in Lexington, Kentucky, was the girlhood home of Mary Todd Lincoln. It is said to be the first shrine in honor of a First Lady.

Lincoln approaches the entry recreated here to scale. During their month-long visit in 1849, Abraham's legal expertise was required in the settling of the estate of Robert S. Todd, Mary's father.

Abe and Mary's first child was named Robert for his grand-father.

The title "First Lady" was originally used while Mary Todd Lincoln was in the White House.

SCENE 5: LINCOLN VISITS FARMINGTON   1841

During a "down" period in Lincoln's three-year courtship of Mary Todd, he journeyed to Louisville to visit his good friend, Joshua Speed at his parents' home, Farmington. The Speed home was lively with the activities of a large family and their friends. Lincoln soon lost his melancholy mood while aiding in Joshua's romance with Fanny Henning.

Joshua's mother, Lucy Fry Speed, presented Lincoln with an Oxford Bible during his visit. Lincoln's "bread and butter" note is well known. The Lincoln-Speed friendship remained strong throughout the years. This scene shows a portion of Mrs. Speed's parlor at Farmington which is located at 3033 Bardstown Road in Louisville. The historic home is open for public tour.

SCENE 6: THE LINCOLN-DOUGLAS DEBATES   1858

The passing of the Kansas-Nebraska Act early in 1854 brought Lincoln back into the political arena. He joined the new

Republican Party and began making speeches opposing the view Democratic Senator Stephen A. Douglas that each new territory be allowed to decide for itself its stand on slavery. This view repudiated the Missouri Compromise.

It was this series of debates, especially the "House Divided Against Itself" speech which resulted in Lincoln's becoming the Republican standard-bearer in the contest against Douglas for the U.S. Senate. Although Lincoln lost his bid for that election, these debates with "The Little Giant" gave him national exposure and eventually led to his becoming the successful Republican presidential candidate in 1860.

SCENE 7: EMANCIPATION PROCLAMATION
SEPTEMBER, 1862

In this scene, you see President Lincoln in his White House Cabinet Room working and reworking his drafts of the Emancipation Proclamation He never completed more than a single sheet each day, reading, revising, and carefully weighing each sentence. In midsummer of 1862, Lincoln called his cabinet together and revealed his determination to adopt the policy. After the federal victory at Antietam, he decided to wait no longer. The Emancipation Proclamation was issued whereby four million slaves were given their freedom and slavery forever prohibited in these United States.

This room is now known as the Lincoln Bedroom.

SCENE 8: THE MATTHEW BRADY STUDIO FEBRUARY, 1864

"Mr. Brady has made me President," said Lincoln to campaign supporters before the election of 1864. This portrait of Lincoln with his youngest son, Tad, was printed in many of the nation's newspapers and became one of the best known. It was "my father's favorite," Lincoln's son Robert later said. This photograph, known as "Brady's Lincoln," is engraved on our five-dollar bill. During his years in Washington, Lincoln sat before the Brady cameras on not less than seven occasions, each time photographed in several poses. Matthew Brady's name has a special place in American history. His work included famous

Americans, places, and the recording of the Civil War. Brady has provided a permanent pictorial history of this era of our country.

SCENE 9: THE SECOND INAUGURATION   MARCH 4, 1865

March 4, 1865, was a somber, drizzly day. Roads were covered with mud and a cold, gusty wind was blowing.

The huge multitude on the plaza in front of the capitol broke into a tremendous shout as Lincoln stood to be sworn into office by Salmon P. Chase, Chief Justice of the Supreme Court.

President Lincoln stepped forward and began to read his inaugural address printed in two columns upon a single page. As his voice rang out, he was interrupted with applause and cheers. As he spoke "With malice toward none, with charity for all," the sun broke through the clouds. Many people saw this as a good omen for an end to the War Between the States and a brighter future for the Union.

SCENE 10: THE GETTYSBURG ADDRESS

NOVEMBER 19, 1863

The ceremonies to honor the 51,000 Americans' who were injured or killed at the Battle of Gettysburg in July, were held on a cold, wet Thursday in November at 10:00 in the morning. The band played as the procession moved through the town toward the cemetery. The dignitaries took their places on the platform and Edward Everett, the principal speaker, began his oration which lasted two hours.

President Lincoln had been asked "to set apart formally these grounds to their sacred use" by a few appropriate remarks. The President stood, glanced at his manuscript, and began what has become one of the world's most famous speeches— learned by countless school children and others around the world. It lasted three minutes.

SCENE 11: SURRENDER   APRIL 9, 1865

Palm Sunday, Lee and Grant meet in the McLean home at Appomattox Court House, Virginia.

U.S. Grant, in his mud-splattered boots straight from the

battlefield, drafts the document while Lee, seated in a simple cane backed chair, rests his hands on the "surrender table." These two great generals signed the agreement which allowed the South to keep her dignity, the North to show compassion, and the end of four bitter years of Civil War.

SCENE 12: FORD'S THEATRE   APRIL 14, 1865

The surrender was signed; Civil War was over; April 14 was a day for thanksgiving. Mrs. Lincoln had chosen to attend Ford's Theatre where the popular Laura Keene was performing in the comedy "Our American Cousin."

The President, who greatly enjoyed theatre, with his wife and their guests, Major Henry Rathbone and his fiance Clara Harris, were seated in Box 7 which had been specially furnished for the Presidential visit.

John Wilkes Booth entered the theatre and ascended the stairs unnoticed by guards. He entered directly behind Lincoln and fired one shot. The President slumped forward in his chair. Booth vaulted the railing of the box, catching his spur in the flag. As he fell to the stage, Booth fractured his left leg, but even so dashed across the stage shouting "Sic Semper Tyranis!" (Thus Always To Tyrants).

Seconds later he had disappeared into the night, while the wounded President was carried across the street to the Petersen house. There he lingered until 7:22 the next morning, never regaining consciousness.

Secretary of War Stanton was to have said, "Now he belongs to the ages."

Other Books from SON-RISE Publication's
Historical Series
1-800-358-0777

0-936369-47-7

0-936369-38-8

0-936369-73-6

0-936369-35-3